stuart,
Thanks so much for read" , my
book! I hope yo ling
it! Keep imaginmg,
– Yuri Jean-Bp

Metamorphs: Return of the Legion

Metamorphs, Volume 1

Yuri Jean-Baptiste

Published by Yuri Jean-Baptiste, 2019.

This is a work of fiction. Similarities to real people, places, or events are entirely coincidental.

METAMORPHS: RETURN OF THE LEGION

First edition. January 7, 2019.

Copyright © 2019 Yuri Jean-Baptiste.

ISBN: 9781792811685

Written by Yuri Jean-Baptiste.

Also by Yuri Jean-Baptiste

Metamorph Anthologies
Metamorphs Anthologies: Volume 1 (Episodes 1-10)

Metamorphs
Metamorphs: Return of the Legion
Metamorphs 2: Ripple Effect

Watch for more at https://yjbliterary.com/.

This book wouldn't be possible without the help of many, God above all else. I'd like to thank my wonderful wife, my #1 supporter, who convinced me to turn my dream into a reality. To my amazing parents and siblings, for your love, and my trusted beta readers, for your support. To my mother, who taught me to read and instilled her love of books within me. Lastly, to Janet Kreeger, who taught a young boy how to use his imagination. Sorry it took so long to keep my promise.

Part One: Origin

Prologue

They told him that when you died, your life flashed before your eyes, allowing you to relive all of your most treasured memories, so Lieutenant Paul Logan was understandably confused at why he was still staring at the cold, dead face of his best friend beside him. He and Private Bill Hurley had served several tours of Iraq together, surviving some of the worst that humanity had thrown their way. However, this evening out in their remote desert outpost, they hadn't stood a chance against the intruders that were now calmly stepping over stray bullet casings and the lifeless bodies of soldiers they had murdered only moments ago. The assault had taken mere seconds, the soldiers caught completely off guard, and by the time they had reacted, it was entirely too late.

Lieutenant Logan felt a burning along his side from where the massive gash was spilling his blood throughout his already soaked pants, the hole revealing his exposed ribs. His entire right side was numb, the burns so severe that his nerve endings had completely fried. He tried to muffle a cough, afraid that they would notice his still breathing body lying in the corner amongst the ruin. The taste of iron stung on his tongue as dark, red fluid dribbled down his chin.

The floor felt slick, covered in the fluid and body parts of the men who had tried to stand their ground against the intruders. The sound of boots reverberated throughout the still room, where only moments ago the air had been filled with the echoes of automatic gunfire and sirens. There were five of them, four males and one female, and from what he could tell, they were all freaks. "Genetically empowered individuals" was the politically correct term for their kind, but Lieutenant Logan knew a monster when he saw one.

He tried his best to lift up his head and listen to what they were saying, turning his one remaining eye toward the cloaked figures before him, and could just barely make out their words over the persistent ringing in his ears.

"Finally...after all these years, we've found him."

"About damn time! After everything we've been through, all the comrades we've lost...it'll all be worth it once we wake him up. I still can't believe he was here all this time! The humans were foolish to think we wouldn't get to him."

"They should have killed him when they had the chance. Lucky for us, their oversight will be our victory over this world and its inhabitants. Once we have the key, he will rise again, and nothing will stand in our way!"

"Still...all of our plans lie in the hands of the boy. Are you sure we can trust him?"

"Of course we can. He's been our most loyal soldier, as ruthless as he is efficient. He's undergoing the application process as we speak. Once he's on the island, he'll get us the information we need to infiltrate it and retrieve the key."

The island? The key? What the hell were these lunatics talking about?! And what were they about to do with the vessel he and his men had been guarding? Lieutenant Logan knew he needed to get a message out to the president and inform them of what had just happened. He needed to warn them of the impending danger. Reaching into his pockets, Lieutenant Logan slowly drew out the emergency pager with his only functioning hand, but as he did, another wave of pain surged through his body causing him to convulse and drop the device.

The five figures quickly turned around, surprised by the noise. Through the bloody haze of his vision, Lieutenant Logan could identify the faces of his attackers, their appearances ranging from the breathtakingly beautiful to the monstrously hideous. His heart pounded in his collapsed chest in what was to be the last time, as the central figure, a man made entirely of shadows, revealed a pearly white grin. Long, black tendrils seemed to emanate from his body before surging toward the military man at an alarming rate.

They said that your entire life flashed before you when you died, but all Lieutenant Logan could see was darkness.

Chapter 1: Ordinary

Tristan Davids slowly opened his eyes to the sounds of screaming alarm sirens. The clock on his phone read 6:30 AM, and his alarm was on full blast, ensuring that the young man would eventually get up.

"Tristan! Shut that thing off already and get up! You're going to be late!" he heard from beyond his bedroom door. Tristan closed his eyes and tried his best to ignore both the cries of his mother and the sounds of ringing next to his ears. *Just another couple minutes,* he thought to himself. *Then I'll be ready to go.*

"Tristan! Did you not hear your mom?! Shut that off and let's get going! I'm not dropping you off! I don't care if you have to walk there this early! Move it, mister!" Tristan's father joined in the cacophony. Groaning in response, Tristan reluctantly got himself out of the warm, cozy bed and shuffled into his bathroom shower.

Scrambling to get ready, Tristan couldn't help but stare at the image reflected back at him from the mirror. Here he was, two days away from his 16th birthday, and he still looked like a twelve-year-old. He was short for his age and undersized. His medium length hair was usually tousled all over the place, but he tried to gel it up to look cool like the other boys in school. *Yeah, like that's ever helped.* Tristan had never been very good at making friends throughout his life, and high school was no different. He was fast approaching the end of his sophomore year at South Miami High, yet the most engagement he had was joining the JV soccer squad, and only at the request of Coach Nibian, who had also coached Tristan's older brother, Allen.

Snapping himself from his pity party, Tristan snatched his school bag beside his bed and made his way downstairs to breakfast. His father was already seated at the table, drinking his coffee and poring over the daily news on his tablet. Despite the heavy-rimmed glasses he wore on his face and salt-and-pepper hair along the top of his curled hair and beard, Oliver

Davids looked fantastic for his fifty years. He was powerfully built, his broad, rounded shoulders complimenting his six-foot frame. He was a successful lawyer who had worked hard to free himself from his rough upbringing down in the slums of Liberty City. He made sure to instill the same values in his children and was a constant motivator to Tristan to push himself to be better.

Tristan's mother set a plate of scrambled eggs, bacon, and toast on the table. "Make sure you eat before heading to the bus."

"Isn't he a little old for you to still be making him breakfast?" Oliver asked, raising his eyebrows.

"I know, I know. I just figured it would help slowpoke here get to school on time," she replied.

Gwendella Davids was the definition of a super-mom: sweet, caring, thoughtful, and one heck of a chef. She was actually the head chef and owner of an upscale, downtown brunch café called Eden, where she served some of the best plant-based meals in the city. Tristan had taken more after his mother in looks; while he had his father's jet black hair, he had his mother's kindly brown eyes and soft features. She was on the taller side, and as she brushed her golden-brown hair aside to kiss Tristan's father before leaving for work, Tristan couldn't help but wonder when he would finally get his growth spurt.

"So, anything good on the agenda today? Don't you have a soccer game this afternoon?" Tristan's father asked as he finished up his coffee and began to close down his tablet. Tristan nearly choked on a piece of bacon. He had almost forgotten about the game!

"Uh, yeah," he sheepishly replied. "We play St. Francis High right after school."

"Well, that sounds fun! I've heard they haven't been doing very well this year. You should be able to get some quality minutes in there!" his father said.

"Yeah, I don't think so, Dad. I'm still probably gonna wind up on the bench today," Tristan mumbled, looking down at his plate.

"Hey, don't sell yourself short. You're a lot better than you give yourself credit for. Don't be afraid to ask for a little bit more playing time. Your brother was never shy about wanting more time on the field. You have his shot, don't be afraid to use it," he advised. Tristan rolled his eyes but grudgingly acknowledged his father.

Tristan hated being compared to his siblings. Allen had been the popular jock at SMH during his time, a dual-sport athlete and class stud. Although twelve years younger, Tristan had looked up to his brother growing up, but once Allen left for boarding school when he was sixteen, Tristan rarely saw him. Elaina, his older sister, was no different, although she was known more for being the brains of the family. An intellectually gifted individual, Elaina left for the same boarding school as Allen, but graduated early, top of her class. Tristan was definitely the runt of the three, despite whatever encouraging lies his parents fed him.

After he finished wolfing down his breakfast, Tristan grabbed his backpack to head out the door. Before he could leave, his father handed him an envelope marked 'Mr. Don Peters'. "If you stop by the comic book shop today, could you hand this to Mr. Peters for me?" he asked.

Tristan nodded to his father, who smiled and patted him on the back before Tristan made his way to the bus stop. Briskly walking the two blocks, he managed to make it to the stop just before the bus started to pull away. He smiled apologetically to the bus driver before spotting Marco and Johnathan toward the back of the bus.

The best part about having friends like Marco Alvarez and Johnathan Woo was that, after seven years of friendship, neither of them had to pretend. They understood that they were all socially awkward and nowhere near the status of their peers when it came to school hierarchy. Marco and his five siblings were all first-generation Americans whose family came from Cuba. Slightly taller than Tristan, he was also overweight, his diabetes and exercise-induced asthma often making him a target for the school bullies. Johnathan, on the other hand, was a string bean. Tall and lanky, he was an only child, whose acne and glasses led to many stereotypical 'nerdy Asian' jokes. For the most part, the boys kept to themselves while in school, avoiding the dumb jocks and planning out their next League of Warriors campaign.

"Dude, did you see the new expansion pack for LOW comes out tonight?" John exclaimed the minute Tristan sat down next to them.

"Seriously?! Already?!" Tristan replied. "I thought it wasn't coming out for another few weeks?"

"Naw, homie," Marco said smiling. "They decided to spring a surprise release tonight to test out the beta. It's only the demo, but we can buy the full version after midnight!"

Tristan smiled at the thought of playing the new expansion pack for his favorite game. *Maybe I can skip out on tonight's game and head home early*, he thought before shaking that idea out of his head. His father would be so disappointed if he pulled that stunt. Besides, he needed to swing by the comic book shop later anyway.

The boys chatted a few more minutes regarding their plans for the night before the bus pulled up to their school. As Tristan exited the bus and stared at the sign reading "South Miami High School", he couldn't help but feel the usual sense of dread. Making their way through the hallways, the three friends headed straight to homeroom, where only a handful of students were present. Once inside, Tristan started toward his locker to grab his textbooks. As he walked, a large, blue Converse sneaker shot out from behind and clipped his foot, sending the poor boy face first to the floor. A chorus of laughter followed as Austin Chatman, the school's star quarterback, and his goons surrounded Tristan.

"Aww, looks like Tiny took a fall this morning, fellas! That's too bad. He should be more careful when he's running beneath people's feet!" Austin teased. Tristan's face burned red with rage as he slowly gathered himself off the floor. Austin held out his hand in front of him, offering assistance. "Need some help?" he asked with a smile. Tristan looked at him, hesitant. "Here, take it," Austin insisted, his green eyes staring mischievously. As Tristan slowly reached for his hand, Austin quickly moved it, slapping Tristan upside the head in one swift motion. "Oops! Guess you need to work on those reflexes, Short Stack," Austin said, nudging Johnathan aside. The boys laughed as they exited the room, each one pushing Marco into the wall when they passed. Alone, the three boys stared at one another in silence.

Sighing, Tristan released his balled up fists, disappointed at himself. He wanted to defend himself, but what could he do against those five jerks? *Who are you kidding? You would've just gotten yourself pummeled.* Austin was a grade-A tool, and he seemed to just get worse each year, especially after his parents' divorce. Tristan had known Austin since the sixth grade, and the stocky blond had been decent enough when they were younger, never anywhere near this cruel. However, between his tumultuous home life and rising popularity, Austin had become a constant source of ridicule toward the three friends. Rubbing his stinging head, Tristan eventually retrieved his books from his locker, while Marco and John debated the merits of impaling Austin and his friends on a broadsword.

The rest of the school day was fairly typical, with Tristan going through the motions as he completed his daily assignments and tried to avoid saying anything to draw attention to himself. Once school was over, Tristan packed up his bag and walked over to the locker room, where he got dressed along with his teammates in preparation for the upcoming soccer match. After listening to a typically uninspiring speech from Coach Nibian, the boys trudged out to the field to play their next opponent. Tristan immediately made his way down to the end of the bench, his usual spot awaiting him. The other boys made sure there was some space between them, not wanting to associate with arguably the worst player on the field.

Tristan knew that the only reason he was even on the stupid squad was because his older brother had convinced Coach Nibian to allow him to join. Despite his numerous pep talks, Coach just didn't understand why Tristan didn't give as much effort into the sport as Allen had. The sad truth was, Tristan rarely gave hard effort because he knew he would never be as good as everyone hoped. In his mind, he was saving them the heartbreak of letting them down.

While Tristan sat on the bench, the game flew by with both sides locked in a scoreless battle. In fact, Tristan had nearly dozed off when he heard his name being called.

"Earth to Tristan! Get over here! We need you on the field!" Coach Nibian screamed. *Wait, what?!* Tristan thought as he ran toward the coach. He had never been called up to play before! As he approached his coach, Tristan saw one of the team's forwards being helped off the field with what seemed like an ankle sprain. "Grossman just got injured, and we need a body up front. All you have to do is run, Tristan. Just wear those defenders out and let Joey do the rest, all right? Can you do that?"

Tristan could barely focus, the fear of actually competing creeping up-on him. Coach Nibian bent down and grabbed Tristan by the shoulders, locking eyes. "Look kiddo, I know this is big for you, but try to relax. You got this. Look deep within yourself...and find whatever gene you and Allen happen to share. Remember what I always tell you, aim for the big white square and not the short, gangly kid in between. Go get 'em!" Nibian said, patting Tristan on the back.

Well, that might have been as encouraging a speech as I'm ever going to get. Tristan ran onto the field as the clock began to run again.

Tristan did as Coach Nibian had instructed, and with the ten minutes still left, he ran his heart out, completely oblivious to the flow of the game. The clock winding down, Tristan was just starting to run out of steam when the impossible happened. In perhaps the most bizarre sequence of events, the ball managed to get through the last defender, resulting in the goalie slipping on the turf as he tried to clear it. The ball slowly rolled toward an empty net, suddenly no one between Tristan and unlikely glory. Tristan heard the roar of the home crowd, and he raced unopposed toward the soc-cer ball. Rearing back his foot to deliver the game-winning dagger, his heart swelled with pride. *It's hero time,* he thought as the crowd erupted in cheers.

It was about 6:30 when Tristan arrived at the local game shop, 'Gamer's Empire'. Only a few blocks between school and home, it was Tristan's fa-vorite hangout. The store had been an abandoned warehouse that was bought by the current owner, Donald Peters, and cleared out to make room for a massive library of shelves completely stocked top to bottom with thousands of games, comic books, and trading cards. Tristan had frequent-ed this store nearly every day since he was a young boy and had fallen in love with the store's vibrant environment from the beginning.

Mr. Peters was at the far end of the warehouse restocking the latest is-sues of 'X-Men' and 'Young Teen Titans' when Tristan entered through the doors. He tried to wipe off the Gatorade from the bottom of his cleats as best he could before walking in, but they still made an audible splotching noise every time he took a step. He was sure he looked a mess, but Tristan hadn't had time to change after the game and wanted to make sure Mr. Pe-ters received the envelope. Mr. Peters filed away the last of the copies in his hand and turned to Tristan, pushing his thick glasses up his nose with a bright smile. His wispy, white hair was all over the place from running around the store and his long, lanky arms were covered in marks from carrying large stacks of games off the delivery truck.

"Well, Mr. Davids, it would seem that you've been a victim of the Willy Wonka factory. Did they mistake you for the other Oompa-Loompas?"

"A short joke, very original," Tristan replied, trying not to smile.

"To what do I owe this pleasure, my orange friend?" Mr. Peters asked in his strong British accent. Tristan reached into his backpack and handed Mr. Peters the envelope his father had given him after breakfast.

"My dad wanted me to give this to you on my way home from the game. I think it's an invitation to my birthday party." Mr. Peters seemed thrilled as he opened the card, revealing a note within.

"Ahhh, yes. Your birthday. I suppose that is coming up isn't it?" said Mr. Peters, a mischievous smile on his face. *Like he ever forgets anything.*

"How was the match, by the way?" Mr. Peters asked while reading through the letter. Tristan's head bowed immediately.

"That bad, huh?"

Tristan nodded. "Yup. By myself with no goalie in sight, and I managed to sky it clear over the bar by a mile. I thought I had given Mr. Nibian a stroke. He told me afterward that I should think about joining the football team."

"Well, that doesn't seem too bad," Mr. Peters replied.

"As a punter."

"Okay, so it's a little bad," Mr. Peters chuckled. "Well if it went so poorly, why did you get a celebratory Gatorade shower?" he asked.

"It wasn't celebratory. That was from the home fans, who threw cups at me when the game ended," Tristan explained, running his fingers through his hair, trying to untangle the ends.

"I'm gutted, Tristan," Mr. Peters sighed, shaking his head. "Sometimes children can be so cruel. Don't let them get to you. Sometimes the greatest weapon we have against the enemy is our own self-worth. Never let them take that from you. There were many who felt this establishment was a mistake and would fail within a year of opening. Good thing I was always a terrible listener." Tristan smiled, feeling somewhat better at the wise man's words.

"So I'll see you on Saturday?" Tristan asked, turning to leave.

"Unfortunately not, mate. I'm sorry but my front desk manager has been away all week on vacation, and I will have to take his place that night." Tristan's head dropped in disappointment. "But fear not! I have a surprise for you up my sleeve," Mr. Peter's said, eyes twinkling. Tristan's mood was immediately lifted at the sound of this and found himself in a much better state when he arrived home.

That evening, Tristan sat down with his parents for dinner. He was famished after all that running this afternoon, and it clearly showed.

"I swear, I do not know where you hide all that food, young man! How you don't weigh 300 pounds is beyond me," his mother said.

"Clearly he got his mother's metabolism," Tristan's father retorted with a wink. Tristan looked at his father in between bites and informed him that Mr. Peters was unable to come to the party. "Well, that's too bad. I know how much you like him. At least the Hernandez and Woo families will be here," his father replied.

"And don't forget, your brother and sister are coming to town that day, as well," his mother pointed out. Tristan had completely forgotten that Allen and Elaina would be there on Saturday. His siblings usually only came once a year during the holidays, so Tristan was understandably surprised when his parents had first announced that they would both be here for his 16th birthday. Not that he minded, but why was this birthday so special?

After dinner, Tristan went upstairs to his bedroom and shut the door behind him. After logging into his laptop, he found that his friends had already downloaded the demo of League of Warriors and were starting a campaign. Tristan quickly joined the game, grabbing his headset and connecting with his friends. "All right fellas. I've had a rough day, and I need to blow off some steam. Who's ready to lay the smackdown on some orcs?"

"Let's get it!" Marco replied.

"For hoooonnnnooorrr!" bellowed John, causing the three friends to break out in laughter at his cheesiness. Tristan had a blast for the next two hours playing campaign after campaign with his friends. As time went on, he forgot about his rotten day and let himself get caught up in a world of heroes and monsters. For a brief moment, he forgot he was Tristan Davids, high school loser, and let himself be something he longed to be deep down inside. Someone else.

"Tristan! You're gonna be late!" Tristan awoke to the sounds of his mother's screams from downstairs. *Oh crap!* Tristan thought, turning to his bedside clock. *I didn't set my alarm!* Tristan hopped out of bed and grabbed his clothes from the closet. He quickly shoved toothpaste in his mouth as he threw on his clothes and hastily packed his school bag.

"Don't forget your lunch!" his mother reminded him as he sped through the kitchen, taking the brown paper bag off the counter. He grabbed his bike from the garage, swung on, and pedaled as fast as he possibly could. If everything went smoothly, there was still a chance he could get to school before the bell rang for attendance. Of course, that's when it started to rain. Not just any rain, mind you, but a full-on South Florida downpour. Tristan cursed his luck, trying his best to increase his speed.

By the time he got there, Tristan was soaked to the bone as he squeaked his way toward his first-period class. He was sure he looked a hot mess when he entered the room, but at least class had not yet started. He managed to compose himself somewhat as he sloshed to the back of the classroom and found the nearest open chair. His cheeks flushed while he tried his best to wring out his damp clothes and slick back his wayward hair. He was pulling out his textbooks and notepads when he noticed several people around him sniffing the air and giving him sideways looks. He too started to smell something a little too ripe in the air. He groaned to himself when he realized the awful truth: in his rush to get ready, he had completely forgotten to put on deodorant! He squeezed his armpits together and held his head in his hands. *Dear Lord, strike me now. This day can't get worse.*

By the time the bell rang for lunch, Tristan was determined that the universe was out to get him. He was blindsided by a pop quiz in his English Lit class, managed to bang his head on the bottom of his desk while picking up his pencil in Geometry, and cemented his status as class klutz in Chemistry by spilling one of the chemicals on his pants, making it look like a perpetual pee stain. Taking a seat beside his two friends, Tristan threw down his backpack and slammed his head onto the table.

"Please tell me that I'm going to wake up from this nightmare at some point today," Tristan mumbled.

"Cheer up, homes. We got four more classes to go then we're outta here for the weekend. I don't know about you, but I'm stoked for your party! And you know your parents are probably gonna buy you the full version of the LOW expansion pack if you ask them tomorrow," Marco stated.

Tristan's head perked up slightly when he heard this. Marco did have a point. The weekend, and Tristan's birthday, was almost upon them.

Tristan was beginning to feel a bit better when he felt a sudden stab of pain behind him. He grabbed the back of his head, still smarting from the football that was thrown across the room by Austin.

"Oops, sorry Wee-man! Meant to throw it toward the wall behind you, but that fat head of yours got in the way!" Tristan's face was beet red with embarrassment, and he tried to hold back tears as best he could. Marco and Jon simply dropped their heads, trying not to make themselves the next target. Feeling abandoned, Tristan started to sense a rage rising within him that he hadn't felt before. As if today wasn't bad enough, he had to sit there and be tormented day by some pea-brained Neanderthal. *I've had enough!*

"Shut up, Austin! Who the hell do you think you are, asshole?!" Tristan cried out, slamming his hands on to the table. He immediately regretted his outburst as the room grew quiet. The raging fire within him had suddenly turned into a sputtering matchstick.

Austin slowly got up and walked toward Tristan's table, the nearby students seeming to part like the Red Sea. Tristan looked around in panic. *Where the hell are the teachers?* Arriving at the table, Austin bent his face toward Tristan.

"What did you say to me, dip weed?" he said menacingly. Tristan swallowed hard. *Don't you chicken out now! Stand up for yourself!*

"I said, who do you think you are?" Tristan stuttered. "You walk around like some hot shot, picking on kids when we haven't even done anything to you. What's your deal?"

"My deal? My deal is that I don't like you nerds walking around my school. My deal is you and the Nerd Crew are an embarrassment. Between Reject Bruce Lee, the Mexican Blob, and Captain B.O. stinking up the place, you're lucky I still let you come around here without paying a fine. So shut your face like you always do, or the next thing I break is you!"

Austin began to turn around, when Tristan muttered, "You're doing it for attention."

"Excuse me?" Austin paused, turning back slowly.

Tristan had his head down put continued to say in a low voice, "You're not fooling me, Austin. I remember what you were like before. I'm sorry about your parents, but you don't have to be like this. We're not your enemies."

Tristan looked up and stared at the stunned sophomore, who for the first time was speechless. Tristan could see, for just a brief moment, a look flicker across Austin's face. Looking back, Tristan liked to believe that for once, the bully had let down his guard to reveal the hurt, confused boy inside. Unfortunately, the moment passed once one of Austin's friends screamed out, "Beat him up already!" The crowd roared in agreeance, and Austin brought his fist thundering down.

Tristan had never been in a fight before, much less punched in the face. It was not something he enjoyed in the least. Tristan flew back off his chair as Austin continued his assault, swinging down on Tristan's head. He tried his best to curl into a ball and cover his head, but that just opened up his ribs to the bully's size 9 Nikes. Tristan could barely make out Marco and John trying their best to intervene, but Austin's friends had set up a blockade and were pushing them back.

A sharp whistle pierced the cafeteria air, and Principal O'Malley and Coach Nibian stormed through the room, knocking kids aside to stop the fight. "That's enough! Get off of him, Chatman! That's enough!" the principal yelled, pulling the boy off of Tristan. He grabbed Austin by the scruff of the neck and began dragging him out of the room. Tristan could hear the schoolmaster yelling at Austin about the years' worth of detention he was going to face, as well as his suspension from the football team.

Mr. Nibian helped pick Tristan off the floor while he told everyone to file out. "Get moving people! Nothing to see here! Nothing to see!" He held Tristan steady and lightly brushed off the bruised, bleeding teen. "Geez, Davids! You all right there, kiddo? Looks like you got yourself a few knocks," his coach said, a look of genuine concern on his face.

Ignoring the coach, Tristan looked around at the students leaving the scene. He saw the kids snickering behind the soccer coach's back, the looks of disappointment on his friend's faces. He had never felt so embarrassed.

Tristan tried his best not to let the tears fall past his quickly swelling eyes, but they came down anyways. "Listen, kid...I'm sorry. I know high school can be tough for kids like you," Nibian began, putting his arm on Tristan's shoulder, but Tristan pushed it aside and ran past him. Tristan didn't know where he was headed, but he knew he wanted to get as far away from this place as fast as possible. Tristan grabbed his bike and quickly pedaled away from the school, his sobs drowning out the shouts behind him.

Tristan didn't remember how he got to Gamer's Empire through the tears. It was all a painful, terrible blur to him. He simply remembered the look on Mr. Peter's face when he walked through the doors. There was no smile, no usual smart quip to tease Tristan. Just a look of understanding and acknowledgment. The young man didn't get two words out of his mouth before Mr. Peters gave him a hug. Mr. Peters simply patted him on the back and gently told him, "It's all right, son. It's all right. We live to fight another day." After helping get the boy cleaned up, Mr. Peters handed him an ice bag to help reduce the swelling on his face and sides.

"That does indeed sound like a bloody rough day from any perspective, my lad" Mr. Peters sighed. "Such a shame what has happened to that Chatman boy, as well."

"Shame?! Who cares about that overgrown troll?! He's a jerk! I hope he gets a lifetime of suspension and kicked off the team!" Tristan exclaimed. Mr. Peters shook his head in disapproval at Tristan's outburst.

"Careful, young man. The hero who is consumed in the hatred toward his enemies and fails to empathize often risks straying down their dark path," he said ominously. Tristan fell silent to Mr. Peter's words but couldn't help but feel a lingering resentment toward his classmate. He was also dreading having to explain his current state to his parents and wanted to make sure he beat them home. He thanked Mr. Peters for his help and biked home while the sun set behind him.

Tristan made it home before his parents and placed his bike in the garage. He slowly trudged up the stairs to his room, locking the door behind him. After a brief shower, he threw on some clothes before getting his black and blue body under the covers of his bed. In his heart, Tristan longed for the comfort of his parents. He wanted to cry to them and have them tell him that everything would be fine and that they were proud that he at least tried to stand up for himself. But all he could think of was how ashamed they would look when they saw him, beaten and battered. As Tristan replayed the day's events, he laid his head down in his pillow, muffling the sound of his sobs.

Chapter 2: The Party

Tristan was sound asleep when the loud pounding on his door began. He awoke with a start, falling out of his bed in shock. The door continued to slam as if about to fly off of the hinges. *What the hell is going on?!* "Who is it?!" Tristan stammered, his heart rate elevated, but all he heard was a menacing growl in response. "Seriously, knock it off!" Tristan exclaimed to no avail. He slowly snuck around his bed and quietly moved beside the door, ready for an intruder to burst through. "Dad, if this is you, you're not funny! Cut it out!" Tristan thought the door was about to fall over from all the slamming, his hands moist when he reached for the handle.

Suddenly, the banging ceased, the commotion abruptly gone. Tristan tried to listen to hear if there was any breathing behind the door, but all he heard was silence. Getting onto his hands and knees, Tristan checked underneath the door but could see no signs of anyone, not even a shadow. Tristan slowly unlocked the door and began to peer out.

Without warning, the door blew back and Tristan yelped in surprise, jumping backward. Before he knew what had happened, he was thrown back onto his bed. Tristan barely had time to scream and curl into the fetal position before he felt a muscular arm wrap around his neck and familiar knuckles quickly rubbing their way through his disheveled hair.

"Noogie Monster!" cried Allen as he rubbed Tristan's scalp raw. Tristan roared in frustration, flailing around, unable to break his older brother's death grip. He heard the sounds of laughter behind him, while his family looked on, ignoring the pleas of their youngest.

"Allen, I'm gonna kill you!" Tristan squealed, but his threats were met with more laughter from his oldest sibling. Finally, Allen released his grip, held down Tristan's swinging arms, and simply sat on him.

"What's up, little brother?! Happy birthday, big guy! Tell me you aren't happy to see me." Tristan snarled in response. "Aww, I love you too! Hurry up and get dressed, Mom made breakfast, and the flight here had me starving."

Tristan's brother gave him one of his trademark playful grins, and despite the mounting pressure on his bruised ribs, Tristan couldn't stay mad at him. Allen's antics matched well with his youthful face, which he tried to make appear more mature by growing out his curly hair to his shoulders and sporting a fairly thick beard. Tristan's older sister walked into the room, shaking her head, trying to hide her continued giggles. She made her way over to Tristan and brushed back his hair before giving him a kiss on the forehead.

"Happy birthday, Trist. Be careful of Allen sitting on you. He had like three enchiladas for dinner last night," she warned. Tristan groaned in despair while Elaina straightened up, letting her dark, brown hair fall across her brown eyes and warm smile. Even she was enjoying Tristan's current predicament.

"All right you three. That's enough mayhem for one morning. Let's get the birthday boy downstairs so he can eat," his mother stated.

"See you down there, bro!" Allen said, pushing off of Tristan's chest before letting out a loud fart. Tristan cried out once the stench reached his nose, Allen laughing as he joined his sister down the stairs. He picked himself off the bed and, despite himself, couldn't help but laugh.

He was still smarting from yesterday's beating, but just being around his siblings again did wonders for his mood. He was sporting a nice shiner around his right eye this morning, and Tristan's left jaw had some residual swelling, not to mention the purplish bruises along his ribs. Starting to feel sorry for himself, he quickly shook his head, pushing away the negative thoughts. *Austin and the jerks at SMH are not going to ruin this day!* This was his birthday, and he would not let them take that away.

The scent of mixed berry French toast, bacon, and omelets filled Tristan's nostrils with a heavenly aroma the moment he entered the kitchen. Walking in to the "Birthday Song", Tristan was beaming before he sat down between his two siblings, who gave him a hug. The family tore into the food once the singing ended, and his siblings began to regale his parents with tales of current events.

Allen was a successful entrepreneur, whose vacation business was located in Alaska and focused on providing visiting travelers with excursions into the wild while staying in one of his several bed and breakfast cabins. From the sounds of it, business was booming, and he was looking to expand upon the property. Elaina's life was a little more reserved than her older brother's, working for one of the top genetic research companies in the United States. She was among the youngest at her company yet had already been involved in the publishing of several high-profile findings, her research focused mainly on the subject of genetic mutation. While Tristan admired his sister, he couldn't help but feel his eyes glaze over anytime she brought up 'genealogical tracing' or 'DNA barcoding'.

Eventually, the family wrapped up breakfast, and Tristan's sister turned to him with a playful nudge. "Alright, enough about us. How's everything going with you, birthday boy?"

"Everything is going fine, I guess," he replied sheepishly. "Same old, same old. You know how it is. Nothing ever really exciting happens to me."

Elaina seemed disappointed at the response before her eyes flashed with a sudden idea. "Hey guys, why don't we swing by the beach for a little bit this morning? I've been dying to see some clear water and white sand! I love the Puget Sound and all, but I'm pretty sure I can use a decent tan at this point," she suggested, staring at her pale arms.

"How about it, Tristan? Your mother and I have to set up for the party, but that sounds like a good plan for you three to catch up in the meantime!" Tristan's father said. Tristan found himself nodding in agreement. After all, he didn't get to see his siblings very often, and it was hard to pass up a morning at the beach when it was such a beautiful day out. Tristan set his dishes down into the sink and ran upstairs to change into his swim trunks. Perhaps it was just his imagination, but as he left the kitchen, he could've sworn he saw his family exchange secretive looks.

As soon as they arrived, the three siblings hopped out of the car and began to sprint onto the hot, sandy beach. Tristan couldn't have asked for more perfect weather, the cool spring breeze helping to negate the high temperatures and toasty sand beneath their feet. The three decided to set up close to the clear, blue water and laid out their blankets, pitching an umbrella to provide some shade. Once they were set-up, Tristan began to remove his shirt when he felt a sharp pain along his side. He lowered his arms back down, grimacing in discomfort. In his excitement for the beach, he had forgotten about the bruises by his ribs. He gingerly started over, taking his time to remove his shirt, revealing the ugly, purple marks beneath.

Setting down his shirt, he noticed Allen was making an effort to stare out into the ocean, but he could feel his brother bristling with anger. Even Elaina had a murderous look on her usually serene face. Tristan bowed his head and tried to act casual. "It looks worse than it feels, guys. Don't worry about it," he mumbled.

"I don't care if he is in high school, I would've knocked him back a grade if I was around," Allen replied softly, unclenching his fists.

"Let's just enjoy the day, boys," Elaina said, although even she seemed to be in agreeance.

The three eventually made their way into the water and swam around over the next few minutes. Tristan couldn't help but admire his brother's aquatic skills, while he maneuvered his way through the crashing waves with ease. It was almost as if he were propelling his body faster than even the water itself. At one point, Allen used the momentum of one of the rising waves to position himself onto his unsuspecting sister's path. Before she knew it, Allen had crashed right into her, taking her under the current. She came up cursing and hitting her older brother, and the two boys laughed themselves into tears. Lying together on the beach, Tristan soon forgot all about his troubles.

They had probably lain around for the better part of an hour when Elaina turned to Allen. "Hey, Allen, you remember how much trouble you used to get into when you were around Tristan's age?" she asked, smiling.

"How could I forget? I still have the marks from my spankings."

"I remember the time when the principal at SMH called Mom and Dad because they thought you were skipping school, and they wound up finding you on the roof!" Elaina said.

Allen thoughtfully rubbed his beard. "Yeah, I still don't remember how I got up there."

"Sure you don't," Elaina said rolling her eyes. Allen glanced at his sister with a look of false shock.

"I don't! And let's not act like I was the only one with a weird streak. Or should I bring up the time you almost got kicked out of school for smoking in the girl's bathroom?" Allen mentioned, his eyes wide with glee.

"I did not! They thought it was me, but it turned out one of the boys had flushed a smoke bomb in the stall next to me earlier that day! I was taking a—never mind! How do you even remember that?!" she said as the boys burst into laughter.

Allen turned to his younger brother. "How about you, Tristan? Any crazy stories to tell? Any unexplainable accidents?" he asked with a playful nudge. Tristan wrinkled his brow in thought. Racking his brain for any good stories, Tristan began to realize he had nothing good to share with his siblings. Tristan was almost never invited to parties and usually spent most his time playing on the computer or hanging out at the game shop. He was never one to misbehave, and he couldn't remember the last time he had gotten himself grounded or in trouble at school. Tristan was as plain as it got, just another face in the crowd.

"Not really, to be honest," Tristan said, looking down. His siblings exchanged skeptical looks.

"Well, it doesn't have to be anything bad. Maybe, something...weird or out of the ordinary?" Elaina suggested. Tristan shook his head. An awkward silence fell upon the three before Allen cleared his throat, turning back towards the ocean.

"Oh well, you're still young. Who knows? Maybe you've got an interesting year ahead," he said, staring off into the distance. Perhaps it was the tone of his brother's voice when he said that, but Tristan began to feel like there was something he was missing that he couldn't quite put his finger on.

The three siblings stayed on the beach for another few hours before packing up their belongings and heading back home. Tristan had just showered and changed his clothes when the doorbell rang, signaling the arrival of the Hernandez and Woo families. After setting aside their gifts, the families all embraced one another, thrilled to be celebrating amongst old friends. After they were done, they made their way into the living room while the three friends slowly drifted away toward the backyard.

Once outside, the boys walked around the yard, finding a soccer ball that Tristan had abandoned a few days ago. Tristan pulled it to him with his feet and juggled for a bit before passing it to Marco. The three friends proceeded to pass the ball around, reluctant to say the first word. His two friends looked as apprehensive and awkward as he'd ever seen them and, after a few moments of embarrassing silence, Tristan broke the deadlock.

"Look, guys, I'm sorry about yesterday. I should've answered your texts and calls. I was just, I don't know, embarrassed," he admitted. The ball stopped at the feet of John, who was looking down in shame.

"No, Tristan. You shouldn't be the one apologizing. We should have stood up for you. I'll be honest, I've never been in a fight before, and I didn't even know how to react until it was too late."

"I could've done something. Anything. I was just...too scared. Look at me, man. Those kids could crush me without even trying. I'm useless," Marco chimed in, sighing deeply. Tristan couldn't help but feel sorry for his two friends. It wasn't their fault Austin kept picking on them, but there was no way Tristan could allow it to keep happening. At that moment, Tristan realized that if he could go back in time, he wouldn't have changed a thing. Well, except for the part where Austin used his face as a punching bag.

"Don't worry about it guys. You know how hard my head is? Austin's fists are probably in worse shape than my face," he joked, and they burst into laughter.

Eventually, Tristan's mother called the boys in, letting them know that dinner was ready. Tristan's mother had really outdone herself tonight: grilled barbeque pork ribs, 5-cheese macaroni and cheese, garlic mashed potatoes, a multicolored salad, and a heaping plate of red beans and rice. The families bowed their heads while Tristan's father led them in prayer before demolishing the assortment before them, everyone praising Gwen with each bite. Tristan's mom kept brushing aside their many compliments, but he could tell she was pleased the way her face flushed red with pride.

After finishing his third plateful of food, Tristan was practically comatose, stuffed from overeating. He couldn't have even dreamt of taking another bite when the lights went out, and his parents walked into the room with a giant, Oreo cookie ice cream cake. *Well, maybe one more bite won't kill me.* The families joined together to sing Happy Birthday, and as Tristan looked around the room, he thought back to what Allen had said on the beach. Once the singing had stopped, Tristan made his wish while blowing out the sixteen candles: *For a year of change, one that I'll remember forever.*

After opening up his presents, the party began to wind down around 9 o'clock, both families starting to say their goodbyes. Tristan walked them outside to their cars and watched them drive around the corner, pleasantly surprised at what a great day it had turned out to be. He was exhausted from the beach and all the time playing with his friends, but this had been a birthday to remember. Tristan was ready to call it a night and read his new comic books before bed, however, when Tristan walked through the door, he found his family waiting for him in the living room. His siblings were standing beside his parents with a tense look about them, but his parents appeared fairly nonchalant.

"Tristan! How was it? You have fun?" his dad asked him with a smile.

"It was a blast! Thank you guys so much! You have no idea how much I needed that. It hasn't been the best week, but today was definitely the high-light, by far," he exclaimed.

"Good, son. I'm glad you enjoyed it. Hey, why don't you come in here for a second? We wanted to talk to you for a moment, if you don't mind."

Concerned, Tristan slowly walked over to the open couch across from his seated parents. "Everything all right? I'm not in trouble am I?" he asked, racking his brain for something he could have done wrong. His mother smiled at him, shaking her head.

"No, dear. Everything is fine, you're not in trouble. We just have some-thing important to tell you."

That doesn't sound good. Tristan gulped nervously, preparing for the worst.

"We'd like to talk to you about our family history," Tristan's father said, a serious expression on his face. Tristan was dumbfounded. This conversa-tion was clearly taking a turn he hadn't expected. His two siblings crossed the room and sat down on either side of him. Allen gave him a reassuring pat on the back, which only served to further confuse Tristan. *What is go-ing on?*

Tristan's father paused for a bit, forehead furrowed while he searched for the right words. "I swear, I've done this two times before, and it doesn't get any easier. Well, here goes." Oliver leaned forward and began his speech.

"Throughout history, there have always been those who have stood out for their amazing contributions to society and unique abilities. Whether it was geniuses, like Albert Einstein, or physically talented athletes, like Jessie Owens, they inspire people to this day and are models of what we all wish we could achieve. Beyond that, you can find individuals who weren't just great at what they did, they were extraordinary. I mean, really and truly special. They were the people who weren't just respected and admired but were revered and practically deified. Are you with me so far?"

Tristan was confused, not sure where his father was going with his speech. *What does this have to do with our family?* Rather than voice this thought aloud, Tristan merely nodded, allowing his father to continue.

"These extraordinary individuals have been removed from our history books, and instead have found themselves classified as legends or myths. Heck, some are even called superheroes. Men who were able to slay lions using only their bare hands and women who were able to turn others to stone with a simple glance. Some had powers so great, they were seen as gods themselves. These unique individuals existed within our world and were referenced throughout all cultures until, one day, they simply ceased to exist."

Tristan looked at his father as if he were crazy. "Uh, yeah, Dad. That's because they didn't exist. They were made up. There's no such thing as gods or superheroes. It was just a bunch of stories. Humans don't have powers like that. It's impossible."

Tristan's father smiled softly, staring at his son with a strange gleam in his eyes. "Son, out of everything you just said, only one statement was true. What if I told you that there are people who are capable of extraordinary things? People, who because of a certain genetic mutation, are able to develop powers and abilities unlike anything this world has seen before? That they didn't simply vanish, but instead chose to go into hiding to protect their species from a world that was growing to turn against them?"

"You see, you're right, Tristan, *humans* do not have these gifts. *Metamorphs* do. These genetically enhanced individuals have these powers. Your grandparents had them, your mother and I have them, as do your siblings." Tristan's father paused as they all turned to stare intently at him now. "And Tristan... there's a chance you do, too."

Chapter 3: Self-Reflection

Tristan blinked, staring at his family for a long time following his father's revelation. Looking back and forth between his siblings, he waited for one of them to burst out into laughter and yell out "just kidding", but they simply stared back at him with smiles of reassurance instead.

"So let me get this straight. You're telling me that everyone here has some kind of super-power, that you're all basically super-heroes?" Tristan asked.

"That's more of a human term for us, but essentially, yes," his mother responded.

"...and that somehow, I could have these abilities as well?"

At this point, his parents looked at one another and exchanged worried glances before nodding their heads again. "We believe that's the case, son, although we haven't seen you display any of these talents just yet. Genetically speaking, you have the trait, however, the gene itself may be recessive," his father explained.

Tristan sighed to himself and rubbed his eyes, trying his best to keep his temper under control. "And to think, that for once in my life, I was about to go a whole day without feeling like a complete disappointment. Glad to know my 'talent gene' isn't turned on."

"Tristan, we are—!" his father began, but Tristan cut him off.

"Look, I get it. I'm not some special, talented superstar like Allen and Elaina. We can't all make straight A's or be named on the All-American team," Tristan stated.

"Tristan, that's not fair. That's not what they're trying to say," his sister replied softly.

"Fair?! Fair?! Try being the turd of the family! Getting picked on every day at school while living with constant reminders of what you're not! All of my life, I've been surrounded by you, who all have these amazing gifts and are great at everything! You think I don't want to be special?! To be liked?! You think I like being...me?!"

Tristan's eyes begin to burn as he held back the tears, a lump rising in his throat. "Life isn't fair, Sis. Apparently, I'm living proof of that. Sorry I got the recessive genes. I'm sorry I haven't displayed any 'talents' like you guys, but some of us have to be okay with just being normal."

"Tristan, that's not what we're saying. Please hear us out. This isn't some metaph—" Allen began, but Tristan was already rising up to leave.

"Tristan, wait!" Allen called to him, making a move to intercept his brother, but Tristan's father rose up to restrain him. Refusing to turn around, Tristan stormed into the garage and grabbed his bike. He began to pedal into the night, making his way past the familiar roads while he tried to clear his head. Still fuming at their remarks, Tristan found himself flying through the empty streets around him. He was pedaling as fast as his feet could take him, chest heaving and lungs burning with exertion. Eventually, Tristan began to feel himself get light-headed, and he hit the brakes, gradually slowing to a stop as he struggled to catch his breath. His heart pounding in his ears and drenched in sweat, Tristan noticed a familiar neon glow beaming down around him. Looking up at the large sign, Tristan scoffed at himself, not surprised at where he had wound up. Without even meaning to, Tristan had managed to bike his way to Gamer's Empire.

The shop was probably locked by now, but he figured since he was here, he might as well see if Mr. Peters was around. Tristan tried the door, but the handle didn't budge when he attempted to pull it open. Disappointed, he turned around to get back on his bike, when he heard the clicking of the lock behind him.

"Mr. Davids, this is the third day in a row you've come to my shop looking like a mess. I'm hoping that you're not thinking of making this a habit." Tristan turned toward the old shopkeeper but couldn't find the words to say. Mr. Peters sighed and smiled at the young man. "Come on in. You can help me reorganize the board games before I close up."

Tristan quietly followed behind and was soon helping the owner return miniature figurines and dice back into their respective boxes. For a while, neither one spoke and simply worked to get everything back in order, until ultimately Tristan decided to break the silence.

"I got into a fight with my family."

Mr. Peters looked at him from atop a ladder he was using to place a board game back, glasses perched on the edge of his long nose. "Is that right?" he asked, waiting for the boy to elaborate.

"They basically went on a tangent about how special and great they all were, but that the jury was still out when it came to me," Tristan said angrily.

"Rubbish! I find it hard to believe they would say any such thing!"

"It's true! They said I haven't displayed any talents like them, and it's because I have recessive genes, or something. They even tried to convince me that they were like superheroes! A meta-something or another, I don't remember. Like I was some five-year-old kid who still believes in fairy tales! Can you believe that?!"

Mr. Peters laughed softly to himself and mumbled something that Tristan couldn't quite make out. He made his way slowly down the ladder and sat down in a nearby chair, pointing to an open seat beside him for Tristan to sit. "Now this, I have to hear!" he said.

Tristan sat down beside the old man and recounted his family's ridiculous conversation following his party. Tristan poured out everything that was running through his confused mind, while Mr. Peters simply nodded his head in acknowledgment, stopping Tristan only when he needed clarification on a point. Even after Tristan had finished, Mr. Peters stared on, unblinking. Tristan began to wonder if maybe the old man had dozed off with his eyes open when his eyes suddenly lit up and he shot out of his chair.

"Oh, sorry, my lad! Allow me to leave you for one brief moment! I need to grab something from my office before I forget!" Mr. Peters started to shuffle off, but stopped abruptly, turning back Tristan. "You were done talking, weren't you?" he asked apologetically. Tristan nodded in amusement. "Perfect. I'll be back with my thoughts on your rather peculiar situation," Mr. Peters said, resuming his exit.

Tristan waited patiently for Mr. Peters to return, listening to the sounds of the old man rummaging through his office. Eventually, he heard Mr. Peters yell, "Aha! Found it!", before making his way back into the room. He strode in the direction of Tristan, and in his hands was a thin, square-shaped box covered in festive wrapping. He handed the box to Tristan with a big smile.

"Happy birthday, Tristan! Wanted to make sure I gave you this before I forgot."

Tristan smiled back gratefully. "Thank you, Mr. Peters. You didn't have to do all that."

"Don't be daft, of course I did. There's no way I could let my most loyal customer go without a birthday present to show my appreciation for his patronage," Mr. Peters said, adjusting his glasses. "Now as for your unfortunate predicament, I have thought about it for a bit and have a few questions of my own before doling out any advice. The first question I have is this: have your parents ever brought up the idea that they were disappointed in you or your accomplishments that you could think of?" Mr. Peters asked.

Tristan thought about it for a moment. He knew there had been times when he hadn't done so well in his classes, but his parents were always pleased as far as his academics were concerned. Even when it came to his athletics, they would still tell him they were proud of him, despite him rarely getting off the bench.

"No."

"I see," Mr. Peters said, thoughtfully tapping his chin. "Well, how about this? Have they ever told you that you weren't capable of something? Or that you weren't as accomplished as your siblings?" Tristan scratched his head, but could not think of any recent times where they had cautioned him away from something or directly compared him to his siblings. He shook his head no.

"Lastly, I ask you this," Mr. Peters began, before leaning in and asking softly, "Can you remember the last time they lied to you?" Tristan stared at the old man in silence. *He can't be serious.* As if reading Tristan's mind, Mr. Peters held up his hand in acknowledgment. "Now, hear me out. I'm not saying that your family dresses up in tights and fights crime whenever you're not around. But maybe they were trying to tell you something," Mr. Peters finished.

Tristan burst into a sarcastic laugh. "What, that I have the potential to become 'extraordinary' like them?! Come on, Mr. Peters. Even you can't expect a loser like me to believe that!"

Tristan immediately regretted his comments as the store owner gave an annoyed snort before removing his glasses and rubbing his eyes. When Mr. Peters placed his glasses back on, a new look had crossed his face, and stern eyes stared back at the young man.

"Are you done? How long do you plan on attending this pity party, or have you realized yet that you're the only one in attendance? Are you seriously going to tell me that you are not every bit as capable as either of your siblings? Tristan, when are you going to realize that you are the only one holding yourself back? What are you so afraid of? You're at the stage in your life when it is time for you to start taking control of your own self-worth and stop allowing others to determine it for you!"

For what seemed like an eternity, Tristan could only look down at the floor, stung by the truth behind Mr. Peters' words. *What am I so afraid of? Why am I so down on myself?* Tristan sighed, knowing what the answer was. He was scared of failing. He was worried that he was letting down his family, unable to live up to the high standards that they had created. And as a result, he was unfairly blaming them for his problems and lashing out at himself in the process.

"Tough to hear, isn't it? But I don't think you came here for sugar-coating or sympathy. You came here for truth." The old man folded his hands together and leaned back against the chair. "What are your dreams, Tristan? What are your goals? Don't lie there and allow yourself to go through life in mediocrity. Don't stand aside and wait for the world around you to change. Be the change." Tristan felt his chest tighten with emotion, and he nodded in acknowledgment at the old man's words. "Now, do me a favor. Open up your gift already!"

Tristan smiled and proceeded to open the wrapped gift, revealing two thick packages of comic books. Tristan looked at the covers of all twelve comic books and was taken aback. Usually, he was well versed in all of the classic comic book titles, but this was one he had never seen before. On the front cover of the first comic was a picture of seven adults, who looked to be standing beside each other, each demonstrating a unique power. The title above them read 'The Adventures of the Magnificent Seven!' in bold letters. At the very bottom of the page was the author's name, and Tristan's mouth dropped in surprise.

"You made your own comic book series?!" Tristan gawked in amazement.

"I sure did. This was many years ago, when I first opened up the shop. We used to have our own printing press in the storage area near the back of the warehouse. The series did quite well, too! It was a personal achievement of mine, and I was proud that I had finally fulfilled my childhood dream. While I'm sure they aren't as good as those you have in your collection, I thought you might like them."

Tristan had no words to express his gratitude, so he stood up and hugged the old shopkeeper.

"I'm glad you like it. Now run along back home before your parents begin to worry," Mr. Peters said, shooing him toward the door.

"Thanks for everything, Mr. Peters," Tristan replied, beginning to walk out of the shop. Before he went any further, Tristan turned around and asked, "Hey, Mr. Peters? One more question. Why did you stop making these comic books?"

Mr. Peters paused before he answered, and Tristan saw his eyes moisten before the old man looked away. "To be honest with you, Tristan, after the events leading to the passing of my dear wife, I came to find that I no longer had the ability to face the characters that stared at me from the pages. Sadly, they no longer came to life for me as they once had," he murmured, patting Tristan on the shoulder. "Now, run on and think about what we discussed."

A few minutes later, Tristan could see his house up ahead and was ready to get upstairs and call it a night. However, he knew that before he did, he had some apologizing to do. He couldn't let his family go to bed thinking that he was still upset at them. Pulling into the driveway, Tristan realized that his mother's car was no longer there, and all of the lights in the house were out. *That's strange*, Tristan thought before he noticed the lone figure sitting on the front steps of the house. Tristan swung off his bike and walked to the door, the shadowy outline becoming recognizable.

"Hey, Dad," Tristan said, slowly walked over to his father, who was staring upward at the stars. Oliver Davids glanced down at his son, a tired look on his face.

"We were worried about you. Thankfully, Mr. Peters gave us a call a few minutes ago to let us know you had gone over there and were just leaving his shop."

Tristan looked down at ground guiltily. "That's my bad, Dad. I shouldn't have freaked out on you guys like that. I could have at least given you guys a heads up about where I was going. It won't happen again." Tristan's father gently patted the brick steps next to him, and Tristan sat down to join him.

"Well, I suppose if that's the worst you can pull off after sixteen years, I'll survive. You're not the first of my kids I've had that talk with, and I have to say, that was one of the better reactions."

Tristan was confused. "What do you mean 'had that talk with'? You gave that speech to Allen and Elaina too? Why did they get the speech?"

Tristan's father seemed to chuckle to himself, shaking his head slowly. "Tristan, I'm sorry if you misunderstood what we were trying to tell you. I don't want you to ever feel that you need to live up to any expectations or feel pressured to be the best. We love you for who you are, and all we want is for you to be happy. It was never our intention to make you feel bad about yourself. The fact of the matter is, Tristan, you are special, whether you believe us or not." His father paused for a moment before turning back toward him. "Why don't we take a ride out in the car before the family gets back? Just you and me?"

"A car ride? Now? It's late! Where are we going?"

Tristan's father flashed a mysterious grin before responding. "It won't be long. Let's just say we've got one more surprise up our sleeves."

Chapter 4: Revelations

B acking out of the driveway in his father's SUV, Tristan turned to the driver's seat and asked, "So where are we going?"

"Oh, we're not going too far. It's a beautiful, clear night out. I figured we could find some place to stargaze a little."

Stargazing? Since when did Dad ever stare at stars? Tristan wasn't much of a stargazer himself, however, he couldn't remember the last time the two of them had hung out and felt that he should make the most of the offer. While they drove on into the night, Tristan realized that he didn't recognize any of the roads they were taking, although something about it seemed familiar, as if they had taken this trip a long time ago. They were driving further away from the lights of the big city and seemed to be heading in the direction of the dark trees of the forest.

"Are we headed to a park or something?"

"You'll see."

Confused, Tristan turned back to the window. Watching the trees fly by, he could feel a growing sense of déjà vu.

"You know son, I see a lot of myself in you these days, especially when I was around your age," Tristan's father remarked.

"Like me? How?" Tristan scoffed in disbelief.

"Believe it or not, I was very much an introvert growing up. I didn't have many friends, besides my—, well, let's just say I wasn't very popular. Living in Liberty City, the kids in the neighborhood were...pretty brutal. I wasn't the strongest as a teenager and used to get knocked around a lot because of it. I was often frustrated at myself and felt that I wasn't good enough."

"Well, what about your parents? Didn't they ever try to support you and stuff?"

His father sighed softly. "They did the best they could, Tristan, but you have to understand..." His father trailed off, and Tristan could tell he wasn't looking at the road before him anymore. His gaze was toward a past he wanted to forget. Tristan's grandparents had all passed away before he was born, but while his mother spoke of her parents, Tristan's father was more reserved. He rarely referred to them and didn't keep any mementos of their time together. Curiosity had led Tristan to ask him on more than one occasion about them, but the discussions were usually brief.

"They were good people, son. Complicated, but good people. I've mentioned it to you before, but your grandmother was a nurse while your grandfather was a soldier in Vietnam when I was growing up. He was a war hero, highly regarded in his unit as one of the best pilots in the Air Force."

"Really?! You never told me that part! That's awesome! How come we've never heard of him?" Tristan asked.

His father merely shrugged. "Back then, there were a lot of great men whom history forgot. He did a lot for the war effort...but sadly it came at a price. When he returned, he wasn't the same. The things he had seen...really changed him. Over time, it changed our family and made growing up more difficult, to say the least."

Tristan's father cleared his throat and seemed to wipe something from his eye before turning back to Tristan with a sad smile across his face. "I guess the answer is no, Tristan. No, I didn't really have my parent's support when I was your age. They tried their best, but they had their own battles to fight. But you do, son. I hope you realize that. You'll always have our love and support."

Grateful, Tristan was about to reply when his father interrupted. "We're here," he said, making a sharp turn off the road and onto an unpaved pathway within a large patch of forest.

"Dad, what is this place?" Tristan asked as the SUV wound its way deeper into the dark, foreboding forest.

"Don't you remember?"

After about a minute, the car's headlights shone brightly on a chained gate up ahead with a large metal sign posted on its front. The sign read: "Davids Private Property- No Trespassers". Putting the car in park, Tristan's father exited the car to unlock the gate. Suddenly, Tristan began to remember why this area had seemed so familiar. "This is where we used to go camping when we were younger!" Tristan exclaimed once his father returned to the car.

"That's right. We used to go here at least once every summer when you guys were kids. Your mother's parents owned this land."

"Man, I haven't been here since I was, what, five? Why'd we stop coming here?" Tristan began to question before something else caught his attention. As the surrounding trees opened up to a large grass opening, Tristan noticed a familiar vehicle near the field. "What's mom's car doing here?"

"I told them to meet us here," his father said softly. The hairs on the back of Tristan's neck began to rise. *What the heck was going on*?

"Let's go, son. They're waiting." Tristan wasn't sure what to expect when he got out of the car. Perplexed, he walked out into the clearing and onto the massive grass field ahead.

At first, Tristan was taken aback by the sheer beauty of his surroundings. They were in a large field the size of a small stadium that was completely encircled by the neighboring woods. The lush green grass was covered in a misty dew while the clear, cloudless sky shone brightly with the stars above. Tristan's gaze was drawn to the center of the field where his father was walking toward three darkened figures.

"Over here, son," his father called out, waving him for him to join. Drawing near, Tristan could make out the rest of his family, softly illuminated by the moon's light. Tristan didn't know what was going on, but there was a sense of anticipation in the air, an eerie silence filling the night.

"Hey, guys? What are we doing here? Is this some kind of surprise camping trip or something?"

His mother smiled and shook her head. "No, son. This is much bigger than that."

"What do you mean? What's going on?"

His father stepped forward and placed his hands on Tristan's shoulders, staring intently into his brown eyes. "Son, there's something you need to understand. We're not what you think we are. I know that it's difficult to believe and you think that we're just trying to mess with you, but you need to trust us when we say you are part of something special. The things we spoke about earlier? About being a metamorph? Tristan, it's all real. Believe me, we've all been in your shoes. Every time we've had to tell one of our children, it's always been the same. The same anger, the same disbelief, the same pushback. It's normal. Heck, it's rational. But I need you to do me a favor here. I need you to suspend your disbelief for a moment. Okay?"

"Dad...guys? What are you talking about?" Tristan whispered.

"I wish there was an easier way, son, but I'm going to have to ask that you give us a chance to prove ourselves." Tristan's father turned to Elaina and said, "Elaina, dear? I'm worried that it's a little too clear out here tonight. I don't want any planes or wandering eyes to spot us."

"Got it, Dad. I'm on it."

With that said, Elaina closed her eyes and spread her arms out beside her, tilting her neck back to face the night sky. She breathed in deeply, and when she opened her eyes again, the entirety of her eyes had turned grey. Tristan felt a noticeable shift in the air pressure around him, and suddenly the surrounding mist that had covered the grassy floor began to rise past his waist and upward into the air. Tristan heard the surrounding trees shake with a mighty force, large pockets of mist rising through their leaves, and he gaped in wonder at the scene before him.

Elaina's forehead furrowed in deep concentration as a massive wall of mist, at least twice the length of the trees in the forest, began to solidify and was now circling the area. The top of the wall of mist began to fold in, eventually joining together, enclosing them all in a massive, ever-shifting dome. While he could still see everything within the field with perfect clarity, Tristan realized that everything else around him, from the stars above to the opening that they came in from, was all smoky and difficult to make out.

Tristan was struggling to get words out of his mouth when he heard his older brother let out a laugh behind him. "Man, I gotta say, that was pretty darn good. You got a lot faster since last time I saw you use the dome technique." Elaina grinned at her older brother, clearly pleased at her handiwork. "Still, it's gotta be tough having the lamest power in the family." Elaina's smile quickly turned to a frown, and she punched her brother in the arm.

"All right, Allen. You're up." Tristan's father said.

Smirking at his younger brother, Allen stepped forward, removing both his jacket and boots. Bringing his hands to his sides, palms facing toward the ground, Allen paused, frowning. "You know, I really need to work on coming up with a catchphrase for this."

Elaina snorted and replied, "Yeah, good luck with that one! Twenty-five years on this Earth, and I've yet to hear you say something cool."

Allen turned his head to his sister, grinning mischievously. "Sooome-thiiing coooool!" he screamed. Suddenly, Allen ignited into a burst of flame, fire exploding out of his bare feet, open palms, and long hair. He rocketed upward, smoke billowing in the scorched air behind him. Tristan could hardly wrap his mind around what he was seeing, barely able to make out the flaming object streaking across the sky. Tristan's screams of terror mingled with his brother's screams of excitement, as Allen flew around the misty dome at a pace rivaling a fighter jet.

"I swear, that boy cannot help but show off anytime he gets a chance," Tristan's father said, shaking his head.

"I wonder where he gets that from?" Tristan's mother jokingly replied. Tristan's father blushed slightly before raising his hands to his mouth.

"All right, Allen, that's enough! I think Tristan has an idea of your powers! Come down now!" he yelled.

"Aww c'mon! Let's do a round of target practice before I land!"

Tristan's mother frowned at her husband. "You know I hate it when you two play that silly game. It's too dangerous."

"We haven't played that game in a long time, and he's an adult now, honey. We barely get a chance to play anymore. What's the harm?" his father asked playfully before dashing around the field to pick up handfuls of nearby rocks. Tristan watched while his dad's arm wound up, preparing to throw. Olly's hand began to shimmer with a soft, iridescent, red glow, and every bone and muscle in his hand became visible, like a bright, red X-ray.

"Here it comes!" his father yelled, before launching the handful of rocks upward with all his might. The red glow immediately left his father's hands and instead transferred to the tiny projectiles as they shot upward in Allen's direction like fiery bullets. The projectiles closed in on Allen, and Tristan braced himself for the sight of impact.

Without warning, each individual rock exploded, one after another, with the force of a hand grenade. Tristan fell backward onto his butt, scrambling for dear life while the sky filled with fiery clouds of smoke and debris reminiscent of 4th of July fireworks. As each rock detonated in a wild blast of energy, Allen expertly piloted himself in between each explosion, pinballing himself in lightning-fast bursts of flaming propulsion to avoid being struck head-on. Tristan heard his brother scream in excitement, flying through each blast unscathed.

When the last projectile had dissipated, Allen took one final launch straight up into the air. Nearing the top of the dome, Allen suddenly turned off, flames extinguishing around his extremities. *What's he doing?!* Tristan watched his brother gradually slow down, and at the peak of his projection, Allen flipped 180 degrees, head facing toward the ground below...and fell.

"Allen!" Tristan screamed and leaped back on to his feet, concerned that his brother was now plummeting toward his death. Halfway down, Allen's hands and feet began to flicker again, almost as if he were building up steam. Suddenly, the sound of cannon fire filled the air, and with a burst of smoke, Allen shot straight down at a speed so fast Tristan's eyes were unable to follow. His brother landed on the ground about twenty feet from him, Tristan nearly flying back from the impact while dirt and debris rained all around them.

Tristan coughed, waving his arms to blow back the smog and radiating heat around him. His ears were ringing from the combined sounds of the overhead propulsion and the subsequent crash landing, but he could still make out Elaina's voice complaining, "Geez, Allen! Did you have to do that so close to us?!"

The smoke clearing, Tristan heard Allen's familiar laugh as he stepped out of the large hole he had made before them. His brother's clothes were singed from the flames, and he was smeared in dirt and soot while steam came off his sweaty body. He dusted off his hands and tried to clean the remaining grime off his jeans as he grinned at his brother. "Well, Trist? What do you think? Pretty cool, huh?"

Tristan looked at his siblings before glancing back and forth at his parents, unable to find the words to say. He felt himself take a deep breath, and before anyone could stop him, Tristan spun around and sprinted as fast as his legs could take him to the car.

Tristan could hear the voices of his family calling out for him to stop, but he had no intentions of slowing down. He needed to get as far away from these people as possible. Tristan was already calculating his route of escape once he sprinted through the clearing and onto the dirt path leading back to the road. *All right, don't panic. My once normal family has been abducted by superpower-wielding aliens from outer space. That explains today's events. The people I've grown to know and love are no longer alive and their bodies have been copied by the aliens as a way to force me to join their evil plans of world domination. Yeah, that makes sense.* He figured he could make his way through the forest, past the wall of mist, and hopefully find some passing car to flag down and help him get away from his abductors.

Passing branches snapped around him when he sped by, thoroughly scratching up his arms and legs, although Tristan barely noticed with all of the adrenaline coursing through his veins. Tristan could hear the sounds of the road up ahead when suddenly his mother appeared a few feet before him. Due to the mist and forest cover overhead, Tristan could barely make out her familiar form as she called out to him.

"Tristan! Tristan! It's okay! It's okay!" she said, arms held up before her as if trying to tame a wild horse. "Try to calm down, sweetheart. We're sorry for shocking you like that. I know it's a lot to take in, but try to breathe, baby. You're okay."

Tristan was hyperventilating at this point, tears coming down his face. He barely had the composure to choke out, "I'm not okay! What the heck is going on?! What's happening?! How are you guys doing this?!" His mom gently shushed him, stepping gently across the forest floor.

"I know, sweetie. I know. It doesn't make sense right now. But come back to us and we can explain."

At that moment, while Tristan's mom made her way toward her son, she stepped into a patch of moonlight, and Tristan screamed. Where his 'mother' stood was a large humanoid with her exact features except it was entirely made up of leaves, vines, and branches. It was as if his mother was some sort of plant version of herself. "Tristan, it's okay!" she tried to say, but Tristan was already sprinting away from her. Running through the path, several plant copies of his mother began to spring from the ground, calling after him. It was like some sort of zombie apocalypse he had seen from the movies! Tristan was hitting full speed at this point and blowing past the animated wooden copies pleading beside him. He could just make out an opening ahead and thought he could hear the sounds of a car.

"Help!" Tristan screamed. "Stop, please!" he begged, bursting through the final trees outlining the forest and onto the dark, mist-covered road. Cold, wet air hit his lungs as he turned toward the light of the passing car he had heard, a sense of relief washing over him. *Finally, I'm safe.*

"Tristan!" he heard his mother scream from behind as the bright, yellow lights of the speeding car surrounded him. Too late did he understand that because of the thick mist, the driver could barely see five feet in front of him. Tristan screamed in terror while the yell of his brother's voice, a flash of light, and the feeling of a freight train smashing into his side joined together, and the world around him went immediately black.

Tristan awoke with a start. He was drenched in sweat and breathing heavily as the morning sun shone through the blinds in his bedroom. *What the heck?* Tristan thought, glancing around in confusion. It was a typical Sunday morning, and he was safe and sound at home in his warm, cozy bed. There were no zombie plants, exploding missiles, or giant walls of mist to be found here. After a moment had passed, Tristan laid his head back on his pillow and breathed a sigh of relief, smiling to himself. *It was just a dream!* He had been sleeping this whole time. He couldn't believe what a strange nightmare he had been just experienced, yet it had felt so real at the time.

Tristan began to roll over to get out of bed when suddenly he felt a pain so sharp throughout his right side that he nearly passed out, crying out in shock. He heard the sounds of hurried footsteps rushing up the stairs, and his parents burst in, a concerned look on their faces.

"Sweetheart! Are you okay?" his mother said, rushing to his side and helping him back onto the bed. Tristan tried to slow down his breathing and attempted to lift his shirt to examine the source of pain. Where there was once a moderately sized bruise along one of his ribs from his fight was now a massive black and blue discoloration running along his whole side. Tristan's eyes bulged at the sight, his fears now realized.

"Son, we are so sorry about last night. You have to understand, by the time they were your age, Allen and Elaina had already begun to experience their abilities. It was much easier to get them to understand what was happening and trust what we were saying. We underestimated the fact that with this being so new to you, you were bound to panic," Tristan's father explained.

"We didn't mean to scare you, sweetie," his mother said. "We should have planned better when it came to having this discussion with you. It nearly ended in disaster." Tristan tried his best to fight back the panic in his chest, his mind wrestling with the possibility that everything he ever believed in was turning upside down.

"What happened? How did I survive? The last thing I remember was the car crashing into me."

"Uh, that would be my fault." Tristan turned to the sound of Allen's voice, who stood outside of the bedroom door with Elaina. "I was tracking you overhead when I saw the car coming. At the rate it was moving, the only way I could get you out of the way in time was to shoot myself down there as fast as I could. I did my best to cushion the blow, but I'll be honest, it's not a move I've practiced with a live target too many times," he admitted.

Tristan stared at the ceiling above, trying to process the millions of questions and emotions running through his mind. Even as a little kid, Tristan could remember pretending to be a superhero, imagining what it would be like to fight crime and have amazing powers. *But things like this only happened in movies and comic books, not real life!* Yet here he was, surrounded by the family he thought he knew, coming to grips with the fact that these beings might actually exist. Tristan took a deep breath and sat up, wincing slightly.

"Tristan, I know you probably feel a sense of betrayal right now, but you have to trust that there's a reason we had to keep it hidden from you. I'm sure you have a million questions, so I'll try my best to explain," his father began.

"Our family belongs to a species known as metamorphs. We're not superheroes or crazy space aliens. We're simply a type of human who has developed a point mutation, which has caused resequencing of our genetic code. It can be passed down from either parent, although some may only carry the trait and not the mutation itself. While this mutation would cause immediate death in a normal human being, we have discovered that we carry a specific gene, the Deus Gene, which allows us to undergo a metamorphosis instead. The mutation is initially latent but begins to trigger around the early teenage years before fully expressing itself around the sixteenth year of age. We don't yet know why sixteen is such an important number for it, but it's one of the things that researchers like Elaina are looking into."

"Once the metamorphosis occurs, our genetic code is fundamentally altered, allowing us to develop superhuman abilities. We are each capable of doing extraordinary things based on our set abilities, which are passed down from generation to generation. Now, we don't all have the same powers. It varies from person to person, as I'm sure you've figured out. On the other hand, sometimes people within a family don't develop any powers. While they may carry the Deus Gene and the mutation potential, it doesn't always become active, and that individual is deemed..."

"Normal" Tristan finished. "They're just a normal person...Is that what I am?" he asked, glancing around.

"We're not sure yet, son," his father replied. "We don't think that's the case. The mutation is...quite prominent between both of our bloodlines."

Tristan slowly shook his head trying to process everything his parents had just said. He could feel a mixture of emotions inside of him: anxiety from this new reality before him, excitement about what this could mean, but most of all, fear that he wasn't like them. Fear that he was, in fact, just normal.

Tristan looked at his brother, a sudden realization hitting him. "The stories you guys were telling me at the beach. You were trying to see whether I'd ever experienced something strange. My powers." His siblings nodded solemnly. "Why is this the first I've heard of metamorphs? If there's more like us, why haven't we seen them on the news or something?"

"Unfortunately, it's not that easy son. That's part of the reason why we've had to keep this a secret, from you and from the world around you. You see, you have heard of metamorphs before. Any time you read a book on Greek mythology or Norse gods, those are all tales of real metamorphs who existed in the past. Those are our ancestors. Any time you turn on the news and hear a story about some mother lifting up a car to save a baby, or a man surviving a plane crash, those are usually metamorphs."

"Well, why haven't we come forward? I mean, you said it yourself, people don't believe in us anymore."

"And that's the way we need it to be, son," Tristan's father replied. "Between being worshipped for their otherworldly powers and being manipulated by the desires of humans, metamorphs eventually became liabilities. We were either corrupted by the glory bestowed upon us or forced into a life of public servitude. Before long, we were feared by those who thought our powers too strong and hunted by those who wished to gain them for themselves. We had to disappear, to hide our true selves, in order to live out our days in peace."

"I know there's still more that you want to know. We have time. For now, try to rest up. You're still healing from last night. Take some time, and when you're ready, we'll meet you downstairs and try to answer more of your thoughts."

His parents rose from his bed and wrapped him up in a gentle hug, making sure not to apply too much pressure to his ribs. Tristan's siblings were next to embrace him, Allen being especially careful not to cause Tristan more pain.

"Welcome to your new life, little brother," he whispered, and they left Tristan to sleep and dream of a new tomorrow.

Chapter 5: The Council

If Saturday was a rollercoaster of emotions for Tristan, Sunday proved to be a much-needed respite to help him adjust to his new reality. While Tristan had thought he had plenty of questions to ask, he soon realized there was much still to learn.

To start off with, due to their attempts to live normal lives, it wasn't until the late 20th century that a number of metamorphs discovered one another and organized to form a group whose purpose was to find and nurture others of their kind. The group was coined The Council, and one of its founding members was Tristan's grandfather. It turned out that he was quite the legend in the metamorph community, something Tristan's father had failed to mention previously.

Vincent Davids was a fighter pilot serving in the Air Force when he met his wife, a military nurse whose ability to miraculously heal wounds was attributed to her medical skills, however, Tristan's grandfather immediately understood how special she actually was. While she initially denied his claims, his ability to produce and manipulate electricity quickly changed her stance. The two were understandably excited about their connection and soon began to actively search for others like them. It wasn't long before they had gathered enough super-powered individuals to form The Council, and from there began a lifelong project to help foster their new community.

After much deliberation and planning, the Council eventually decided to create a small school on an uninhabited island between Japan and the Philippines. Their purpose was simple: along with the fundamental foundations of education, they would teach the students how to use their powers for the good of society, so that one day they could reveal themselves to a world that was ready to accept them. The island was named New Pararaiha, and soon the Academy was built, enlisting dozens of teenagers every year who showed promise as metamorphs. During what was viewed as the "Golden Age of Heroes", Vincent Davids had been the first headmaster of the school and taught alongside his six other colleagues. The Academy was quickly viewed as the pinnacle of metamorph society and helped develop some of the greatest metamorphs of their generation, including, to Tristan's surprise, his parents.

Tristan now understood why Allen and Elaina had to leave for "boarding school" when they turned sixteen, both his siblings having trained at the Academy for four years before integrating back into society. As it turned out, not everything about their current lives was what Tristan believed it to be, either. When they weren't back in the States, both of his siblings were teachers at the Academy themselves! This brought up the next question Tristan had wanted to ask his family. It was gnawing at him from the moment they had all revealed the nature of their powers, but to his relief, his parents were already thinking the same thing.

"Listen, son. We don't want you to feel any pressure to say yes, but if it's something that you'd be interested in, we would love to send you to the Academy yourself in order for you to learn and develop your powers," his father proposed. Tristan immediately felt a wave of excitement and anticipation overcome him. This was an opportunity that he could never have even dreamed about, and for a moment he imagined what his life could be like if he accepted. Unfortunately, there was a small fact everyone seemed to be dancing around.

"Um, guys? Not that I'm not excited about the idea, but aren't I supposed to have powers by now? How am I supposed to even go to this school if I don't meet the most important requirement?"

"Well, son, we're not all the same. Some mutations trigger later than others. It's not an exact science. Heck, maybe you've been using your powers and never even realized it!" his father stated.

"Are you sure you can't think of anything? Maybe something that happened to you at school or with your friends that you couldn't explain?" his mother questioned. Tristan tried to rack his brain for anything out of the ordinary that had occurred in his life but could find nothing of significance.

"Well, there are some cases where people's powers don't manifest until placed in certain situations. Look at Aunt Lorie!" Elaina chimed in. Tristan's mother's face brightened at the suggestion.

"That's right, my sister was also a late bloomer. Navi didn't realize her abilities until her senior year of high school when she discovered that her power was to instinctively know her present location no matter where she was. In the air, out at sea, didn't matter, she knew."

Allen shook his head and chuckled to himself. "Man, what's with the girls in this family and having the worst powers?" Tristan's father gave a snort of laughter, which quickly turned into a cough at the sight of his wife's stern eyes.

"Wait, why did you call her Navi?" Tristan asked, ignoring his brother.

"Oh, it's a time-honored tradition at the Academy. At the beginning of the year, each new student is renamed based upon their abilities. It's a sign of letting go of their past lives, and their "rebirth" into the community of metamorphs," Tristan's mom explained.

"So, it's like a superhero codename or something?"

"Yes, I guess you could think of it that way," Tristan's father said with a smile.

"Well, what are your names?" Tristan asked, pointing to his family members.

"Mist," Elaina stated.

"Rocket," Allen said proudly, arms folded across his chest.

"Gaia," his mother answered.

Tristan's father paused for a moment, reminiscing. "Comet. They called me Comet."

Up until the evening, Tristan's family did their best to answer any other questions he had, and before he headed off to bed, his father pulled him aside. "Hey, I know today was a lot, but keep your head up. Like we said before, sometimes it takes time or a certain situation before you find out what your powers are. This doesn't change anything. Powers don't define us, Tristan. Don't you ever forget that, got it?" Tristan gave his father a small smile and nodded. "Good, now get some rest. Tomorrow's another big day."

"Tomorrow?" Tristan frowned. "What's happening tomorrow?"

His father paused before turning and looking at his son. "Tomorrow...you meet the Council."

The next morning, they made their way to the garage where Tristan said his goodbyes to Allen and Elaina. The Council meeting would take up his entire day, and his siblings had flights back to the Academy that after-noon. As he embraced the two, Tristan felt at a loss for words. This was the most momentous weekend of his life, and he was grateful that they had been there through it all. For the first time in a long time, they were united again by this common bond, this now shared secret. Tristan smiled at this thought, and it gave him the courage to face the day ahead.

Tristan and his parents piled into the car and backed out of the drive-way, waving goodbye before making their way to the meeting place.

"So where are we meeting them?" Tristan asked. He imagined that an organization of this magnitude would be located within a major city, per-haps downtown Miami, in a massive headquarters masquerading as a busi-ness or maybe an abandoned, shadowy government building. He pictured a group of costumed superheroes surrounding a large table discussing the fate of metamorph affairs, prepared to take action at a moment's notice, like the Justice League.

"It's actually quite close by," his father said with a smile.

"Really? Have I seen it before?"

His mother burst into laughter at his comment. "Oh yes, sweetheart. You have definitely seen it before," she said, with a mischievous smile. Con-fused at the reaction to his question, Tristan decided to leave it alone for now. He didn't have long to wait, however, once his father pulled into a fa-miliar parking lot.

"We're here," he said, turning toward Tristan's stunned face.

"You have got to be kidding me!" Tristan cried out, staring through the window while Mr. Peters waved at the three from inside of Gamer's Em-pire. "Gaaahhh! What else don't I know?!" he moaned, rubbing his head in frustration. His parents simply grinned as they stepped out of the car.

Since it was noon on a Monday, the store was a ghost town when they walked in, the usual crowd of customers either in school or at work. Tristan could only gawk in disbelief watching his parents and Mr. Peters greet one another like old friends.

"Comet! Gaia! Always a pleasure seeing you two! How are my favorite pupils doing?" Mr. Peters exclaimed.

"Wait, what?! Pupils?!"

"Of course!" Mr. Peters responded. "These two were among the finest to pass through the Academy when I was a teacher!" Tristan felt like his head was about to explode.

"Back in our day, Mainframe taught history and literature. The class was a tough one, but you couldn't ask for a better teacher," Tristan's mother remarked.

"Oh stop, Gaia! I'm lucky any of you learned a thing from this old quack!"

"Hold up, Mr. Peters! You're...a metamorph?" Tristan said stunned.

"Goodness, I thought that was obvious by now!"

"How come you never told me?! What are your powers?! Mainframe?!" Tristan fired off. Mr. Peters let out a chuckle, holding out his hands to slow down the impatient teen.

"Easy there, young man. I didn't say anything for the same reasons that your family could not. Also, I'm quite certain you would've thought I was quite trollied. As for the name Mainframe, I got that from my powers. I have the gifts of photographic memory and the ability to store infinite amounts of knowledge within this little beauty," he said, tapping the side of his skull. "Quite useful when learning and teaching the history of our species."

"So you're like a human...supercomputer?"

Mr. Peters nodded thoughtfully. "Yes, you could say that. Back in those days, I was still useful."

Tristan's father patted the old shopkeeper on the back, saying, "Useful? Don, you were one of the originals! The Seven would have never been formed without your guidance!" *The Seven? Why did the name sound so familiar?*

"Wait a second...the Seven? As in the Magnificent Seven? The comic books you wrote?" Tristan gushed. Mr. Peters nodded and tried to remain nonchalant, but a proud smile escaped his face. Tristan felt a new sense of respect for the man he considered a mentor. Not only was he a powerful metamorph, he actually knew Tristan's grandfather personally, and was one of the members of a superhero team!

"Well, enough of the past! You lot didn't come here to discuss this old man's former adventures. You came to begin a new future! Let us head to the chamber so that we can start the screening process and identify our young protégé's talents," Mr. Peters stated, waving them to follow his lead.

What screening process? Tristan thought as he trailed behind the three. Once they reached the far corner of the back wall, Mr. Peters opened a door marked 'Storage Room' and led them inside. The room was about a quarter of the size of the main floor, completely filled with labeled shelves stocked top to bottom with various marked supplies. They continued to walk past the shelves to the back of the room which led to yet another door, this one made of steel and unmarked. There was a hand scanner where the doorknob should have been and an eye scanner located to the right of the doors. Mr. Peters placed his palm on the screen, causing an audible click before pressing his face against the eye scanner. Once the scanner confirmed recognition, the doors opened, revealing an elevator within. *What could possibly warrant this much security?* Tristan pondered when they stepped into the elevator.

The doors shut before him, and Tristan felt the elevator shoot downward, plummeting them quickly for what seemed like only a few seconds. When the doors opened back up, Tristan couldn't believe his eyes. Before him was a massive room, perhaps bigger than the store above. The room contained computers and lab equipment, even a small workout gym in the back corner. There were TV screens mounted on the back wall and shelves filled with what looked to be old history books. But what really caught Tristan's eyes were the costumes and paraphernalia. Throughout the entire room, there were plaster models of various costume-clad metamorphs protected in glass displays, as well as numerous accessories, ranging from giant crossbows and staffs to antique pistols and jet packs. It was like a shrine dedicated to metamorphs of lore.

"Welcome to the Chamber of Seven, Tristan," Mr. Peters began, proudly waving his arms before him. "A reminder of our once great past, I've continued to maintain this fortress as its warden, ensuring that our proud history is not forgotten. Once headquarters to the Magnificent Seven, this has now become one of the several testing centers for the Council around the world. Here we will be performing various screens in order to determine your genetic markers, physical and academic aptitude, personality, and abilities. The process is rather extensive and personal, so I would ask that your parents leave you at this time so that we may commence."

Tristan's parents met his worried gaze with reassuring smiles that helped to slightly ease his anxiety. They gave nods of acknowledgment to Mr. Peters before turning back to the elevator, leaving Tristan to his fate.

"Well now, young Davids, shall we begin?"

Tristan gulped nervously but nodded his head. Mr. Peters waved for Tristan to follow him, and the two walked through the display floor to the section of the chamber that resembled a high-tech lab. Mr. Peters pointed toward a large steel chair in the center, similar to those seen at the dentist's office but with restraining straps.

"We will have you take a seat in that chair, Tristan. We're going to start by taking a look at your genetic markers. I will need to take a blood sample and electrical impulse reading before we begin our tests."

Tristan took a deep breath, making his way to the chair. He hated needles and was always squeamish whenever he had to go to the doctor, but he didn't want Mr. Peters to think he was a wimp. Tristan laid down in the chair while Mr. Peters secured the straps around his ankles, wrists, and forehead.

"This looks a lot scarier than it actually is, so try not to panic."

Tristan tried to slow down his rapid heartbeat and could feel his palms soaked in sweat while Mr. Peters reached into a drawer and pulled out a small needle, syringe, and vial. Tristan's eyes widened as the old man gathered his supplies, and he turned his head so he wouldn't have to watch. He felt the cold, moist wipe of the alcohol pad and winced slightly once he felt the prick of the needle and subsequent pressure of the blood being drained. The process was over almost as quickly as it began. By the time Tristan glanced back at Mr. Peters, the old man had already covered the area with a Band-Aid and was making his way with a small vial of blood toward a centrifuge. He placed the sample inside the small device and pressed a button, causing it to spin around Tristan's blood rapidly.

"Next up, we will perform a quick shock to the system, which will cause some minor discomfort but nothing painful or life-threatening, I assure you." Mr. Peters reached for another nearby drawer and pulled out two tiny, circular electrodes, connecting one end to a machine while placing the other end on Tristan's forearm. He proceeded to walk up to the computer and type furiously on the keyboard before turning to Tristan and saying, "Standby for a slight shock."

Mr. Peters hit a button on the keyboard, and Tristan suddenly felt a tickling sensation, like his arm was falling asleep, as a small electrical current zipped through his arm. He had no idea what the test did, but he thought that he could feel the current traveling around his body, from the bottom of his toes to the tips of his hair, before eventually returning to the electrodes on his forearm. Tristan took a look at Mr. Peters, who was staring intently at the computer in front of him. Tristan saw the old man's eyes briefly widen as he muttered "My word" softly to himself.

Tristan furrowed his eyebrows, curious at what Mr. Peters had seen. "What is it? Do you see something?"

Mr. Peters hurriedly clicked on the computer before saying, "Oh nothing, nothing. I just saw something that stood out a bit, nothing to be concerned about," he said, shuffling back to the centrifuge and removing Tristan's sample. He walked back over to the computer and placed the sample in the opening of a small metallic box on top of the workstation, which lit up red, yellow, green, in that order, before beeping. Mr. Peters glanced again at the computer screen, analyzing the results. The shopkeeper raised his eyebrows in a look of confusion before shaking his head and returning to Tristan, releasing the straps around him.

"Everything all right?"

"Of course! Like I said, nothing to worry about! Now, let us begin our testing!"

Mr. Peters then led Tristan to the workout gym on the other side of the room, where a bench press, weight racks, and a large treadmill full of weird devices awaited. "Here we will be testing your physical capabilities. I will attach a heart rate monitor to your chest, as well as some electronic markers to analyze your biomechanics while you go through some exercises. Give me just a moment to set everything up!"

Within a few minutes, everything was up and running. Tristan had a heart monitor placed across his chest and small Styrofoam balls attached to his arms and feet, blinking with built-in sensors. Over the next hour, Tristan was asked to perform various exercises, from maxing out on the bench press to doing a VO2 max test on the treadmill, and by the time it was done, Tristan was physically drained. After Mr. Peters brought Tristan a glass of water to drink and some protein bars to munch on, he explained the next part of the testing process.

"Now, we will be moving on to the academic and personality aspect of our test," Mr. Peters said, pointing in the direction of a large desktop computer toward the side of the room. "You will be taking a computerized test that will be scoring you based on your aptitude of both math, written, and verbal skills, similar to most standardized tests in high school. The final portion will be a personality exam, to which we ask that you answer as quickly and honestly as you can. Remember, there is no right or wrong answer for this portion. It simply allows us to get a feel for who you are as a person and what we can expect going forward," Mr. Peters said with a smile.

Tristan groaned at the prospect of taking an exam after all of that activity, wanting nothing more than to take a nap, yet despite his feelings, he slowly got up and made his way to the desk. Upon beginning the computerized exam, Tristan was pleased to find that this was quite similar to most standardized tests he had taken in the past. Before he knew it, he had cruised through the academic portion of the exam in a little under two hours, and the computer prompted him to subsequently begin the personality assessment. Having never taken a personality test before, Tristan wasn't quite sure what to expect. Some questions were relatively straightforward, such as:

"An armed man walks into the bank while you are attempting to deposit your paycheck. He fires his weapon before ordering everyone to the ground. He demands the bank's money, along with everyone's personal valuables. Do you-

a) Pretend that you are defenseless, before springing into action while the assailant isn't looking, taking him on yourself

b) Do what the man demands and hand him your belongings quietly. This is not worth risking lives for.

c) Ask the robber if you could join him in his nefarious plans, before backstabbing him in the end and making off with the goods yourself.

d) Secretly hide in the bathroom, while you call 911 to alert them to the situation. The more help, the better."

Other questions were more opaque and confusing, leaving him to simply guess:

"During your sixteenth birthday, you are given the power to turn into any form of elemental matter. Would you rather have the ability to transform into air, water, fire, or rock? State your answer and provide reasoning in five or less sentences."

"All right, Tristan, I think we have everything!" Mr. Peters told him, once Tristan had wrapped up the final question.

"So now what? Will I get my scores today?"

"Oh, yes. All of your results will be processed and analyzed within the hour before I submit them to the council members. Following submission, we will have to wait for the Council to view the results before we all meet to discuss your admission. Generally, in order for a student to be admitted to the school, they must obtain a majority of the Council's votes. While it usually does not come down to this, the student is allowed an appeal if denied initially. In the meantime, there is a small lounge to the far right of the room by where we first came in. You may remain in there while we wait."

Tristan thanked Mr. Peters for his help before walking to the lounge, admiring the fantastic apparel and armaments along the way. One day, he would need to take a closer look at all the gadgets that the Chamber housed within these walls. When he swung open the large glass doors and walked into the lounge room, Tristan was pleased to find several couches surrounding a large screen television, small eating table, and refrigerator. Tristan chose the sofa closest to him and sat down on the plush cushion. He found the remote and began flipping through channels, sinking deeper into the comfortable cushions. While channel surfing, Tristan felt himself grow more and more sleepy, the fatigue from the rigorous testing finally catching up to him. Within minutes, he was dozing off.

Tristan awoke to the muffled sounds of what appeared to be angry arguing. Initially, Tristan was disoriented as to where he was, before his memories flooded back to him in a wave. *What time is it?* he wondered, glancing at his watch. *6:00 PM! I've been asleep for nearly three hours!* At this point, his results should have been up and analyzed already! Bolting off the sofa, Tristan quickly made his way to the doors but hesitated when he saw the scene through the glass before him. At the far end of the main room, four of the seven mounted TVs were all on, revealing the large faces of the Council members, who appeared to be fervently arguing with Tristan's parents below.

Two of the faces on the left belonged to females, one containing old, wizened features, wispy white hair, and the greenest eyes Tristan had ever seen, while the other was a pretty, middle-aged blonde with a kindly demeanor. Tristan couldn't make out the features of the person to the far right, as they wore a shroud which completely covered their face except for eyes of radiant gold. The middle screen, however, contained perhaps the most intimidating face of all. A stern, weathered façade, complete with cold blue eyes and greying brown hair, stared downward, and the man seemed incensed about whatever was being discussed. From his appearance, the man looked to be someone of great importance and experience.

"This is a complete travesty!" Tristan's father roared at the screen. "How could you not accept him?! His scores were comparable to those we've received in recent years! This is B.S., Morgan, and you know it!"

Tristan felt his heart plummet into his cold stomach at the sound of this statement, his worst fears becoming true. He felt the room spin around him as he attempted to steady himself. He could see Mr. Peters shaking his head solemnly while his mother looked like she was about to punch through the television screens herself.

"I told you, Oliver, I don't care what his scores are! How are we supposed to allow a child into the Academy when they have not been found to have any abilities?! It has never happened before in the history of this great school, and I am not about to tarnish our name for the stupid sake of your family legacy!" the man named Morgan shot back, growing red with anger.

"Gentlemen, please! That's enough!" the old woman yelled out, trying to restrain the men from going at one another. "We are not here to attack the integrity of the Council! We are here to determine whether or not this young man has the requirements to succeed at this school. I, for one, am at a loss on how we can expect him to succeed when he does not have any abilities to begin with!"

"But he does have abilities, Agatha!" Tristan's mother pleaded, waving in the direction of Mr. Peters. "Don, you've seen his markers! He is a metamorph!" The televised heads turned toward Mr. Peters, who could only sigh softly in disappointment.

"Well, Mainframe? Is this true? Does the boy have any powers to speak of?"

"The results were...inconclusive, Principal Winter," Mr. Peters replied, glancing briefly at Tristan's parents. "The impulse screening revealed something I hadn't seen in quite a long time. His readings were through the roof. I'm not exaggerating here when I say we may be talking about...Power 9 potential." There was a murmur of disbelief among the group, even among Tristan's parents, as Mr. Peters continued. "And the boy does indeed have the Deus gene present, however...the mutation is dormant. For some reason, it has yet to activate despite numerous provocations."

"What does this mean?" the shrouded face asked.

"It could mean one of two things. Either the boy discovers what we could not and finds a way to trigger his mutation, or...he is to remain simply human," Mr. Peters replied.

A tense silence hung in the air while the Council considered the old man's words. Meanwhile, Tristan was trying to wrap his mind around what was just said. *Power 9 potential? Dormant genes? What did all this mean?* His thoughts were interrupted when his mother broke the silence.

"Morgan, I know this is an unorthodox situation," she began. "I know how highly you value the standards of the school, and I'm not asking you to show favoritism here just because we are members of the Council."

"Even though he probably should!" Tristan's father interjected before backing down at his wife's glare.

"All I'm asking is for you to give him a shot. The potential is there, you know this! Any other kid, this would be a no-brainer. He just needs to find his trigger, and if anyone is capable of bringing out the best in a student, it's you! If we leave him to this life, he will never become who he was meant to be, but if he's taken under your tutelage, I have no doubts my son will become one of the best you've ever had. He just needs a chance, Morgan. Please, set aside your biases and trust that this is a risk worth taking." At that moment, Tristan didn't think he could possibly love his mother any more than he did right now.

Morgan Winter's face softened a bit at his mother's statement, and he appeared deep in thought. He closed his eyes and sighed, and when he opened them back up to stare at Tristan's mother, there appeared to be a newfound softness in them, as if for a brief moment he had let down his guard and removed his gruff exterior.

"Gwen, you know much I care about your family. Believe me, no one here wants to see your boy fail, least of all me. I know how much this means to you all to have him here at the Academy, but how can I possibly justify having a non-gifted student at the school while denying so many others who clearly show talent? How can I believe that this boy can succeed here when he will already be starting so far behind the others? As the headmaster, I have to set aside my biases, look at the facts, and not let my personal feelings get in the way of these difficult decisions. I'm sorry, but my vote is no," the principal stated, bowing his head.

Mr. Peters sighed before stating, "Then it is decided. The vote is 2-4 in favor of rejection."

"Wait!" Tristan cried, bursting through the glass doors, all eyes turning to him in surprise. For a moment, there was stunned silence while everyone stared, and Tristan immediately regretted his decision. Mr. Peters was the only one who looked somewhat amused, smiling at the embarrassed boy with a knowing gleam in his eyes.

"What is this? Why is he here?" the golden-eyed metamorph demanded.

"I believe the boy is allowed to appeal the decision, as per the Academy bylaws. I'm certain these are his intentions...am I correct in my assumption, Tristan?" Mr. Peters asked with a mischievous grin. Tristan slowly nodded, trying hard not to let his jaw drop. *He had known all along this would happen! That's why he mentioned it beforehand and had me wait in the lounge!*

Mr. Peters gave him a reassuring nod before waving him forward. "I believe the floor is yours," he said, and Tristan slowly made his way before the row of intimidating faces.

Tristan cleared his dry throat and tried his best not to appear as the scared child he felt like inside. "Umm, hello. My name is Tristan Davids, and I would like to make an appeal to be admitted into the Academy," he mumbled, his voice barely audible even amongst the silence.

"Speak up, boy!" the old woman shouted. "These hearing aids can only go so high!" she said, tapping her ear.

Tristan closed his eyes and took a deep breath, familiar doubts flooding his head. Images flashed through his mind: Austin and his goons shoving him aside and pushing around his friends. His classmates booing him when he missed the open net during the soccer game. All the hurtful, mocking looks from his peers while they watched him get beat up and thrown to the floor. Tristan felt a wave of emotion start to build up and could only manage to stutter. "I—I—"

He felt his face flush as he heard Principal Winters sigh in annoyance above him. About to give up, Tristan suddenly heard a voice in his head that he had never heard before, a woman's voice that overpowered his thoughts:

"*Go on, child. Don't be afraid. You're more special than you realize. It's not us you need to convince, but rather yourself...*" Tristan opened his eyes, startled. He looked around, but everyone else was simply looking at him. Perhaps it was his imagination, but he could have sworn he saw the pretty blonde glance knowingly at him. A calm seemed to sweep over him, and Tristan took a deep breath, staring straight into the eyes of Principal Winter.

"I know I've placed you all in a difficult situation, and for that, I apologize. I want you all to know that I get it. I'm not like you, at least not yet, and if accepted, I would probably be the only one at a school full of super-humans who was...unusual. Trust me, the irony isn't lost on me. But if I can be honest, how would that be different from how my life is now? I'm sure you guys don't really care, but I've been picked on and made to be an outcast my entire life, treated like a freak because the kids see me and my friends as different. All I've ever wanted was to feel accepted and to be normal, but it turns out I am different! I'm not normal!

"Council, I don't know anything about 'Power 9' or 'Deus genes', but I do know this: I'm done trying to be like everyone else. This is the first time in my life that I've finally found something I'm willing to fight for, and I can't turn back and take no for an answer. After all this, knowing what I know now, there's no way I can go back to my old life, hoping that people will finally accept me. While my powers may not have shown up, that doesn't mean they still can't. I'm *going* to discover my powers, Mr. Winter, with or without your help. If anything...I hope you believe in that."

There was a long pause once Tristan finished, his heart still racing in his chest. For what seemed like an eternity, no one said anything. Breaking the silence, a familiar voice spoke: "I recast my vote. Yes."

Tristan looked up toward the blonde Council woman, his earlier suspicions confirmed. Tristan's parents both smiled in gratitude at her image and said simultaneously, "Our vote is yes."

The old woman above seemed deep in thought before she gave her answer: "No."

"I second that," the golden-eyed person replied.

Tristan's heart felt like it was about to implode as he looked desperately to the principal's cold eyes. The older man seemed to waver for a bit, his eyes softening when Tristan whispered, "Please, sir."

Principal Winter sighed and rubbed his forehead in vexation before saying, "I'm sorry, but my answer remains the same."

Tristan was crushed, the weight of disappointment threatening to engulf him. *How could this be? After all this, I don't even get a chance to try?* Tristan looked down at the floor, not wanting the Council to see his eyes welling with tears, when suddenly he heard, "Perfect! I vote yes!"

Tristan jerked his head up in surprise at Mr. Peters, who stood beside him with a smile on his face. The Council members all looked at once at the old man with stunned expressions.

"No disrespect to you, Don, but this is not your decision," Principal Winter scoffed from above. "The Council has voted, and he has not received a majority vote."

"On the contrary," Mr. Peters began. "In the event that all members of the Council are not present, former members are allowed to represent them and cast their vote in order to achieve a fair result! From my understanding,

Professor Stellios was sick this morning and, sadly, was unable to be present today, meaning that only six votes would be cast. As a former member of the Council, it is, therefore, my duty to cast the vote in her stead, which to my calculations, would give Tristan a 4-3 count toward acceptance into the Academy!"

"This is preposterous! Where in the rules does it say this?!"

"Article 9, Section 4-3, Sentence 2," Mr. Peters said matter-of-factly.

"How could you possibly know that?" Principal Winter questioned.

The old shopkeeper simply laughed before stating, "Because I wrote it, young man."

Tristan nearly fainted with joy as Mr. Peters turned at him and said, "Congratulations, Tristan. Welcome to the Academy."

As Tristan's parents rushed to embrace their son, he glanced at the faces on the screens above. While the other three seemed to be pleased or at least accepting of the final decision, Tristan noticed the narrowed eyes of Morgan Winter, who was clearly still upset. This was one of the happiest moments of his young life, yet Tristan couldn't help but feel that he had now made a powerful enemy.

Chapter 6: Saying Goodbye

Still in disbelief and floating on air, Tristan followed his family back up to the main floor of Gamer's Empire. The first thing they did upon leaving the Chamber was let his siblings know that he would soon be joining them at the Academy. They didn't go into detail regarding the difficulties behind his acceptance, and thinking back on it, Tristan felt overwhelmed with gratitude toward Mr. Peters. Tristan's parents were nearly in tears thanking him afterward, but their old friend remained humble as always.

Once they returned home and Tristan had gotten over the high of successfully appealing the Council, the reality of the situation began to sink in. His parents would soon be notifying his school, letting them know that this was Tristan's final semester attending SMH. Most likely everyone would think that his departure was because of the recent fight, but to his surprise, Tristan wasn't really concerned regarding this false perception. The thing that did bother Tristan was the fact that he would be leaving everything he had ever known behind, including his parents and best friends. Prior to getting accepted, Tristan hadn't really given this fact too much thought, but now that he was in, Tristan wasn't sure how he would break the news to Marco and John.

Not wanting to delay the inevitable, Tristan decided to let them know that evening, though he knew that he couldn't reveal the whole truth to them. Besides, Tristan highly doubted that they would believe him anyway, and he took a few minutes to decide on the right words before making the call. As expected, his friends were devastated by the news, and Tristan tried his best to explain to them his decision to carry on the family legacy. It was for the best, Tristan told them, and would give him a better shot at starting fresh and getting into a prestigious college.

Try as he might to soften the impact of the news, Tristan couldn't help but have a heavy heart at the sounds of his friends' pleas not to go. Besides growing up together, the three of them had shared something deeper that the other kids couldn't relate to: together, they had suffered the same difficult experience of being bullied. They had been made outcasts and stuck together when no one else cared. That was something that could never be replaced, and even though he knew it was for the best, a part of Tristan wondered whether or not he was making the right decision.

From the moment, he stepped back on campus, Tristan was prepared for the looks of ridicule and the verbal jabs his classmates would throw his way following the humiliation he had endured the week prior. When he ran into Austin and his goons during homeroom, Tristan didn't pay them any mind, despite all the dirty looks and banter. The most difficult part about returning to school was facing the disappointed looks of his friends in person.

"Guys, I'm not dying! I'm just switching schools, that's all. I know California is a long ways away from here, but I'll still visit. And we'll still play LOW together, right?" he said trying to console them. The two nodded in agreement at that thought but didn't appear convinced. Tristan wasn't even sure himself if the words he was saying were true, but it helped him feel like he wasn't being a total sellout to his friends.

The next few weeks were an absolute blur to Tristan, and before he knew it the school year had come to an end. There were no teary goodbyes, no heartfelt good lucks from any of his classmates or teachers. It was as if he had never existed within these halls, just another generic face in the school yearbook. In fact, the only person besides Marco and John who acknowledged his departure was Austin, who made sure he knocked the books out of Tristan's hands at the end of the day when the two were alone in homeroom.

For a second, Tristan saw red and considered giving the jerk an unexpected rematch. However, he stopped when he realized something that changed his mind: Mr. Peters was right. Austin was just a hurt kid, lashing out at the world. At the end of the day, he went home to a silent house and a broken family, where he looked forward to returning to this alternate reality. If Tristan was going to live up to his family name, he needed to start acting like it, he realized.

"Hey, Austin!" Tristan called out to the boy before he left the room. Austin turned around as Tristan thought of the right words to say. "I know you don't like me, and I'm not really sure why. You've bullied me and my friends for no reason, and you've done everything you could to make our lives miserable these past few years. I'm not gonna miss you, and I definitely don't regret leaving you behind. But I want you to know...I'm not angry at you. I wish things could've been different between us, but the past is the past. I don't hate you, and I know that you're not really a bad guy. I hope things work out for you and your family. I guess what I'm trying to say is...good luck, man." With that said, Tristan calmly walked out of his classroom for the last time, leaving his books and stunned classmate behind forever.

The rest of the summer went by just as quickly as his school year had done. When Tristan wasn't at the game shop learning from Mr. Peters, he was spending his remaining time getting ready for the big trip to the Academy. Tristan had never seen his usually calm mother so fretful. It seemed like every day she was finding new things they needed to get done: getting new clothes to wear for school, heading to the post office to get a new passport for Tristan, setting up bank accounts to help him pay for school supplies when he arrived at the Academy, among a million other things. And here, Tristan thought getting the school to accept him was going to be the headache!

One of the best things to come out of the summer was being able to gain more knowledge at the game store. Mr. Peters was a wealth of information, a literal human database, and Tristan tried to soak in as much as he could. He learned about how The Council had people in the Department of Education who managed to work around the system to make the Academy an accredited preparatory school. Tristan would be completing his final two years of high school there, as well as the first two years of college. Once graduated from the Academy, he could either leave with his Associate's degree or transfer to a human college to complete his Bachelor's. There was even a school sanctioned-competition called the Battledome, where students contended with one another utilizing their powers.

There were some downsides, however. Because of their efforts to remain hidden from the world, travel to the island was very restricted. As a result, there really weren't opportunities for students to see their families. Even calls and internet usage were limited in order to avoid human satellite detection. Once a year, they would be allowed to return home, however, that was all.

Along with going through a variety of books and references to identify great metamorphs of the past, Mr. Peters allowed Tristan back into the Chamber of the Seven to go through the various artifacts and treasures that were preserved in the displays. Tristan was fascinated by the costumes and weapons that were stored there and was curious as to why they were ever used.

"What do you mean why?" Mr. Peters said with an incredulous look. "For the very same reason you've read about hundreds of times upstairs!"

"Wait a second, you mean to tell me that there were actually superheroes? Like in real life?" Tristan exclaimed.

"Of course! How could there not be?! Wherever there are individuals blessed with extraordinary powers there has always been the push to use them...whether for good or evil. That is how the notion of superheroes and villains came to be. Metamorphs of the past were often called into action to protect humans from their brethren who wished to use their powers to subjugate the 'weaker species'. It was up to superheroes, like your grandfather and the Magnificent Seven, to protect mankind from radical members of the metamorph community. They used these same aliases and costumes before you to protect their identity from both humans and metamorphs alike."

"My grandfather was a superhero?!" Tristan gushed, eyes wide with wonder. Mr. Peters' eyes seemed to glaze over, lost in memory.

"Oh yes. Vinny was quite the marvel. Captain Thunder, they called him. He was a crucial part of the Vietnam War. In fact, the president himself gave him the Medal of Honor following the great war, but this, of course, had to be done in secret. Any records or files regarding your grandfather's involvement were deemed highly classified and destroyed in order to keep the existence of metamorphs from reaching the public."

"How can something like this be kept from the public for so long? Surely someone would have caught on and made a fuss about it," Tristan wondered.

"Oh, believe me, there have been many who have tried to bring it to light," Mr. Peters agreed. "They have speculated, somewhat correctly, that the government is hiding all of these secrets from the people of the world, keeping any knowledge or evidence of such foreign beings in one highly guarded central location. Area 51, they call it!"

As the summer sped along, Tristan's time with Mr. Peters eventually drew to an end. The old shopkeeper was needed on Council business and had been asked to travel to England in order to confirm the authenticity of a recently discovered relic which may have belonged to an ancient meta-morph. While the old man seemed thrilled to be sent on assignment back to his home country, a part of him was sad to leave the despondent Tristan behind.

"Don't you worry, young one. This is not good-bye. We shall see each other before long. You are capable of extraordinary things, and I look forward to seeing what the future has in store for you. Remember what I told you and make sure you give your best at everything you do. You are indeed special, Tristan, powers or no. When the time is right, you will know, and you will determine the change."

Tristan hugged the old man in a fierce embrace, trying his best not to cry, before Mr. Peters picked up his bags, locked the shop doors, and made his way into the waiting Uber transport.

"Tristan! It's time to go, sweetheart!" Tristan heard his mother yell from downstairs. The day had finally arrived, and it was time for him to be taken to the airport to make his way to the Academy. It seemed like just yesterday Tristan had been told that he had been accepted into the Academy, and now here he was, about to leave behind everything he had known and forge a new life halfway across the world. He had said his goodbyes to John and Marco the night before, the three friends reminiscing about the fun times they had shared together. Even though they had struggled to finally part ways, it had been a great way to send him off.

Tristan took a deep breath when he entered his father's SUV, trying to contain his rising emotions. The anticipation was killing him.

"All right, son. Big day today!" Tristan's father said, looking back at him from the rearview mirror. "I know this is a bit intimidating, but believe me when I say you'll be fine." Tristan nodded in acknowledgment.

"So which airport are we going to? Miami International?" Tristan asked.

"Actually, we'll be going a little further...Key West," his mother replied.

"Key West?! Are you serious?! Why all the way down there?!" Tristan questioned, surprised at the three-hour stretch he would be facing.

"That's where The Hanger is," his father stated.

What the heck is The Hanger?

His mother seemed to read his mind, as she explained, "Because we metamorphs exist in secret and the Academy is hidden from the world, we've had to find ways to meet and travel there discreetly. New Pararaiha is not located on any man-made maps, and we have done everything in our power to keep its location a mystery, erasing it from geological records and visibly cloaking it from passing ships and planes. That's how it earned the nickname 'Island X'. The only way to get there is for one of our private planes to transport you directly. Therefore we built this facility in secret to allow us to travel between locations without being compromised by human interference."

"We call it 'The Hanger', a desolate aircraft base privately owned by the Council and containing these transport airplanes for those who wish to attend the Academy. The planes were constructed by our own people and are technological marvels, capable of reaching incredible speeds while remaining hidden from any visual or electronic detection. Once you're on, you should make it to New Pararaiha in a little under a day."

Tristan's mother seemed to choke up on that last part, and for the first time, Tristan began to realize how hard this must be on his parents, sending their youngest child away for several years.

With a long trip ahead of him, Tristan placed his headphones on, and for the next few minutes, stared out the window, listening to music. Thoughts of the island played through Tristan's mind while they steadily got closer to their destination. Between his wild imagination and the peaceful oceanic scenery rolling by outside the window, Tristan found himself almost in a trance-like state. Before he knew it, he was slowly nodding off and fell into a restless sleep.

Tristan awoke to his mother softly nudging him and gently removing his headphones. "We're here, son. Grab your bags."

Tristan sprung up from his seat. *They were here already?! I only closed my eyes for a minute!* As reality set in, Tristan began to process his surroundings. They were one of many cars parked inside a massive airplane hangar. Tristan saw teenagers around his age walking around the large, steel building with their families, arms full of luggage. Some were joking around and laughing, excited to travel abroad, while most seemed sad to be leaving, hugging and crying as they said their farewells.

Tristan exited the car, dragging his bags behind him when his eyes locked onto the gigantic aircraft before him. Whatever images he had conjured earlier were nothing compared to the actuality of the behemoth ahead. The plane was built similar to a regular 747, but for the fact that it looked to have two additional floors added on above and was at least twice as wide. It had six turbines attached to each wing, and rather than enter through the side door by staircase, there was a massive hatch that opened from the back for the students to enter, revealing some of the coolest features Tristan had ever seen. The top two floors contained private, medium-sized rooms complete with beds and a desk. The bottom floor was a common area that contained several comfortable looking sofas and television screens. Toward the side was a dining area with long tables, refrigerators, and buffet style catering. *It's like a flying hotel!* Tristan thought, awestruck.

Tristan turned around to find his parents crying as they came forward to hug their son. He had tried so hard to not let his emotions get the best of him, but now that they were here, he couldn't stop the tears. Sobbing into her shoulder, Tristan heard his mother whisper in his ear, "I'm so proud of you, son. You will always be my special boy, you hear me? Always. I love you!"

She kissed him on the forehead before turning away to wipe the tears from her eyes. Tristan's father held on a little longer while he tried his best to compose himself.

When his dad finally broke away, he locked his wet brown eyes onto his son's and said, "I want you to know how much this means to us, seeing you grow into this amazing young man. It's been a privilege to raise you three and call you my own, and I hope you know that you kids are my heart. I love you, son. Go embrace your destiny, and just know that no matter what, your family will always be behind you."

With that said, Tristan's father joined his wife, and they watched their son reluctantly trek to the aircraft, holding his bags while trying to wipe away the steady stream of tears rolling down his face.

Boarding the plane, Tristan joined the line of about forty students walking up the large metal ramp and onto the soft, carpeted common area.

"Please have your ID ready to show as you make your way to the back! We will have your tickets for you once confirmed, and you can begin to make your way to your assigned rooms. Please make sure you place all baggage in the silver compartment located in the back of your rooms and make sure you are seated prior to takeoff!" a short, middle-aged man with greying hair and large grey mustache shouted once Tristan entered. The man had on a pilot's uniform and seemed to be the one in charge of the transport. After the students flashed their passports to the older gentleman, they were each handed a ticket with their names and room number on it and pointed to the stairs in the back of the room.

When it was Tristan's turn to hand in his passport, the man glanced back and forth between it and Tristan's face. Finally, the man broke into a grin and said, "Davids, eh? Another one?! Hope you're as nice as your sister but not as much trouble as your brother!" he said jokingly. Tristan gave him a half-hearted laugh, trying not to blush in embarrassment when he heard people muttering curiously behind him. He grabbed his ticket, which read "Third Floor, Room 13", and walked to the stairs before him.

When he reached the third floor, Tristan walked down the hall to the door marked R13. He inserted his ticket into a slot next to the door, and the metal doors slid open, revealing his cozy accommodations. Walking to the back wall, Tristan located the silver storage box and opened it. Once he placed his luggage inside and shut the top, a male voice came on over the loudspeaker:

"All right, everyone, this is Condor, your pilot speaking. Please make sure you are seated upright on your beds and buckled in with the seatbelts provided. We will be taking off in the next minute so please make sure you are secured in, as the plane hits high speed quite quickly. I'll let you know when it's safe to unbuckle yourselves and move around the aircraft. Thank you for allowing me to be your pilot, and I hope you enjoy the flight!"

With that said, a robotic voice replaced the pilot's over the loudspeaker, and a countdown began: "T-minus, 60...59...58..."

Tristan hurried away from the window and sat on the bed, the turbines outside growing increasingly louder while the plane began to power up. "45...44...43..." His back propped against the wall, Tristan looked around his bed and found two belt buckle straps located beside him. He buckled himself in, trying his best to make himself comfortable. "20...19...18..." Tristan closed his eyes and felt the plane vibrating with warm, contained energy, the sounds of the engines starting to roar. "3...2...1!"

Suddenly, everything seemed to stop. There was no more vibrating, no more heat, no sounds of the turbines to be heard. Just silence. For a second, Tristan opened his eyes and looked around, confused. *Did something happen to the plane? Did it blow a fuse or something? What was going on?* Without warning, Tristan's head flew back from the force of gravity crashing against him as the plane rocketed out of the hanger in one loud blast, racing forward at the speed of sound.

Chapter 7: New Beginnings

It took Tristan several minutes to leave his bed, even after Condor announced that it was safe to move around. He was still a bit freaked out and wanted to make sure he wasn't going to splatter himself into the wall if the plane decided to pick up speed again. Unsure of what to do at this point, he decided to open up the storage container and retrieve his backpack. Inside were the many comics Tristan had received on his birthday, and he figured now was as good a time as any to read some of them. He took out the pile of "The Adventures of the Magnificent Seven" first, plopping himself down on the bed to read.

By the time Tristan had finished the last novel, several hours had already gone by and he was growing hungry. He gathered all of Mr. Peters' comic books and neatly placed them away into his backpack before walking outside the bedroom door. Tristan felt butterflies zip around his stomach when he stepped outside the room, nervous about actually having to interact with his new classmates for the first time. Walking down the hallway, Tristan nonchalantly nodded his head at a passing student, trying his best to appear cool. The boy returned the nod with a smile, and Tristan began to feel a little better about his ability to make new friends. *Just take a deep breath and try not to say anything stupid!*

Descending the two flights of stairs to the first floor common area, Tristan found a large group of kids already down there. Some were seated in the kitchen area, gobbling down the food at the buffet, while others were lazily reclining on the couches, watching television and talking. *Okay, just be cool.* He prayed that he didn't look as nervous as he was feeling and quickly walked over to the kitchen.

Drawing closer to the food line, Tristan was pleasantly surprised at the inviting aroma of the impressive spread before him. There was a variety of foods to choose from: crispy fried chicken, gooey mac and cheese, steaming mixed vegetables, and even various seafood and tofu dishes. Tristan licked his lips, salivating as he began to pile food on top of his plate. Balancing two full plates of food in his hands, Tristan grabbed a Mountain Dew from the fridge before sitting down at one of the tables closest to the sofas. Tristan started to shovel down his meal while he listened to the conversation currently going on amongst the group beside him.

"Dude, I can't wait to finally get there," a dark-haired, baby-faced boy said. "I hear the Academy is massive! And with all the technology they have on this plane, I can only imagine how high-tech the school is!" From his accent and dark skin, Tristan picked up that the boy was Latino, and from the looks of it, he appeared to be younger than any of the other nearby students.

"You can have the technology, Juan. I hear the beaches are more beautiful than the ones I've got back home in Jamaica," said an athletically-built black boy with dreads beside him.

"I hear it's the same when it comes to the lasses, if you catch my drift," another boy replied, causing laughter amongst the guys while the girls rolled their eyes, audibly groaning in annoyance.

"Wow, Brandon. If you're gonna even try to pick up a girl, you better hope you have better pick-up lines than that!" Tristan smiled at the tall, bronze girl who had spoken, deciding that he liked her immediately. Her brash, confident demeanor was complemented by her strong features. Tristan didn't know her, but he could tell she wasn't someone to be trifled with.

"Aww relax, Cynthia. You know I was just having a bit of fun! Didn't mean nothing by it," the boy beside her said with his thick Scottish accent, giving her a friendly nudge of the shoulder. The boy had pointy ears that were nearly covered by his dark, wayward hair. He had a long face and soft eyes that for some reason made Tristan think of a puppy dog. The girl named Cynthia scoffed before playfully returning the nudge.

"I could care less about all that. I just want to figure out how to use my powers. It'd be nice to finally eat a full meal for a change without my hamburger turning into a popsicle halfway."

Tristan stared at the boy who had made the last comment, curious at the idea of a hamburger popsicle. The boy was on the taller side, his long, brown hair coming down to his shoulders, which he had to comb over to avoid falling in front of his serious looking eyes. He had movie-star features, but there was an air of coldness about him, despite his overall friendly demeanor. He gave them a smile, which revealed unnaturally long, sharp incisors. Tristan was practically mesmerized by how white they were, equally matching his pale complexion.

"Don't worry about it, Christian, you'll figure it out. If anyone can teach you how to control your powers, it's Principal Winter. That man is a legend!" said the Jamaican.

"Appreciate the vote of confidence, Malcolm," Christian responded.

"Legend or not, you better hope you figure it out quick, Chris. Last thing you want is to be facing me in the 'Dome unprepared," a commanding voice spoke from the middle of the crowd. Tristan craned his neck to see past some of the bodies blocking his view before spotting the one who spoke. The boy was slouched comfortably on the couch and had his feet propped up on the ottoman before him, looking more fascinated by the Sportscenter highlights playing on the TV than his peers.

He was a well-built kid with dark skin, short, curly hair, and a face that made him appear like he was always frowning. He wore a cut off t-shirt, revealing muscular arms, and a long necklace with a small glass bottle full of sand attached at the end. The boy turned his head casually toward Christian and sneered, "Don't worry, *chommie*. I might take it easy on you if I'm in a good mood."

The room grew still as the students looked amongst each other, an uneasy feeling of tension in the air. Tristan could have heard a pin drop with all the awkward silence when the boy burst into laughter. "I'm messing with you, Chris! Chill! We probably won't even see each other during the season. All I know is, I'm making sure my squad is stacked. Who knows, maybe we'll be teammates," he said absently, returning his gaze back to the TV.

"Sure, Gabriel...maybe," Christian replied, but from his tone and the look in his eyes, Tristan could tell that was the last thing on his mind.

"I wonder how our teams will be decided? I heard that your team basically determines if you pass or fail. If that's the case, I just really want a group that's going to hold their own in the classroom," said a girl next to Gabriel. For a second, Tristan completely forgot where his mouth was and nearly poked his eye out with his fork. He felt his breath leave him as he stared at the most beautiful girl he had ever laid eyes on.

She had long, wavy, dark hair and mocha skin, and he found himself drawn between her full lips and deep brown eyes. Despite her seemingly relaxed tone, Tristan noticed her fidgeting her hands and chewing her lip as if she were nervous about something. Tristan could tell that people in the group were responding to her statement, but for some reason, he couldn't make out what anyone else was saying. For what seemed like forever, all Tristan could focus on was the way she twirled her hair around her finger and the way the light seemed to reflect upon her skin. Her eyes eventually caught Tristan's, and as quickly as it had started, the trance was broken. Tristan hastily averted his gaze to his food and prayed that he wasn't blushing in embarrassment.

"—each member of your team," Cynthia finished, the group nodding their heads in agreement. Tristan mentally kicked himself, wishing he hadn't drifted off and missed what she had said. "Besides, you know I've got you if they name me a captain," she said with a confident smile.

"Not if I get her first!" Gabriel shot back, grinning while he stared ahead. "We all know Belle is a perfectionist. She might as well join the best squad," he said, patting his chest with unabashed bravado.

"Oh, please! What makes you so sure you'll even be named a team leader?" Cynthia asked, raising her eyebrows.

"C'mon Cynth! You know I hate to brag," Gabriel said, shooting her a sly wink, "but I'm probably the most powerful one in this class. You saw what I could do earlier! Imagine how much better I'm gonna get once we start getting stronger. *Jislaaik!* Watch and see, I'm gonna be better than that old-school super team that used to run around there. What's their name? The Super Six? The Fab Five?"

"The Magnificent Seven," Tristan interjected absently, and all eyes turned in his direction. It was the first time the group had taken notice of his presence, and Tristan wished he could have disappeared into his seat.

"*Ja, Nee,* that's it. I knew it was something like that. I was close," Gabriel mumbled to himself, and Tristan could have sworn that Belle smiled in approval.

"Look at the wee genius over there, hanging out by his lonesome!" Brandon exclaimed. "What are you doing over there, being all quiet and whatnot? Anyone that can get Gabe here to finally shut his yap deserves to be hanging out with us! Where were ya when he was going off about his basketball skills?" he asked, garnering a few laughs and a dirty look from Gabriel, who didn't seem to appreciate Tristan's intrusion. "What's your name, lad?"

"Uh...it's Tristan" he said, barely getting his voice above a whisper.

"Speak up, boy! No one can hear you over here!" Malcolm yelled out from the back.

"It's Tristan! Tristan Davids!" Tristan responded, trying his best to sound more confident.

The room suddenly froze, and Tristan looked around at the open-mouthed faces that were now all staring his way. Even Gabriel had lost interest in the basketball game playing on the TV screen.

"What did you say your name was?" Christian asked.

"Tristan Davids...did I say something wrong?" Tristan asked, finding himself incredibly unnerved at the silent stares.

"Davids. As in related to the school's founder, Davids?" Christian pressed.

Tristan nodded slowly as he responded, "Yeah, that Davids. He was my grandfather, but I didn't know him or anything. He died before I was born, but—"

"Dibs!" Cynthia interrupted. "Dibs! He's on my team! I'm calling it! Dibs!"

"What?! You can't do that! You can't call dibs yet! You don't even know what his powers are! That's cheating!" Juan protested indignantly.

"Who cares? He's a Davids! That's gotta be like a free pass for the year!" Cynthia shot back with a laugh before turning to Tristan. "What are you doing by yourself over there? Come over and hang with us!" she said with a friendly wave.

Tristan had thought about a moment like this for years, and now that it was actually happening, it took everything in him not to panic. *Remember, act like you've done this before!* Tristan told himself, taking a seat in one of the open sofas beside Belle. He tried not to make eye contact with her as he nervously sat down.

"So what's it like being a Davids? Did you grow up around famous metamorphs or something? Have you ever met Dr. Chronos? Were you—Oww!" Juan spouted out before Cynthia finally smacked him upside the head.

"Take a breather, Juan! Let the kid get a word in or two!" she said, rolling her eyes.

Tristan smiled gratefully at the girl before saying, "Well, to be honest, I never really knew about metamorphs until this year. My parents kept it hidden from me until I turned sixteen, so I never got a chance to meet anyone famous or anything. At least, not that I know of. Except for Mr. Peters—I mean, Mainframe. I've known him since I was a little kid. What about you guys? How did you all learn about metamorphs?"

"Our families, for the most part. The metamorph community is pretty tight-knit. We try and stick together, especially if we know there are others like us around. Kinda strange that your parents keep such a low profile, but I'm sure there's a good reason," offered a short Asian girl who suddenly appeared beside Cynthia. Startled, Tristan jumped back, causing two twin boys sitting nearby to laugh simultaneously at his reaction.

"Oops, sorry! I didn't mean to scare you!" she apologized.

"It's not your fault. I just...didn't see you is all. I hadn't realized—wait a second..." Tristan began to explain when he noticed something unusual about the girl. While he could make out her clothing quite easily, her skin tone seemed to blend into the cream-colored cushions of her surroundings. Tristan squeezed his eyes together and tried to refocus them, but it seemed the more he tried to look at the girl, the more she seemed to be indistinguishable from the sofa.

"Yeah, sorry, I don't have the greatest control over my powers just yet," she said in her squeaky voice. "Sometimes, when I'm in crowds, I get a little nervous and start to camouflage myself."

"Dope!" the twins said, nodding in approval. The Asian girl giggled before slowly coming into clearer contrast.

"I wouldn't worry about it too much, Emily. We have a hard time ourselves controlling our powers. It's pretty much reflex at this point," one of the twins said reassuringly. To demonstrate, his brother raised his hand up to strike the back of his head. As he swung down, the other brother literally became transparent, a gaseous imprint of himself, and the hand went right through his head. As soon as the hand had passed, the boy became solid again, although his shirt was now on the floor, and he glared at his sibling in embarrassment. His brother simply shrugged and gave him a sheepish smile. "We still haven't perfected not losing our clothes. At least you kept your pants on this time!" he laughed.

Tristan couldn't believe his eyes and was trying hard not to freak out over how amazing this all was. It was all so surreal, flying on a plane full of super-powered kids, headed to their own private island. It was like a dream world he didn't want to wake up from, until he heard the question he had been dreading since he had arrived:

"So what about you, Tristan? What're your powers?"

Tristan slowly turned his head to Belle and tried to give a half-hearted smile. "Uhh, well...it's kind of...complicated," he began to explain, before being interrupted by Malcolm.

"Ahh, don't be shy, brother! Even if it's something complex, it's probably much cooler than ours!"

Tristan felt his neck burning as he shook his head slowly, facing the crowd. "No...that's not what I meant. I, umm, I actually don't have powers...yet. Uhh, they're kinda dormant or something. I have the Deus gene, or whatever, but we're just waiting for the mutation to happen..." Tristan's eyes fell to the floor, an awkward silence filling the room.

Gabriel let out an angry scoff, slowly turning to Tristan. The boy's dark face had taken on a look of indignation and disgust, a look Tristan had seen countless times before on Austin, and a familiar feeling began to creep inside of Tristan's gut.

"*Voetsek!*" Gabriel exclaimed, his voice barely above a whisper. "Are you serious?! Are you seriously telling me that you got accepted into the Academy...with no powers?!" Everyone seemed to either be glancing away from Tristan at this point or shooting him accusatory glares. "This is some bull—!" Gabriel began, before Christian interrupted.

"It's whatever, man. Just drop it. It's cool. We're all good here."

Tristan attempted to shoot Christian a look of gratitude for the save, but even the pale boy wouldn't make eye contact with him.

"*Nee*! We're not all good here, pretty boy!" Gabriel shot back, standing up and throwing the television remote to the side. "How is it that we all had to bust our asses to get into this school, meanwhile he gets in scot-free because of a name!?"

"Gabe, I said drop it! It's not his fault!" Christian retorted, but Gabriel had a full head of steam, sauntering his way to Tristan.

The tension in the room was palpable at this point, and while Tristan could hear the cries from his classmates pleading for Gabriel to back off, all he could focus on was the bottle of sand around the looming boy's neck. It was as if a miniature sandstorm was occurring within the vial, the sand violently swirling around in a constant tornado, beating against the glass like the sound of a heartbeat. *What the hell was that?* Tristan wondered as the boy leaned in, menacingly, a look of contempt radiating from his dark brown eyes.

"You know where I'm from, Davids?" Gabriel questioned, teeth bared with each word. Tristan continued to meet his gaze, refusing to back down.

"No, I don't."

"I'm from the Namib desert, in South Africa. I didn't get to grow up in a famous family like yours. I didn't grow up with money, going to all the fancy schools and driving around in all the fancy cars. I grew up in a wasteland, one of the hottest places in the world, alone. I grew up with no family and only a few friends to watch my back as I struggled daily to get enough food and water to survive the next day. I grew up in dirty streets, where people won't hesitate to take your life if it means that they can take away anything of value. What do you know about that life?"

Tristan could see the lifetime of pain within the eyes of the young man and did his best not to let it get to him, not let it intimidate him into silence. He tried to appear composed before standing up, face-to-face with Gabriel.

"I'm sorry to hear that, Gabe. You're right, I've never had to deal with any of that, and I wish you hadn't either. But what does that have to do with me? What gives you the right to try to push me around? Because you think you're better than me, tougher than me?"

Gabriel barked out a harsh laugh, which reverberated throughout the room, before looking into Tristan's eyes and shook his head. "You don't get it, *laaitie*. This got nothing to do with me thinking I'm better than you. You see, when you sat down in that comfortable bed upstairs after punching in your first class ticket to Island X...when you sat down at that table over there to enjoy your plateful of delicious food and drinks...you did it at the cost of someone else. Someone else with an actual power. Someone else who didn't have the luxury of a privileged upbringing and had to fight and claw their way to even be offered a chance to test for the Academy! You see, my friend Yannick had powers too. He, too, lived alone on the streets of South Africa, dreaming of an opportunity for a different life, a better one. But Yannick didn't get accepted, despite the fact that he was smart and would use his powers to protect me anytime the street gangs tried to harass us. So yeah, this has everything to do with you."

At that moment, an overwhelming sense of guilt struck Tristan. Not once since he had been accepted had Tristan even considered the ramifications of his admittance. Standing before all of his peers, Tristan realized that it wasn't Gabriel who was seen as the villain, but rather himself. He had kept someone, perhaps someone more deserving, from a spot at the Academy. And it was all because of who he was and who he knew. It was all because he was a Davids.

As Tristan opened his mouth to apologize, a pale hand suddenly shot out to push back Gabriel, and Tristan watched Christian step between the two.

"I said that was enough, Gabe. We get it. We all have sob stories of our own. That doesn't mean we get to dump our baggage on each other and act like jerks. It wasn't his fault, it's the Academy's decision. Now back off."

For a moment, a look of wild anger swept across Gabriel's face as he moved forward to get face-to-face with Christian. "Easy there, Chris. Touch me again, and we're gonna have some problems. I'll put you and your boy here down for the count before your next photoshoot!"

To Tristan's surprise, Christian simply laughed in Gabriel's face, his gaze moving downward. Once he gradually stopped laughing and lifted his head up to Gabriel, Tristan noticed a change in his appearance. Gone were his soft brown eyes and easygoing smile, replaced by black irises and a menacing sneer, revealing razor-sharp fangs. His normally pale skin had become the color of snow, a sharp contrast to his now jet black hair that seemed to have straightened slightly past his shoulders. Tristan felt the hairs on the back of his neck rise up and thought he felt the temperature in the room drop fifty degrees. He could see the vapor in the air when Christian breathed, the boy stepping closer toward Gabriel.

"Trust me, Gabe, I'm not a stranger to problems...I am one. And if you ever step to me like that again, it'll be more than just the thermostat that I'll be adjusting." For what felt like an eternity, the two boys glared at one another, practically daring the other to make the first move.

"Christ...are we done here, or am I going to have to watch you two arm wrestle for who's the king of the jungle gym?" Belle asked, breaking the silence as she stood up. "Honestly, I know we're in high school, but I can't wait for the day you guys start to act like men instead of...boys." The pretty girl shook her head disapprovingly before walking away.

"Amen, sister," Cynthia muttered, following her lead. "Guess the party's over, boys and girls. I'm going back to my cabin. Thanks for ruining the flight." The others began to gradually disperse, leaving the three boys standing alone in the common room. Gabriel walked past Christian, bumping him aside with his shoulder before turning to Tristan.

"You're lucky your boyfriend here had your back, Davids. But he can't stop you from being exposed the minute you step onto the island. You might have been something special back home, but out here, you're just another nobody."

"You don't know me, Gabe. And you don't scare me either," Tristan growled back, hoping he sounded more intimidating than he actually felt.

"We'll see," Gabriel retorted.

Tristan let out a sigh of relief once Gabriel left and turned to Christian. "Hey man, thanks for sticking up for me back there. You didn't have to do that. Glad to see that not everyone hates me right now," he said, extending his hand. To his surprise, Christian simply walked past him.

Tristan swallowed hard and tried not to let his sinking feelings overwhelm him. Despite all his hopes, nothing in his life had changed. He was still a loser, no matter where he went. He didn't belong back home with the humans at his high school, and now he was facing a potentially worse situation here at the Academy. It seemed like no matter where he was, Tristan would always find himself an outcast, rejected by both sides.

Tristan slowly turned around to head back to his cabin, only to find Christian standing by the stairs staring at him. He once again appeared like his normal self, brown hair and all. "Listen, Tristan, I know you mean well and didn't ask to be in this situation, but you need to learn to keep your head down. You just put a huge target on your back today, and as much as I can't stand that jerk-off, Gabe is right. You're standing in someone else's spot because of your family legacy. I'm not saying that to make you feel bad. I'm saying it because you're going to have work twice as hard as the rest of us to prove that you truly belong here. It may not seem fair to you now, but it's your reality. Stay away from Gabe...and let's hope there's more to you than just a name." With that, Christian walked up the stairs, leaving Tristan behind, alone with his guilt and the growing thought that he had made the biggest mistake of his life.

The flight took nearly an entire day, and Tristan spent the remaining time in his cabin, avoiding the rest of the students. For the next several hours, Tristan was either taking restless naps or reading The Dark Phoenix comic books that he had received from his siblings. Condor, their pilot, would give updates as they grew closer to their destination, letting them know how soon before they arrived.

Finally, Tristan heard the announcement over the loudspeaker: "All right everyone, this is your captain speaking! Please make sure to buckle up as we make our descent into New Pararaiha, located a few hundred miles off the coast of Japan. I will let you know once it's safe to leave your seats and disembark from the plane. I hope you all have enjoyed your flight, and I wish you all luck for the school year ahead!"

Tristan placed the belt buckle around his waist securely as the countdown began again. Once the timer hit zero, Tristan felt the familiar rush of gravitational force when the aircraft rocketed downward into a freefall toward the earth. Tristan was happy he hadn't eaten since his earlier lunch, certain that he would have left most of his dinner in the atmosphere above. Suddenly, the plane began to slow down, bringing into focus a large patch of empty, open water outside of the cabin windows. Despite it being a beautiful, sunny day out, there were large clouds surrounding the plane and a thick mist above the water making it quite difficult to see and discern anything. The plane continued to head straight down, and for a moment, Tristan began to worry that Condor had suffered a heart attack during the descent and was plummeting them to a watery grave.

Just as he was about to scream in terror, they broke through the clouds below in a flash of sunlight. The aircraft burst through what Tristan realized was an illusion, and before his eyes lay the most beautiful, massive expanse of land he had ever witnessed. Island X was as close to a paradise as he had ever seen, clear blue ocean surrounding the white, sandy borders of the triangle-shaped island. Large mountains encircled the expansive greenery of large tropical trees while birds circled overhead. Growing up in Miami, Tristan was used to a tropical environment, but even he had never seen exotic, colorful plants such these. As they circled around a landing pad atop one of the beaches, Tristan could make out a large, grey dome hidden between an alcove of mountains to the north. His eyes could also see the outline of a massive building nearby that he could only assume was the school itself.

Tristan felt the aircraft right itself before it gently slowed down to a complete stop, landing quite softly on the landing pad below. Tristan could sense his anxiety rise after the plane powered down and the announcement came on to begin disembarking. He unbuckled his seatbelt and slowly trudged to his storage compartment, removing his bags and backpack. Tristan walked to the cabin door and found himself frozen in place. He closed his eyes and for a moment, he thought about staying on the plane, hiding until it made its way back home. He could sneak off the plane without anyone even realizing and contact his parents, letting them know he had made a huge mistake and just wanted everything to go back to normal again.

The image of Mr. Peters returned to his mind: "Be the change, Tristan."

He heard the words of his father: "Go embrace your destiny, son."

He remembered the look on Christian's face: "Let's hope there's more to you than just a name."

Tristan opened his eyes again, a resolute expression forming across his face. *No.* There was no going home for him, not anymore. *This* was his home now. And it didn't matter what anyone else thought, he was going to prove them all wrong. No matter what, he wasn't going to go down without a fight. And with that, Tristan took a deep breath, pressed the button to open the cabin door, and stepped out into a brave, new world.

Part Two: Hero in Training

Chapter 8: The Academy

When it was finally his turn to walk down the metal ramp and out into the bright, sunny day, Tristan found himself smiling, soaking in the sun's rays. He marched forward out onto the warm sand, allowing the tiny granules to trickle into his sneakers while he plodded along. The tropical paradise had to be at least 90 degrees, but the cool breeze coming in from the ocean made it feel like a lazy spring day. Tristan's gaze fell to the brilliant blue ocean beside him, the clear, frothy waves crashing along the shore and filling the air with a cool mist.

Still mesmerized by the ocean's beauty, Tristan caught Belle from the corner of his eye. She walked along the water's edge, allowing it to wash over her sandals, a smile slowly forming along her face with each passing wave. She seemed at home beside the water, and Tristan felt his heartbeat pick up slightly at the sight. Tristan was so focused on her smile that he nearly missed the large wave approaching beside her. Edging closer to the shore, the wave's crest rose up and increased speed, throwing itself where Belle was walking.

Tristan dropped his suitcase in panic and started to yell out a warning, but before he could get the words out, Belle spun around at the last moment, arms spread wide. Tristan's jaw dropped as he witnessed the impossible, the wave splitting into several sections and washing over Belle—no, not over—around her! Tristan rubbed his eyes, thinking that he was imagining things, but when he opened them again, there she was, walking backward while the strands of water followed her every step, streaming around her arms, legs, and torso, without ever touching her. Tristan watched Belle's radiant smile grow even larger as she giggled to herself, manipulating the water's movements like a skilled puppeteer.

"You probably shouldn't stare that long. I'm pretty sure there's a fifteen-second limit. Anything after that, you might as well take a picture."

Tristan was so entranced, he hadn't even realized Christian standing beside him, smiling and shaking his head. Tristan felt himself immediately turn red, quickly gathering his luggage out of the sand.

"I didn't—I wasn't trying to—!"

"Dude, relax. I'm just messing with you. Belle is amazing. It's pretty cool what she's able to do with her powers. I can't even imagine what will happen once she actually unlocks her full potential."

The two boys stood and watched Belle finally release the water from her control and turn in their direction. Christian smiled and applauded while she approached, and despite shaking her head, Tristan could tell Belle seemed pleased. Sighing to himself, Tristan turned around and walked past Christian, continuing over to where the class had gathered in front of a tall woman in khaki shorts and a t-shirt.

The woman had short, dark hair that was spiked up and large eyeglasses that nearly covered her whole face. She had deep blue eyes behind her lenses and heavy eyeliner, which combined with her hair, made her look like a punk rock star. Tristan guessed she was in her late twenties and wondered who she was. Once all the students had made their way over, the woman placed her hands on her hips and shouted:

"Welcome, new students! My name is Professor Sophia Cameron, although you may refer to me by my alternate, Cam, and it is my honor to be your host on your first day here! I will be your guide today and will be showing you around Island X. The island is obviously quite large, so we will only be going around the areas that you will need to know about during your first year. As you advance throughout your four years at the Academy, you will gain access to areas of the island usually reserved for the upperclassmen.

"Today, we will be going through the training grounds, Battledome, and some of your outdoor classrooms before we finish with a walk through the central campus! You may leave your bags where they are, and our groundskeepers will pick them up and bring them to your dormitories. If anyone has any questions during our tour, please do not hesitate to ask me! All right, let's begin!"

With that said, Cam spun around and began to march down the beach, the students following behind as they made their way north along the coast.

"As you can tell by the sun's positioning, we are making our way northwest along the coast of the island. These beaches are absolutely gorgeous and full of some of the most unique coral reefs and aquatic life in the Pacific Ocean. While swimming and aquatic activities, such as surfing and snorkeling are allowed, please be careful as the deeper waters do contain some predatory creatures!" Cam announced. "Now as we make our way between these two mountains, we will be coming upon the training grounds!"

Tristan looked past where Cam was pointing and could make out a wide path that had been created in between two small mountains. As the beach area became mountainous, the white, sandy terrain began to grow slightly darker and tougher while the ground level rose slightly, forming a hill. The walk up to the top of the hill was a relatively short one, and once there, Tristan had a clear view of what awaited on the other side.

Up ahead at the bottom of the path, lay a large circular enclosure surrounded on all sides by the mountains. The bowl-shaped expanse contained several grass fields and clay courts with large chain link fences around their perimeters, as well as a small building toward the back. Walking past a large arched sign overhead reading "Academy First Year Training Grounds", Tristan counted eight total fields and courts, evenly distributed, and couldn't help but be impressed at the sheer size of them all.

"Ahead of us lies the first year training grounds. We separate classes when training to ensure we have enough room and avoid any potentially dangerous situations. This area allows you to hone your talents while ensuring your safety and the safety of your classmates. The open fields are for anyone's use, however, the courts and weight room must be reserved ahead of time," Cam explained to the group.

Walking through the grounds, Tristan could see various training tools within some of the courts, everything from wooden targets to plastic human-shaped dummies. Tristan heard whistles of appreciation from his classmates and several of them were already discussing plans to train together once the opportunity presented itself. After they took some time to explore the area, the students continued along another mountain-bordered path on the opposite end of the enclosure. As they walked along the path, Cam spoke to them regarding the outdoor classrooms:

"Just a few hundred yards from the training grounds are your outdoor classrooms. As first years, you will have two classes that are taught out here. They require a bit of a hike, so make sure you give yourselves plenty of time to get to your class period to avoid being late. The terrain isn't bad, but expect to get a little bit of a workout throughout the year, especially if it rains or snows!" Tristan took the professor's words to heart as his quads were already feeling like jelly from all the walking they had done.

The path was a steady incline that wound between the mountains in a snakelike fashion, forming a large U from end to end. Toward the top of the mountain, just as the main path began to curve around, two ancillary passages were seen, one on either side.

The passage to Tristan's left was marked with an arched sign that had the symbols "TA 101" and led to a massive grass-covered overhang the size of a hardwood basketball court. The overhang overlooked the ocean in a stunning view and was carved into a flattened semi-circle with chest-high stone barriers preventing students from falling off into the treacherous waters. While the students toured around the area, Tristan walked over to the edge of the overhang, leaning over the barrier to get a look at the ocean below.

After they had taken a look at the first classroom, Cam took them across to the opposite passage, which led them to a large cave entrance with the label "DP101" carved out in the awning overhanging the entrance. At first, Tristan expected to find themselves in pitch blackness and wondered how they would be able to see anything, but to his surprise, the inside of the cave was actually well illuminated, revealing an amphitheater within. The amphitheater was quite large and the seats were all carved from the mountain itself, encircling a wide open floor about fifteen steps below. The sun's rays shone throughout the room, and Tristan's gaze followed them up to the open ceiling. It looked as if someone had taken a scoop out of the mountain top, allowing for maximum light to permeate through without exposing them too much to the elements.

Cam once again gathered the students together and began to guide them back along the main path, leading them around the curvature and down the other side of the hill. The descent was much smoother, and Tristan was grateful they were no longer heading up an incline. Once back on flat ground, the terrain changed from the dirt gravel of the barren mountain to the lush green grass of open fields. If the beachside view had taken his breath away earlier, Tristan was just as impressed by the colorful variety of flora that surrounded him now. Everything from mango and coconut trees to exotic plants and flowers he had never even imagined was spread out throughout the open land.

Stepping through the tall grass, Cam lectured them about the various types of plant and animal life that existed on the island and how their resources allowed the school to be self-sufficient. The class walked for about another mile before they got to the massive alcove Tristan had seen earlier. Within the pocket of surrounding mountains loomed a gigantic grey dome. The mountains blocked the sun's rays from shining on it directly, and it gave off an ominous appearance lying in the shadows of the giant rocks.

"Before you lies the Battledome!" Cam called out, sweeping her arms behind her like a curator unveiling a museum's finest piece. "Here is where legends are made, forged in the heat of battle! Each year, teams are permitted to submit their names to the League Commission to become eligible for competition and earn the right to raise the coveted Golden Cup!" This last statement brought about several whoops and cheers from the crowd before Cam raised her hands to quiet them down.

"The Battledome is a time-honored tradition amongst the students who have attended, but be warned, it is not to be taken lightly. Currently, the only teams to have claimed the trophy have belonged to the third and fourth years. But who knows? Maybe this is the year that all changes..." Cam said theatrically.

Next, the students headed south and soon found themselves walking down a narrow dirt trail that was outlined by tall grass and large palm trees with unlit torches attached. They followed the trail for about another mile before they identified the outline of several large structures through the branches. As they approached the buildings, Tristan spotted a large metallic gate up ahead.

"The school grounds are protected by a steel enforced barrier that surrounds the property. The gates are closed during certain times of the day to ensure the safety of our students. Only the teachers are given access to open them, so make sure you abide by the rules of curfew!" Cam remarked before pulling out something from her back pocket. She clicked on the small grey device, and the metallic gates ahead slowly opened, revealing the campus within.

Once they walked through the metallic gate, they entered into a massive grass courtyard that was practically the size of Tristan's old school. It had several small lakes scattered throughout the open grounds, with patches of shady trees spread around the area. There were brick walkways leading to various destinations, from the dormitories to the school itself. There were also small recreational areas throughout: miniature soccer fields, basketball courts, tennis courts, or just places to lay out on a hammock.

To the far right of the courtyard were the student dorms, two massive two-story buildings that were physically connected by a smaller one in between. While the small building resembled your typical square-shaped dorm building, the two beside it were enormous brick cylinders with domed roofs, modeled in the same fashion as an Italian basilica.

If the dorms were meant to draw the eyes with its design, the Academy itself was on another level. The building was essentially a four-story Pantheon made up entirely of pristine white marble, glistening in the afternoon sun. "The Metamorph Academy for Higher Learning" was etched into the stone overhang above, and the sheer size and beauty of the school overwhelmed Tristan.

"As you can see, our open campus is quite expansive! The lakes are open to swim in during the warmer months and there are several areas to play sports or simply relax, if you so choose. To your left is the magnificent Academy, where we will visit later this evening. Along with your classrooms, the building houses the library, student store, and cafeteria for all of your snacks and meals. While the classrooms and store will be locked nightly, you will have access to the study hall and cafeteria, day or night."

"To our right are the student dorms. They are separated by gender and split top to bottom, the first and second years above, while the upperclassmen have the bottom rooms. The connecting building in between is the common area, where there are a variety of tabletop games and a lounge area to watch TV, movies, or play video games. For obvious reasons, we do not use normal satellite reception for phones or electronics but instead utilize our own encryption devices. As a result, cellular reception will not function while on the island and your access to the internet will be restricted to only the university server."

By the time Professor Cam had finished explaining, they had reached the crossroad between the two dorms. The teacher pointed in either direction, instructing the girls to head left toward their dorms while the boys would head to the right. Their belongings were already waiting for them in their rooms, where they could shower and change before meeting at the Academy entrance for their final tour of the evening. Granted an hour's respite, the students quickly made their way to their respective dorms, eager to finally shower and get into some clean clothes.

Tristan followed behind the rest of the boys into the air-conditioned building, grateful for a temporary reprieve from the sun. Past the glass doors, Tristan was surprised to see that the inside of the building seemed in sharp contrast to its red-and-grey brick exterior. The inside looked like a modern hotel building, from the soft carpeted floors down to the beautiful oaken walls. The stairs were directly to the right of the entrance, with the common area to the left. The long hallway before them extended quite a distance to the back and contained doors on either side which opened to the boy's rooms. They found the second floor to be structured the same way and proceeded through the doors on the left labeled "First Year Sleeping Quarters".

The first thing Tristan noticed upon entering the room was how spacious it was. The room was shaped into a semicircle, with the closest wall containing all their beds with the headboards lined along it. The twin-sized beds were evenly spaced apart with a nightstand and gentleman's dresser alongside each. On the opposite, curved side were couches, reading tables, and windows with small sitting ledges that could be used to admire the clear view of the beautiful landscape outside. At the end of the room was a door leading to the communal bathrooms.

Tristan found his luggage beside his bed near the back of the room and noticed Gabriel was on the opposite end. Tristan was quietly grateful that he wouldn't have to deal with having him nearby. While Tristan unpacked his items into the drawers and cabinet space, Christian walked over to the adjacent bed, throwing himself face-down across the sheets in exhaustion.

"Dude, after all that walking, I'm just ready to nap! I hope this next tour is quick so we can relax or something!"

Tristan smiled at his neighbor, shaking his head. "I wouldn't get your hopes up, man. Did you see the size of that place? Odds are, we're gonna be exploring the school until dinner!"

Christian groaned in response. After pouting several more minutes about how the climate was damaging his hair and giving him a sunburn, he eventually rolled himself over and unpacked as well. While he still wasn't sure what to make of him, Tristan was more than happy to share the space with someone who wasn't going to give him a hard time all year.

By the time he was showered and dressed, Tristan had about fifteen minutes before the next part of their tour began. As they exited the building to head over to the Academy, Tristan noticed Juan walking beside him with a smile across his face.

"What?" Tristan asked the shorter boy, eyebrows raised.

"I don't know, it's just kind of ironic, you know?"

"What are you talking about?"

"The whole not-having-powers thing! Initially, I thought you were just trying to mess with us, but once I realized you were being serious... I suppose it's just unexpected to think that someone with your bloodline might be one of the underdogs around here."

"Well, I appreciate you not rubbing it in," Tristan said sarcastically.

The boy appeared taken aback by this, the smile immediately leaving his face. "There's nothing wrong with not having powers, it's just surprising is all! I'm not trying to rub it in, but it's only natural that you would be viewed as an underdog. Logically speaking, if you were to be matched up in the Battledome against anyone here, the odds would not be in your favor. I was merely making a point!"

"Yeah, well point made!" Tristan shot back angrily. Tristan surprised himself at the intensity of his outburst and could see some of the nearby kids staring. Juan didn't seem to be fazed by Tristan's emotional reply, however and simply shrugged in response.

"I apologize if I have offended you, as it was not my intention. At times, I struggle to empathize with those around me due to my powers and, from what I've been told, lack of social skills. I genuinely didn't wish to cause you any distress, and if it makes you feel any better, I myself have been an under-dog my whole life. Between my diminutive size and polarizing personality, I was never quite good at making friends and was often on the receiving end of school-yard harassment. One thing I've discovered from my experiences is this: never count out the underdog. Some of the greatest things can come from places least expected."

Tristan didn't know what to say and felt slightly guilty for his earlier outburst.

"My mom liked to tell me that before she—." The small boy suddenly paused before giving Tristan a half-hearted smile and quickened his pace, leaving behind a confused Tristan.

Eventually, the students reached the Academy entrance, making their way up to the front doors, where Professor Cam awaited. Once everyone was accounted for, Cam began her speech:

"All right, everybody! I hope you're feeling refreshed and ready to start the second part of your tour! I will be showing you all the details of your new school before we go to the mess hall for dinner, where you will also be greeted by Principal Winter himself! If everyone is ready, we can be-gin!" Cam said, escorting the students through the front doors and into the school.

After walking through the large front lobby, the students found them-selves in a massive circular expanse containing a gorgeous fountain with a golden statue of the Magnificent Seven at its center. The large glass rooftop overhead reflected the beautiful outdoor conditions in a colorful array of light. Tristan looked upward at the three stories of classrooms overhead, all of which were situated in a circular arrangement around them. The back wall contained elevators and stairs with classrooms aligned on either side.

"Here on the first floor, you will have access to most of your first-year classrooms. The room numbers go clockwise, so make sure you're paying at-tention to avoid getting lost. Straight ahead are the stairs and elevators to get you to the floors above."

Cam pointed to a set of glass doors to the left through which Tristan could make out rows of long tables and a buffet-style set-up at the far end of the hall. "To the left lies the mess hall, where we will host meals and snacks. Directly across the mess hall is the study hall, where you will have unrestricted access to the Academy library and resources," she said, gesturing to opposing glass doors, which revealed a massive room full of computers, tables, and more books than Tristan had ever seen in his life.

"The second floor contains additional classrooms while the third floor is reserved for labs. Lastly, the fourth floor is where the professors are stationed. Office hours vary for each professor so make sure you read your syllabus to know when those are! Now, follow me and we will take a quick tour throughout the facility!" Cam said, directing the students along.

It took about an hour for the students to explore each floor and familiarize themselves with the layout. Although the building itself was quite large, it was fairly easy to get around, the circular hallways making navigation pretty straightforward. The classrooms were all quite standard, and the professor's floor was also nondescript except for Principal Winter's office, which stood separate from the others at the far end with its large, wooden double doors.

After the tour, Professor Cam brought the students back down to the mess hall, where the cafeteria staff had set up dinner for them. Tristan had forgotten how long ago it had been since he had last eaten and made sure to load up his plate with all of his favorites before finding an open seat to sit down. Once he sat to eat, Tristan noticed that the other students had already formed little cliques of their own. Belle and Gabriel were sitting and laughing alongside the twin boys, while Cynthia, Brandon, and Emily were deep in discussion at the table beside him. Before he could feel too sorry for himself, however, he was soon accompanied by both Christian and Juan.

"Bro, with all this excitement, I had completely forgotten how hungry I was! The hike earlier was no joke!" Christian said through a mouthful of baked beans.

"You're telling me! I can't remember the last time I've walked around this much! Usually, the only things I'm working out are my fingers when I play League of Warriors," Juan replied. Tristan immediately perked up at the mention of his favorite game.

"Juan, you play LOW?" he asked, prompting a strong nod from the young boy. This launched the two into a full-blown conversation about the video game, while Christian merely stared in bemusement.

"Man, you two need some human friends."

Grateful for the company, Tristan continued to chat amongst the two boys over the next few minutes. He had completely forgotten about their scheduled visitor until he heard a hush go through the room. Tristan was turning in his seat to see what the commotion was when he spotted the tall, powerful figure of the man known as Principal Winter. He wore a black business suit and walked into the room with the air of a man who commanded everyone's attention, his piercing blue eyes sweeping across the class.

"Welcome, first years! My name is Principal Morgan Winter, and it is my honor to have you all here. You have been gathered from across the world, from all different backgrounds and life experiences, for the opportunity to learn and discover your true potential as metamorphs!

"While I know that it is difficult to leave behind the family and home you have known all of your life, I hope you all discover New Pararaiha to be your new home and that each and every one of us are all family here. If you would allow me to indulge myself, I would like to spend a little time explaining the importance of this special place before I dismiss you to your dorms."

"This wonderful institution was founded by the very men and women whom you saw immortalized upon your entrance to this building. The Magnificent Seven, led by the great Captain Comet, felt that it was vital to discover those of their kind and teach them the rich history of metamorphs, empowering them to control and utilize their abilities for the benefit of society. We have had many great legends pass through these halls, and I have no doubt that many future ones are right before my very eyes," he said looking toward Belle and Gabriel with a smile, both of whom seemed to glow at the words.

"One of the defining aspects of our school is the focus on teamwork, and that is the key thing we look for when it comes to our grading system. Starting today, several of you will be chosen to become team leaders. These leaders are decided based upon their personality tests and aptitude scores from the admission process, and they will be charged to recruit three other members from their class to form a team. Not only will you form a lasting, unique bond amongst your teammates, they will also be essential in deciding your final grades, your semester scores averaged together as one," Principal Winter said.

This last part shook Tristan to his core. Now it made sense why most of the students were avoiding him. If all of their grades were averaged together, Tristan was a huge liability for anyone hoping to make it through the Academy. He was already facing an uphill battle by attending the school with no powers to speak of, but getting his classmates to accept that risk as well was a big ask. Tristan's heart plummeted with the realization that there was a good chance he would not be recruited by anyone.

"While at the Academy, you will no longer be bound to conform to the society which your human cousins have designed. Rather, you will be reborn into a new world, one in which the possibilities are limitless! Over these next four years, you will be pushed to your physical, mental, and emotional limits, challenged in every aspect of your lives. If you are to overcome all of these challenges, I offer you these words of advice: One, you must learn to love and trust one another. Lean upon each other, as your strengths may be someone's greatest weakness. Two, perfection isn't expected, but progression is required. Lastly...have fun, my children. Understand, you are amongst the most fortunate beings on the planet. Take advantage of these moments before you, and live your lives to the fullest," Principal Winter finished, and the students clapped in appreciation.

After a short period of applause, Principal Winter held out his hands to quiet down the crowd. "Now that my speech is finished, you are all free to return to your dormitories, except for the following students, who have been chosen to be team leaders!" Principal Winter cleared his throat before listing off names: "Cynthia Perrotta...William Conrad...Gabriel Jackson... Juan Parra..."

Tristan smiled as Juan's face lit up at the sound of his name being called, and Tristan wondered whether he could convince the young boy to take him on as a teammate. While Winter continued on, Tristan tried to see if he recognized any of the students being named, his eyes eventually stopping on Belle. The girl's face seemed to drop with each name announced, and Tristan found himself hoping that hers would eventually be called.

"—and lastly, Tristan Davids!"

A hush fell across the room, while Tristan took a minute to process what he had just heard. *What?! Team leader?! How?!* The students began to whisper amongst each other, shooting glances of disbelief in his direction. *Surely this had to be some sort of mistake!* Tristan caught Belle's eyes, and his heart nearly broke at the mixture of disappointment and bitterness across her face.

Christian patted the two boys on the back as he stood up to leave and whispered, "Congrats boys! I'll try to keep your fan club from swarming you both once you leave. I'm sure people are just gonna be knocking down the doors to join your squads!" He gave them both a cheeky grin before strutting out the doors, leaving all but Principal Winter and the ten team leaders alone in the room.

"First, I would like to congratulate each and every one of you for not only making it into the Academy but for also being chosen as team leaders. This decision was not made lightly and know that you all earned this great honor!"

"Yeah, some of us," Tristan heard Gabriel scoff from across the room. Tristan felt his neck burning while some of the students stifled their laughter. If Principal Winter had heard the remark, he pretended not to notice.

"Moving forward, teams are to be formed no later than the day prior to the start of school and submitted to my office directly. While each member will earn their own individual grades, your scores will be averaged as one twice a year, during mid-semester and at the end. Your team will be ranked accordingly and will determine your success as a unit, so it is vital that you choose your teammates wisely."

"I think we already know who's gonna be last!" Gabriel muttered, inciting more silent chuckles.

"As leaders, your role within the group is absolutely paramount. Besides carefully selecting your teammates, your job is to find a way to develop them, encouraging growth on an individual level and as a whole. You will get to know and understand each of them personally, their strengths, their weaknesses, and help them to unlock their potential for the good of the team. Each of you has exceptional leadership potential and personality traits that will allow you to be successful in this role, and I hope you all realize the honor that has been bestowed upon you!"

"Can't be much of an honor if anybody can get chos—!"

"Mr. Jackson! Is there something you wish to share with the group?! It appears that you've been quite the comedian over there in the corner since I've started speaking! As a team leader, I would have hoped that if there was something pressing that needed to be discussed, you would have the courage to bring it forth to the assembly!"

For a moment, there was silence as everyone looked on at the two. It began to appear like Gabriel would back down from the icy stare of the principal, but before Winter could continue his speech, Gabriel stood up.

"Yeah, you're right. I should've been more forthcoming, and I apologize for that. I just don't see how you can tell us that we've earned this title and how this was carefully decided upon when you let people like Davids become team leaders! He has no powers and no legitimate reason for even being at this Academy! He got in because of his name, and now he gets to be a leader because of it as well?! What about the other students, with actual powers, who scored higher than him?! How can you expect people to take orders from this...human?!"

Tristan could feel the tension in the air as the students gaped in shock. While they seemed surprised at the audacity of Gabriel's outburst, some nodded their heads in approval at the points he had made. Tristan felt his stomach turn sour and, not for the first time, wondered if he had made a mistake. To his surprise, Principal Winter's stone cold expression broke into a smirk of amusement as he slowly walked over to Gabriel's table. It could've been his imagination, but Tristan could've sworn the room grew darker with each step Winter took.

"20, 19, 19, 20, 20." There was a look of confusion across Gabriel's face as Winter rattled off the numbers. "16, 15, 17, 15, 16. Do you know what those numbers are?"

"No, sir," Gabriel replied.

"Your acceptance into the school and selection as team leaders is based on the cumulative score from a total of five attributes, which are weighted on a scale of 20. The first set of numbers are the scores that Mr. Davids earned on his way to being accepted into the Academy. The second set...belongs to the next closest student. So tell me, is there anyone else who objects to the idea of Mr. Davids being selected into this Academy? If so, I will glad-ly list off your individual scores to see how you compared."

The room was dead silent at this challenge, and Gabriel slowly sat down, head hanging in embarrassment. Tristan was absolutely floored. Out of all of the people at this school, Principal Winter was the last person Tris-tan had expected to stand up for him being here. *Maybe I was wrong about him after all.*

As quickly as the room had darkened, it suddenly was brought back to light, Principal Winter resuming his speech with a smile on his face like nothing had happened. "Being team leaders, it is essential that you are able to enlist a group of individuals who will be best suited to fit your leader-ship styles. Over the years, we have developed a system of student pairing that has proven to be successful based on abilities, personalities, and team potential. I have here a list of names for each one of you whose scores pre-dict the best match for your team. You may use these as guides for those you wish to recruit, or you can ignore them entirely and decide for yourselves. It will be your call either way."

With that said, Principal Winter reached into his jacket and produced ten sheets of paper, which he handed out to each of the students present. When Winter got to his table, Tristan felt like he needed to say something to show his gratitude for standing up for him.

"Thank you sir...for everything," he managed to say, reaching for his pa-per.

Winter paused before speaking, his voice barely above a whisper. "Don't thank me yet, Davids. I warned you beforehand regarding your ad-mittance into this school, and I still stand by my words. I merely delayed the inevitable. For your sake, let's hope you prove us all wrong." Fixed on those cold eyes, Tristan felt himself gulp hard before Winter moved on. *So much for believing in me.*

Unsurprisingly, there were only a handful of names on his sheet com-pared to the long list Juan was currently poring over. None of the names were familiar, and one was crossed out in black marker to make it illegible. If Tristan thought this would be a challenge before, he now knew that even the teachers wouldn't be making it any easier for him.

"I hope you all are excited for the year ahead and the prospect of what's to come! I have high hopes for your class and can already tell that great things are in your future. Congratulations again on your accomplishments, and good luck going forward! You are dismissed." With that, Principal Winter turned around and made his way out of the mess hall, leaving the students alone in silence.

Slowly, the students stood up and exited the room, Tristan and Juan among the last to leave. Walking across the open grounds to the dorms, Juan chatted away about who had made his list and who he thought would make the best teammates. Tristan barely heard a word that came out of the excited boy's mouth. He was already in his own world, calculating the best way to make new teammates. When they got back to the dorms, Tristan decided to head to the common area.

It was his first time seeing the lounge room, and when Tristan walked through the wooden double doors, he was greeted with a welcome sight. The lounge, impressive in its sheer size and warm brown walls, looked to be a giant den, complete with pool tables, ping pong, pinball machines, air hockey tables, and foosball. There were shuffleboards in the corner, gaming systems connected to multiple televisions, and soft, maroon couches all around. A handful of students were gathered in the room, some playing PS4 while others were having a pool competition. It seemed the perfect environment to recruit. *All right, just relax and be yourself. You got this!* Tristan took a deep breath, ready to begin.

It went about as well as he could've predicted. While the students were nowhere near as hostile as Gabriel, they were clearly not interested in starting off as underdogs right out of the gates. News of his not having powers had spread quickly amongst the students, and they openly acknowledged this as the main reason they were not interested in joining his team. Tristan tried his best to be understanding of their reasoning and appear optimistic as he moved throughout the room, but with each rejection, his spirit fell further and further. Before long, he had spoken with all the students in the room to the same result, and despite a few other new students trickling in through the doors, he decided it was best to call it a night and head to bed.

Tristan opened the bedroom door to find the room empty except for Christian, who appeared to be getting dressed up to go out. Christian was staring at his reflection in the mirror while running hair gel through his thick hair and adjusting his shirt. Tristan didn't want to talk to anyone at the moment but felt awkward walking out after he had just entered, so he grudgingly made his way to the back of the room.

"What's good, bro? You're just in time! I'm about to head over to the courtyard. A few of the girls had mentioned they wanted to meet up over by the hammock area in a few minutes. You wanna join?" he asked. "Come on, I know you've had your eye on a few of them! And I could definitely use a good wingman! What do you say?" Tristan shot him a beleaguered look and shook his head in silence. Christian frowned at the cold response. "What's wrong, man? You look like someone kicked your puppy or something."

At first, Tristan considered ignoring the boy but decided against it. It seemed that only two kids around the school actually liked talking to him, and he wasn't prepared to push one of them away. "No one wants to join my team," he finally said, collapsing onto the bed and staring up at the ceiling. "It's like I have the plague or something. I mean, I get it. Without any powers, I'm a liability. But it still sucks, you know? It's not like I asked for any of this! I didn't ask to be in my family. I didn't ask to be a team leader! All I wanted was to finally be accepted, to get away from my old high school and start fresh. Now here I am, in the same predicament, looking in from the outside. I just...I just wish people gave me a chance, you know?" He sighed in frustration, the room falling into silence.

Tristan continued to stare up at the ceiling awaiting some sort of response until he heard the sounds of Christian combing through his hair once more. "Hey, are you even listening to me?!"

"Geez, I thought you were done! You were saying something about how terrible your life is, you have no friends, why me, yadda yadda yadda. Not gonna lie, I forgot the last part. I was zoning out, but I think I got the gist," he replied. Tristan rolled his eyes in defeat, concluding that talking to his self-absorbed neighbor was next to impossible.

Tristan laid there while Christian finished prepping himself, spraying his clothes with a sweet smelling cologne before walking to the door. As he reached for the doorknob, Christian suddenly paused and faced Tristan.

"Hey Davids, I gotta admit, I was wrong about you. I thought for sure you were gonna be some stuck-up, self-righteous, preppy boy when we first found out who you were, and yet here you are, all emo and up in your feelings," he proclaimed with a laugh. "Anyways, you definitely need to work on your sales pitch if we're gonna get people to join our squad. That move might have worked on me, but I doubt anyone else will buy it. I'll see if I can convince any of the girls to join too, but that might be the last thing on my mind, if you catch my drift. I'll see you tomorrow, and we'll figure out who else we can sucker into this," he said, flashing his pearly grin. With that said, Christian walked out the door, leaving an open-mouthed Tristan alone in the room to realize that he had not only just made a new friend, but a new teammate.

Chapter 9: Recruiting

"So you're sure Jillian Murphy was a no?" Tristan asked, crossing off the last name on his paltry list of candidates while they sat together at one of the tables in the common room.

Christian nodded and replied, "Oh, yeah. Hard pass. Nothing good came from that conversation. She basically laughed at me the entire time and kept saying 'You've got to be kidding me!' in between each pause. It was rough."

"If it went so bad, how come you're smiling?" Tristan inquired.

"Because I got her number afterward. Apparently, she thinks I have a great sense of humor along with being cute, so...yeah. Besides that, it was awful" he said, still smiling. Tristan continued to give his friend a blank stare. "All right, we may have made out afterward, too. But I felt really guilty the whole time, I promise! All I could think about was your sad face when I broke the news to you...actually, no, that's just a lie. And a little weird."

Tristan shot Christian a feigned look of contempt before groaning aloud, his head falling on to the table in frustration. "Chris, it's been three days! I need you to stop making out with our potential recruits and actually get people to join our team! We have nobody! Right now, I'm basically a walking plague, and Lord knows I'm already socially awkward! You are my ace in the hole here. I need you to work your magic!"

Christian shrugged to Tristan and leaned back on his chair. "Dude, I'm trying, but you knew this was never gonna be easy! You're powerless, and while the girls may dig the hair, let's not forget, I'm still considered a freak myself around here." Christian's last statement caused Tristan to look back toward his friend guiltily for overlooking the struggles that he had been going through himself.

The past few days with Christian had helped improve Tristan's mood, however, as they got to learn more about one another, Tristan also got to witness firsthand the downside of having abilities. While Tristan longed to discover his unique powers, Christian had struggled to control his own. As far as he could tell, Christian's powers encompassed transforming into a vampire-like state (long hair, translucent skin, and all), while manipulating the temperature around him.

While it seemed cool at first, Christian had little to no control over when his "transformations" occurred. One occurrence happened their second day in when he accidentally got himself and a girl stuck in one of the small ponds they were swimming in together. They were on a "recruiting date", as he liked to put it, and he somehow managed to freeze part of the surrounding water, trapping the two until one of the professors managed to hear their cries for help and thawed them out. Needless to say, the students were a little wary of Christian's powers.

"Let's get out of here, man" Tristan sighed. "We're going to need to create a whole new list since we've run out of names, and I'm tired of thinking about this. I need to relax for a bit. Let's go chill by the beach."

Christian nodded in agreement, and the two boys grabbed their belongings, making their way out of the common area. As soon as his feet hit the sand, Tristan began to remove his sneakers, the warm, soft granules sliding in between his toes while he walked toward the water's edge. It was a typically beautiful day out, and the cool winds kept the sun's rays from being too oppressive. Tristan and Christian removed their shirts and laid out by the water, allowing the tide to splash around them while they relaxed and discussed their thoughts on future teammates.

Without warning, the sand beside Tristan exploded with a massive impact, sending the startled boy flying through the air and into the water ahead. He was still screaming in terror when he eventually broke through the water's surface and was greeted with the sounds of familiar laughter and recognizable faces.

"Hahahaha! You should've seen your face! And that scream! Honestly, Elaina can't hit those high notes!" Allen called out to his younger brother, holding his sides with laughter. Elaina was beside him, trying her best to give the elder a disapproving look while shaking with silent laughter. The immediate annoyance toward his brother's prank was soon overcome by his sheer joy at seeing his siblings again. Tristan swam his way back to shore and immediately tackled his brother onto the ground, a battle which eventually resulted in Allen sitting atop his younger sibling. After he had admitted defeat and suffered yet another disgraceful blast of subsequent flatulence from his brother, Tristan was let back up and properly embraced by his siblings.

"What are you two doing here?! I thought you guys didn't arrive until school started!" Tristan asked.

"The teaching staff for the upperclassmen usually report about a week ahead of time, so here we are. We typically have to report to the northwest quadrant of the island once we arrive, but we were given permission to come see you first," Elaina explained.

"How has everything been going? Was it everything you imagined?" Allen asked, tousling Tristan's sand-filled hair.

"Well...it's a long story," Tristan admitted, but before he could get into any details he was interrupted.

"Ahem!" Christian had his arms folded across his chest and an expectant look on his face as he awaited his introduction.

"Excuse Mr. Hollywood over here. He gets a little jealous whenever he feels neglected. This is my new friend, Christian Josephs. Chris, these are my older siblings, All—"

"Professors Rocket and Mist!" Christian jumped in, vigorously shaking Allen's hand. "I've heard a lot about you two! You guys are the only siblings to have fought against each other in the finals of the Battledome! You both are legends around this school!"

Tristan was taken aback at Christian's knowledge, this being the first he had heard of it himself. Christian paused when he got to Elaina, gently taking her hand and bringing it to his lips as he shot her a dreamy smile. "An honor indeed, Ms. Davids." Tristan groaned aloud and pushed his friend aside from his red-faced sister.

"All right, lover boy, that's enough! Go find someone else's sister to swoon over!"

Soon, the four were having lunch together in the school mess hall, catching up on the events of the past week. Both his siblings seemed pleasantly surprised at Tristan's new role and were happy to give him advice regarding things they had learned from their time as team leaders. The sight of them all together attracted more than a few stares from his surrounding classmates, and secretly Tristan hoped that it would encourage them to join his team.

Enjoying the time spent together, Tristan was disappointed when they eventually announced that they had to return to the teacher's quarters. The two said their goodbyes to Christian, who was very appreciative that they had allowed him to tag along, and embraced their youngest sibling before gathering their belongings. Tristan watched while the pair exited out one of the metal gates on the northeast side of the campus, an off-limits access point for the students.

The two friends decided to take the rest of the day off from recruiting to recharge their batteries, spending their remaining time playing games of pick-up basketball with some of the other students and hiking around the mountain area near campus. By the time his head hit the pillow, Tristan was exhausted from the day's activities and fell into a restful sleep.

During the previous night's dinner, Professor Cam had made an announcement regarding the student's annual uniform fitting. This mandatory event required the students to be evaluated at the school's design studio on a first-come-first-served basis in order to have uniforms designed for them based on their particular powers. While his fellow classmates seemed ecstatic about the prospects of having their own custom outfits, Tristan was understandably less than thrilled.

By the time Tristan had dragged himself out of bed and gotten dressed, there were only a handful of students still in the room, including Christian, who was still debating which sunglasses he wanted to wear. Rushing, they managed to make it to the Academy, only to find the line of students extending out past the main lobby. The design studio was among the labs on the third floor, and the students were waiting to get on the elevator and join their fellow classmates above. In the meantime, Tristan and Christian chatted together while they waited, gradually moving forward whenever the elevator doors opened to allow students off and take up the next group.

Some of the outfits were subtle and unassuming, like Brandon's, who wore a loose-fitting grey t-shirt and long, black sweatpants, while others' seemed quite extravagant and complex, like Emily's ornate camouflage jumpsuit that seemed to shift colors whenever light reflected off of it. The shy girl seemed appalled at drawing so much attention to herself, and Tristan watched as both she and her suit began to blend into the background, making her practically invisible.

As time went on, Tristan saw more familiar faces come down. Juan's outfit seemed quite plain, a glossy, all-white jumpsuit with a hoodie that looked like it was swallowing the boy's head, however, he seemed quite pleased with the selection. "The fabric is made out of Kevlar, so it can stop projectiles! It's fireproof too! I can't wait to start our training and test it out!" the young boy said, his eyes practically glowing with excitement. Tristan couldn't help but wonder who would be excited about testing out projectiles and having fire aimed at them.

Cynthia came out soon after the boys finished talking, dressed in one of the most impressive outfits they had seen yet. She had a full-on blast-resistant suit, similar to ones used by explosive technicians in the army, although this one seemed much more lightweight and streamlined. The black and red suit was custom fitted to her taller, slender frame, and the blast plates were smaller to accommodate greater mobility. She had no helmet attached either, which allowed everyone to catch her confident smile as she walked past her classmates, who gaped in apparent intimidation.

Finally, after nearly an hour, it was their turn to enter the elevator, and they made their way up to the studio. Before he could step off, Tristan was met with a sight that caused his heart to skip a beat. Belle stood before him wearing her new outfit, a seafoam-colored sleeveless wetsuit that showed off her toned, brown arms and stole Tristan's breath away. He could only smile awkwardly at the girl standing before him, his mouth open as he struggled to find words to say. An eternity seemed to pass until he felt Christian pat his shoulder.

"What's good, Belle! My friend here says hi also! Don't mind him. Juan was just showing off some of his telepathic powers and accidentally stunned Tristan with some memory lapse, so he's having a hard time speaking! You know how that goes, right? Well anyway, it was nice seeing you again! That outfit is slaying by the way!"

Belle smiled and nodded at the two, Christian gently guiding the still frazzled Tristan into the hallway. Once the elevator doors closed behind them, Christian burst into laughter. "Smooth, Trist. Man, we've got to teach you how to talk to girls."

Walking down the circular hallway, the two spotted Gabriel and Malcolm leaving the design studio. If they had inflated egos before, their new looks didn't help the situation. Malcolm's outfit was a sleek, one-piece track uniform, the all-black skintight suit resembling an Olympic athlete's. He had on shoes that looked like extremely lightweight slippers with thin, razor-sharp steel studs underneath and wore thin, black, futuristic goggles with dark red lenses across his eyes. Even Tristan had to admit, he looked impressive.

Next to him, Gabe looked equally imposing, his outfit consisting of a dark brown leather jacket over a dry-fit, black shirt underneath. The shirt seemed to contain protective padding built within and complimented his black cargo pants which were held up by a belt containing several circular vials of sand. His black boots rang across the hallway as they made their way to the elevator doors.

While passing by Tristan, Gabe shot him a look of amusement. "Wow, they're just letting everyone get a uni today, huh? Might as well get this man a lunch lady's uniform and hope he can at least be somewhat useful while he's here!"

Before he could reply, Christian placed his hand on Tristan's chest and shook his head. "Relax, bro. Not worth it, not now. He's looking to throw you off balance. Don't let him," he advised under his breath. Tristan took a deep breath and turned back around, doing his best to compose himself while they resumed their walk.

Upon entering the design studio, the boys found themselves within a blindingly white room with two steel tables in the middle covered with art supplies and sketches. Directly behind the tables were high-tech machines which Tristan had never seen before, containing a stockpile of different fabrics and materials. Tristan wasn't sure what he was seeing, but he knew that technology like this wasn't available in the world he had left behind. To the left were several mannequins and mirrors, while to the right were the dressing rooms.

Tristan had expected to see some old spinsters sitting around a sewing machine and was surprised to find three tall women and a male sitting behind the tables staring intently at the two boys. The four wore heavy makeup on their skin, giving them an appearance of porcelain and were all shaved bald with several hooped earrings on either ear. They wore thin, white turtleneck sweaters and flowing gowns of various shades that seemed to change color based on which direction Tristan was looking at them. They all appeared to be in their mid-twenties, but there was something behind their eyes that told Tristan they were much older. The two boys approached the center of the room where they were greeted warmly by the four, who seemed to double in size upon standing.

"Welcome to the design studio, gentlemen! We are the Designers and will be responsible for creating your custom outfits! Each year you will have an outfit designed specifically for you based off of your ever-evolving powers and personalities, and our goals are to provide you with products of the highest protection, quality, and comfort!" the yellow-eyed woman to the left said. "My name is Dori, and beside me are Tori, Lori, and Kori" she continued, pointing at her red, blue, and green-eyed companions respectively.

"In order to ensure efficient outfits in a timely manner, we obtain your testing records prior to your arrival and have them pre-designed. We will take your measurements and have you try on your outfits before explaining them to you. Come this way!" Dori said. The two boys followed Dori and Tori to the fitting stations while the two others made their way to the machines behind them, arranging certain materials and fabrics into the chrome machinery.

The boys were placed in front of the mirrors and measured by the two women, who periodically shouted out numbers to their colleagues. Tristan could barely focus on the instructions that Tori kept giving him, distracted by both the image of Lori and Kori hard at work punching in calculations into the machines and the ever-changing colors on their gowns.

"Perfect, your measurements are all complete! Let's make our way over to the dressing rooms," Tori said and proceeded to guide him across the room to the changing stalls. Tristan walked into one of the pearl-white stalls and closed the door behind him while Tori went to go get him his clothes. After a few seconds of waiting, Tristan heard her call out from the other side of the door, and a suit bag came up over the top.

Tristan wasn't sure what to expect as he removed his outfit and held out the uniform in front of him. He had received a white one-piece leather suit similar to what bikers wore. The zipper extended from his navel to the top collar, and the suit had built in padding around his abdomen, chest, shoulders, elbows, and knees. Tristan slid into the suit before turning around to look at himself in the stall mirror. While he wasn't sure how the suit worked, it looked surprisingly good on him and felt great with its lightweight design. Tristan unlocked the stall and stepped out to the smiles of the Designers.

"Tristan, that looks great on you!" Lori exclaimed while Kori gave him a thumbs up of approval. Tristan heard the stall beside him unlock, and he turned to see Christian revealing his outfit as well.

Christian had on a fashionable, black coat jacket which extended down past his knees and seemed to billow around his lower legs. He wore a thin white shirt that was all wrinkled up underneath like some kind of punk Goth. He had skinny, black jeans to match his black boots and, combined with his glasses, looked like the perfect new-age rebel vampire.

"Dope gear, my man!" he said staring at Tristan. "You look like you're about to wreck shop at some biker bar!"

"Nice look yourself!" Tristan acknowledged, and they both turned to the Designers as Kori began to explain their outfits.

"Tristan, your outfit was designed with quite a few issues in mind. Obviously, without knowing when or how your powers will manifest, we needed to come up with something a little more general. This suit will provide you with top-of-the-line protection against any type of moderate level projectiles and close range piercing weapons, especially around the joints, chest, and vital organs. The lightweight design will allow for ease of movement while protecting you from mild elemental damage, ranging from heavy rain and snow to most fires."

"Christian, as for you, yours was a more complex and custom design, built around your unique capabilities. The coat is extremely lightweight, allowing you to move freely, similar to what we would normally see in a cape, and your clothes have been woven with thermal materials to help maintain your body heat when you undergo your transformation. The material is frost resistant, so you never have to worry about freezing your clothes or unwanted splitting," Kori concluded. The suits would be theirs to keep, with duplicates made and sent to their rooms by the day's end, Dori promised before escorting the two boys out of the studio.

Tristan was in much better spirits after their time in the studio and felt a new sense of confidence wearing his new uniform. The outfit helped him feel like he actually belonged, and by the time they reached the main floor, Tristan was ready to resume his search for their remaining teammates. Unfortunately, the two boys were greeted by the sight of some unwanted classmates. Gabriel stood by the lobby fountain deep in conversation with Malcolm, Brandon, and, to Tristan's surprise, Belle. Tristan resisted the urge to walk past the girl, in the hopes of her being impressed by his new suit, and instead started toward the entrance to avoid Gabriel.

The two boys had barely made it halfway before they heard the sounds of mocking laughter behind them.

"Hahaha! Wow, look at the dynamic duo of Captain Figure-Skating and Mr. Clean! Not even the Designers could save these two from looking like a bunch of lames!" Gabriel crowed. Tristan could no longer contain his anger at this point, despite Christian's attempt to hold him back.

"You know what? Screw you, Gabe! What the hell is your deal?! Didn't you have anything better to do besides just sitting around for an hour coming up with some insults for when we got out?!"

Seemingly amused by the outburst, Gabriel broke into a laugh, holding his sides before slowly approaching the two boys. Tristan tensed in expectation of a fight and could feel the air around him gradually grow colder, clouds starting to form with each breath Christian took beside him. Gabriel stopped short of Tristan, a cocky smirk across his face.

"You don't have to worry about my act, homie. I got my squad assembled already. Me, Brando, Malc, and Belle...we 'bout to own this place. You think you're special now, *laaitie*, just because they gave you that sorry outfit? Why don't you take a look over there in the mess hall? See the black boy with the thick hair and dorky glasses sitting over by the far left?" Gabriel asked, pointing in the direction of the cafeteria. Sitting by himself was a skinny black boy with a long mane of disheveled curly hair and thick-rimmed glasses—and a blue uniform the exact same style as Tristan's.

"Will is a team leader like us with the unfortunate lame gift of speaking and understanding any language he encounters. As a result, he got stuck with the same generic outfit as everyone else who doesn't have decent powers, or in your case, none at all. You see it doesn't matter that you got yourself some new threads. It doesn't matter that you managed to convince re-ject Dracula over here to join your sorry squad. You're not one of us. You never will be."

Before he knew what was happening, Tristan heard a roar from beside him as Christian shot forward with superhuman speed, shoving the unsus-pecting Gabriel back several feet in a rage. Brandon leaped to his feet, run-ning forward to help his teammate, while Malcolm became a literal blur, already beside Gabriel by the time Tristan had taken a single blink.

"You wanna keep talking shit about my friend, you're gonna have to go through me, sandboy!" Christian snarled, fully transformed into his vam-pire state at this point. "Why don't you tell your boys to stop holding your hand, unless you're too scared of getting your ass kicked by a figure skater?"

Enraged, Gabriel held back his teammates and stepped forward, crack-ing his knuckles. "I'm gonna enjoy breaking that pretty face of yours!"

Tristan could only watch in stunned amazement at the scene unfolding before him, both boys springing forward, ready to clash. Suddenly, a flood of water rose out from the fountain behind them and shot forward, knock-ing the two boys off of their feet before they had a chance to collide. Sliding across the slick, wet floor and coughing up water, they looked up in surprise at a furious Belle, who stood before them with hands on her hips.

"Enough! Both of you! When are you guys gonna grow up already?! We get it! You don't like each other! God, save it for the Battledome! Do you idiots realize that if you're caught using your powers to harm each oth-er, you'll get expelled? You know what that means for your teammates? Yeah, we drop in the rankings, too! I'm not gonna fail out of this school because you testosterone-fueled airheads can't get your act together!" she yelled, shaking her head in frustration.

"Belle!" Gabriel called out as the girl stormed out into the afternoon sun. He slowly got back to his feet with the help of his other teammates, shooting the two boys a glare. "This aint over!" he shouted before they ran out to follow after Belle. Tristan quickly rushed over to the drenched Chris-tian, his friend slowly morphing back into his human state.

"Well that escalated quickly," Christian chuckled, trying to wring out his hair. "Good news is, at least the suit works! My boxers might be soaked but at least my coat's still gucchi!" Tristan shook his head with a laugh, a sense of gratitude coming over him.

"Hey man, thanks for sticking up for me," Tristan said in appreciation.

"Don't worry about it. We stick together, remember?"

Tristan nodded in acknowledgment and offered his hand to Christian, helping his friend back onto his feet. Team or no team, Tristan felt proud to have someone like Christian by his side.

The rest of the morning was fairly uneventful, the boys deciding to join some of their classmates in a pool tournament. It seemed that, for the most part, people had already decided which team they wished to join, and if Tristan didn't find more teammates soon, he would need to let Principal Winter know.

During their last round of pool, an announcement came over the loud-speakers:

"Attention, all first-year students! Please report immediately to the Academy mess hall. Your class schedules have been assigned, and we will be going over your courses and professors. Please be present no later than 1600 hours."

Tristan looked at his watch, which read 3:40, and realized that they had twenty minutes before the meeting began. With a few minutes to spare, the boys joined their classmates in the mess hall, taking the two seats in between Juan and Cynthia. The two leaders already appeared to have a full squad of their own beside them, and while Tristan didn't recognize the three sitting next to Juan, he did know the Anderson twins and Emily, who had joined with Team Perrotta.

After a few minutes of small talk, the room settled down once Professor Cam walked through the glass doors, five additional teachers coming in behind her. The first was a lovely older woman, whose fiery red hair and auburn eyes, further enhanced her regal features. The second was a shorter, Middle-Eastern man with thick black hair and a clean goatee, his olive eyes analyzing all the students in the room. The third was a tall, gangly man with greying brown hair and a tweed jacket which held his glasses and pocket protector. He had an awkward way about him as he swung his long arms and waved toward the students. The fourth professor was the clear favorite among the female students, his handsome, youthful features blending in well with his well-coiffed salt and pepper hair and facial stubble. The last professor was a face Tristan recognized as the pretty blonde present during his school interview.

"Good afternoon, students! We apologize for the short notice but wanted to make sure we presented everyone with your Fall semester schedules and introduced you to your first-year professors," Professor Cam announced. While she spoke, Professor Cam began to pass out sheets of paper with each student's name on top of it. When Tristan received his, he quickly glanced at the five classes to which he had been assigned and compared them to Christian's schedule. He was pleased to see that for all but two classes, they would be together, which helped ease some of his fears.

"As you can see, your classes are separated into two categories: team building and standard curriculum. While your two team building classes require you to take them alongside your group, the three standard curriculum classes will be taken at various days and times, allowing you the opportunity to interact and work with your other classmates! Behind me are your first-year professors, who will now take this moment to introduce themselves! Please give them a round of applause and your utmost attention!" Professor Cam concluded, stepping aside. The students clapped politely as the red-headed woman stepped forward first.

"Hello everyone!" she began, Tristan picking up on her British accent. "My name is Professor Jane Stellios, also known as Tremor, and I will be teaching you all Teamwork and Ability Management 101! I come from the UK and have been a professor here for the last thirty years. I hope you are all as excited to be here as I am to help you develop!" She stepped back to applause while the Middle-Eastern professor came forward, his booming voice echoing across the room.

"Hello, *al'atfal*. My name is Professor Arman Coffman, also known as Crusher, and I will be teaching you Self-Defense 101. I am from the nation of Afghanistan and have been teaching here for ten years now. I specialize in not only increasing your physical toughness but challenging and enforcing your moral values as well. I look forward to seeing you all!" he said with a short bow before turning aside for the third professor.

The tall, slender man strode forward with a smile across his face, waving again to the students. "Hello and welcome, my young metamorphs! My name is Professor Anthony Fisher, better known as Five, and I have the pleasure of teaching about the fun-filled topics of World History! Yeah, let's give it up for history!" he said clapping his hands enthusiastically. The professor received a handful of weak claps from around the room, but mostly awkward silence and blank stares. Tristan was surveying the students' mixed reactions, when he caught Gabriel staring intently at his class schedule, a concerned look across his face. Tristan wondered what could be so worrying when Professor Fisher resumed his speech.

"I come from the great state of Vermont and have been teaching here for thirty-two years! My passion is molding young minds and helping you all learn about our rich metamorph history! All right!" he finished, pumping his fists excitedly in the air. Tristan tried his best to suppress joining his classmates in silent laughter, but it was hard with Christian practically keeling over in tears.

Next up was the handsome professor, who seemed oblivious to the swooning young ladies around him. "My name is Christopher Muelman, also known as Empath, and I teach World Literature. I am originally from Switzerland, though my mother is Greek, and I've been here for fifteen years. My job is to help you all get in touch with your inner voice and really express yourselves!" he finished, hands over his heart. Tristan snorted when he caught Professor Coffman roll his eyes at Meulman's last statement.

The last professor was the blonde, who seemed to command the attention of the entire room when she stepped forward, her voice entrancing the students despite its inherent softness. "Hello. My name is Michelle Tullage, and I teach Psychology 101. My alternate name is Psyche, I am originally from Denver, Colorado, and have been here for about eight years now. I look forward to expanding your knowledge on the wonder that is our mind and hope you are all ready for the great year ahead." Tullage stepped back to join her fellow professors before they lined up and exited the mess hall, one after the other.

Prior to dismissing the students, Cam reminded them that the deadline for team recruiting was two days away and to make sure they took the time to identify where their classes were. Walking out of the mess hall, Tristan and Christian found themselves passing by Gabriel's table, where the boy still seemed to be struggling to read his schedule. He had a confused look across his face, and his brow was furrowed in concentration.

"You all right there, Brainiac?" Christian called out as they walked past. "It's called a schedule. If you can't understand it, maybe you should see if Will can translate it for you with his 'lame powers'. I'm pretty sure he's fluent in Jerkoff," he said with a smirk. Tristan watched as Gabriel shook with rage, but couldn't help feeling a sense of pleasure from getting the last laugh at the expense of their rival.

The two boys left the Academy and were headed for the dormitories when Tristan spotted Belle up ahead. "Hey, Belle!" Tristan called out behind her.

"Well look at who finally hit puberty!" Christian said, nudging his friend. Tristan shot him an evil glare before running over to join Belle. She gave him a small smile as he approached, and Tristan felt the familiar feeling of butterflies in his stomach.

"Hey, Tristan. What's up?" she asked.

"Nothing much! Pretty excited about the class schedules and all. And the professors seem really cool, too!" he replied, trying his best not to sound nervous.

"Yeah they do!" she agreed, brushing back her dark hair while they walked beside one another. "How's everything been going otherwise? I know it hasn't been the easiest few days for you..."

"Oh, the teams? Psssht, that's fine, it's fine. No worries. I knew it was gonna be an uphill battle, and I get it. Honestly, I'll be happy with whatever happens, whether people decide to give me a chance or if I get demoted. I'm just happy to be here," he said with a smile. "How about you? Are you liking it so far? I see you're on Gabe's team. That must be pretty...exciting."

To his surprise, Belle simply shrugged. "Yeah, it's all right. The group seems like they're going to be really powerful so..."

"'They'?" Tristan repeated, raising his eyebrows. "You say it like you're not part of the team."

"Well, honestly, sometimes it feels like I'm not," Belle sighed. "Like I'm just there because I can give them the upper hand, not because I actually fit in. It's like I'm in some sort of stupid fraternity or something, you know?"

"Well then, why did you join them?"

"I don't know," Belle shrugged. "I guess I feel like they give me the best chance at being at the top of the rankings. I just don't get it. With all my scores, why didn't I get chosen to be a team leader?" Tristan felt a pang of guilt remembering the disappointed look on her face when his name had been announced.

"Listen, Belle...I'm sorry about all this. And for what happened this afternoon. I know you probably don't see me as the leader type, especially the way Gabe and I have been going at it. I never meant to take anything away from you or put you in the position of being a mediator between us. You deserve better than that." Belle looked up at his earnest face and smiled. She began to reply, but whatever she had intended to say was lost in the sounds of familiar shouting behind them.

Tristan quickly spun around to find a fully transformed Christian facing off against a clearly enraged Gabriel with Brandon and Malcolm close behind. "Damn it," he muttered, leaving behind Belle as he sprinted toward the commotion.

"I'm gonna make you pay for what you said to me back there, vampire boy!" Gabriel yelled out as he circled Christian, who merely sneered.

"Sorry, I can't cure stupid! How'd you get into this school anyway? You pay someone to take your SATs or something?" Gabriel roared in anger as he charged forward, fists swinging toward Christian. With his enhanced speed and reflexes, Christian clearly had the upper hand and maneuvered around each punch thrown his way, spinning and ducking with deliberate movement.

Gabriel threw a haymaker at his head, but Christian ducked underneath with a smile, his body tensing as he rose up to deliver a return uppercut of his own. Unfortunately, this forced him to move closer to the inside of Gabriel to fire off the blow. Before Christian could react, one of Gabriel's glass vials shattered, sending sand all across Christian's rising body. The sand appeared possessed, moving all around his friend before condensing into a solid block in the blink of an eye and completely encasing Christian's body from shoulders to knees.

"Gotcha!" Gabriel sneered while raising his arms, manipulating the sand block and lifting Christian into the air. *No way!* Tristan thought, continuing to race to his friend's aid. While he had figured that Gabriel could manipulate the sand in his vials, he had never expected this level of control from his enemy. Tristan could hear Christian groan under the pressure of the sand block squeezing around him. "Who's the idiot now?!" Gabriel taunted.

Disregarding his own safety, Tristan launched himself at Gabriel's chest, hoping to catch the boy off guard and tackle him to the ground. Unfortunately, he was not fast enough. Spotting Tristan in midair, Gabriel managed to release Christian from the sand block in time to redirect the particles at an unprepared Tristan. The sand rushed forward and hit the airborne boy like a brick wall, thrusting him back into a nearby pond.

Crashing into the cool water, Tristan's neck whipped forward from the force of the impact, disorienting him. Ears ringing from the landing, Tristan took a few seconds to gather himself before swimming toward the water's surface. Nearing the top, he felt a slight nudge from below and soon found himself speeding upward. He rocketed out of the pond, the water molding around him and gently placing him feet first onto the ground. He was soaking wet and still a little dazed but could make out the figure of Belle standing before him, shielding himself and Christian from a still fuming Gabriel.

"Are you kidding me right now, Belle? You really gonna stand up for these jerks?! Stand down!" Tristan heard Gabriel shout, pointing in their direction.

"That's real funny, Gabe, seeing as the only jerk I see around here is you! And those threats might work on the other kids, but they don't scare me!" Belle said menacingly, the nearby pond beginning to ripple violently. Tristan could see doubt creep across Gabriel's face as he continued to glare at Belle.

"Last chance, Belle," Gabriel said in a low voice.

"That's cute. I was about to say the same thing."

For a moment, Tristan thought Gabriel was actually going to go through with it, but Belle had called his bluff. Shaking his head, Gabriel dusted off his jacket before starting to turn around. "Guess this means we know which side she's really on, huh, boys? That's all right. We'll find someone else. The geek squad over here can have her. I think we all know what would've happened if she hadn't saved y'all today," Gabriel taunted, before turning to leave.

"Yeah, run off with your little girlfriends!" Christian muttered as he weakly rose to his feet. Unfortunately, his comment reached the keen ears of Brandon, whose eyes narrowed at the remark. Stepping forward, Brandon brought his fist back, ready to swing upon the unprepared Christian. Tristan tried his best to warn his friend, but before the words could leave his mouth, the oncoming fist was caught in midair, swallowed up by a massive palm before impact. Both Christian and Brandon looked visibly surprised as they looked up at the colossal hand's owner.

Standing at around 6'6 was a large, muscular boy with sandy-blonde hair and a square-shaped head. His stern expression and rock-jawed face was utterly intimidating, and it didn't help that he possessed the body of a gladiator. "You really shouldn't hit people when they're not looking. It's bad manners," the boy said to Brandon, a country twang in his voice. Flustered, Brandon glanced back and forth between his trapped fist and the boy's face before deciding that his best option was to use his other hand. That was the wrong choice.

When Brandon's free fist hit the tall boy's exposed face, several audible cracks emanated from his hand. Unmoved, the large boy seemed undisturbed at the sight of the screaming Brandon and raised his eyebrows in annoyance. "Are you done now?" he asked politely, to which Brandon vigorously nodded his head. "Good. Now run along with your other friends and leave this poor boy alone." He released his grip on Brandon's uninjured hand, allowing the three boys to sprint their way across the courtyard toward the infirmary.

For a while, there was only stunned silence before Christian broke the tension, clapping the large boy on the back. "Dude, I have no idea who you are or where you came from, but you just provided me with quite possibly the greatest moment of my life! That was awesome!"

The boy turned to Christian, arms crossed over his burly chest, clearly not amused. "You need to learn to watch that mouth of yours! You had a free pass, but you just needed to make a smart comment to rub it in. Next time, I'm gonna let him get his lick in if you pull a stunt like that again." Christian raised his arms in surrender and nodded.

Tristan slowly made his way over to the giant boy, shooting Belle a nod of gratitude along the way. "Excuse me, but what's your name? I haven't seen you around campus before, and no offense, but a kid your size doesn't just move around incognito around here."

The boy looked down at Tristan, his hard expression softening. "The name's Dan. Dan Samus. I actually just got here this afternoon. I'm a late arrival. Had some stuff going on back home that needed to be taken care of before I could fly out here."

"Well, Dan, my name is Tristan. And my friend Chris here owes you a soda for saving that ugly mug of his," Tristan said, extending his hand.

"Hey!" Christian proclaimed as Dan smirked at the comment. He looked down at Tristan's hand before grasping it in a firm handshake which, to Tristan's surprise, was quite gentle.

"Well, Mr. Tristan, I'm glad I could be of help to you folk. Now if you don't mind, I need to find some place called the Design Studio. I asked around, but I cannot find that darn building for the life of me, and I need to get there before they close."

Tristan broke into a grin as he folded his arms across his chest. "Dan, I think I know how I can start to return the favor."

Chapter 10: A Team Assembled

It didn't take much for Tristan to convince Dan to join the team, the soft-spoken giant quite happy to be around friendly faces. Upon his arrival, he had been treated like some kind of freak, the other students intimidated by his defensive-lineman frame made every effort to avoid him. Belle had also seemed to unofficially join their squad, choosing to accompany them while Dan was fitted for his outfit, which was more than fine by Tristan. By the time Dan walked out of the design studio, wearing what looked to be a full-on Roman gladiator outfit, Tristan was silently congratulating himself, convinced that he may have just pulled off the impossible two days before the deadline.

That evening the four of them sat down for dinner together, and he soon found that his expectations were wildly off the mark. The four began with some small talk, explaining the school grounds and campus layout to the newcomer, but quickly found themselves in awkward silence, unable to come up with any other topic of conversation. While they ate, Tristan finally found the courage to ask Belle if she would like to join their team, now that it seemed that she and Gabriel had fallen out. Belle's eyes fell to her plate when Tristan brought it up, and he could sense her hesitation.

"Honestly, Tristan, it's been a really long day. I don't think I'm in a good place right now to say yes for sure. I need a little bit of time to reevaluate my options at the moment. Do you mind if I let you know by tomorrow?"

Tristan did his best to appear unfazed, despite his disappointment at the words. "Absolutely. No problem. Take as much time as you need. I get it."

"Tristan, it's not—"

"Belle, I get it, trust me. No worries. Just let me know if you change your mind." Tristan went back to picking at his plate, although he found he was no longer hungry. After a few minutes, Belle silently gathered her belongings and left to go back to the dorms.

Once she had left, Dan leaned over to Christian and whispered, "Is it always this awkward with those two?"

Christian shook his head and shrugged. "Only on days that end in 'y'. You should see them when she's in her swimsuit!"

"Shut up," Tristan muttered, grabbing his belongings, and together they made their way back to the dorms. Tristan and Christian showed him to the first year room where his belongings had been placed in one of the middle beds. They made sure to steer clear of Gabriel and his crew, who seemed slightly more subdued at this point. Brandon had a cast around his hand and was still clearly in some amount of discomfort. The two boys said goodnight to Dan before making their way to the back of the room. Tristan didn't realize how tired he was until he had showered and hopped into bed. By the time his head hit the pillow, he was already sound asleep.

The morning seemed to come almost immediately, the early sun's rays creeping through the window curtains and dancing across Tristan's face. Unable to fall back asleep, Tristan rose up and got dressed. Christian and Dan were still sleeping, so he decided to take a jog around the campus before breakfast. He walked downstairs and exited the building, starting his light jog around the open grounds. Opening up his stride, Tristan found himself easily picking up the pace and was pleased with how good it felt.

After a few laps around the grounds, Tristan spotted Belle coming out of the girl's dormitory, waving in his direction. He had planned on avoiding her, dreading the eventual rejection he knew was coming, but apparently, she had other ideas. Tristan slowed down his pace and headed over to the smiling girl, who seemed vaguely impressed.

"Wow, you move pretty fast out there! You sure you don't have any powers?"

Tristan smiled and shook his head. "No, unfortunately, I have to give my brother credit for that particular gift. Trying to actively avoid wedgies as a kid taught me to pick up my pace." Belle laughed aloud at the image, and Tristan felt his face grow warmer at the sound.

"Listen, I was hoping to catch you out here. I wanted to talk about last night," Belle began before Tristan held out his hand to stop her.

"Belle, I told you, no worries. I get it, okay. I know you take your grades seriously and being on my team could potentially be a huge risk to that. I didn't mean to put you in an awkward spot last night, and I'm sure you have other people fighting to get you on their squad. Believe me, there's no hard feelings." At first, Tristan felt relieved to get the words off his chest until he saw the annoyed frown across Belle's face.

"You know Tristan, you really need to do a better job with the whole leader thing. You keep trying to convince people to join your team but spend half your time apologizing for your flaws and assuming you're going to fail. People aren't going to follow someone they can't trust. How are we supposed to have confidence in you when you're barely showing any in yourself?" Tristan's mouth hung slightly, clearly unprepared for the response, and was unsure of how to respond.

Belle gave him a smirk, apparently reading his mind. "Just say 'Yes, Belle. You're right'. Trust me, you'll be saying that a lot these next four years." Tristan barked out a laugh and nodded, repeating her words. "Look, Tristan, my problem has never been about you not having powers. You can't be blamed for that. Besides, there are plenty of students here whose powers are underwhelming at best. That doesn't mean they can't be special and make a difference. My hesitation with joining your squad, Tristan, is wondering when you're going to stop feeling sorry for yourself and figure that part out. Own the gifts you do have, stand up for yourself, and be the leader you were charged to be."

Tristan could only nod in acknowledgment as he marveled at the wisdom behind the girl's words. Finally, he looked at Belle and extended his hand.

"Welcome to Team Davids, Belle. Happy to have you on our squad."

Belle raised her eyebrows playfully. "Oh really? Just like that? Who said I was joining?"

"I did. Because you're going to challenge me to become a better leader. And because I'm going to do everything in my power to make sure you stay at the top of the class. We may not be your first choice, Belle, but I promise you won't regret your decision. You have my word."

Belle smiled, taking his hand in acceptance. "Well, Mr. Davids, you certainly have my attention. And if my calculations are correct, I believe you have yourself a team."

After his talk with Belle, Tristan rushed to the Academy to deliver his team submission to Principal Winter's office before the deadline. Winter wasn't in during that time, so Tristan filled out the application form and submitted it to the principal's secretary, Ms. Dorregard, who promised to process it immediately. By the time he had finished, Christian and Dan had already gotten up and were eating with Belle in the mess hall.

Walking in, Tristan spotted Gabriel, along with his newly formed team, across the room. They had apparently found Belle's replacement in the form of another late addition to the school, a strikingly attractive raven-haired girl by the name of Sofia De Rossi. Tristan couldn't help but wonder how they were faring as his squad continued to struggle to develop quality rapport. Between Chris' wise-cracking personality, Belle's perfectionist persona, Dan's humble demeanor, and Tristan's shy disposition, they were indeed a motley crew of individuals, and Tristan began to realize the complexity of the task before him.

After breakfast, the team decided to hunt for their school supplies and took the elevator down to the basement level of the facility, which was previously restricted to the students until now. The basement contained a massive bookstore, which held all of their supplies for school. The store had just about anything the students required during their four years on the island with its impressive inventory of items, and they helped each other find what they needed among the overwhelming rows of supplies.

As the day went on, the group continued to experience difficulty gelling together, their personalities each vastly different from the next. Belle found herself increasingly frustrated by Christian's never-ending quips and constant affixation to his looks. Tristan found Belle to be overly methodical and micromanaging when it came to doing things, at times being downright bossy. Christian was frustrated by Dan's seemingly dry personality and silent demeanor, while Dan couldn't understand why everyone felt the need to complain so much. Tristan's growing anxiety was not aided by the fact that the school assembly was only a day away, with classes beginning that following Monday.

The school assembly was apparently a big deal at the school, the moment in which the first-years would decide upon their alternate names.

While his teammates had apparently put a lot of thought into their new aliases, Tristan could not think of anything despite hours of reflection.

"Dude, just pick a name, who cares? It doesn't have to be anything fancy" Christian said in exasperation after Tristan brought it up for the millionth time.

"On the contrary, Tristan needs to seriously think about this. His name will help define his legacy at this school, for better or worse, and shouldn't be taken lightly. This is kind of a big deal," Belle retorted, earning an eye roll from Christian.

"I think what they're trying to say, Tristan, is try not to stress about it. Your name will come to you eventually. You don't have to force it, and once it does, I'm sure it'll be great," Dan said reassuringly.

Belle shook her head firmly and replied, "No. Not at all. You should definitely be worried about it. I think that..." Christian let out a loud groan as she began her tirade, and Tristan felt a small migraine start to come on. By the time the day was over, the four students had had just about enough of each other's company and went off separately to bed in silence.

The following day, Tristan woke up with a sick feeling in his gut. He was not prepared for the class assembly and still couldn't think of a suitable name. He could barely finish his breakfast and was not very good company, his mind deep in thought about possible nicknames. Thus far, his best ideas had been Captain Unknown and Mystery Boy, which only made his teammates roar in laughter. Well, maybe just Christian, but the rest definitely snickered.

Eventually, 6:00 PM rolled around, and Tristan proceeded to get dressed for the occasion. Christian helped him and Dan put on their neckties, demonstrating what he referred to as "the art of the proper knot". Tristan hated to wear ties, and from the way he was slowly turning deeper shades of red, Tristan could tell Dan was also ready to strangle Christian if he gave him one more correction.

Arriving a few minutes early, the boys got to the Academy and walked to the back of the building, where the school's outdoor amphitheater was located. It was fairly large, consisting of several levels of smooth stone lined with soft grass. It had the capacity to seat well over a hundred students, so they were all able to fit comfortably for the event. Belle had saved them a spot near the front, and the boys filed into the seats around her. Belle wore a long, sky blue dress and had her hair straightened, making her look slightly older. She had on a little bit of makeup for the occasion, and Tristan could feel his palms start to sweat when he sat next to her.

"Wow, Belle, you look...nice. I mean, not nice, beautiful...like in a friendly way! Like we're friends. And you look...nice." Tristan cleared his throat, his face turning bright red. Tristan could see Christian and Dan snickering silently behind her at his awkward compliment. He gritted his teeth and made himself a mental note to dropkick the two of them whenever this was over. The corner of her mouth raised slightly before Belle turned to Tristan.

"I know what you meant. Thank you, Tristan, that's sweet. You guys are looking handsome yourselves."

Once the last of the students found their seats, the first year professors, led by Principal Winter, made their entrance. They all wore white hooded robes, except for Winter, who wore purple, and walked down the tiki-torch lit path down the center aisle. The professors all filed to the stage, which contained several seats on either side of a large projection screen and came together in a line before the students. Winter stepped forward from the middle and removed his hood. His icy blue gaze swept across the room before he spoke.

"Good evening, my children! We are honored to have you all join us tonight for your commencement ceremony. As you all know, this is a special night, one where we continue a time-honored tradition. Tonight, you will shed the chains of your past and allow yourself to be remade as a member of this proud community! We will continue to live out our creed and instill in you the values that we hold so dear at the Academy: to teach and mold the youth of today in the hopes of creating a better tomorrow, for us and for all of mankind!" The students gave Winter a round of applause before he held up his arms for silence. "Now, let us watch a short video detailing the legacy behind the commencement ceremony." Winter and the professors took a seat on either side of the large screen, and a hush fell over the students as the video began.

The short film was about ten minutes long. Narrated by a familiar voice, it went through the early years of the school and the people who helped found it. Old photos of former students and teachers were shown, as well a few grainy videos featuring the Magnificent Seven. There was even footage of Tristan's grandfather and his parents, which he was absolutely mortified by.

While the video continued to play in the background, Tristan began to develop an unusual sense that he was being watched, a feeling as if his very soul were being exposed. Seemingly out of nowhere, a sense of vertigo started to overwhelm him, and he looked around to see if anyone else was having a similar experience. His classmates all seemed normal, however, thoroughly engrossed in the film above. As Tristan continued to look around, his eyes were drawn to the seat to the left of the screen, where Principal Winter sat, staring directly at him.

For a moment, Tristan was unsure whether he was imagining things, but the more he glanced up at Winter from the corner of his eyes, the more the feeling of vertigo increased. *What the heck is happening?* The more he tried to resist, the stronger the feeling became. Tristan felt beads of sweat trickle down his forehead in concentration as he tried to mentally push away whatever strange effect Winter was having on him. His head was pounding at this point, and he felt like he was going to scream.

Just then, the video ended, and the class began to clap, breaking whatever trance Tristan had been in. His palms were drenched in sweat, and he was breathing hard as if he had just done some strenuous exercise. "Hey, Tristan, everything okay?" Belle asked with a worried look. Tristan turned to her and nodded quickly, giving her a weak smile. He looked up at the stage where Principal Winter had resumed speaking, a large smile on his face and looking like nothing had happened.

"I'm fine. Think I just had a little panic attack or something. I'm good though," Tristan responded unconvincingly. He had no idea what had just happened, and a part of him still wondered if he was imagining things as he caught the tail end of Winter's speech.

"—your name a reflection of your inner self, your identity! It signifies your desire to enter into your new community and embrace your cultural heritage! Now, we have a special guest here today who will be in charge of the ceremony. You will each come up individually and reveal your chosen name, to which he will announce you to the community. It is my joy and privilege to introduce to you our guest of honor, the legend himself, Mainframe!"

The class erupted in applause as Mr. Peters came from behind the stage and waved to the students, grinning from ear to ear. Tristan nearly fell out of his seat in shock at the sight of his old friend and mentor! The old man politely shook Winter's hand, who gave a short bow to the elder metamorph and proceeded to sit back in his chair. Once the applause died down, Mr. Peters stepped forward and stared into the crowd, giving Tristan a quick nod.

"Thank you all for your warm welcome! It is truly an honor to be given this task of granting you your new names! As you come on to the stage, I hope you all feel the same sense of pride and renewal as I did when I first chose mine! Today begins the first day of your new lives, so, without further ado, let us commence!"

With that said, the students rose up from their seats, starting with the first row, and lined up on the stage to be named. Tristan watched while his classmates walked up to Mr. Peters, who gave them each a small speech before they whispered their new name to him. He would then turn to the crowd and announce in a booming voice, "I give you...!" filling in their chosen name, to which the class roared in approval.

Cynthia's group was among the first ones on the stage, and she beamed with pride when Mr. Peters called out "Detonella" to the crowd. Mike and Tom Anderson chose the names Fog and Smoke, respectively, while Emily went with the name Camo. The poor girl went completely invisible at the sound of applause, and Mr. Peters laughed in surprise at the empty dress that stood before him. Juan's group followed closely behind, the small boy deciding upon the name Psyborg, which somehow Tristan felt suited him perfectly.

A few more groups went through before Gabriel's team sauntered up to the stage. Tristan watched as his rival spoke his name, which Mr. Peters seemed to take a strong liking to, before announcing "Agayu" to the crowd. While a majority of the students seemed confused at the name, Tristan noticed a few of the African students were particularly pleased. As for the rest of his team, Brandon went with the name Wolf, Malcolm chose Blaze, and Sofi was renamed Twister.

Finally, it was Tristan's row that was called up, and he felt his chest tighten up in anticipation. While Belle kept insisting it was bad luck for him to do so, Tristan had his teammates go before him in order to buy himself a little more time. Belle went first, beaming from ear to ear when she whispered her name to Mr. Peters. "I give you...Ariel!" he announced, holding her arm aloft. Tristan found himself smiling as she blushed before making her way off the stage.

Next up was Christian, who shot him a sly grin, and Tristan silently prayed that it wouldn't be anything inappropriate. "I give you...Vamp!" Mr. Peters announced, Christian throwing up his hands in a rock and roll gesture, tongue flaring out. "All right, keep it moving," Mr. Peters said with a laugh as he shooed him off. Dan came up after, completely dwarfing Mr. Peters with his size, bending down to whisper his name. Mr. Peters nodded in acknowledgment, and since he was too short to lift up his arms, pointed to the boy and said, "I give you...Samson!"

Approaching Mr. Peters, Tristan felt his heart clench in his chest, the old man's familiar smile not enough to help quell his churning stomach.

"It is my honor to welcome you into the metamorph community, young man. Today, you join the rich culture of your people and are reborn into a new society! What have you decided your name to be?" Mr. Peters said, eye's seeming to glow in expectation. Tristan felt like his knees were going to collapse. His mouth felt unusually dry, and it had suddenly grown deathly quiet in the amphitheater. The tiki lights seemed blinding, and Tristan's thoughts seemed at an impasse.

"Go on, child," Mr. Peters encouraged.

"I...don't know Mr. Peters...I don't have one."

A look of surprise quickly flashed across the old man's face, and Tristan could tell the gears in his head were turning. Without missing a beat, his mentor spun toward the crowd and announced: "Quite a bold move, Mr. Davids! While unorthodox, it is not unheard of for some metamorphs to humble themselves and keep their given name as a sign of respect and unity toward the world they have come to know and love!" Tristan saw Winter raise his eyebrows at this statement, clearly taken aback by the impromptu speech. "While one day, fate may decide upon a new alias, for now, I give you...Tristan!"

There was a smattering of confused applause heard, and Tristan quickly walked off the stage, shooting his mentor a look of gratitude at the save. He tried to avoid the eyes of his confused teammates when he sat down beside them, and once again, wished he were anywhere else but there at that moment.

Following the naming ceremony, Principal Winter gave a final parting speech before announcing that there would be a banquet provided for them in the mess hall. Tristan had no desire to attend the banquet, but he didn't want to appear out of sorts and felt that he had already let his team down enough. He trudged along behind them, the three speaking excitedly about some of the names that had been chosen. He attempted to seem interested, chiming in half-heartedly, but couldn't bring himself to do much else.

Upon entering the mess hall, the room was buzzing with energy. While the students feasted on the delicious spread placed before them, the professors walked around congratulating everyone. Tristan watched his teammates separate, spreading out to talk with some of the other students, and soon found himself alone in the corner.

"So tell me, was my introduction video so boring that you completely forgot to come up with a name or were you just trying to keep an old man on his toes?" Tristan gave a silent laugh as he turned around to give Mr. Peters a hug.

"I thought I recognized the voice on the video. Thanks again for saving my hide back there, Mr. Peters. I was really struggling up there tonight."

"Tonight?" Mr. Peters asked skeptically.

"Okay, maybe every night since I've gotten here. It's been a bit of an adjustment," Tristan reluctantly admitted.

"Yes, most changes are. But you control how you deal with the adversity, young man. It can either break you or mold you into the man you're destined to be."

"Yeah...looks like I'm still figuring that part out, you know?"

For a while, neither of them said anything, watching the students mingle before them. Tristan broke the silence, turning to the old man and asked, "Hey, Mr. Peters? What's up with Gabe's name? What's Agayu mean?"

"It's the name of an African deity, the guardian of the desert. While he was often viewed as warlike and irascible, he was known to soothe the turbulent rivers and thought of as the strength that comes from deep inside the soul. It is quite the name to live up to." Tristan was taken aback by this, watching Gabriel joke around with his teammates from across the room.

"Funny, who would've thought Gabe could actually think past his next insult? I can see the first part in him for sure, but that last bit is a bit of a stretch."

"I wouldn't be too quick to judge the boy just yet. Like you, he, too, is having to make a difficult adjustment to his new surroundings and may not have the maturity to properly process his emotions. Give him time. He may yet surprise you." Mr. Peters gently patted the young boy on the shoulder before leaving to go mingle with the other professors. Tristan thought about what Mr. Peters had just said but couldn't get past the image of Gabriel flinging him into the pond earlier that week.

Still feeling out of place, Tristan decided to sneak out of the banquet and take a walk. Stepping out into the cool, breezy night, Tristan loosened up his tie and removed his shoes. A walk on the beach always helped him get his mind off things, and he decided to give it a shot. Tristan made his way onto the beach, kicking the sand beneath his feet while the tiki torches helped illuminate his path. The ocean water seemed to shine from the strange iridescent glow of the nearby coral reefs. He eventually sat down beside the water's edge and stared out at the waves beyond, outlined by the lights of the starry night sky.

"Mind if we join you?" Tristan heard Christian's voice and turned to find his teammates behind him.

"Yeah, sure. I don't mind," Tristan replied as they sat beside him. Neither of them said anything for a while, staring in silence at the stars above.

"I swear, it's like a picture book sometimes, you know?" Christian said, initiating the conversation.

"What is?" Dan asked.

"This island, man. It's amazing. The beach, the mountains, the weather. It's like it popped out of some fairy tale or something. It's almost too perfect sometimes."

"You say that like it's a bad thing." The three teens turned to look at Tristan, who was staring at Christian. "The island being too perfect. You say that like you don't believe it. Why?"

Christian thought for a moment before shrugging to himself. "I dunno. I guess I had envisioned a few more Sports Illustrated models walking around is all." Dan and Belle let out an immediate groan. "What? I'm serious! I'm pretty sure this is where Sports Illustrated does their swimsuit edition! They've got to be some—"

"Stop! Just stop!" Tristan shouted, shocking everyone into silence. "Why do you always do that?!"

"Dude, I was just messing around."

"That's just it, Chris! You're always messing around!" Tristan blurted in anger. "You're always making smart comments, trying to deflect anytime we bring up something real! I'm being serious right now! Why are you so worried about this island?! What is it about this place being too perfect that's such a bad thing?!"

"Because it can't last!" Christian screamed back. A pause fell over the group as Christian's demeanor seemed to completely change, the somber look Tristan had first seen on his face returning. "Because...it can't last. Nothing good ever does." Tristan stared at his friend, unsure of what to say.

"Look, man, I know I can be a bit...much sometimes. But that's just how I deal. My parents left me when I was just a baby, and I've spent my entire life bouncing around from foster home to foster home. Every time I thought I had found the perfect family, the one who would finally take me in for good, they changed their minds and sent me away. Maybe it was my attitude or the way I would always find myself in some kind of trouble. Or maybe it was the unexplainable things that would happen whenever they took their eyes off of me. My hair suddenly growing seven inches in a matter of minutes. My skin turning translucent whenever I threw a tantrum. The way the room turned cold whenever I had nightmares."

"I still remember my last night at a foster home. My guardians had a school conference they needed to attend and had made me dinner before they left. That night, my powers started to really manifest, and every time I tried to take a bite of my food, it would just freeze. Just freeze in my mouth. You ever stick your tongue on a metal pole during the winter?" Christian asked, staring straight at Tristan, his eyes red with the tears he was struggling to hold back. "Imagine doing that. With every bite. By the time they got back from their meeting, they found me curled up in a ball screaming and crying, blood all over the place. Alone, cold, and afraid. They were so freaked, the next day they packed up my bags and sent me back."

Tristan could hear Belle sniffle beside him as Christian continued to stare with his cold, empty eyes. "Nothing good ever lasts, Tristan. The homes, this island...they're all temporary. So I'm gonna keep smiling and joking. I'm gonna keep messing around because at the end of the day, all that matters is who gets the last laugh."

"Chris, I'm...I don't know what to—" Tristan began before Belle interrupted.

"I hate myself," she said matter-of-factly, earning a confused look from all the boys. "What? I do."

"Why? What could you possibly hate yourself for? You're perfect!" Tristan asked, immediately regretting the last statement, but Belle didn't seem to notice.

"Well, that's the problem, isn't it? I'm not. I'm not perfect, at all. Something that my parents loved to remind me over and over growing up. I didn't have your background, Chris. I come from a fairly affluent family in Marseilles, and I'm an only child. As a result, my parents put all their focus on making sure I turned out to be their perfect progeny. From childhood, they had me enrolled in music lessons, spelling bees, art class, you name it. They threw everything at me and expected me to be perfect. At everything. I was top of my class every year at school. I won every award. I dominated everything they set before me, but the only one I actually enjoyed was swimming."

"I swam distance, and the 10k was my specialty. I loved it. The feel of the water, the sense of competition, the complete silence as you entered into your own little world. Just me and the water. I was the best at my age level and was competing nationally before I even hit my teens. Last year was nationals, and I was the favorite to win. I remember feeling a little different that day. Not bad, just different. I jumped into the water, got off to a great start, and absolutely crushed it. I swam without a care in the world. Beat the national record by three minutes, barely even trying."

"Belle, that's amazing! Congrats!" Tristan replied. To his surprise, a tear fell from Belle's eye as she seemed lost in the memory.

"Yeah...amazing. I was disqualified and had all of my medals stripped away for cheating. Performance enhancing drugs and metabolic manipulation they concluded, although they could never prove it. You see, while I was busy being lost in my own world beneath the water's surface, I forgot to come up and breathe. I just swam straight through. The people above were freaking out, but I just kept going, speeding along and picking up the pace. The only ones who weren't freaked out were my parents, who refused to defend me."

Belle sighed, looking down at the sand beneath her. "My aunts and uncles...my cousins and grandparents...they're all metamorphs. But not my parents. To them, they were the only perfect ones in a family full of freaks. And in a space of a day, I went from being their perfect little girl to just another embarrassment." Tristan felt his heart swell with emotion. He wanted to hug Belle, hold her, and convince her that she wasn't some freak, that her powers were a beautiful gift. But seeing the look in her brown eyes, he knew no words could heal the disappointment she felt.

"Well, shoot, my family ain't so bad," Dan proclaimed, rubbing his thick hair. "I ain't got no sad story like y'all folk. I come from a family of hard-working dairy farmers out in middle-of-nowhere Milwaukee. Me and my seven siblings helped out on the farm our whole lives when we weren't in school. My parents never went to school themselves, so they're real proud of me right now," he said with a soft smile. "I'm the only one in the family with powers, 'cept my sister, who thinks she can talk to the cows, but I just think she's crazy." The group burst into laughter at this, Dan included.

"My parents, they always knew I was special. I was the oldest of the eight, and they always told me to make sure I protected them as best I could and keep them outta trouble. So I did. Anytime they would get into scuffles at school or if they needed help moving the tractor to the shed when it got a flat tire, they would just call on me, and I'd be there." Dan sighed, looking out over the water, but Tristan could tell that his eyes were seeing something else. "I sure hope they're doing all right. Pop ain't doing too well, his heart being weak and all. Wasn't gonna come, but he made me promise to get on that plane. Said I better not come back until I was finished...no matter what happens to him..."Dan stopped at the last part, and Tristan placed his hands on his broad shoulders.

There was a long pause of silence until Tristan looked up and realized that they were all looking at him. "What?" he asked.

"Don't 'what' us! You got us all in our feelings and we're waiting on you, Dr. Phil!" Christian remarked, causing Tristan to smile.

"You all know my story already! It's nothing special. I'm a nobody. A nobody in a family of somebodies. I have a great family, a great life, great friends. Ironically, the only thing that's not great seems to be me. I am...underwhelming. I'm currently enrolled in a school founded by my grandparents, where my parents and siblings all became legends of their own, and then there's me: no powers, no cool alias, no special outfit."

"And it's hard, you know, trying to live up to a name that's permanently stuck to you. It's like a destiny that's being forced upon you, except you don't know whether or not you're the main character or just a cameo in someone else's story. I've spent all my time wishing I was someone else because, at the end of the day, I still can't figure out who I am! Maybe I am just a regular human after all, the one speck of normalcy in a family where the extraordinary is just the usual."

"I just...want to belong, whether its back home as a regular guy or out here as a metamorph. But I think I'm starting to realize that's not my fate. Maybe I'm meant to be an outsider, to be different. Maybe I need to stop whining, feeling sorry for myself and start taking control of my future. Maybe I need to stop letting people tell me who I should be, and start becoming the man I want to be."

Tristan breathed out a sigh of relief, a weight lifted off of his shoulders. He was greeted by silence in response, and Tristan looked back and forth expectantly at his teammates. "Well? Is that it? Aren't you guys gonna say something?"

Dan seemed to pause in reflection before turning to Tristan with a serious face. "Yeah, you were right. That was pretty lame," he said, face breaking out into a smile. Tristan lunged forward to playfully throw a handful of wet sand at the big guy, which quickly escalated into an all-out war. The four friends were laughing now, sandballs and playful shouts filling the night air.

By the time they were done, they were completely covered in sand, their formal attires ruined, and exhausted from their game.

As they laid out on the sand, attempting to catch their breath, Christian turned to Tristan and said, "Hey, Tristan. Thanks for doing all that. Getting us to open up to one another and finally bond, that was pretty cool."

"What are you talking about?" Tristan asked, confused. "I didn't—I hadn't planned on—"

"Sure you didn't, bud. Sure you didn't," Christian said sarcastically, standing up to brush off his clothes.

"I'm serious!" Tristan exclaimed, but he could tell none of them seemed to believe him.

"I swear, that mopey, emo thing he does. Gets you every time," Christian said with a laugh. "I'm heading back to the dorm. Care to join me, Farmer Samson?" Dan nodded and soon joined Christian in walking off the beach, joking and laughing along the way.

Tristan turned to Belle and gave her an incredulous look. "What just happened?" he asked. Belle smiled as she continued to work the sand out of her hair.

"You did something special, Tristan. You turned a group of misfits into a team," Belle replied while she fixed her dress. "And then you turned that team into friends." She flashed him a grin before turning to the dorms, and Tristan felt his knees grow weak. For a moment, he stood by himself in silence, watching her silhouette fade into the distance. Gathering his shoes and tie from the ground, Tristan looked up at the stars with a smile, and for the first time in his life felt like he finally belonged.

Chapter 11: Classes Begin

After a restless night, Tristan woke up a few minutes before his alarm went off, nervous energy swirling around in his gut. The previous day, all of the remaining students and teachers had made their way back to the island, the once calm dorms a hive of activity. Tristan and his friends had managed to avoid most of the commotion, and after their night on the beach, the four had really begun to click and get along. Tristan smiled to himself, still amazed that he had pulled it off.

Before he could get too far into his thoughts, the sound of alarms filled the room, and he shot out of bed, excited to begin his first day of school. He punched the still-sleeping Christian on the arm, laughing aloud while his friend's obscenities follow him into the bathroom. Since he wasn't with Professors Stellios or Coffman today, Tristan changed into a loose fitting t-shirt and khaki shorts, grabbing his backpack on the way out the door.

It was about 7:15 when the group met in the mess hall for breakfast, and the four discussed their class schedules for the day. While Dan had Psychology first, the other three had World History. Tristan would then join Dan for World Literature before their lunch break, and he would end the day by himself in Psychology. After Tristan had gobbled down his meal, the school bell rang, announcing the end of the breakfast period.

Tristan, Belle, and Christian said their goodbyes to Dan before heading over to room 107. Tristan had never been particularly fond of World History, however, he was very much excited to learn about metamorphs. Upon entering the room, Tristan was met with the familiar sight of your typical high school classroom, fixed tables lined up in rows with two stools paired with each one. Each table was marked with their names atop the desk, and to his disappointment, Tristan was not paired with either of his teammates. As a tall, dark-skinned boy approached, he pushed back his thick glasses and gave Tristan a friendly nod.

"What's up, Tristan? Glad to see I'll be hanging out with a fellow leader!" Will Conrad said, smiling.

"I wouldn't get too excited. Pretty sure you'll be singing a different tune come test time."

Will laughed at this and shook his head. "Honestly, man, I'm just glad I don't have to take this class with that jerk over there," he responded, pointing his thumb at Gabriel, who had been paired with Tom Anderson. "I don't know about you, but I've got too much self-respect to help some tool get an A off my hard work." Tristan nodded in agreeance.

The two boys took out their books and writing materials just as Professor Fisher walked through the doors, a large smile on his face while he attempted to juggle the mound of books and papers in his hands. "Hello, my bright-eyed, young pupils! Good morning, and welcome to your first class of the school year! As you know, my name is Professor Anthony Fisher, and I am thrilled to welcome you all to World History! We will be beginning our day by going through the basic class rules and our syllabus for the year. Afterward, we will explore the first chapter of our World History books, briefly going over the start of human civilization. While I know many of you are anxious to begin learning about the rich history of our people, we must first discuss and come to understand the world that had existed around us before we first came to be!"

After passing out the syllabus and going over class expectations, the professor spent the remaining time going over the beginnings of human civilization, from the Neanderthals to ancient Mesopotamia. As it turned out, Professor Fisher's class was a lot more interesting than Tristan had expected. The old man was extremely knowledgeable, and his passion for the subject he taught was downright infectious.

When the school bell rang, Tristan left class, intrigued for what the rest of the day held for him. Tristan's subsequent class was World Literature, located two doors adjacent to the classroom he just came from. Tristan waved goodbye to Belle and Christian before detecting Dan lumbering in his direction through the crowd. Tristan waited for the big fellow to catch up to him prior to opening the classroom door.

When the two boys stepped into the classroom, they were immediately greeted by Professor Meulman, who was sitting cross-legged on his desk, dressed in torn, faded jeans and a turtleneck, despite it being at least eighty degrees outside. The room smelled like jasmine, and there were sounds of relaxing music, dribbling waterfalls, and distant chimes coming from a Bluetooth speaker system set up beside the professor.

"Good morning, gentlemen! Welcome to class! Please feel free to grab a chair and sit wherever you would like. We believe in a positive, relaxed environment here, so don't worry too much about where you wind up, just let your seat find you!" Meulman said with a serene smile. Tristan and Dan both exchanged glances of skepticism before looking around the room for a place to sit.

The room was fairly wide open with several small circular tables set up throughout. The tables were short, perhaps two feet off of the marble tile floors, and rather than having seats, soft, plush pillows were around each table, three to a spot. Tristan and Dan chose a table closest to the back of the room and set down their bags.

Among the last of the stragglers was Cynthia, who took a long, hard look at her remaining options before locking her eyes on the seat beside Dan and Tristan. With a resigned look across her face, she walked toward the back of the room and sat across from the two boys. Neither of them said anything while they took out their supplies and waited for class to begin, until, finally, Dan broke the silence.

"I don't know about y'all but I'm a little nervous about this class. Meulman seems cool and all, but I hate reading. I can talk Harry Potter all day, but if he pulls out Shakespeare, I'm taking a nap," the large boy said.

"I hear ya, big guy. I'm decent enough, so if you need any help, just ask!" Tristan reassured his friend.

"Aww, that's too cute! You two could have little study dates and hold hands!" Cynthia teased.

Dan's face turn slightly red at Cynthia's remark, and Tristan could sense the boy was about to shoot off an angry reply. However, before Dan could get the words out of his mouth, Tristan answered back.

"That's right, Cynth. And if you play nice today, we may save you some of our ice cream. Careful that you don't eat it too fast though. I don't want you to get a brain freeze, seeing as you think slow enough as it is!" The words left Tristan's mouth before he even had time to think them over, and he realized that he had been hanging around Christian way too much. Cynthia looked up at Tristan with narrowed eyes, before a smile slowly spread across her face.

"Touché, Tristan. That was actually a decent comeback. You might survive a semester with me after all."

After their little back-and-forth banter, the three chatted for a few more seconds before Meulman started his class. Meulman began by passing out copies of "Bulfinch's Mythology", which they were to read for the beginning of the semester. The professor was eager to look over and discuss the various tales that had been passed down, exploring the meanings behind each one. The class briefly went over the first two fables together in detail. As his powers implied, Professor Meulman was about more than just scratching the surface of a story, wanting to delve into the emotions they invoked upon both the characters in the stories and the readers themselves.

Despite her initial teasing, Cynthia was actually quite helpful when it came to literature and seemed more than happy to assist Dan whenever he had questions in regards to plot threads and character backgrounds. The two seemed to get along surprisingly well, and by the time the bell rang, it appeared they had made a new friend in Cynthia.

Once class was over, the teammates walked over to the dormitories to switch out their books and take a short power nap before meeting back at the Academy for lunch. Tristan had just finished polishing off his plate when the lunch bell rang, indicating the start of their final class for the day. Tristan separated from the group to go to Psychology 101, which was located next door.

Compared to his previous two classes, the Psychology classroom contained individual seats and chairs arranged in rows. Professor Tullage was busy writing down things on the whiteboard when Tristan walked into the classroom, and he decided upon an open seat in the middle of the room. This being the only class in which he didn't have a teammate, Tristan felt more relaxed once he saw Juan take a seat next to him, the youngster giving him a wave while unpacking his belongings. The seats around him filled up quickly, and Tristan soon found himself surrounded by familiar faces in Emily, Brandon, and Sofia. Emily gave Tristan a reserved smile, while Brandon looked none too pleased with the fact that he had to sit in front of Tristan.

This was also the first time Tristan had been this close to Sofia, who sat to his right. He had assumed that the strikingly beautiful girl would immediately adopt the hatred of him that their leader emanated, so it was of great surprise when she turned her brown eyes toward his and extended out her hand.

"Hey! Tristan, right? My name is Sofi, pleasure to finally meet you!" Tristan briefly looked around to make sure he wasn't being pranked before slowly extending his hand and shaking hers.

"Uhh, yeah, thanks," he said with uncertainty.

"Don't worry," she laughed, "I'm not a stan! It's just that Gabe talks about you a lot, and it's not like I don't have to walk by your grandparents every day."

"Yeah, I bet he does. Guess that makes us enemies for life, I suppose."

Sofi rolled her eyes at this last remark, her smile quickly disappearing. "Wow, typical guy. I'm more than capable of thinking for myself, thank you very much. I don't need Gabe to brainwash me on who I can and cannot be friends with. Now that you said that, though, I can see where he's coming from. Maybe he was right about you after all."

Tristan felt his face grow bright red in embarrassment, realizing how that must have come off. "No, Sofi, I'm sorry. I didn't—!"

Suddenly, the girl let out a snort and broke into a smile. "Relax, Trist! I'm messing with you! You should've seen the look on your face though! Priceless!" Tristan sighed with relief and shook his head. "I did mean what I said about thinking for myself though. So leave whatever beef you've got with my Supreme Leader at the door because I want no part of it. Besides, it kinda sucks, you know? Gabe's actually a really nice guy. You two might actually be friends if you didn't hate each other so much."

Before Tristan could reply, the bell rang, and Professor Tullage turned around from the whiteboard to begin. As with the other professors, Tullage started by passing out the syllabus and discussing the expectations for the year. They would be going through the assigned textbook and learning about the various theories associated with the mind, from mental training techniques to personality assessments. Professor Tullage did a great job at keeping the students interested, using videos and demonstrations, and Tristan didn't struggle with the material as much as he had originally anticipated.

When the bell eventually rang, Tristan was mentally exhausted, and it seemed that his friends felt the same. They decided to unwind by the lake for a few hours before supper and spent the time talking about their class experience. The rest of the day was fairly uneventful, the four friends playing a few rounds of pool before heading off to bed. As Tristan fell into a quick, restful sleep, he hoped the next day's classes would prove to be as interesting as today's.

The next morning found Tristan hiking up the mountain path past the training grounds while the heat of the morning sun beat strongly upon his head. They were all wearing their assigned outfits, and Tristan was already regretting the Designer's decision. The suit might be capable of stopping a knife from piercing his side, but it didn't stop him from sweating up a storm wearing all this leather. Belle seemed much more comfortable in her swimwear, while Dan had the look of someone who had grown used to wearing heavy clothing on a warm day. Tristan had the impression that the boy barely felt the additional weight of the armor he had on. The only person who looked more miserable than Tristan was Christian, whose fair skin didn't take well to the sun and seemed to never grow any darker, despite his many painful attempts to tan.

The four students passed underneath the sign reading TA 101, joining the other two groups of Team Jackson and Perrotta. Each team sat together on the ground, spread across the grassy surface of the overhang while Professor Stellios stood before them, positioned next to a large, auburn boulder. She had on an all-grey leather outfit, complete with a small cloak and matching gloves and boot. There was an air of unbridled self-assurance about her, which intimidated Tristan. The older woman cleared her throat, silencing the class.

"Today, we begin our first day of Teamwork and Ability Management 101, and I hope you all are as excited about the year as I am! You all know me as Professor Jane Stellios, but out here, you will refer to me and each other by your metamorph names. So starting now, you may call me Professor Tremor. In this class, I will be showing you all how to work as a highly-efficient unit geared toward achieving a common goal. We will focus on helping you all discover your gifts, ensuring that you are able to utilize and manage your powers as a team."

"There are no books for this class, all I will require are your outfits and your effort. I am a known perfectionist, and I will not settle for anything less than your best. At the end of our teaching session, you will have an hour of application time during which you will be working alongside your teammates to help each other hone your abilities. Now that we have that out of the way, are there any questions?"

Tristan joined his classmates in shaking their heads. "Good! Now everyone stand up and make your way to the front. Find an open area in which you and your teammates have some space to utilize your abilities."

With plenty of space along the overhang, Tristan and his team were able to find a large area a comfortable distance apart while they awaited further instruction. Professor Stellios paced around the class as she spoke, moving among each group. "Today, you will be activating your abilities and demonstrating how quickly and efficiently you can manage them. Be patient with one another; this is not an easy task and may take several attempts. Some may not get it today, or for quite some time." Tristan lowered his eyes as she shot him a glance. "But rest assured, that if one such as I could control this power, there's no doubt in my mind that we can do the same for you!"

Professor Stellios spun on her heels to face the boulder and extended her right arm, palms open and fingers spread apart. Tristan felt a pulse of energy, the air around her hand bending in waves, and the rock shook violently for a brief second before shattering into a million pieces in the air. The professor flicked back her red hair and looked at the awestruck class. "Shall we begin?"

For the remaining time, the students stood with their teammates, practicing how to activate their abilities while Tremor walked around offering advice. As a whole, the students were able to demonstrate their powers fairly easily, although there were those in each group that had a harder time than others. Among Team Perrotta, Emily probably had the easiest time, changing her skin tone anytime Professor Tremor seemed to get remotely close to her. Tristan noted, however, that her powers seemed to be based on subconscious control rather than conscious manipulation. Tom and Matt were also similar in that regard, able to morph in and out of their ethereal forms whenever they were physically hitting one another but unable to do so just by concentrating. They had on form-fitting, black-and-yellow bio-hazard suits made of a unique synthetic material that helped to hold their gaseous forms together, collapsing upon impact before re-inflating whenever they became corporeal again.

Out of everyone in her group, Cynthia was probably the biggest surprise, as she was extremely reluctant to activate her ability. "You don't understand, things could go very badly!" she tried to explain to Professor Stellios. "Anytime I use it, something bad happens! I can't control it around these people, and someone could get hurt!"

Tristan was shocked to see her eyes start to tear up before Professor Stellios placed her hands on her shoulder. "It's all right, Detonella! I understand you are scared, but you need to trust your outfit. It was designed for your powers and helping you harness this energy. It can withstand some of your biggest energy outputs, and as you gain more control over your abilities, you will learn how to manage even without it. But you have to trust me, dear. You will not hurt these students."

Cynthia closed her eyes, a look of worry still across her face, and gave a reluctant nod. Professor Stellios and the other students stepped back while Cynthia took a deep breath to steady her nerves. When she opened her eyes again, her normal dark brown eyes were no longer there, replaced instead by searing balls of fire. Her bronze skin took on a radiant glow as light began to seep through every pore.

Before he knew what was happening, Tristan was nearly rocked backward as Cynthia literally exploded before his eyes in a wave of fiery energy. The blast was contained, however, extending no further than the girl's outstretched hands. The grass surrounding her was completely scorched, and her suit was steaming from the heat and smoke of the blast. Eventually, the flames extinguished themselves, retreating back down into her skin, and piecing her charred face back together. In a matter of seconds, Cynthia looked completely normal again, albeit covered in soot, and Professor Stellios ran up to give her a hug.

As for Team Jackson, they all seemed well versed in activating their abilities. Gabriel's manipulation of sand was nearly flawless, the particles acting as extensions of himself, while Malcolm literally ran circles around his group, a visual blur to Tristan's eyes. Sofi was also proficient in her powers, which turned out to be wind manipulation, and she used it to comedic effect.

When Gabriel continued to show off with his sand, swirling it around and twisting it in circles across his body, Sofi's eyes went completely white while extending her palms in a subtle gesture toward the group leader. Before Gabriel could react, he was suddenly caught in a whirlwind of sand, the violent winds whipping the grains into his open mouth while he sputtered for her to cut it out. This earned a well-deserved laugh from the class, which she accepted with a gracious bow. Despite her teasing, Sofi made sure to help the disgruntled boy to his feet, blowing him a kiss for forgiveness. Gabriel tried his best to look upset, but even Tristan could tell it was just an act.

Brandon was the only one who Tristan couldn't figure out. The boy seemed unable to activate his powers and seemed to be encouraging his teammates to berate him while he paced back and forth with closed eyes. After a few minutes, he opened his eyes again and shook his head. "Sorry boys, I don't think it's enough. I think I need to genuinely feel it in order for it to work."

Tristan's group fared about the same as the others. Belle, of course, stole the show with her water control when she lifted a spiraling stream from the ocean below up to the overhang. She received quite the praise from Professor Stellios, and Tristan could tell she was pleased, her smile practically lighting up the room. Dan wasn't far behind either, deciding to do push-ups with the entire team standing on top of his broad back for good measure. Tristan wasn't sure what to do himself, so he made sure to offer encouragement to his teammates, but he couldn't help but notice the look of disapproval across the professor's face while she looked on.

Next was Christian, who continued to be an enigma. His powers seemed to emerge based on his emotions at the time, but he was reluctant to allow himself those opportunities. Despite their best efforts to scare, anger, or simply agitate Christian, he simply deflected each time, refusing to give in. At most, they could get the boy's eyes to change and his hair to lengthen, but Tristan could feel no change in the air temperature, and Christian's fangs were never fully on display.

Professor Stellios was growing frustrated with his flippant attitude, but before she could speak, the bell rang for the lunch period, snapping her out of her thoughts. "All right everyone, gather your belongings and head off to lunch! We will pick back up where we left off on Thursday! Enjoy the rest of your day!"

Following lunch, the team returned to the mountain, this time entering the cavern to the amphitheater of Self-Defense and Metamorph Philosophy. The students took a seat upon one of the various stone rows looking down on the middle of the open circle where Professor Coffman stood. The Middle Eastern man wore a traditional white thawb, his robe flowing in the gentle breeze emanating from the top of the opening above.

"Welcome, my *altalmidh*! As you may have already heard from Professor Tremor, we will be going by our metamorph names while we develop our skills as a team, so you may call me *Duktur* Crusher! My class is run similarly to Tremor's, as we look to develop your skills and teach you how to manage your abilities. While Tremor focuses mainly upon your offensive abilities and team cohesion, my focus lies on individual adaptation and defensive capabilities. In time, you may come to see that the greatest tactical weapon in your arsenal is a well-organized defense!"

Following his speech, the rest of the class was spent learning about the importance of self-defense and the philosophy behind its practice. It was not, as Professor Coffman stated, a means to "beat up" their opponents, but rather, a way to disrupt their game plan until you gained the advantage. After class, Tristan was planning on leaving with his teammates, when he heard his name called out by the professor. He told the others he would catch up with them later before walking toward the shorter man. When the two were finally alone, Professor looked up at him with his cold brown eyes and folded his arms across his chest.

"Mr. Davids, I was hoping to speak with you privately regarding your status in my class."

Tristan felt his stomach drop, knowing where this conversation was heading. "Look, Professor Crusher, I know what you're going to say."

The older man raised his eyebrows, questioningly. "Really? What would that be?"

"That this class is pretty much impossible without powers. That I can't really compete with my peers until I figure this whole metamorph thing out."

To Tristan's surprise, Professor Coffman barked out a laugh and shook his head. "Let me ask you something, Tristan. What does having powers have to do with defending yourself?"

Before Tristan could respond, the older professor lunged forward, pulling back his fists as if to throw a punch. Instinctively, Tristan let out a yelp and ducked, lunging to the side while trying frantically to get his arms up to defend himself. Professor Coffman looked on in quiet amusement. "You just successfully maneuvered your way out of an oncoming attacker's assault. Tell me, what powers did you use for that? I don't expect you to be able to utilize your powers any time soon, Mr. Davids. What I do expect is for you to find a way to compete with your peers, despite this handicap. While in this class, expect to learn things differently from your team, and do not grow discouraged. You'd be surprised how little I've had to use my own powers over the years in order to overcome my adversaries." With that, Professor Coffman gathered up his satchel and walked out of the cavern, leaving Tristan still holding up his fists, wondering what to make of his new professor.

Over the next few days, Tristan and his friends began to grow accustomed to their new schedule and classes. They were each challenging in their own way, but Tristan found himself enjoying them all, except for maybe Professor Stellios' class, whom he was still convinced didn't like him. By the time the final bell rang on Friday afternoon, he was ready for the weekend, the group having made plans to go surfing on the beach and possibly snorkeling out along the reefs. Before he could get too far, however, he was stopped by Principal Winter's secretary waiting for him beside the inner fountain. She was a tiny woman bent over with age holding a glossy, wooden cane at her side.

"Excuse me, Mr. Davids?!" she called out when he passed her by. "Principal Winter would like to speak with you for a moment and has sent me down to retrieve you!" she yelled in a squeaky voice, causing several students to turn around and stare.

Tristan felt his ears burn. "Principal Winter? Is everything all right?" he asked when she began to direct him toward the elevator.

"What?! What did you say?! You'll have to speak a little louder, young man! The ears don't quite work like they used to, ya know?!"

"Uhh, nothing, ma'am! I'll gladly follow along!" he yelled back.

Upon entering through the double doors, the old woman led them across the wood-paneled waiting room. There was an electric fireplace burning in the corner surrounded by several couches and a large coffee table covered in magazines. The old woman shuffled over towards a tall desk made of wood with a name tag atop of it that read "Ms. Dorregard". As she took a seat at the table she pointed to the door marked "Winter" and yelled, "You can go right in, dear!" Tristan thanked her before turning the metal knob and stepping through the door.

Within the large office was a massive mahogany desk, behind which Principal Winter sat, staring at his computer. Behind the older man were shelves, completely filled to the brim with texts of various sizes and colors. Beneath the desk was a large rug and there were several comfortable chairs before it.

"Mr. Davids, thank you for coming in," Principal Winter said, standing up to shake Tristan's hand and gesturing toward an open chair. Tristan took his seat, trying hard not to appear nervous. For a moment, neither one spoke, Winter staring intently into the young boy's eyes as if trying to read his thoughts. Tristan began to feel a familiar sense of vertigo before Winter smiled politely and broke the silence.

"So, Tristan, how are things? Are you finding everything all right?"

"Uhh, fine sir. No complaints. I'm enjoying being here."

The man continued to stare at Tristan, nodding his head, but appeared distracted. "Glad to hear! It's always good when our students enjoy their time here with us. It's not very often that we get students of your...status, and it's important for me to know that there's no differential treatment being shown toward one such as yourself."

"What do you mean differential treatment? Like students picking on me or something?"

"Yes, I suppose you could put it that way."

Tristan shrugged in response. "I'm used to it. I've survived in the past, I should be fine here as well."

"Unfortunately, Mr. Davids, *here* is not like what you are used to back home. This isn't some regular human school where you are on equal ground, surrounded by your peers from the neighborhood. The Academy is full of the most gifted, talented metamorphs from across the world. *Here* can prove to be quite difficult for one such as yourself and even quite dangerous. I don't mean to dissuade you, but—"

"Then what are you trying to do exactly, Principal Winter?" Tristan interrupted.

"Excuse me?"

Despite his best efforts to keep his cool, Tristan felt a burning sensation in the pit of his stomach. "Why did you call me into your office? To warn me about bullies? Make sure the teachers aren't making me feel too inadequate? You've made it perfectly clear from the beginning what you think my chances are to succeed at this school, but with all due respect sir, I'm pretty sure William Conrad hasn't been in this office and given this speech."

Principal Winter simply stared back at the boy, jaws clenched. Tristan met the principal's cold glare, refusing to back down. "Despite all the pushback I've gotten, I've actually liked it here. But you know what's been disappointing? How much you guys have in common with the 'regular human schools' that tried to break me down, too. Unfortunately for you, I'm tired of getting pushed around, and I'm really sick of people telling me what I'm capable of."

The principal took a deep breath, and Tristan thought he noticed the lights in the room flicker briefly before the man exhaled. He gave the boy a cold smile, gesturing toward the door. "You may leave now, Mr. Davids. As always, it was a pleasure to hear your thoughts. I look forward to what the future has in store for you."

Tristan slowly got up and walked toward the door. Placing his hands upon the metal knob, he fired one parting shot at the man behind the desk:

"You know, Principal Winter, you really shouldn't be too concerned about what would happen should I fail out from your Academy."

"Oh, really?"

Tristan nodded as he walked out the door. "I'd be more worried about what it means if I manage to pass."

Chapter 12: Enter the Battledome

Tristan decided not to speak to his teammates regarding his meeting with Principal Winter. Not wanting to worry them, he tried to focus on enjoying the weekend rather than dwelling on his encounter. Besides, the beautiful weather they had over the next few days made it hard for him to complain. The water was perfect, and they spent their weekend among the waves and the colorful reefs. Perhaps the best part was snorkeling with Belle as they swam alongside some of the massive sea turtles and exotic fish. Her face lit up with excitement with each new discovery, and Tristan easily found himself entranced with her smile, much to the obvious delight and subtle teasing of Dan and Christian.

When the following week rolled around, however, the island was in a much different mood. Tuesday was a full on downpour, lightning and thunder coursing through the blackened skies while a fierce wind whipped stinging water droplets from every direction. This, of course, happened to be the day that Professor Stellios had scheduled a class field trip to the Battledome, and the students were none too pleased to have to traverse across the harsh elements to get there. The students had on rain gear while they trudged through the muddy fields toward the alcove, but not even their waterproof attire could stop them from getting completely drenched from the downpour. Even Belle, who usually loved being out during the rain, looked positively miserable at the current conditions.

Walking toward the mountains, Tristan could see the circular outline of the Battledome grow clearer with each step. The dome was made up of giant chrome-colored metallic plates that seemed to shine with each flash of lightning overhead and was double the size of a professional football stadium. The dome was built upon a concrete foundation, which required a ramp to gain access to the pair of revolving doors.

Passing through the entrance, Tristan could see that they were among the last to report and were greeted by their sopping wet classmates, who also looked like they would rather have been in the Academy. The only one who seemed oblivious to the weather was Gabriel, who was busy trying to force his way through the double doors that led into the main floor. Professor Stellios simply watched with amusement while the stubborn boy tried to peer through the tiny crack between the doors to get his first glimpse of the arena. When everyone had finally gathered together, Professor Stellios cleared her throat and walked before the arena doors, gently pulling a reluctant Gabriel to the side.

"Thank you all for showing up on time, I know getting up in this weather was quite the challenge. I hope you all are ready to learn about one of our greatest traditions: the Battledome! The arena has undergone many changes and upgrades over the years, but the pastime of pitting your wits against those of your peers remains the same! I know you all are chomping at the bit to get inside and see for yourselves, so without further ado, I present to you...the Arena!"

Professor Stellios placed her hands onto a fingerprint scanner beside the door and an audible click was heard before the doors swung open automatically, revealing the contents within. The students gasped in unison once the lights within the gigantic building lit up the arena before them, the grandeur of the Battledome finally seen. The expansive, chrome hallway opened up to a gargantuan glass dome that extended all the way up and attached to the roof itself. Surrounding the dome were stadium-style seats, the bleachers extending to just below the rafters. The bleachers wrapped around the glass dome and ended near the back of the building, where the locker room tunnels were placed on either side. A third tunnel made of glass looked to extend from the locker room area into the glass dome and was clearly the entrance point for the contestants.

Professor Stellios pointed to the middle section of bleachers, and the students took their seats along the steel benches. From his viewpoint, Tristan could clearly observe the dome's interior. The flooring consisted of thousands of large metallic panels, gleaming from the stadium lights above, and throughout the field were tall, cylindrical beams of metal that varied in width and height. Tristan had heard tales of epic battles within the Battledome, teams braving the elements and fighting through mazes and traps, but looking at the futuristic battlefield he was confused as to what people were referring to. *This just looks like a giant chrome pegboard surrounded by glass. What's all the fuss about?*

"As you all can see, this facility is among the most advanced buildings currently on the island and the only one of its kind in the world. It is specifically designed to host Battledome events and allows the contestants to be placed within simulated environments in order to battle. Before we get into the architecture of the building, let us rewind and first discuss the sport itself!

"Battledome was a game originally created in the 1970s by a metamorph named Gordon Irving, better known as Hercule for his gift of super strength. He and his friends loved to utilize their powers out on the Training Grounds, honing their abilities in one-on-one sparring sessions. Obviously, this caused some friction within the group as the abilities of some didn't always translate toward a level field of competition. For example, those with strong physical abilities could dominate their less imposing classmates through their aggressive tactics, while those with mental abilities could dismantle their foes with a simple thought or command. It made it difficult for the friends to determine the true value of their abilities, that is until Gordon decided to add more competitors to the fray. By recruiting their various teammates to play alongside them, the friends were able to balance out the strengths and weaknesses of each individual player, the focus becoming who could tactically outwit the other and become proficient in the art of teamwork.

"Initially, only a handful of teams competed against one another, but soon it generated interest throughout the school. Before long, they had formed their own recreational league with permission from Principal Davids. With the sport growing in popularity, it became clear that the students needed a larger area to participate in, and from this, the concept of the Battledome came about by the innovative genius, Christophe Okacha, who is regarded as perhaps the most influential metamorph of his generation. The Nigerian-born metamorph was the first recorded child born with an active Deus gene, entering into the world as a half-boy, half-machine. He is better known as Tech for his ability to create unique marvels of technology based on his unusual DNA and physiological material. 90% of the high-tech machinery you see on this island, from the Hyperjet to this very building, was designed and constructed by his hands."

"The preliminary structure of the Battledome originally began construction in 1978 and finished two years later. The original model was nowhere near as intricate as it is today, however, the basic structure remains the same, a coliseum-style arena surrounded by stadium seating. There was also a new addition to the game, as various "obstacles" were set in place within the field to make the battles more difficult, forcing the teams to start to rely more heavily on tactics rather than simply charging forward into a battle royale. Attendance for the sport skyrocketed amongst the student population, and the sport was soon recognized as the official sporting competition of metamorphs," Professor Stellios stated.

"Over the years, the technological boom helped transform the Dome into the 40,000 seating capacity marvel you see before you. The field was surrounded by reinforced glass that contains holographic disks capable of displaying any environmental setting our judges decide upon prior to the start. While the crowds are able to clearly see everything from this side of the glass, the participants cannot see us. Rather than the previous mixture of dirt and sand flooring, the field was instead outfitted with these current chrome plates, which also contain holographic properties. Obviously, the images themselves cannot convey a realistic enough image to be confused for things like water or sand, which is why just below the plates are actual environmental particles which can be called forth at a moment's notice! The plates can separate to filter in sand and dirt, while machines below can manufacture things like snow and ice. In fact, the plates can be altered in order to allow water to enter the dome and simulate lakes and ocean frontiers! The possibilities are endless!"

"The obstacles were also replaced by these metallic cylinders, which can be altered in terms of length and width and moved around magnetically. They also contain holographic material to appear like trees, columns, walls, you name it, and they allow the participants to utilize their environment to create a more realistic battle setting. Now, that you are all caught up with the backstory of the game. I bet you're wondering how it is played!

"You and your teammates are pitted against an opposing faction, equipped with nothing but your assigned outfits. Three judges, selected from amongst the faculty, decide what environment they wish to place you in, as well as what obstacles will be present. Each team begins on the opposite side of the field, and once the countdown reaches zero, the holograms are immediately turned on. Each team has exactly twenty minutes to completely incapacitate all members of the opposing team or have more teammates in play once time has expired. Judges can halt the game at any time if there is any form of cheating suspected, such as suit modifications or breach in code of conduct."

"Battledome teams must submit their forms to Principal Winter's office, where they will each be ranked and seeded according to their projected power levels. Each team plays a total of eight matches during the season, and the top sixteen are selected based off of their total record and strength of schedule. From there, they will be placed in a playoff bracket to determine who will go to the finals to fight for the glory of being crowned World Champions!"

For the next few minutes, Professor Stellios continued to explain the sport, discussing the various records set within the Battledome: fastest victory, most consecutive wins by a team, the top ten teams of all time, etc. Tristan was very surprised when he heard several of his family members named among those who held records. Unbeknownst to Tristan, his father was the leader of the #3 team of all time, while his sister was a member of the greatest underdog team to be crowned champion. In fact, his sister faced the defending champions in the finals, which happened to be Allen's team.

"It was an epic match for the ages, Mr. Davids, and you would have been quite proud of your siblings! Believe me when I say that all spectators that day got their admissions worth!" Tristan felt his neck grow hot and a nudge from beside him.

"No pressure right, superstar?"

"Shut up, Chris," Tristan muttered.

Eventually, Professor Stellios concluded her lesson, dismissing them for the day. The students exited the dome and walked back in the rain, abuzz over what they had just witnessed, several of them declaring that they wanted to compete in the upcoming season. Gabriel of course, was the loudest of these voices, determined to let everyone know his would be the first first-year team to win the competition outright. While normally Gabriel's boasting grated upon Tristan's nerves, he hardly paid him any mind the entire walk back. He was too busy thinking of ways to convince his teammates to sign up for the season himself.

For the next two days, Tristan spent all of his energy attempting to convince his teammates to submit their names for the Battledome season. He had been watching clips of famous matches on the computer, enthralled at the various matchups and tactics he observed. He didn't know where the spark had come from. He had never been particularly athletic, and with no powers of his own, he was severely handicapped. For some reason, however, he felt the pull toward competing. Perhaps it was hearing his family's legacy within the sport itself or watching videos of matchups where competitors used their tactical prowess rather than powers to overcome. Whatever it was, Tristan had the itch, and desperately wanted his teammates to agree. Unfortunately, they were not as keen to throw their names into the mix.

"Dude, we would get smoked," Christian said at lunch when Tristan first brought it up.

"Speak for yourself!" Dan shot back.

"Okay, Captain America and Aquagirl over here could hold their own, but you have no powers, and there's no way I'm letting this pretty face get bruised for the sake of a medal!"

"It's not a medal, it's a cup," Tristan corrected. "And stop underestimating us! I'll be fine, and I'll talk to our opponents ahead of time to make sure they punch you in the gut instead!"

"As much as it pains me to admit it, Tristan, but Chris is actually right on this one," Belle said with a shrug. "We don't stand much of a chance against some of the teams in our class, let alone the upperclassmen."

Despite their initial rejection, Tristan refused to let it deter him from getting them to sign up. He spent the rest of the week speaking to them individually, doing everything he could to convince them. With the deadline to submit teams looming, it wasn't until breakfast that Friday morning that Tristan was able to get them all to cave in.

"Fine! Oh my gosh, you're being so annoying! If you want us to get wrecked on a weekly basis, just throw our names in already! It'll be better than listening to you mope around for the whole year," Christian exclaimed. The others nodded in agreement. Beyond excited, Tristan practically leaped from his chair and raced out of the mess hall. He was out of breath by the time he got to Principal Winter's office but managed to scream out that he needed a form to Ms. Dorregard, and he hastily filled it out in front of her.

For the rest of the day, Tristan's stomach was in a knot, nervous excitement coursing throughout his body. Their squad was one of four first-year teams that submitted their forms, the others being Gabriel, Juan, and Cynthia's teams. He was anxious to see the schedule and where his team would be ranked amongst the school. He had never been this excited about any activity before, and his energy soon became infectious, his friends checking their school emails periodically to see whether the schedule had come through.

Finally, a few hours following dinner, Belle let out a squeal of excitement while they were hanging out around the hammock area of the courtyard. The three boys huddled around her as she opened up the email. The schedule listed their eight matches, which included matchups against Juan and Cynthia. While he was quietly happy that they had not been paired against Gabriel's team, Tristan was not pleased with their overall ranking. Despite having Belle and Dan on the team, they were ranked dead last among all of the teams submitted.

They didn't say it aloud, but Tristan knew what his teammates were thinking: he was the reason they had been placed so low. Staring at the computer screen in silence, jaw clenched and eyes narrowed, Tristan was determined to prove the judges wrong. He wasn't going to let his friends suffer and be humiliated because of him anymore. Whatever it took, Tristan was going to become a leader like those he saw in all of the Battledome videos he had pored over, developing his team into a cohesive, unstoppable unit. He was going to find a way to compete alongside his peers and show them all what he was truly capable of. After all, it was in his blood.

Chapter 13: Raging Sands

That Saturday, the team attempted to find time to practice on the Training Grounds. Unfortunately, they discovered that the facilities and on-site weight room had been signed out by other Battledome teams eager to start their training as well. Thankfully, Christian managed to find a nice, secluded space along the southernmost portion of the beach where they could train their powers without fear of injuring anyone nearby.

Their first session was incredibly awkward, each one of them reluctant to compete for fear of injuring each other. Tristan had them all stand apart to begin with before charging forward, every person for themselves. This line of thinking turned out to be a disaster. Belle had an obvious advantage against her teammates, since they were so close to the water, and it was clear Dan was holding back on any blow he attempted to throw. Christian just kept running around and giggling, trying to avoid any contact, while everyone seemed to actively ignore Tristan. After a few minutes of getting nowhere, Tristan halted their session and brought them into a huddle.

"All right, this is pretty useless. We're accomplishing nothing training like this. I understand we're all friends here and don't want to hurt one another, but we're not even using our powers effectively or with any purpose. There's no way we can actually compete if we can't figure out how to best use our abilities." The team nodded in agreement.

Tristan furrowed his eyebrows and tried to come up with a solution. After a few seconds, he snapped his fingers together, a smile crossing his face. "I got it. This might take some time, and we may not be able to get to training today, but at least we'll be ready for tomorrow," he said, walking in the direction of the mountain region.

"Where are you going?" Belle called out behind him.

"C'mon! We're gonna grab supplies! If we can't find a way onto those training grounds, we're gonna build one of our own!"

Over the next few hours, Tristan and his friends gathered and brought back wood, rope, and various other supplies from around the island to their training area. Tristan found that wood was easy enough to break down and gather when you had someone with super-strength on your team, and as for the rope and other supplies, the student store never ceased to amaze him with its inventory. By the time they had gotten everything set up, Tristan and his team were physically exhausted and ready to call it a day.

They had managed to secure rows of wooden blocks into the ground, made from parts of the smaller coconut trees Dan had knocked down and snapped, carving out target rings onto the thick outsides. They used the coconuts as markers to create an agility course and tied ropes around the nearest boulder to use as a drag for Dan. They had filled one of their large duffel bags with sand to use as a punching bag and filled some of their smaller ones to mimic weighted bags. There was even a rope climb, attached to the tallest branch of one of the nearby coconut trees. All in all, Tristan was pleased with the day's work and let his team rest, dismissing them for dinner.

The following morning, the group got up early to begin their training, determined to make the most out of the day. They began with hill sprints up the mountain, the morning sun peeking its head over the horizon. After about thirty minutes of this, their calves and quads felt like they were on fire, and Tristan tried his best not to go into a full-body cramp. They followed up their incline workout with a hard two-mile swim out in the ocean, Belle tracking their distance and speed all the way. When they had finished, they took a break to fuel up at breakfast.

After they had eaten, it was back to their homemade training grounds, where Tristan had each of them separate and complete a workout circuit. Tristan, Christian, and Belle each rotated between the punching bag and makeshift weight bags, while Dan wrapped the ropes around his torso and forearms, dragging the large boulder behind him through the dense sand. They all took turns going through the agility course, working on their speed and footwork, and followed that up with a rope climb workout. Tristan's body felt the sorest it had ever been, and he could tell they were all fatigued by the time the workout was finished.

Rather than call it a day, however, Tristan pushed them further, this time focusing on each of their individual abilities. He had Belle channel the water from the ocean into large orbs, aiming them at the wooden targets they had set up. This required an intense amount of concentration on her end, and she struggled initially. Calling forth a steady stream of water was simple enough, but separating that stream into individual spheres while maintaining their forms and pushing them forward was much more complex. With Tristan encouraging her, however, she soon became more proficient at it and could launch a water sphere halfway to the target before it fell apart.

For Dan, it was more about finding a suitable challenge. The giant boy was plenty strong, and while he had never actually pushed himself to discover how far he could take it, it seemed that if he willed it, he could do it. After several minutes of wracking his brain for ideas, Tristan came to realize that the answer was next to them all along.

Tristan led the muscular boy into the open ocean beside them and had Dan stand neck deep in the waters while he yelled orders from the shore. "All right, Samson! Today you've met your match! Here is a target that hits back just as hard as you can and won't break no matter how hard you punch! When I tell you to, I want you to get into your fighting stance and throw the hardest punch you can come up with! Ready?!"

Dan turned to the side in a boxing stance and muttered, "I hope you know what you're doing, bud."

"Hit!"

Dan's body tensed as he cocked back his right arm and threw all of his weight forward, punching with all his might. Due to the resistance of the water around him, he was not able to generate much speed or power when he threw his first punch. That being said, the results did not disappoint.

The water before Dan literally split down the middle for about three yards in front of him, the waves spreading away from his body as if in slow motion. The three teammates' jaws dropped simultaneously at the sight of the exposed ocean floor, and even Dan appeared stunned. As quickly as the water had parted, however, it came right back at the unprepared boy. Dan let out a yelp before being pummeled beneath the water, the pressure holding him below for several seconds.

Coming back up, sputtering for air, he was welcomed by the sounds of his teammates' laughter at the sight of his miscalculation. Initially, he seemed embarrassed at their reaction, but Tristan managed to convince him that they weren't laughing at his expense and were very impressed at his results. While he never could manage to stay on his feet once the waves rebounded, Dan was able to continue to work on his power and seemed to actually enjoy doing so by the end.

Christian was perhaps the most difficult problem to solve out of Tristan's three teammates. While his vampire state bestowed him with enhanced speed, reflexes, and agility, Tristan could not figure out what the temperature variation had to do with it. It seemed fixed that whenever he turned, Christian could cause the surrounding air to get colder, however, it also randomly occurred even when he was not in his altered form. The one thing Tristan knew for sure could transform his friend was getting him emotional, but getting the boy to let down his guard for even a moment was a rare occurrence. The good news for Tristan, however, was that he had been around Christian long enough to know how to get under his skin.

After wasting nearly a half hour trying to goad Christian into altering his form, Tristan threw his hands up in defeat, a look of exasperation across his face. "What's it gonna take, Vamp?! I get that your powers freak you out, but how the hell are you supposed to learn to control them if you don't even try?!"

Belle and Dan stopped their training at this point to observe what the commotion was as Tristan began to step toward Christian. "Dude, chill! We're just training!"

"Don't tell me to chill! You're not training! We're training!" Tristan replied, pointing towards his teammates. "You're just standing around like a jerk-off, wasting our time!"

The smirk that was on Christian's face quickly disappeared, his eyes narrowing slightly. *There it is.*

"Easy, Trist. Let's not be stupid here," he warned while Tristan continued to walk forward until they were face to face.

"I might be powerless, Vamp, but I'm sure not stupid. Stupid is being more concerned about how my hair looks every morning than actually being useful to my team!" Christian's pupils rapidly dilated, blackness swallowing them entirely. "Stupid is cracking jokes out here while my friends bust their ass to make sure I don't get jumped again by Gabe!" His skin began to grow translucent and his hair fell down to his shoulders, black and straightened. *Almost there! You've got him!* "Stupid is not using my powers because I'm too scared I might bite my tongue again!"

Christian snapped and before he knew what was happening, Tristan was hanging in the air, squirming while his friend held him aloft by one hand. As Belle and Dan rushed to his aid, Tristan looked down at what was once his friend's face in bewilderment. The creature that stood snarling before him no longer contained Christian's jovial demeanor. His now muscular skin practically radiated a sickly, pale glow, his teeth bared into a snarl displaying razor-sharp teeth. His nose had sunken into his face, two narrow slits replacing it. But what scared Tristan the most were the eyes. There were no joy in these eyes, only cold darkness and relentless hate. There was no semblance of humanity here.

Tristan felt a burning chill along his throat where Christian was holding him and only then realized how intense of a cold wave his friend had conjured up. The sand below them had frosted over despite the sweltering heat of the sun. The damp spots of sweat on Tristan's t-shirt were stiff as glass, and it felt like a strong breeze could shatter it into pieces.

Before his friends could intervene, Tristan looked out to them and held out a hand, motioning them to stop. They slowed their run, but their bodies were tensed up, ready to step in if needed. Tristan returned his gaze back toward Christian, locking their eyes together. He still couldn't breathe, and his neck was really starting to hurt from Christian's freezing vice grip. He tried to speak but couldn't get any words out due to the pressure. *Maybe I didn't plan this one out as thoroughly as I thought.*

As stars began to slowly creep into his vision, Tristan had one last idea to get him out of this situation, straight out of Allen's playbook: With his eyes still locked on to Christian, Tristan let out a loud fart. Christian's eyes widened and the snarling expression was quickly replaced by one of pure bewilderment. For a moment, Tristan was convinced his friend was going to kill him for that desperate tactic, but instead, a smile slowly crossed the boy's face. His eyes started to shift, gently returning to their original brown.

His skin morphed back to its usual pale tone, while Christian shook with laughter, loosening his grip.

The two boys collapsed beside one another in a heap, Tristan starting to cough as air began to fill his lungs while Christian held his sides with laughter. Despite his current condition, Tristan couldn't help but join his friend, laughing alongside him.

"Bro, you are the worst team leader, ever!" Christian said through his tears.

"It worked didn't it?"

Dan glanced back and forth between the two of them before throwing up his hands. "That was the plan?! Piss him off to get him to transform, then save yourself by farting on him?! I swear, boy, I still don't know how y'all convinced me to join you lunatics," he said, walking away.

This just made the two boys laugh even harder causing Belle to roll her eyes at the scene. "I'm surrounded by idiots."

While Belle followed Dan, Tristan and Christian slowly began to regain their composure. Christian looked at Tristan with an apologetic smile and began to speak, but Tristan held up his hand for him to stop.

"Don't. I knew what I was doing. We may not be able to control your powers but we at least know a trigger. It's your rage. Especially when I brought up a traumatic moment from your past. Look, I know this isn't easy for you. Maybe, at some point, we can find another, less painless way to get you to turn, but for now, this could be your answer. If you could allow yourself to go back to that memory and harness it...maybe you could use the darkest moment of your past to your advantage. I know you're scared, but you're not alone. Not anymore. We're a team, and we're not going anywhere."

Tristan picked himself up and walked over to his friend, extending his hand. For a moment, Christian hesitated, looking like he was about to say something, probably one of his usual smart remarks. Instead, he closed his mouth and allowed Tristan to help him up, and the two boys made their way back to the school.

The following week was business as usual, with Tristan and the team continuing to adapt to their new academic and physical demands. The combination of classes throughout the day and training in the late afternoons left them all exhausted by the evening and struggling to keep their eyes open. Tristan was doing quite well, for the most part, however, he continued to struggle in Professor Stellios and Coffman's classes due to his lack of powers. While Stellios seemed to simply ignore the boy, Coffman at least tried to make Tristan feel involved, placing him aside and having him go through defensive stances and movements while the class focused on protective techniques.

Over time, Tristan's growing obsession became the Battledome and with the season opener that week, the school was abuzz with excitement. There would be three matches that Friday, and Gabriel's team would be the first event. There was a lot of hype surrounding the match as Gabriel's team was ranked 18th and would be matched up against a third-year team that was projected to be fairly good this year. When Friday evening rolled around, Tristan could barely contain his excitement as he and his friends joined Juan, Will, and Cynthia's teams in making their way to the arena.

When they arrived at the arena, the stands were packed with their fellow students, all of whom were chatting and yelling at one another while they waited for the matches to begin. Tristan and the crew managed to find seats on the right side of the stadium, getting in a few minutes of conversation before the lights dimmed. The glass dome flashed bright with a sudden burst of lights and pyrotechnics, and a large square box descended from the top of the glass dome, two sides made of glass while the remaining sides were video screens. Five figures appeared from within, three standing behind an equipment and video area, while two sat behind a central desk with headsets and microphones. One was a shorter, heavy-set black man with a barrel chest, while the other was an extremely tall, lanky white man whose bald head practically glistened with the reflection of the bright lights.

"Good evening, ladies and gentlemen!" the husky black man said from the booth. "Welcome back to another season of the Battledome! We're excited to be here! My name is Cedric Monroe, and I'm here in the booth with my main man, Jay Fletcher! What's going on, Jay?"

"Nothing much, Ced!" the bald white man replied. "I'm stoked to be here with you. Been bored out of my mind since last season ended. Half the time I just put on football or basketball to help me sleep better, but it's nice to finally have some real competition to root for, you know?" The crowds roared with pleasure, while the two commentators smiled, their faces shown on the two main screens above.

"Well, let's not keep these people waiting, Jay, and give 'em what they came for! We have a heck of a showcase for you all tonight, so sit back, relax, and let's get this show on the road!"

"Before we begin, let's introduce tonight's guests, as well as our matchups!" Jay said before switching the camera over to the equipment area behind them. "We have our judges here with us over by the World Organizer and Reconstruction zone. For those who are unfamiliar with the W.O.R. zone, this is where the judges deliberate and design what scenarios and environments they will place our contestants in. Speaking of design, let's welcome our first judge, Kori, of the Designers!" As Jay announced each name, the students gave out a cheer and respectfully clapped while the cameras focused on each judge's face. "Our next judge is a familiar face to everyone here, let's welcome Professor Cam! Last, but certainly not least, it's everyone's favorite assistant, Ms. Dorregard!"

"What?! Who called me?! What's going on?!" Ms. Dorregard cried out, looking about in confusion at where the omnipresent voice was coming from.

"No, Ms. Dorregard, we're just calling out your name. He's just—!"

"Who's talking?! How do you know my name?!"

"Good Lord, never mind. Just move on, man, move on," Cedric said rubbing his forehead.

"Tonight's matchups start off with a bang, as young, first-year upstarts Team Jackson take on veteran participants Team McElroy!" Tristan laughed as Will and Cynthia started booing at the team photo of Gabriel's group that appeared on the screen. The roar of the crowd was deafening, and Tristan felt his pulse quicken from the energy flowing through the packed stadium.

"All right, kiddos! Hold on to your seatbelts because we're about to get this place lit!"

"What the heck is 'lit'?"

"I dunno," Cedric shrugged "I heard my daughter use it. Now, entering the arena, let's give it up for our first two teams! On your left, Team McElroy, and on your right, Teeeeaaam Jaaaacksoooon!" Fireworks exploded along the roof of the glass dome, sending showers of sparks down among the contestants who were starting to walk in through the glass tunnel entrance. Gabriel's team sauntered in to the sounds of applause, and Tristan could see the smug, confident look across the boy's face.

Tristan's attention turned toward Team McElroy, who were led by Erwin McElroy, a tall, redhead whose alternate name was Torch due to his power of fire manipulation. There was Lightner, a smaller blonde boy who could generate blinding light from his hands. One of the two girls on their team was Jet, a girl with spiked blue hair and heavy piercings, who could fly. Lastly, there was Arachne, a stout, hairy girl who could shoot out sticky webs from her fingertips.

The two competitors made their way to opposite sides of the arena, huddling up and whispering while they waited for the battlefield to be generated. Within seconds, the glass began to shimmer, and the field began to shift around, the metallic obstacles starting to change their shapes. Soon the silver interior of the dome had been transformed, appearing as a massive open courtyard with various trees and small ponds all around. Tiny flakes of snow fell from above while the glass ceiling painted itself into a cloudless, starry night. Tristan nearly forgot he was watching a live battle for dominance, lost in the beauty of the Japanese landscape painted before him. The moment faded, however, once the timer began counting down and the announcers returned. "Ladies and gentlemen, here we go! Our first match begins...NOW!"

As soon as the bell went off, the two teams sprinted forward, trying to keep their balance while moving across the wet grass, slick with frost. The battlefield didn't appear expansive, but the scattered trees and ponds made the surroundings difficult to navigate smoothly. Closing in on each other within the coverage of the trees, Jet pushed off the ground and began her ascent into the sky above. Around the same time, Arachne shot out two strands of web from her hands and used them to swing herself into the tree branches.

Smart. They're hoping to gain advantage off the higher ground. Sofi is the only one whose powers can affect them and it'll be two against one. The tactic made sense to Tristan, and he expected the third-year team to be able to use their experience against the rookies to great effect.

If Gabriel had noticed what Team McElroy's game plan was, he wasn't showing it, and they continued to sprint between the trees. When they were about twenty yards away, Torch and his crew began to take the offensive. From her position forty yards above the thin cluster of trees, Jet made her descent, aiming to fly through the thin openings of the foliage and surprise Sofi below. Sofi, meanwhile, had been tracking Jet's movements and slowed her run in order to brace herself from the upward attack. Unfortunately, due to the leaves and branches above she did not have a clear line of sight, which forced her to wait for Jet to make the first move and expose herself. Simultaneously, Arachne had anticipated this and was making a beeline straight at Sofi, swiftly swinging from branch to branch with barely a sound. Her stealthy movement and supernatural speed allowed her to avoid the onrushing boys below, apparently oblivious to the movement above.

While this was happening, Torch had removed a small lighter from his back pocket and flickered it to life. He and Lightner halted their run, and he proceeded to draw forth the flames from the lighter into three small spheres of fire. Torch furrowed his eyebrows in concentration and launched the balls of fire at the three boys. Gabriel pressed on, shattering a sand vial on the ground ahead of him and quickly generated a wall of sand before him, the shield quickly extinguishing the flaming ball. Malcolm easily dodged the projectile meant for him, shifting to the side in a blink of an eye before it could hit him.

I don't get it. Why doesn't he just speed his way through this and knock them all out? He has super speed, and there's no way they could stop a fist moving over 100 miles per hour! The last thought brought about a revelation to Tristan, uncovering Malcolm's true weakness. While he could move at blazing speeds, it did not make him invulnerable to its effects. He could theoretically strike someone down at that pace, but that also meant his fist felt the same impact. A blow at that speed could shatter every bone in the boy's arm.

The third ball of flame whizzed next to Brandon, narrowly missing him. It did strike the tree beside him, however, the impact knocking the boy off his stride. He tried to adjust himself, but with the grass being so slick from the frost, his feet slid out from under him, and he stumbled to the ground. Tristan watched in horror as the flaming tree fell over, Brandon struggling to get up in time. The boy tried to hold his arms up and shield himself, but there was no way his body could hold off the tree as it fell directly on top of him.

If they were concerned regarding their teammate, Gabriel and Malcolm certainly didn't show it, continuing their approach and were now within ten feet of their opponents. Torch was now generating a large ball of fire the size of a basketball and preparing to launch it at Gabriel, while Lightner began to close his eyes, his hands emitting a faint glow. Jet's slow descent turned into a steep dive, and she tucked in her arms and straightened her legs, speeding toward the tops of the trees directly above Sofi. Concurrently, Arachne was timing her swings perfectly, preparing to meet Sofi at around the same time.

They planned this well. Sofi is in a two-on-one situation, and Brando is incapacitated. Lightner can take out their vision with a blast, and Torch is ready to toast Gabe to a crisp. They've got Gabe right where they want him, and he's too arrogant to realize it. This match is over and we're barely four minutes in.

In a matter of seconds, everything Tristan thought he had figured out flipped on its head. "Wolf, stop messing around and get over here! Now!" Gabriel yelled out, throwing another two vials of sand onto the ground. A low growl began to reverberate through the stadium, steadily growing in volume and intensity before transforming into an overpowering roar. Suddenly, the ground exploded in a furious rain of fire and wood as a massive wolf-like humanoid leaped into the air towards the shocked Torch and Lightner. Tristan's jaw dropped in awe while witnessing the giant beast easily soar above the tree line and come crashing down in the space between the two opponents, the impact of the landing causing Torch to momentarily fumble his ball of flame and knocking Lightner to the ground. The beast stood about seven feet tall and looked to weigh at least 300 pounds of rippling, furry muscle. His massive jaw held razor-sharp teeth between which drool steadily fell.

"Blaze, let's roll! Just like we planned!" Gabriel ordered, a smile crossing his face. Tristan was on the edge of his seat as he watched three events happen simultaneously. First, Jet blasted through the foliage above, aimed directly at Sofi. Sofi saw her burst through the trees and reacted, bringing her arms above her head, the air around her swirling violently. Next, Arachne flew out of the branches in a gracefully timed leap, extending her hands and launching several strands of webbing at the unsuspecting girl. Once the strands connected, Sofi would be tied up, allowing Jet a clear shot at her head. Malcolm, however, had stopped on a dime just before he reached Lightner, and suddenly, he was gone.

After the match, it would take several camera angles and slow-motion replays to break down what had actually occurred. In the split second it took Malcolm to arrive, he had managed to catch each individual strand of webbing before they struck his teammate. The boy then proceeded to circle around Arachne, literally running sideways on the trees while tying her up. The replays showed the boy's unbelievable ability to partially ignore the rules of gravity due to his immense burst of speed, confining Arachne in her own trap. All the crowd could see with the naked eye was that mid-way through the air, Arachne was suddenly completely covered in her own webbing and crashed headfirst into a nearby tree, knocking her out completely. The shocked Jet tried to slow down her descent only to be blasted by a vicious whirlwind generated by Sofi and was violently thrown to the ground, her body curled up and unmoving.

While this occurred, Lightner had regained his bearings, and his hands started to glow again. As Brandon lunged, Lightner threw out his hands, a blinding flash of light exploding from his palm. The glass dome quickly became tinted, blocking out a majority of the glare, but even then, Tristan had to shield his eyes, spots forming around his field of vision. The blast of light stunned the onrushing Brandon, who roared in bestial rage, momentarily blinded by the light. While Brandon held his eyes with his large clawed hands, Lightner grabbed a large block of wood from the ground and attempted to quietly make his way behind the beast.

As the boy got closer and prepared to swing his weapon, Tristan watched the monster pause, subtly sniffing the air. *It's a ruse! He's baiting him!* Once Lightner's arms came down for the swing, Brandon spun around with superhuman speed, catching the wood in mid-air. With a roar of triumph, Brandon backhanded the exposed chest of Lightner, launching the boy into the nearest pond, where he remained below the shallow waters.

Meanwhile, Gabriel had stepped onto the pile of sand he had thrown down a few seconds earlier and threw his arms downward, palms facing the golden grains. When Torch threw the large ball of fire at Gabriel's chest, the sand immediately lifted the boy safely into the air, his knees tucked into his chest. Gabriel's leap took him completely over the flustered Torch, the projectile flying harmlessly beneath his feet. Clearing the head of Torch, Gabriel reached back with his right hand and called forth the sand on the ground behind him. He quickly swept his arm forward, bringing the sand with him. The wave of sand crashed directly into Torch, forming a giant fist that mimicked the shape of its creator. Once Gabriel gently landed on the ground behind Torch, he brought the sand fist down with him, sending the immobilized Torch onto his back, covered from foot to neck.

The whole thing happened in a space of fifteen seconds. Three blue dots appeared in quick succession on the screen, the audible pings following closely behind. Gabriel slowly stood up, a look of supreme confidence on his face. He held the struggling Torch to the ground, who continued to squirm unsuccessfully against the ever-tightening grip of the sand. Murmurs were heard among the crowd looking on, and Torch let out a yell, struggling to get air into his compressed lungs. There were no more cheers now from the crowd, some students starting to boo the poor sportsmanship Gabriel was displaying.

Suddenly, the timer ceased and the holograms all shut off, the final buzzer going off. The judges had stopped the match, allowing the school medics to rush onto the field and care for the wounded. Gabriel immediately released Torch's body at this point, seemingly snapped out of his battle rage. He nodded at his teammates before they marched back through the tunnel to the awkward smattering of applause from the concerned audience.

"Well, there you have it, folks! In a savage display of sheer power, Team Jackson overwhelms the favorites, Team McElroy!" Jay proclaimed, the match replay appearing on the screen.

"Absolutely, Jay! A quick change of tactics just left McElroy's team exposed and quickly overmatched! Let's go through the video footage and break this game down!"

For the next few minutes, Jay and Cedric went through play-by-play commentary on the matchup, but Tristan could barely follow what they were saying, doing his own replay in his mind. The crowd seemed a little more subdued following the match, the next two battles going the full twenty minutes and not providing anywhere near the excitement. Once the night was over, all everyone could talk about was the match between Team Jackson and McElroy, people now starting to take Gabriel's earlier proclamations more seriously.

That evening, Tristan and his team hung out in the common room going over each team, breaking down their strengths and weaknesses and ways to best match up with them. It wasn't a long talk, and they went to bed shortly after, their minds mulling over the evening's events. Lying in his bed, Tristan knew they were not prepared for the Battledome, as it were. They could not realistically expect to compete against teams like Gabriel's unless they got a lot better and fast. Tristan had to figure out how to unlock his team's potential within the next two weeks, and time was running out.

Chapter 14: Helping Hand

"All right, everybody! That's enough for today! You may discontinue whatever you are currently working on and gather by the center of the room."

It was the Tuesday following Team Jackson's debut, and Professor Stellios was just wrapping up their latest lecture. Today's lesson was about using proper technique when calling forth their powers, and Tristan's team had been working hard to nail down the basics. Following the weekend, the team had been doubling up on their training sessions, pushing one another to improve upon their skills, and the results were starting to show. During class, Christian had managed to partially transform into his vampiric state in under fifteen seconds, while Belle was starting to perfect her water spheres. Dan wound up just doing pull-ups, and Tristan had stopped counting after 800. Even though the muscular boy was soaked in sweat, he didn't appear tired, and Tristan was starting to wonder what Dan's limits actually were. Tristan was still the odd duck, using the class time to either motivate his teammates or do little things on the side.

Once the students had all gathered around her, Professor Stellios continued with her announcement. "As a whole, you have all been doing well in my class, and your progress should be commended. With that said, you will all be faced with an exam next week in which I will be asking you to demonstrate a progression point in your ability levels. This will be a pass/fail exam, so please be prepared to bring your best, as I will not take subpar or mediocre effort from anyone! Is that understood?" The class murmured in understanding. "Good. I shall see you all on Thursday. You are dismissed."

As the class gathered up their belongings, Tristan stayed back, nodding for his friends to head over to lunch without him. After the last of his peers had left the classroom, Tristan walked over to his professor.

"May I help you, Mr. Davids?"

"Yes, ma'am. I just had a quick question," Tristan mumbled nervously. "I was just wondering...while the other students are taking their exam next week, what would you like me to do?"

"What do you mean 'what would I like you to do'? You are to do what everyone else is doing. Take the exam."

"But...I don't have any powers, ma'am."

"That is none of my concern, Mr. Davids. I was under the impression that you were accepted to this school, without restrictions, were you not?"

"Well, yeah, but—"

"Which means that you are expected to comply with all of our terms and regulations. While I am expected to teach you how to use your powers, you are expected to be able to perform to the same level as your peers."

"But how can I do that without any powers, Professor Tremor? No offense, but I don't think that's exactly fair!"

"Rules are rules, Mr. Davids. Perhaps it would be more 'fair' to give your place at the Academy to someone with lower scores and active powers." Tristan's face burned at this last comment. "While I have no issues with you being at this school, how could you possibly think it's 'fair' if I allowed you to be treated any differently from those around you? I'm sorry if you feel that you are not up to the task of competing with your classmates, but I refuse to lower my standards."

Dejected, Tristan stared down at the ground, unsure of how to respond. "You can pass this test, Mr. Davids, though you'll need to be creative. Prove that you are not willing to settle for mediocrity. Prove it, Mr. Davids, if not for me than for yourself. Now, head over to lunch and think about what I've just said."

Tristan quietly walked out of the classroom, and during lunch, he thought about what Professor Stellios had discussed with him. Inside, he knew she was right. He could not reasonably expect her to treat him differently from his peers when he himself had fought so hard to make that point to Principal Winter only a few weeks before.

Later on, Professor Coffman began the afternoon's lesson by allowing them fifteen minutes to stretch and warm up prior to their lesson. Today, he announced, they would be working on utilizing their powers for counterattacks. While the other students began to warm-up, Tristan ran his hands through his hair in frustration.

"Mr. Davids!" Tristan looked up to find Professor Coffman calling him by the far end of the room. "A moment of your time, if you could spare it." Tristan wondered what he had done wrong as he quickly walked over to the older man.

"You wanted to see me, sir?" he asked nervously.

"Is everything all right, Mr. Davids? You haven't seemed quite yourself this afternoon."

"I'm fine. Just a little tired is all," he replied, avoiding the man's piercing gaze.

Professor Coffman raised a greying eyebrow and shot a quick look behind Tristan before turning back to look at the boy. "Mmhmm. Are you sure it had nothing to do with the talk you had with Professor Tremor?"

Tristan groaned and finally met the professor's eyes. "Seriously? She told you?"

"Yes, Tristan. Believe it or not, despite our vastly different personalities, Jane and I are quite good friends. We also are directly across from one another, and I can hear her yell from across the blasted mountain!"

"I don't know what to do, sir. I mean, she's not wrong, but even in this class, I struggle whenever we have days like today. They're all getting better with their powers, but me...I don't know how I can get any better with my self-defense when I'm not able to actively participate."

Professor Coffman rubbed his thick beard, his brow furrowed in thought. After a brief moment of silence, the man folded his arms across his chest. "Well...there is a way. But it is going to require much effort and time on your part. You must be willing to open up your schedule if you wish to pursue this course of action." Tristan nodded eagerly, curious to what the professor had in mind. "I teach an additional class for upperclassmen as an extracurricular activity or students who are having difficulty in my class. It is taught in Lab 310 at 7:00 on Tuesday and Thursday evenings and usually lasts about an hour and a half. There will be no need for your outfit, only athletic attire is required. Are you interested?"

"Absolutely! Yes! Thank you, sir!"

Professor Coffman smiled at this, giving a quick nod of approval. "Good! I'll see you tonight, then. For now, let's plan on you working on your footwork during class today."

Tristan thanked the professor again before making his way back to his friends, who were again staring at him in concern. This time, Tristan met their expressions with a reassuring smile, his mood beginning to lift for the first time since earlier that day.

After class was done, Tristan immediately set to completing all of his homework prior to dinner. Once he had finished his assignments, Tristan threw on some athletic clothes before walking over to the Academy. While crossing the courtyard, Tristan spotted Christian sitting beside the lake. His pale friend had his chin in his hand, and he was staring intently on a half-eaten sandwich before him.

"What's up, Chris? Contemplating the existence of sandwiches and their meaning in our everyday lives?" Christian continued to stare, unmoving. Tristan frowned, concerned at the lack of a reaction from his teammate. "Everything all right, man?"

Christian paused before answering. "It happened again."

"What did?"

Christian picked up the sandwich and tossed it toward Tristan, who promptly dropped it in surprise as the frigid food struck his hands. The sandwich hit the ground with a soft thud, the frozen toppings falling out and rolling across the grass.

"I don't know what's going on, bro. I was just having a snack out here, minding my own business. I was thinking about this exam, what I should do, and what would happen if I don't pass. What if I keep screwing up, you know? My grades slip, I can't figure out my powers, and before you know it they're just kicking me out. And now I'm back where I started, you know?! A high school dropout with no family and no future! And...it just happened." Christian held his head in his hands, shaking gently as tears ran down his face.

Tristan knelt down and grabbed his friend by the shoulder. "Look at me, Chris. We're going to figure this thing out! You have to trust me. You're not going to fail this test. You're not going to get kicked out!"

Christian nodded, trying to compose himself. "Why do you think this happened to me, bro? Why now? I wasn't even transformed!"

Tristan shook his head, at a loss for words. "I don't know. At least we know it's not triggered by you transforming. I mean from the sounds of it, you were suffering from a panic attack. I had a friend back home, Jon, who used to get them every now and again. Whenever he was stressed out, he would get these reactions: his heart rate went up, he started hyperventilating, he'd freeze up during tests, and—!"

Tristan paused, a thought hitting him as he looked up at Christian. "That's it!"

"What's it? What happened?"

"It's a reaction! It's a defense mechanism!" Christian looked at Tristan like he was crazy. "That night, when it first happened, you said your foster parents were at a parent-teacher conference at the school, right!? Were you concerned that you would get in trouble or something? Stressed that you weren't doing well in your classes?"

Christian thought hard about what Tristan was saying and slowly nodded his head. "Come to think of it, I had gotten back one of my grades earlier that day and had failed a test. I was scared that the teacher was gonna rat me out."

Tristan grabbed his friend by the shoulder, unable to contain his excitement. "That's it, Chris! Don't you see!? This stuff happens as a defense mechanism, as a way to protect yourself! Whenever you're feeling an increased stressor, you trigger the reactions: whether you're scared about your grades, angry with Gabe, or sneaking around with a girl and things get a little too...intense."

"Totally worth it, by the way."

Tristan rolled his eyes as he continued. "All of those things trigger your reactions, allowing you to not only transform into some weird vampire state but also allow you to manipulate the temperature around you! We know what the cause is, now we just need to figure out how to manage it!"

Christian thought about this revelation for a moment, continuing to stare at his friend. Slowly, he broke into a smile. "You know something, Trist? If you keep sticking with me, I might turn you into a leader yet. Thank God I'm around to make sure you do your job, or else this gig would be way too easy for you." Tristan groaned and tried to repress the urge to strangle his chuckling friend.

Later that evening, Tristan was walking around the third floor of the Academy, stopping once he reached the door marked "L310" on its glass window. Through the glass, Tristan could make out several shapes and see the mirrored walls and blue padded floors. Tristan could hear several voices from within, and he thought there was at least one that sounded familiar.

Upon entering, Tristan was greeted by the sight of familiar faces. Among the group of what looked to be about fifteen students, Tristan saw Emily, Juan, and Will mingling in the crowd of chattering people.

"Tristan! What's good, man? I didn't know you were in this class!" Will called from across the room, waving Tristan over.

"*You* didn't know? Heck, I thought *I* was the only one struggling in Crusher's class!"

"Please, between Tremor and Crusher, I'll be lucky if my behind doesn't get kicked out next week! Apparently telling Crusher 'please don't hit me' in Mandarin doesn't count as self-defense!"

The four of them laughed at this, and Tristan explained how he came to be invited to the class.

"Yes, but at least you have an excuse, Tristan. Theoretically, I should be doing well in both classes with my abilities. However, my powers are still so raw. Until I learn to harness them a bit better, Professor Crusher thinks it's best for me to learn how to physically defend myself rather than risk frying some poor kid's brains!" Juan said.

"I'm pretty much in the same boat as you guys," Emily said softly, gesturing toward Tristan and Will. "My powers are great for hiding, but that's about it. It doesn't do much when you're going toe-to-toe with kids like Sofi or Belle. So despite the obvious intimidation factor of these big guns," she said, flexing her tiny biceps, "Professor Crusher thought it'd be best for me to learn how to actually do more than just curl in a ball and hope no one notices me."

Listening to their stories, Tristan felt a wave of relief. It was nice to know that he was not alone in his struggles.

While they continued to talk, Professor Coffman shuffled into the room carrying four large duffle bags on either shoulder. He walked to the front of the class and deposited the bags beside him onto the cushioned floors. "All right everyone, settle down! As you all are familiar with me, I will not go into any lengthy introductions. This class is designed to be a supplement to what many of you are either learning or have learned from my Self-Defense course. You will discover, in time, that powers can only take you so far, and that the real battle is often decided in here!" Professor Coffman said, pointing to his head.

Professor Coffman bent down and unzipped the duffel bags that were on the floor, revealing a variety of red body pads with Velcro straps attached. "I would like everyone to select a partner from those around you. One of you will start off wearing the body pads while the other will be practicing the various defensive techniques. We will switch halfway through each lesson, so you will have plenty of time to practice. Let's get going!"

Tristan glanced at Will, who nodded in acceptance, and the two friends walked up to receive their pads. Will agreed to be the training model first, outfitting himself in the red pads and mouthguard Professor Coffman was passing out. After each group spaced out within the large training lab, Professor Coffman began his demonstration.

"The first move we will be working on is the art of the dodge, or 'slipping' a punch. While fools may view this as being cowardly or weak, I promise you, it is the key to every good fighter and will open up your opponents to a variety of counterattacks. First, I would like each of you to get into your fighting stances. Remain in your normal stance when your opponent punches and slightly bend from the waist, avoiding the blow. You will then quickly move to the outside of the punch, slipping to the side from which the punch was thrown. This will not only help you avoid the shot, but it also opens up the outside of their body for an attack of your own. Right now, I want the padded assailants to work on throwing punches, while their partners focus on slipping the attacks. While it's important to get your technique down first, don't be afraid to change it up once you're comfortable and increase your speed and how many punches you throw. Now, begin!"

Will stepped forward and began to slowly throw steady jabs toward Tristan's head with his padded hand. Will was a southpaw, so Tristan bent out to the left, narrowly avoiding the blows while moving his feet and sliding to the outside of Will's left side. The move seemed fairly easy, until Will switched stances and hit the unprepared Tristan square in the forehead with a right cross. "Don't go sleeping on me, Tristan!" Will grinned.

Tristan nodded his head in acknowledgment and started to pay closer attention to his friend's body movement, tracking his shifting feet and swaying body in order to better anticipate which fist would come his way.

"Switch up!" Professor Coffman said, and the partners switched roles. After they finished practicing that move, Professor Coffman taught them a couple of other dodge techniques: avoiding hooks and step backs into a lunge position. All of these blocks and dodges opened up the opportunities for counters, which Professor Coffman promised they would go through on Thursday.

All in all, it was a great session, and Tristan was exhausted by the time they were dismissed. He walked with Emily, Juan, and Will back to the dorms, and that night, Tristan went to bed with a newfound sense of accomplishment, ready to continue to build upon his success.

Thursday morning, Tristan woke up and quietly got dressed before sneaking around to Dan's bed, shaking the giant boy awake.

"Huh?! What the—! Tristan! What the hell are you doing this early?!"

"Shhh! Stop yelling or you'll wake everybody up!" Tristan hissed. "Get up! I had an idea for you, but could only get the weight room reserved during this time. I know you're tired but grab your clothes and let's go!"

Dan groaned in displeasure but reluctantly got himself out of bed. Tristan waited patiently while Dan changed into his workout clothes, before following Tristan out of the dorms and to the weight room. While Dan stretched in the corner, Tristan grabbed weights and loaded up the Olympic barbell nearby.

"All right, you ready?" Tristan asked once Dan had finished warming up.

"What's all this about, man? Why are we here so early?" Glancing at the weight on the bar, Dan laughed in disbelief and shook his head.

"When was the last time you really tried to push yourself, Dan? How do we know what you're really capable of? I mean, I've seen you move those boulders in the sand. That's gotta be at least 120 pounds, easy. I've seen you punch through those small coconut trees to get our wood. Hell, I've watched you literally split an ocean!"

"So what? I'm strong. It's not that complicated."

"That's just it, Dan. What if there's more to it?"

"What do you mean?"

"Remember when you did those pull-ups during class? You seemed to do more the second time around. How is that?"

"I dunno," Dan shrugged. "Just seems easier the second time around. Like my body knows what to expect, you know?"

Tristan laughed aloud and shook his head. "No, I don't. In fact, I don't think anyone does. Whenever we do strength exercises like that, it gets harder the next few times because our muscles fatigue and lose the ability to generate that kind of power!" Tristan looked up toward his friend expectantly. "Dan, what if your powers extended beyond just super strength? What if you were...invulnerable? Like, your body literally adapts to whatever pressure is demanded on it?"

Dan looked down at Tristan trying to wrap his mind around what his friend was telling him. "So you're telling me that I pretty much have no limits? That I'm as strong as I want to be?"

"There's one way to find out." Tristan gestured toward the bench. Dan stared hard at Tristan, contemplating the request. Tristan was almost certain Dan was going to refuse his proposal and walk out, a part of him hoping that the boy would do just that and not risk injuring himself. Before Tristan could stop him, Dan shot his friend a smile and laid flat on the bench, gripping the barbell above. He gave out a large roar and attempted to lift the weight.

On his first attempt, the barbell didn't budge, and after several seconds Dan released his hold with a grunt of frustration. Tristan tried to mask his disappointment. He had been certain that he was correct in his theory. Before he could step forward and help his friend up, Dan's meaty hands shot up once again for a second attempt. This time, there was no doubt, as Dan managed to lift up the weight and slowly control it toward his barrel chest. After he set the barbell down onto the start, Dan let out a gasp and let his arms fall beside him, heaving with effort. He didn't speak for several seconds before turning his sweat-soaked face toward Tristan with a smile. "Good...call...boss-man. How much was that? 400? 500?"

Tristan swallowed hard, shaking his head in disbelief. "Dan...that was 1,000 pounds. You just lifted a truck."

That evening, Tristan met again for Professor Coffman's Defense Mastery class, and they built upon their previous session. Rather than simply dodge to avoid the attacks, the professor had them progress into counter attacks as well, throwing short jabs and hooks after they had successfully slid to the outside of their partners. Tristan worked with a smaller second-year student name Caleb this time, and the shorter boy's fast feet and sharp jabs were a welcome challenge for Tristan, who had to quickly adapt to his more advanced partner's techniques. At the end of the night, Tristan had bruises throughout his body but was more than happy for the experience, hungry to continue to challenge himself.

Friday night, Tristan and his friends kicked off the weekend by attending the Battledome matches, where Juan's team fought for the first time against a second-year team. While they lost a close match that nearly went to time, Tristan cheered them on enthusiastically throughout. With Professor Stellios' test only three days away, Tristan and his friends used the rest of the weekend to practice their individual progressions. Tristan understood that he could only offer encouragement to his teammates and made every effort to find time to work with them individually. He found himself focusing on Belle, who was still struggling to maintain her water spheres over twenty feet, her frustration mounting with each failure.

Tristan knew Belle was her own worst enemy. When things didn't go her way, she tended to blame herself, getting into her own head and psyching herself out. Interestingly, whenever they were together having fun, things seemed to come naturally to her. Tristan could remember her walking along the lake with the three boys, casually flicking her wrist beside the water. He had observed how the lake's surface responded, a thin, delicate rope of water trailing behind her, adjusting and moving with each intricate motion of her hand. It was at times like these Tristan would catch himself staring at his friend for far too long, a dopey smile across his face, until either Christian hit him upside the head or Dan gave him a subtle nudge.

While Belle appeared to never notice these embarrassing moments, Tristan couldn't seem to help himself.

Watching Belle cry out in frustration, her latest sphere bursting around ten feet, Tristan thought back on those moments and decided to interject in her training. "Hey, Belle? You got a minute?"

Tristan walked to where she stood, hands on her hips. "What do you want?" she shot at him. Tristan raised his arms in surrender, and the girl closed her eyes and sighed. "I'm sorry, I didn't mean to snap at you. I'm just...frustrated."

"Really? I couldn't tell. You seem so serene and Zen-like."

"Don't you tease me! Maybe I'll start using you as target practice!"

Tristan grinned and shook his head. "No, you won't. I put it in my will that I want Chris to succeed me as leader should anything happen. Consider it my life insurance from you." This time, Belle genuinely let out a laugh. Watching Belle smile, Tristan again found himself staring a little too long at her dimples. *God, I love making her laugh.* He caught himself, however, and nodded toward the target ahead. "Try it again," he suggested, smiling.

Belle gave him a questioning glance but faced off against the wooden bulls-eye. She gently generated a sphere of water, calling forth the liquid from the nearby ocean. Slowly spinning the globe between her hands, she pushed it forward, getting it to within five feet of the target before it fell apart. Despite the improvement, the girl sighed and hung her head. "I can't do it. I can't figure this stupid thing out, and it's driving me insane."

"You're too hard on yourself, Belle." He placed his hands in his pockets and began to rock back and forth on the warm sand beneath. "I remember when we got here, and the first thing you did was go over by the water's edge. You called it forth and manipulated it around your body like it was your puppet. It was so smooth and natural. It blew my mind the way you could do that. I'd never seen anything like it." Tristan smiled and looked toward his friend. "I bet that was how you were when it came to swimming too, huh? Just in your element, having fun, not worrying about anything but you and the water. Just...free." As Belle stared deep into Tristan's eyes, he placed his hand on her shoulder and pointed to the target. "Remember that feeling, Belle. Stop thinking. Be free again."

Tristan hadn't even noticed the water leave the ocean with how quickly Belle seemed to generate it within her palms, and before he knew it, it was off, spinning steadily toward the wooden target. It took less than five seconds to travel across the sand, but when it burst along the carved etches of the bulls-eye, Tristan let out the air he had been holding in his lungs in relief.

For a moment, neither of them said anything, Tristan's hand still on her shoulder while they stared at the target. "So...I didn't realize you were watching me so intently on that first day. How long were you—?"

"Well, that's quite enough training for one day! I think I'm gonna head over to Chris and see if he needs help. See ya!" Before he turned around to briskly walk away, Tristan could have sworn he saw Belle grin.

When Tuesday rolled around, Tristan was in good spirits heading into Professor Stellios' class. He was a little nervous for his demonstration but had full confidence in all of his teammates. Professor Tremor began the class by announcing the order in which the teams would be tested, with Gabriel's team leading the way and Cynthia and Tristan following suit. The teams performed as Tristan had expected, with little to no surprises.

Eventually, it was Team Davids' turn to show Professor Stellios what they had been working on, and Tristan announced that he would be demonstrating his newfound defensive techniques. He asked Christian to step forward in order to spar with him, but when his friend stood up, Professor Stellios suddenly stated, "No." Tristan was stunned for a moment, unsure of what to do as his friend shot him a confused look before reluctantly sitting back down.

"Having your teammate as a partner is not a good enough test for so weak a demonstration of your progress, Mr. Davids. For all we know, you two have choreographed your movements." Tristan felt a flush of rage and indignation at the idea that he would stage this and began to speak up, when she cut him off. "Agayu! Please step forth!" Tristan felt his heart skip as his cocksure rival rose up to face him, a sneer creeping across his face.

"This should be fun," the boy said, cracking his knuckles.

"Begin!" Professor Stellios shouted, and before Tristan could properly ready himself, Gabriel was already in the process of throwing a right hook. Instinct kicked in, and despite Tristan's training, he stepped back to avoid the blow. *Wrong move!* Stepping back, arms up to deflect the punch, Tristan left his core open for Gabriel's follow up jabs, which struck him on either side of his ribs in quick succession. Tristan let out a grunt of pain and reeled from the strikes, the air forced from his lungs. For a moment Tristan felt his mind go blank, and panic crept in.

Gabriel was pressing forward, throwing jab after jab at the stumbling boy, occasionally connecting and throwing Tristan off balance. The class could tell things were not looking good and a murmur began to go through the room as Gabriel pressed onward. Through the flurry of blows, Tristan caught a glance of Professor Tremor, a resigned look across her face, and she appeared to sigh in disappointment. Time slowed down for Tristan, the image burned into his mind.

Suddenly, Tristan felt a surge flow through his body, fire coursing through his veins. He narrowly dodged a blow to the head, deftly shifting his body back into the proper defensive stance. Gabriel swung again at Tristan's head, but this time he was prepared. Leaning to the right, Tristan narrowly avoided the punch and quickly glided his body to the outside of Gabriel's fist. Calling forth the lessons from his last class, Tristan delivered two quick jabs at Gabriel's passing face.

Maybe it was the adrenaline of the moment itself or the pent-up rage of several years' worth of bullying, but Tristan had never felt that much power surging through his hands before. Both punches connected with aplomb and sent Gabriel stumbling sideways. Tempted to press his advantage and rush his opponent, Tristan began to move forward, but stopped in time, remembering his training. He took a quick deep breath to regulate his heartbeat and maintain his composure. Meanwhile, the now enraged Gabriel was fuming, spinning around and rushing forward, throwing a vicious hook with his right hand. There was no mistake this time. Tristan ducked his head toward his opponent's raised armpit and slid beneath the blow, shooting to the outside to deliver a hook of his own to Gabriel's midsection.

Check. Tristan heard his rival grunt in pain while he smoothly swiveled around, prepared for the next attack. Tristan's mind was clear at this point, a sense of calm resonating throughout his body, and he shot the boy a condescending smile. The crazed look in Gabriel's eyes said it all, and Tristan had a feeling he knew what was coming. Enraged, Gabriel ran forward and smashed a vial, sand encasing his fist into a block of stone. He threw everything he had into a crushing blow to Tristan's head.

And mate. Tristan stepped back into a lunge, the strike passing harmlessly above Tristan's head while he looked upward at Gabriel's now exposed chin. Tristan brought back his fist and put everything into his upward jab to Gabriel's jaw. The shock of the blow reverberated down his arm, and he heard a crack as Gabe's neck snapped back. The boy crumpled in a heap at Tristan's feet, a look of surprise across his face.

Tristan looked down in shock at his downed rival, and when he lifted his head was greeted by the sight of equally stunned classmates. The only person who seemed undisturbed by what had just occurred was Professor Stellios, the teacher quietly clapping as she gave Tristan a nod of approval. "Well, Mr. Davids! It would seem that you are just full of surprises. Congratulations! I believe you can consider this a passing grade!"

Chapter 15: Fallout

Pacing nervously around the stuffy locker room within the arena, Tristan felt beads of sweat start to form on the edge of his brow, and his hands were moist, practically sticking to his leather suit whenever he tried to wipe them off.

"Bro, would you relax? We got this," Christian said with a smile. His feet were propped up on a nearby chair, and he laid supine on the floor, arms behind his head. Tristan wished he had his friend's confidence, but he couldn't stop running through scenarios in his head. Last night, he had sat down with the team after his Defensive Mastery class and went over film of their upcoming opponents.

"So here's what we're up against," Tristan had explained, enlarging the video on his laptop. "Team Gomez is our next matchup, and right now they are 1-0 in the Battledome. They're a third-year team led by Michael Gomez, aka Machina, a metamorph with the ability to control machines. He's a solid leader but nothing too special, so I wouldn't worry about them throwing us a curveball. The other members of the squad are Goo, who can turn herself into a green gelatin-like substance, Hazard, who can emit a toxic gas from his pores, and Starlight, who, like Lightner, has the ability to generate a blinding light, except it comes from her eyes and not her hands."

"So creative" Christian mumbled.

"As you guys can see, they run basic formations, usually a 2-2, with Starlight and Hazard leading the pack while Machina and Goo provide support. Because of Machina's ability to take control of machinery, people often mistake him as the main threat, but the real threat is Starlight. She's the one we need to focus on."

Tristan heard Belle clear her throat loudly, and the boy had to take a deep breath in order to keep his tone level. Over the last few days, Belle had started to grow increasingly vocal when it came to disagreeing with Tristan's tactics, and it was starting to wear on him.

"Yes, Belle?" Tristan asked through gritted teeth.

"Not to step on your toes or anything, but I'm going to have to disagree."

"Really, Belle? Why is that?" Tristan asked, rubbing his forehead.

"Because we've already seen what Lightner could do, and it wasn't very effective when it came to slowing down Gabe's team. So what if she can flash a light? All we would need to do is turn our heads and look the other way! Machina, on the other hand, is much more of an immediate threat, as he can basically control everything that's in the room and turn it against us! I say we target him first, and then worry about the rest of his team."

"She does have a point, Trist" Christian said apologetically. "I don't say this often, but maybe she's right on this one."

"Taking out Machina should give us the upper hand in the battle as the other powers seem more manageable between the three of us," Dan said, immediately turning red. "Umm, I meant the four of us...I didn't mean to single you out, man. I just—."

"I know what you meant, Dan. Don't worry about it," Tristan quickly replied, although a part of him was bothered that they still tended to discount his ability to contribute in a fight. "Fine. We do it your way, Belle. But if that's the case we need to make sure Starlight is taken care of right after."

"Well..."

Here we go.

Frustrated, Tristan threw up his hands in surrender. "Fine, Belle! Why don't you tell us what we should be doing?"

Belle gave Tristan a feigned look of surprise, but Tristan could tell this was the opening she was looking for. "Tristan, I'm not trying to boss you around, believe me. I know how hard you've been studying these films. But if you're genuinely asking me what I think we should do...here it is."

For the next ten minutes, Belle broke down the revised game plan she had thought up while the three boys listened in silence. While Tristan found Belle's reasoning to be sound, there were key flaws that she appeared to overlook. Tristan was concerned that the team was being mismatched against their more experienced opponents, but the others seemed oblivious to his arguments. Despite his attempts, Tristan could see the writing on the wall: without powers, Tristan would never be viewed as their true leader. He was their moral support, a cheerleader who would help them focus when things got tough. The real leader was always the one who was the smartest and most talented. And in this group, that meant Team Davids was really Team Lecroix.

Which brought him to the present day, pacing back and forth in the musky men's locker room while they waited to be called out. Tristan heard a gentle knock from outside of the room, and the three boys made their way out to join the waiting Belle. She gave them all what Tristan was sure she thought was a confident smile, but he could tell she was just as nervous as he from the way she kept playing around with the four plastic water vials that were around her waist, looped to the new thin belt which the Designers had created upon her request.

They waited for a few more minutes, their opponents gradually making their way to the opposite side of the hallway until they saw the referees exit their locker room in the middle. The refs waved the two teams to join them in front of the glass tunnel, and once they were all together, proceeded to go through the rules. Tristan could barely remember a single word they were saying, focusing entirely on Michael Gomez, the tall, black-haired boy who kept sizing him up. Tristan met his gaze, unwilling to be fazed out by the boy's tactics.

While they waited for the referees to finish their long-winded speech, Tristan took inventory on his opponents. Machina was muscular and lean and had on a chrome-plated, mechanized bodysuit. To his right was Goo, a tall, slender girl with green skin and large eyes that looked like they were trying to pop out of her head. On his left was Hazard, a bald, dark-skinned boy who lacked any form of hair, with everything from his eyebrows to his legs completely smooth and unblemished. Behind them all was Starlight, a pale, older looking girl with hair so blonde it was practically white, and a pair of thick goggles that were tinted completely black. Even concealed, Tristan could still make out the barely visible outline of her irises behind the lenses.

Eventually, Tristan saw a red light turn on overhead. It was time. The two teams lined up side-by-side and proceeded to walk through the tunnel to the entrance of the field, the referees branching off to take a glass elevator to the control booth above. With each step, Tristan felt the blood rushing to his head, his heartbeat pounding in his ears. When they finally stepped onto the field, Tristan heard the deafening roar of the crowd surrounding the glass dome. He looked around in awe at the spectators around them as they walked to their end of the field.

"Hello, Battledome fans! It's your boy Cedric Monroe, and the big dog Jay Fletcher! Back here for week three of our Battledome season, and we have an exciting one here for you guys today! Kicking off the action, it's Team Gomez against Team— wait a sec, Team Davids?! Dang, how many kids they got?!"

Tristan groaned aloud as Dan and Christian snickered beside him. After what felt like an eternity, Cedric and Jay wrapped up their opening commentary. The hairs on the back of Tristan's neck and arms began to rise, a sense of electricity filling the air. Suddenly, the sounds of the raucous crowd were completely muted, silence surrounding the dome. The glass became opaque, blocking the image of the people outside, and the room began to morph around them. It was a little disorienting for Tristan, the ground shifting beneath him while the glass dome took color.

Within seconds, the steel field was entirely transformed into what looked to be a water treatment plant. They were inside a large, square-shaped room surrounded by several rows of sealed metal vats that nearly reached the ceiling. The vats were all connected by thick steel pipes, in which the sounds of churning water could be heard. The room was dimly lit, the light from the evening stars barely trickling through the window panes above. Aside from the eerie glow of the buttons on the electrical panels around them, this was their only source of light. They were standing on the bottom of what appeared to be two floors. The steel stairs were on the far end of the room and led to the floor above, which appeared to be an open-square, grated platform that went entirely around the facility. The platform was lined with computers and mechanical stations, and there on the opposite side, were the four shapes of Team Gomez.

Tristan took a quick glance around the room, evaluating their new environment and how this would affect their plans. The metal vats contained the water they needed to quickly get the upper hand with Belle's powers, but it would be nearly impossible to break through those thick layers. They needed to also avoid the second level, as Machina clearly had the advantage there. Their only hope would be to try and get their opponents down to their level and hopefully find a way to access the water within the vats. *Perhaps if Chris could alter the temperature and freeze the pipes...*

"Guys, I think we need to—!" Before Tristan could finish, the sound of a large bell went off, and a massive timer appeared in the air above.

"Stick to the plan!" Belle shouted and led the charge. Tristan gritted his teeth, and against his better judgment, followed his friends. Belle uncapped two water bottles while running forward, calling forth the water within them. As two large spheres began to form in both of her open palms, Tristan kept an eye on their opponents. Something was fishy about their strategy. None of them were moving. From Tristan's viewpoint, he could make out their shapes and the red, mechanized glow coming from Machina's eyes, but there was something different that left Tristan unsettled. Why were Goo and Machina standing in the front of their teammates...?

"Time to fly, Samson!" Belle cried out as Dan came striding in from behind.

"Allez-oop!" the big boy said, grabbing her waist with both hands and throwing her up into the air. Dan threw her like he was launching a basketball from mid-court, making it look easy and not even breaking his stride. Belle flew through the air like an arrow, aimed straight at Machina and Goo. While she prepared to fire her water spheres toward the two, Tristan heard Machina yell out, "Now!" Before anyone could react, Goo transformed into a green, translucent blob, forming a large, gaping hole from the center of her gelatinous chest. Directly behind the hole was a waiting Starlight, who removed her goggles.

Realizing her mistake, Belle immediately burst the water spheres in her hands, wrapping herself in a protective layer of water. Instinctively, Tristan glanced toward their opponents as these events unfolded. The blinding beam of light exploded from Starlight's eyes, and he felt his vision go white, no longer able to see. *It was a setup!*

Tristan stopped his run and tried to feel around for a metal vat to try and take cover. He could hear the cries of his teammates around him and thought he could make out the loud crack of metal and subsequent moan of Belle flying straight into the steel railings above. Tristan rubbed his eyes, trying to blink the spots out of his vision, but it was no use. For the time being, he would have to rely on his other senses.

Tristan fumbled around in the dark, his hands grasping the cold slab of metal beside him, and slid behind the massive canister. He called out to his teammates but only received a response from Dan, who seemed like he was a few feet away from him. He knew it wasn't a good idea to reveal his location to his opponents, especially with his vision down, but Tristan needed to know what the current state of his team was. *This is definitely not going according to plan!*

Tristan continued to keep himself low to the floor in order to avoid making himself an open target. He tried to control his breathing and not generate as much noise, hoping to detect any nearby movement. Unfortunately, Tristan didn't get very far before his searching hands fell upon what felt suspiciously like a pair of leather boots. His vision gradually returning, Tristan didn't need his eyes to figure out whose boots they belonged to.

"Like shooting fish in a barrel!" Hazard laughed above, and before Tristan could react, he felt a blast of air rush across his face, inhaling a lungful of noxious gas. Tristan immediately went into a fit, the gas burning like fire in his lungs, and he couldn't stop himself from coughing as the chemicals began to work their way into his system. He felt his lungs start to close up and his eyes water uncontrollably, the feeling of suffocation sweeping along his body. He felt his muscles seize up and tighten, his joints locking up in tension from the bottom of his toes to the tip of his head.

As Tristan continued to cough violently, he surveyed the extent of his predicament. He was all alone with Hazard, who was continuing to surround the area with the green, toxic fumes streaming out of the pores of his body. At this point, there was nowhere to go within the surrounding few feet that would remove Tristan from the gas' radius. He was starting to get light-headed from the lack of oxygen to his brain, and Tristan felt the heaviness of his body start to overwhelm him.

Suddenly, Tristan heard a mighty clap, and the gas immediately dissipated, flying back from a violent gust of wind. He watched Christian soar through the air, delivering a haymaker to the jaw of Hazard. Tristan turned his head and saw Dan from afar, his hands still held together in front of him from the force of the impact. He stood beside Belle, who looked to be shaking off the force of her crash landing. Tristan turned back to watch the flurry of blows Christian was now landing upon the reeling Hazard.

It was like watching a fight scene in slow motion, except that Christian was the only one moving at normal speed. Fully transformed and in a battle rage, he was throwing combination punches like a seasoned fighter to the face and torso of Hazard. As Hazard crumpled to the floor, Christian grabbed him by the shirt before tossing him into a nearby computer station, sending sparks flying everywhere. Tristan looked on in awe as he heard a loud beep from above, signaling the end of Hazard's time in the arena.

Tristan tried to regain his normal breathing, taking in deep gulps of fresh air while his vision returned to normal. Without warning, the shattered pieces of machinery beside him sprung to life, the electrical cords and wiring from the computer wrapping themselves around Christian. The cords tightened and began to lift the struggling boy into the air. Tristan tried to stand up and aid Christian but immediately fell to the laminate ground as wires from the surrounding machinery also began to tangle themselves around his feet. Looking up, Tristan could see Machina through the grates on the platform directly above them, directing the cord's movements.

Machina gave Tristan a cold smile while the two teammates squirmed, his red eyes whirling around the sockets. Electrical sparks shot out from the mechanical wires, and Tristan's heart raced, realizing what was about to occur. A shockwave raced through Tristan's body as a surge of electrical energy rushed into him, sending him into convulsions of pain. It was only a split second, but the moment felt like an eternity, burning pain flowing through every nerve in Tristan's body. He heard the scream from his best friend floating beside him and smelled the burning hair on his scalp. It was inescapable, enveloping him in blinding pain that tore through the cells of his body, lashing out along every fiber of muscle. And just as quickly as it happened, it was gone.

Tristan gasped in pain as the wires around his body went limp, and Christian's smoking body thudded beside him on the floor. Tristan could feel what he thought was blood slowly coming out of his ears and nose, while he stared at the grating above them. Machina was lying completely prone, his face pressed up against the platform, eyes closed. His body seemed to be smoking and twitching involuntarily, and through the ringing in his ears, Tristan heard the second beep from above.

What the heck? Did he short circuit himself? Counting his luck, he heard the sounds of footsteps nearby. Still on his back, Tristan slowly turned his head, only to find Goo and Starlight racing toward them. There was no way he would be able to get up in time to defend himself, but he knew he needed to try. Tristan could see the wounded Christian out of the corner of his eyes struggling to crawl to him and wondered how his friend had managed to survive a shock of that magnitude. If Christian hadn't been in his transformed state, Tristan was convinced he would've been another marker up above.

While the two struggled to sit up, Tristan found that his friends had already formulated their own plan of attack. Dan had ripped what appeared to be a rather large, thick metal rod from one of the devices and was gripping one of the ends like a baseball bat. Belle was giving him instructions while holding the back of her head to stem the flow of blood coming from her scalp. Dan arched the rod back like a batter and with perfect form swung it full force into one of the connecting pipes between the water vats. When he pulled the rod back for another swing, a large dent had already formed from the impact.

Unfortunately, Goo and Starlight were closing in too quickly. Belle and Dan would never be able to assist them in time before he and Christian were taken out by their remaining foes. From this distance, Tristan could already tell that Goo's face was starting to melt, her extremities morphing into a gelatinous blob. Starlight's goggles were giving off a bright yellow aura again, and she was lifting her arms to her eyepiece. They were about five feet away now.

Starlight put on a burst of speed and was in front of Tristan in a flash, her right foot planted as her left swung behind, ready to follow through with a crushing kick to Tristan's exposed face. Goo had completely transformed into an amorphous blob and shot herself forward through the air, aiming to hit Dan about twenty feet away. Tristan closed his eyes and prepared himself for the taste of Starlight's leather boots between his teeth. Suddenly, he saw a blur of motion, and Christian appeared out of nowhere. With a last-gasp effort, Christian stretched out both arms as far as he could, one hand making contact with Starlight's exposed skin on her planted right calf and the other touching Goo's gelatinous form.

For a moment, no one moved, time seeming to stand perfectly still. Goo hung motionless in midair, and Starlight struck the perfect soccer pose while Christian held them both. Tristan heard the noise of a strike against the metal pipe and the subsequent burst of pressurized water escaping. It wasn't until then that Tristan realized that it wasn't time that had been frozen, it was their two equally surprised opponents, whose eyes frantically searched back and forth for the answer to their sudden state of suspended animation. Tristan shot a glance at Christian before him, whose brow appeared furrowed in intense concentration.

"Any time now, ladies!" he screamed at Dan and Belle, visibly shaking from the effort. Tristan turned his head just in time to see Belle standing behind them, a vision of awesome majesty as hundreds of gallons of water gathered behind her in a massive wave of relentless fury.

"You boys may wanna hold on to something. Oh, and hold your breath." With that, Belle swept her arms forward in dramatic fashion, and the fearsome tidal wave stormed ahead in a roar of thunderous power.

Tristan didn't remember too much about the subsequent events following their match. He remembered being transported to some room in the back with his fellow schoolmates and being tended to inside of a clinic. The memory was fuzzy, and he didn't really remember heading back to the team locker room to change back into his normal clothes. What he did remember, however, was the blowup that occurred later.

It should've been a happy meeting. They had just won their first Battledome matchup, one in which they were heavily predicted to lose, and they had managed to pull it off without a single incapacitation. This, however, was not the case once they had all gathered together.

"Told you guys my plan would work!"

Tristan paused, incredulous, before reminding Belle that her "so-called plan" was a disaster and had nearly cost them the match. "What are you talking about?! I said we needed to take out Machina and Hazard first in order to stand a chance against them, and we did! The only reason they got the jump on us was that the arena environment gave them the upper hand to begin with! If we hadn't dealt with them early on, you'd still be in the

Triage Chamber getting smoke pumped out of your lungs, and Chris would be on life support! You should be thanking me!"

"Are you out of your mind?! Why can't you just admit you were wrong?!"

This led to what felt like an hour's worth of screaming and yelling, Belle standing firm in her belief that her plan and her actions were what got the team the victory, while Tristan insisted that there was a better way. Christian and Dan seemed non-committal to either side, and their demeanors told Tristan that they just wanted to go back to the dorms. They did seem to concede that Belle's actions, in the end, did save them. After all, breaking the pipes to access the water was her idea.

But that was my idea in the beginning! Tristan wanted to tear out his hair in frustration but instead wound up throwing up his hands in defeat. *How am I supposed to be their leader when they won't even listen to me?* Tristan knew that Belle was the smartest and most talented of their group. There was no denying this fact. How she wasn't one of the leaders selected at the beginning of the year, he didn't know, but the bottom line was this was *his* team now. And he needed them to believe in *his* leadership. Imagining Belle commanding the team, a plan began to formulate in Tristan's mind.

"You know what, Belle? I'm done fighting with you. You're right. You always are. You seem to have all the answers. So from here on out, you're getting what you want. The team's yours." Dan and Christian's jaws visibly dropped as they stared on in shock at Tristan's announcement. Even Belle seemed stunned by his resignation, but the boy only shrugged. "It's not like this wasn't coming. You're the best one out of all of us. You have the smarts, you have the drive, and you have the skills. You've wanted to be a team leader from the beginning and were overlooked. Here's your shot. Besides, the only reason I was probably chosen was that Winter expected me to fail as soon as I stepped onto this island."

For a moment there was only silence as Belle tried to regain her bearings. "Tristan, I—"

"Don't worry about it, Belle. It's fine, really. You got this." Tristan extended his hand, and after a few seconds of deliberation, Belle seemed to compose herself and accept his handshake. "I'll let Winter know first thing on Monday." Tristan released her hand and coldly walked past her, leaving his teammates behind. He didn't look back to see if they were following and prayed that he knew what he was doing.

The rest of the weekend was awkward, to say the least. The friends barely spoke to one another, hanging out only to train, and even then things seemed lackluster and unfocused. When they were around their other friends, they made no mention of the blowout or the change in leadership, accepting their congratulations with quiet gratitude.

It helped that one of the main talking points had become Christian's unexpected ability to "freeze" people, something that Tristan had nearly forgotten about due to their current issues. It had been an unbelievable feat by Christian, who seemed genuinely confused at how he had done it himself. According to him, he had just tried to block the two with his body as best he could but wound up stopping them dead in their tracks.

When Monday came around, the four friends couldn't have been happier, their busy schedule a welcome distraction. That morning, Tristan got up early to go to Principal Winter's office, hoping to catch the headmaster before breakfast. Walking into the waiting room, he found the fireplace on, but Ms. Dorregard was nowhere to be found. The door leading to Principal Winter's office was slightly ajar, and Tristan could hear the rustling of papers. Tristan knocked loudly on the door, clearing his throat for emphasis.

"Yes? Is someone there?"

"It's me, Tristan Davids!"

"Ah, Tristan, come in! The door's open!" Tristan opened the door all the way, revealing the principal standing behind his desk, arranging papers into the massive steel cabinet on the side. He removed his glasses with a smile. "I believe I should start by saying congratulations on your first victory, young man! That was quite impressive for your team to snatch a victory from the jaws of what appeared to be defeat. You four should be proud!"

"Thank you, sir, we are."

"What can I help you with this morning?"

Tristan cleared his throat again before proceeding. "Actually, sir, it's about the team."

"What is it?"

"Well, sir...I'd like to resign from my position as team leader. I'd like to remove myself and install Belle Lecroix in my stead."

The smile on the principal's face disappeared, a confused look replaced it. "I don't understand. You won. Why would you be replaced?"

Tristan shook his head. "The decision was my own, sir. It's complicated, but I believe I can use this to my advantage."

Principal Winter frowned at this statement. "That's quite the gamble. And you're teammates? They're on board with this decision?"

"They are, although they're unaware of my intentions."

"Which are?"

"They need me, sir. They're all extremely powerful metamorphs individually, but they need someone like me to guide them, someone impartial who can set aside their ego for the good of the group. With no powers currently, I'm the only one who can truly make tactical decisions without bias. It may not be as impressive as water manipulation, but it may be the most powerful tool we have and can potentially bring us together as a unit. I believe that it won't take them long to come to the same conclusion."

Principal Winters seemed to consider this before eventually nodding. "Very well. I will submit the paperwork this morning and reassign her as team leader."

"Thank you, sir."

As he grabbed the handle to close the door behind him, Tristan heard the principal say, "Excuse me, Mr. Davids! Before you leave, out of curiosity, if you had to do it all over again, would you have kept the same tactics?"

Without hesitation, Tristan responded. "I would've taken out Starlight, sir."

"Why? Machina and Hazard are easily the most powerful of the group, and they present with the greater power level. Why would you go after her?"

"Because as they proved in the opening minutes, tactics triumph over power any day. We got lucky last match. That won't fly a second time." With that, Tristan turned away, leaving the principal alone to contemplate his response.

Chapter 16: Put Your Trust in Me

"Over the past few weeks, we have gone over the basic overview of early civilizations and their cultures," Professor Fisher began. "Metamorphs originated during these time periods, and we need look no further than the religions of the time to determine their existence!"

"Beginning in early Mesopotamia, the people followed a polytheistic religion, where certain 'gods' were viewed as superior to others by their specific followers. The physical description of these 'gods' tend to vary from culture to culture throughout the ages, but each civilization seemed to have those with similar powers. An example would be Ekni of Sumeria, Mazu during the ancient Chinese dynasties, Poseidon and Amphitrite of Greece, and Neptune of Rome. What did each of them have in common?" Belle's hand immediately shot up into the air. "Enlighten us please, Ms. Lecroix."

"They could all command the waters!"

"Exactly, Belle! Well done! Each one of them had the ability to generate and manipulate the properties of water. I believe that we have someone in this very classroom who demonstrated this very ability over the weekend," he said, causing Belle to flush with pride. Tristan had to restrain himself from rolling his eyes. Will's hand shot up into the air beside him. "Question, Mr. Conrad?" Professor Fisher asked.

"What does that mean exactly, Professor Fisher? Each one of them was identified during different generations and locations. Even their gender changed depending on which culture you look at. It's not like they were the same deity."

"Exactly, Will! Good for you!" the old man said, practically jumping with excitement. "You've pointed out a major fact, and in doing so, confirmed a suspicion that has defined our race for generations! These were all separate entities. Despite their similar abilities, they were not all the 'same god', as some historical researchers claim, but were different people entirely. Aside from their physical differences, some had greater control over their powers than others. While some could control the sea, such as Njord of Norse mythology, Devi, one of the Celtic goddesses, could only manipulate the nearby lakes."

"Another interesting fact is when and where these similar 'gods' were identified. Metamorphs were consistently being born over the course of history, and not just in a single location but across the globe. In fact, the idea that some locations had several metamorphs with the same ability during differing timeframes revealed another important truth on the matter. These powers were being passed down from generation to generation. This wasn't just some freak event, but a matter of genetics itself!"

The wheels in Tristan's head turned as Professor Fisher spoke and a thought popped into his head, escaping his lips before he could raise his hand.

"So if all of these so-called 'gods' were actually metamorphs and were passing down their genes from generation to generation, that would mean that we're their direct descendants! We could basically trace back our family tree based on our powers!"

"Yes, we can, Mr. Davids. Now, obviously, some sired children with other metamorphs of wildly differing abilities, and even some humans. The results were children whose powers bore some similarity to at least one of their parents and those with an amalgamation of both. However, for the most part, we have been able to roughly estimate our ancestral counterparts due to the meticulous research of recent metamorphs, like Mainframe and Cerebrum. In fact, one of the ways we screen you prior to your acceptance to the school is through a scientific method that Mainframe designed that uses electrical impulses to temporarily 'pull' genetic markers from your chromosomes and identify the more obvious compatibilities." With that, Professor Fisher picked up a thick folder that contained what looked to be many bound sheets of paper. "So...who wants to search for their origins?"

The rest of the class period was spent going through their individual genetic profiles that Mr. Peters had compiled during their screenings. The students were deep into their textbooks and laptops trying to read up on their associated metamorphs to determine whom they were most likely to be related to. Not surprisingly, Belle was the first one finished, proudly handing in her paper to Professor Fisher with a beaming smile. Normally, that smile would've caused some butterflies in Tristan's stomach, but today it just seemed more annoying than anything.

"Excellent, Ms. Lecroix! You are absolutely correct! Here is the full copy of your report to compare. Class, I introduce to you, the direct descendant of Neptune and Anuket!" Christian needed nearly the entire class period to discover his roots, but the results did not disappoint. In fact, he seemed happier than Tristan had seen him be in quite some time. "Now here is an interesting combination, Mr. Josephs! The combination of bloodlines between the Mayan bat-like metamorph, Cama-Zotz, and the Norse giantess of winter, Skaoi! My word, now that is quite the mixture!"

"Honestly, Professor Fisher, I can't thank you enough for this. This actually helps answer a lot of the questions I've been having with my abilities."

While he was happy for his friend, Tristan was still struggling himself to narrow down his options. The names on his sheet seemed completely random, from Aztecan goddesses of the stars to Roman gods of lightning. The fact that he had no powers to pull information from didn't help, and as far as he knew, his family members were all over the place with their abilities.

Looking around the room, Tristan could see that he was one of a handful of students left who had not yet completed their assignment. Curiously, Gabriel was one of them. Observing his classmate, he noticed Gabriel furiously scratching his head and rubbing his eyes. He kept squinting at the sheets of paper before him and erasing his notes.

Thinking about it, Tristan realized for all of his bravado when it came to their abilities classes, Gabriel was unusually reserved when it came to the classroom. The few times he was called upon, he struggled to remember information they had discussed previously, and he seemed to have a hard time reading passages from the textbook aloud. Tristan had always figured it was just nerves, but looking at Gabriel now, it seemed like it was more than that. Gabriel threw down his pencil in frustration, glancing up and meeting Tristan's eyes. Embarrassed to be caught staring, Tristan quickly turned around and shifted his attention back to the assignment.

Grrr, this is so frustrating! My whole family has different powers and none of these names on this stupid paper cover them all. All of these names could be my ancestors for all I know! What do they all have in common?! That was when it hit him. Tristan looked over the names listed again and spotted the two he was looking for. After he had circled their names, Tristan brought the paper before Professor Fisher.

"How'd you figure it out?" he asked with a smile.

"The list was all over the place. None of the names on here really made any sense. After all, between the five of us, none of my family members have any powers in common, not even with my grandparents. So rather than figure out what I had in common with them, I thought about what these names had in common with each other. All of the names you gave me were basically the sons and daughters of powerful metamorphs and were well known from mythologies of the past. All except for two. Those two names weren't descendants, but were in fact, the creators themselves. They didn't have specific abilities because theirs encompassed so many. It made sense that it would be those two, which is crazy to me," Tristan admitted, realizing its implications.

"I think you're beginning to understand why your family line is so highly regarded, Mr. Davids. And why we are anxiously awaiting what lies in store for you." The professor looked up as he handed Tristan his detailed forms and announced, "Ladies and gentleman, the descendant of the first known metamorphs, An and Ki!"

The next day, Tristan could hardly wait for the evening to come so that he could continue his fighting progression. They would be going over takedowns tonight, starting with how to properly shoot at their partners. Learning how to quickly bring his opponents to the ground would be a huge boost to Tristan's arsenal, and he was eager to get started. That evening, he arrived early to the mess hall, planning to eat and get to the lab before people started to arrive and get in a proper warm-up.

Walking over to lab 310, Tristan noticed a familiar figure near the end of the hallway. Approaching his classmate, Tristan could see Gabriel pacing around, peering within several classrooms, apparently lost. His instincts told him to leave the boy alone, but something inside of Tristan couldn't let this slide.

"Hey, Gabe? Looking for something?"

Startled, Gabriel quickly covered up his surprise with a shrug of his shoulders. "Naw, just waiting on someone." The boy didn't seem like he wished to divulge further information, leaning up against the wall and glancing at his watch. Tristan nodded and was about to turn the handle to walk into the room, but he couldn't shake this feeling.

"You taking an extra course or something?" Gabriel closed his eyes and clenched his jaw, obviously perturbed at the line of questioning.

"Not that it's any of your business, but no, I'm not taking an extra course. I'm waiting on a tutor."

"Huh," Tristan said, frowning. As far as he knew, the tutoring rooms were all located on the second floor. He removed his hand from the doorknob and walked over to where Gabriel stood. "Are you sure this is where they wanted you to meet?"

"Do I look like a *domkop* to you? It says right here!" Gabriel produced a sheet of paper from his pocket and held it aloft.

"Mind if I take a look? I might be able to help."

Gabriel gave Tristan a long look of distrust, but he eventually conceded, handing Tristan the paper. Opening up the sheet, Tristan could see that it was an email sent to Gabriel by one of the Academy's academic advisors. It read:

"Mr. Jackson,

Taking into account your acceptance scores, recent grades, and request for assistance, we will be more than happy to assist you in being paired with a tutor in order to help you overcome the difficulties you've had in your assigned courses! Thank you for reaching out to us, and we will be more than happy to pair you with someone who fits your needs and can give you the best chance at success. Your tutor, James Ingles, will meet you on 9/25 at 5:00 PM in room 113. Please make sure you arrive on time, and if you have any issues, please let us know!

Sincerely,
The Academy Academics Council"

Tristan sighed as handed his classmate back the paper. *Damn it, Gabe. Why'd you have to go and make me feel bad for you?* "Gabe, what time were you supposed to meet them again? What room?"

Gabriel frowned as he took back the paper and began to read, slowly and deliberately, squinting as he did. "7 o'clock in room...311."

Tristan shook his head slowly. "It's room 113. And it was at 5." Tristan watched as Gabriel stared down at the paper, his hands shaking in frustration. "Gabe, do you ever zone out during class, lose track of time? Ever get headaches when you read or feel like things are moving around the pages?"

"How did you—?"

"One of my friends back home. His name is Marco. He had the same problem growing up. His parents thought he might've had something wrong with his vision but the docs all told them he was fine. Turned out he had dyslexia. Thankfully they spotted it early enough and were able to help get him help when it came to schooling. It was nothing to be ashamed of, and in fact, he was one of the smartest kids in our class. He just needed to have someone work with him individually."

Gabriel said nothing, continuing to stare at the paper in his hands. Finally, the boy looked up and folded the paper into his back pocket. "So...what do I do if I have it? Dyslexia, I mean?"

Tristan shrugged. "My friend spoke with his doc and his professors about it. The school was able to set things up. I can only imagine what resources they have here at the Academy. I would speak with your advisor."

Gabriel nodded thoughtfully, and without a word, walked past Tristan. Before he had gone too far, he paused and turned to Tristan.

"Hey, Davids."

"Yeah?"

"You tell anyone about this, I'll use your face as my personal punching bag."

Tristan smiled, shaking his head. *God, what a toolbag! What did I expect?* "Sure thing, Gabe. You're welcome." With that, Tristan entered his classroom to begin warming up.

Over the final two days, Tristan researched Team Donovan, since Belle proved to be no help in understanding their tactics. She seemed to be focused solely on her abilities rather than utilizing the group to its potential, and it showed. She often took them through battle scenarios where she was practically taking on the entire team single-handedly, using Dan and Christian only as backup. Their new leader was also lacking when it came to altering tactics during battle, one of Tristan's strong points. Tristan eventually pulled up video on his own, hoping to glean some information that could potentially give them the upper hand. What he found was not promising.

Team Donovan was a lot better than Belle was giving them credit for. The group was led by Brittany Donovan, aka Marionette, a tall, skinny American girl who had the power to release psychic energy from her finger-tips in the form of elongated, blue strings that, when wrapped around an individual, could place them under her control. While it required intense control and focus on her end, this allowed her to take over the body of an opposing student, gaining access to all their abilities.

Their next best metamorph was Dreamweaver, a muscular, Native American girl with the ability to put people to sleep simply by touching them. Next was Powerfist, whose stature nearly rivaled Dan's. The thick-necked boy from Denmark was built like a wrestler and below his elbows were large metallic forearms and hands, strong enough to bend steel. Rounding out the group was Reptile, a lizard-like boy with dark red scales for skin, a shock of spiked red hair, claws on his hands and feet, and a tail.

Tristan had a bad feeling about the match heading into it, and when Friday night arrived, he had already formulated a backup plan in case things went south. They were the second match of the evening, and while they waited in the back hallway for the first match to end, Tristan could see Belle tapping her feet impatiently. Oddly enough, Tristan felt completely calm while he glanced across the room, observing their opponents.

Marionette looked like a true performer, wearing a thin purple suit, tie, and black dress shoes. Reptile had on fairly tight sweatpants with a hole in the back to accommodate his tail, and his bare chest revealed thick ar-mor-like scales. Powerfist wore the classic spandex one-piece whose sleeve-less top displayed his metallic arms. Lastly, Dreamweaver had on a tradi-tional Native American garb, and Tristan's eyes were drawn to the various symbols and pictures woven throughout her attire.

Eventually, it was their turn to compete, and the students got into their respective lines and made their way into the area. The audio cut out within the glass dome, leaving the sounds of the two teams walking toward their respective sides the only thing Tristan could hear. Arriving at the edge of the dome, they turned to face their opponents.

"All right, boys, keep your cool. Regardless of what the landscape is, stick to the plan like last time, and we'll be fine. Remember, we take them down individually. Find your matchup, track them down, and try to eliminate them as soon as possible. If you manage to take out your opponent early, help out the person nearest you. This should be a fairly routine battle."

While Belle spoke, the Battledome began to shift around like before, and Tristan closed his eyes so as not to let all of the shifting make him queasy. His eyes shut, Tristan's other senses could account for the changes occurring around him. He could hear the wind begin to pick up, slowly at first, before becoming a powerful gale, strong enough that he needed to set his feet and brace himself against its pull. He could make out the strong smell of salt, thick in the air and his surroundings, feeling sand creeping up his shoes and whipping across his exposed face. He felt a blast of heat, and he opened his eyes immediately, wondering if somehow he had been placed before a furnace of some sort.

This was not good. They had been placed in a desert scenario. It was mid-afternoon, and all around them were massive sand dunes, forming hills that were large enough to obscure their vision past twenty yards on either side. Additionally, they were in the middle of a sandstorm, making their visibility next to nothing. Tristan could feel his mouth drying up from the arid climate and sweat ran down his face.

Tristan immediately recognized that they were not favored in these conditions. Belle was practically useless, the high winds and sand capable of diverting and soaking up her stored water respectively. Dan was already the least mobile of the group, and the deep sand would sink him down with each step. Christian's cold abilities would be difficult to have any sort of effect in these conditions, and Tristan was...well, pretty much no different than any other scenario. Tristan also realized that Reptile and Dreamweaver had now become their most dangerous targets. This environment suited Reptile perfectly, while Dreamweaver would be more difficult to keep track of. They needed to change tactics and draw their opponents in to them.

Tristan heard the loud beep of the match beginning and tried to call out to Belle above the sound of the raging winds. "Ariel! There's no way I can track Dreamweaver like this! I think I should—!"

"Stay back!"

"What?!"

"I said stay back! You're gonna be a sitting duck out there if you try to go out there and take her on! Leave her to me! I'll take her out once I handle Marionette!"

Tristan was furious. "That's stupid! We can't just have you take on their two strongest players! We need a better plan!"

"Look, Tristan! I'm the leader now, remember?! We go with my plan! Worst case scenario, you stay hidden long enough to earn us a draw! Otherwise, we go with what I just said, got that?!"

Tristan was about to say something in response but caught himself when he saw the looks on Dan and Christian's faces. Both of them looked worried, uncertain with what they were supposed to do. *You knew how this would go. Remember, this is what you wanted.* Tristan looked at Belle and nodded his head in submission.

Belle signaled the other two boys, and together they turned away from Tristan, running straight to the nearest sand hill. Tristan retreated to the bottom of the dune to reduce his chances of being seen and kept an eye out on the surrounding hills. He watched his friends run over the top and down into the valley below, disappearing into the swirling sand.

While he lie there, Tristan tried to come up with ways to keep the sand out of his face and protect himself. Unzipping his jacket, Tristan removed the leather material and took off his white undershirt beneath. Tristan tore a thin hole in the middle of the shirt and stuck his head in the bottom. He was then able to get his face inside, wrapping the shirt around his face. Pulling and securing the ends tightly, Tristan's entire face was now completely covered. He was able to see through the thin hole and the moisture from his sweat kept his skin from drying out.

After a few minutes, Tristan decided to head to the top of the hill he had watched his friends go over. Surveying his surroundings from the top of the dune, he tried to detect any movement that could clue him to where his opponents may be. Several seconds passed by without event, and Tristan felt boredom creeping in.

Suddenly, a bell rang overhead, and glancing upward, Tristan saw the updated score. A red mark was now beside his team name. One of his friends had been incapacitated. Tristan stood up and sprinted down the hill as quickly as he could, throwing caution to the wind. There was no way he was going to sit back and do nothing while his friends went down one by one. He crossed the valley in a matter of seconds and was on his way up the next sand dune when he heard the sounds of yelling over the prevailing winds. He slowed to a jog and crouched down to give himself some cover as he got closer to the top. Once he reached the hill's peak, Tristan peered from above to get an idea of the situation.

Before him, Belle lay prone on the ground, Dreamweaver standing directly beside her. A few yards away, Marionette had Dan firmly wrapped around her psychic chains, strands of blue, radiant energy coiled around his arms and legs. His friend looked distressed, but could not stop himself from taking large swings at Christian, who was trying his best to dance around Dan's blows, Reptile's claws, and an oncoming Powerfist. Even in vampire mode, his enhanced speed couldn't save him from taking on three challengers. Christian apparently felt the same way, as he turned around and sprinted in the direction that Tristan lay. Hidden on the other side of the hill's crest, Tristan watched Reptile and Powerfist follow his retreating friend, and an idea formulated in his head. Christian was about ten yards away, and Tristan positioned himself to be perpendicular to his friend when he ran by.

Once Christian got over the hill, Tristan got his knees beneath him, preparing for an explosive launch. Christian noticed the movement and glanced at Tristan, a look of momentary confusion crossing his face. Powerfist was close behind, his focus entirely on his pursuit. The boy had taken two steps over the top of the hill when Tristan shot forward, his front knee going in between the sprinting legs of his opponent while he lowered his shoulder, wrapping both arms around Powerfist's torso. The unsuspecting Powerfist didn't see it coming, and Tristan heard a grunt of pain as the air rushed out of the boy's body. Tristan landed directly on Powerfist and drove him into the ground as hard as he could, a loud crack ringing next to Tristan's ear upon impact.

Powerfist's scream let Tristan know he had, in fact, broken the boy's ribs, but Tristan did not let that stop him. In one fluid motion, Tristan pushed himself up off of the ground and bent his right elbow, opening his palm and anchoring his thumb along his chest the way Professor Coffman had taught them. At the apex of his launch, Tristan rotated from his core, and as his body fell, brought his elbow down onto the exposed temple of his opponent. Tristan felt the reverberations from the blow shoot up his arm as he heard another crack from his driven elbow. Powerfist went immediately limp, and the bell rang above.

Before he could even think about celebrating, however, Tristan heard a piercing screech behind him. Tristan spun around just in time to see the slithering Reptile speeding along the sand on all fours, the boy's razor-sharp teeth exposed and roaring in fury over the fall of his friend. Unable to get up in time, Tristan did his best to get his arm between him and the raging lizard-boy. Reptile shot forward with his long claws extended, however, he was suddenly thwarted. Christian had positioned himself between the two, catching Reptile's hands within his own. His opponent's charge nearly knocked Christian back, but he managed to anchor his shoes into the sand as the two grappled.

Tristan could see the veins on Christian's neck strain with effort, and his clothes were already drenched with sweat. The two were locked in a ferocious matchup, each one trying to use their grapple to topple over the other, but Tristan knew that even if his friend managed to pin down Reptile, he was still at a disadvantage. Reptile was known for using a variety of different submission moves, including using his tail to tangle up his opponents and choke them into defeat.

These thoughts raced through Tristan's mind within a matter of seconds before his eyes caught on to something that gave him a ray of hope. Like most cold-blooded animals, Reptile was protected by a hard outer layer. His underbelly, on the other hand, was quite soft. "Vamp, push him back!" Tristan cried, racing forward to aid his friend.

"What the hell do you think I'm trying to do here? Learn to tango?!"

"Push him, now!" Christian locked his knees and gave a powerful burst of effort forward. He leveraging his full body weight to cause Reptile to lean back, arching his opponent's spine and exposing his chest. Tristan ran full speed at Reptile before leaping into the air and driving his knee underneath the rib cage. Reptile immediately deflated like a burst balloon, collapsing forward and dropping to his knees. As Reptile fell forward with a loud groan, Christian released his hand lock and grabbed the scaled head before him, bringing it down onto his rising knee. With an audible crunch, Reptile went face first into Christian's knee, and Tristan heard the beep from above before the body even struck the floor. The two friends nodded in mutual appreciation before doubling back to their original location.

Tristan took a quick glance behind to see if they were being followed. So far, he didn't see Marionette or Dreamweaver over the horizon. "I take it the plan fell apart?"

"Yup!"

After the two had gotten a safe distance away, Christian elaborated on what had occurred. "We spotted Marionette and Powerfist down in the valley below with their backs turned and tried to sneak up on them. Joke was on us, though. Ariel could barely get the water out of her vials with the winds this bad, and by the time she could even generate a sphere, Dreamweaver had been hiding in the background and ambushed us. She put Ariel to sleep while Reptile came out from the sand and knocked Samson down with his tail. Marionette used her powers on the big guy, and it was game over from there."

"Yeah, well, not anymore."

"Clearly," Christian retorted. "So now what, fearless leader?"

"Now we do it my way and draw these guys out."

"What'd you have in mind?"

After briefly explaining what he wanted to do, they didn't have very long to wait before things fell into place. A few minutes had gone by when the two boys spotted Dreamweaver and Marionette coming over the top of the hill, a still-controlled Dan leading the way. Rather than situate themselves in the valley below, Tristan and Christian had actually positioned themselves on opposite ends at the top of the hill, covering themselves with sand in order to mask their appearance. This vantage point also gave the two boys a leg up on their opponents, who were too focused on the valley before them than keeping an eye on the hilltop's surface. After the two opponents made their way past the two prone teammates, Tristan looked across and gave Christian the signal.

Stealthily, the two boys crept out of their holding position in the sand and snuck behind their unsuspecting opponents. With a quick burst of movement, Christian swooped behind Marionette and got his arms under and around her armpits, placing her into a headlock. Her hands still hold-ing on to her psychic chains, she was defenseless, and Tristan capitalized on this with a quick strike to her solar plexus. Between the shock of the attack and the pain of the blow, Marionette immediately lost focus on her hold of Dan, his blue restraints disintegrating into the sandy air. Using his lever-age, Christian lifted the girl straight back into the air, and rotated around, slamming her face-first into the sand while he lay on top. Christian had her dead-to-rights, unable to move her arms and head, and there was no way she was going to be getting up without assistance.

Having heard the sound of Tristan's strike, Dreamweaver turned just in time to see her friend body-slammed into the ground and quickly rushed to her aid, hoping to touch Tristan and Christian into a state of unconscious-ness. Unfortunately, in her panic to save her friend, she lost track of the hulking, and quite angry, behemoth behind her. Dan merely swatted the back of her head with a flick of his wrist and the girl immediately closed her eyes, falling prone into the sand beneath her. "Now, I'm not the kind of man who'd ever justify hitting a woman, but I think it's time y'all ladies took a nap," Dan muttered as the remaining two beeps went off above.

Tristan sat beside Belle's bed in the triage room. It had been an hour since their match had ended, and he had managed to convince the other two boys to head on back to the dorms while he waited for Belle to awaken. They had given her medicine through IV fluid to help speed up the effects of Dreamweaver's powers, and it was just a matter of waiting for them to take effect. Team Donovan had already been taken care of and had shaken Tristan's hand before walking out. In fact, there seemed to be a new look of respect in their eyes when they looked at him, something he had never ex-perienced but felt that he could get used to.

At that moment, Belle stirred in the bed, and her eyes fluttered open. "Hey there, Sleeping Beauty. You finished napping and ready to go home?"

"Wha...What...happened? Where am I?"

"Long story. I'll explain on the way back," Tristan said with a smile.

By the time they had reached the entrance to the dorms, Tristan had filled Belle in with all that had happened, only stopping to answer any ques-tions she had about their battle. "Wow, Tristan. I don't know what to say. That was incredible what you pulled off!"

"Aww, it wasn't anything special. You could've done it better, I'm sure."

"No, Tristan. I couldn't have," Belle responded, stopping in her tracks and staring intently at him. She had a serious expression on her face and was looking at Tristan in a way that made him feel like she was seeing him for the first time. "I don't think you fully get what you did tonight. They had us beat! There was no way we would've won if you hadn't saved us. You changed up the tactics mid-battle and exposed their weaknesses. Tristan, you managed to turn the tide against one of the better teams at the school when we were down 4-2. And you did it without powers. As far as I'm concerned, that's something I could never do."

Tristan didn't know what to say. He hadn't really thought of it in that light and definitely hadn't expected this reaction from Belle. He had been merely trying to protect his friends, nothing special. Belle walked closer to him, barely a foot away, as she kept giving him that look.

"I know we've had our differences in the past, Tristan, and I'm sorry for undermining you. I guess I've been holding on to the feeling that I was overlooked when they were choosing leaders. But I was wrong. There was a reason why you were chosen, and it's not just about your family name. You were meant for this, Tristan. And I, for one, can't wait to see what you do next."

With that, Belle turned around and walked toward the girl's dormitories, leaving the flushed Tristan behind. Tristan shook his head, trying to gather himself before calling out, "So does this mean what I think it does?"

Belle turned her head, flashing that perfect smile. "Looks like you're back in the driver's seat, captain!" Tristan felt his heart soar as he returned the smile. Yeah. He could definitely get used to this feeling.

Chapter 17: Within the Criminal Mind

The following Monday, Tristan sat before Principal Winter's desk, hands folded on his lap, while he patiently waited for the headmaster to arrive. Tristan wasn't sure what this meeting was about, but he had received an email late last night from the man himself asking him to report to the principal's office prior to breakfast. Tristan had arrived promptly at 6:30 and found the doors open but the room empty. Ms. Dorregard was also nowhere to be found, however, the fireplace continued to blaze on with its seemingly eternal flame.

Around 6:45, the principal finally arrived, slightly out of breath. He was hastily arranging his tie as he walked over to his side of the desk. "My sincerest apologies, Mr. Davids. Unfortunately, we had a bit of an emergency situation over by the north section of the island. There seemed to have been a structural malfunction in one of our water purifier stations on the island resulting in several burst pipes. The situation was odd for this time of year, but we managed to—never mind, I'm sure it's of no interest to you," he said hastily, taking a deep breath to compose himself.

"On to better, more interesting, topics, such as your performance from last weekend. That was quite the response after last week's near disaster. Impressive."

Tristan shrugged, unsure of what to say. *Is this what Winter wanted to talk to me about? Some Battledome result?* "I suppose you can say that, sir. We haven't exactly been at our best, but we've been able to get the end result that we need."

"That is quite true, Mr. Davids. A victory is a victory, no matter how ugly the path it took to get there."

For a moment, neither said anything, staring blankly at one another. Finally, the principal cleared his throat and leaned back into his chair. "You know, I've been keeping an eye on your progress since we last spoke in this office. You seem to be doing quite well in all of your classes, besides your two ability courses. You're just getting by in Professor Crusher's Self-Defense class, while Professor Tremor is still not convinced that you will be able to succeed in hers. I'm inclined to agree."

I bet you do, Tristan thought but said nothing. He simply nodded in acknowledgment while Winter seemed to study his reaction.

"Two of the best evaluators at this school seem to think you don't have what it takes, Mr. Davids. And yet...you keep proving us wrong. And I, for one, am beginning to wonder if I've made a mistake in doubting you."

This time Tristan was, in fact, caught off guard. "Wait, what?"

"Don't get too ahead of yourself," Principal Winter said with a smile. "I said I'm beginning to wonder, not that I've come to the conclusion. There is still a ways to go when it comes to those two classes. Professor Coffman is quite pleased with your progress in his class and speaks highly of your skills when it comes to his Defense Mastery course. I encourage you to continue to work with Arman and hone your skills. Hopefully, we will begin to see more of these miraculous comebacks in the Battledome."

"Hopefully, it won't need to come to that anymore."

"Anyhow, continue to progress, Mr. Davids, and make sure you get those grades up. I'll have my eyes on you." He gestured to the door, indicating the end of their meeting.

Before Tristan proceeded out of the room, a thought popped into his head. "Oh, before I forget! I've been reinstated as leader for my team, so I was hoping we could cancel those transfer forms before they got processed!"

Principal Winter removed his glasses, and the older man smirked. "I'm glad to see your gambit paid off. For the record, I never put in those transfer forms. I may question your metamorph abilities, Tristan, but not your God-given ones. Now, off you go."

Later that day, Tristan reported to Professor Tullage for his Psychology class. Upon arriving, he observed a long, thin metal table in the middle of the room containing what appeared to be a large, rectangular box with a thick black sheet over it. He also found that there were name tags on top of the spaced-out desks, each student assigned a partner. To his chagrin, Tristan discovered his name beside Brandon's. He reluctantly took his seat and awaited further instruction as students began to gradually file in. When

Brandon finally arrived, the shaggy-haired boy frowned deeply but held his tongue when he sat down next to Tristan.

"Good afternoon, class!" Professor Tullage began. "Today, we will be doing something a little different than we've been used to. We will be starting off with a discussion before breaking out into a live demonstration. We will be discussing the topic of good versus evil, particularly in the case of metamorphs. I've set you up with partners and would like for you to really explore this topic. What drives people to commit these acts? How do you think they view themselves? Try to dissect these individuals and understand that no two people are alike. It's okay if you disagree with your partner, as long as you are going into this conversation with an open mind. Now, feel free to begin whenever you're ready."

Tristan sighed to himself before turning to Brandon, who seemed just as motivated as he was. They stared in silence until Brandon began the conversation. "This is so stupid. Everyone knows what makes bad people bad. We don't need to spend twenty minutes on it." Tristan shrugged but said nothing. "People are bad because that's who they are. You can raise a kid in the perfect home, with the perfect parents, and they still may grow up to become a serial killer. Just like you can raise a kid in a crappy environment, and he grows up to be a famous basketball player."

Tristan found himself frowning at this. "So you think people are destined to be good or evil?"

"I think our paths are already laid out for us. Call it destiny, fate, or whatever. Some people are destined to be the bad guy, but how they wind up there is up to them."

"Well, that's just bleak. You're saying that there's no way for someone to change their path in life. That we might as well give up and not even try to fight against some predetermined destiny, even if it leads to a horrible outcome."

"No, what I'm saying is that some people can't be saved because they don't want to be. Some people actually prefer a life of crime."

"That's too black and white, Brando. There's always going to be some shade of grey here, and at the end of the day, it comes down to their intentions. There are those who commit certain acts because they genuinely believe they are doing the right thing. You can't pigeonhole someone into a good or bad category just because you think they're 'destined' to do so! What about you? Should we make sure you don't end up as the next supervillain?"

"What's that supposed to mean?!"

"From the moment I got here, you and the goon squad did everything you could to make me feel like an outcast. Hell, you physically attacked me and my friends before classes even started!" Brandon's eyes widened before he glanced down, guiltily. "I don't know what kind of world you live in, but last I checked, those sound like things the 'bad guys' do. And if that's the case, what's your excuse, Brando?"

Silence came between the boys, and Tristan turned back to face the front of the class. A few minutes passed before Tristan heard two words that he was not expecting: "I'm sorry." Tristan turned to Brandon, who was staring directly at him.

"I'm sorry, all right? I get why you would think that after how things went down. I guess I've been so used to being the one on the outside that it was nice to finally be with the 'in crowd'. I thought if I went along with them, I would finally be accepted, you know? It doesn't help that with these abilities I have something of a quick fuse. I think that's why my parents were so glad to finally get me out of their hair and into this school. So I could be someone else's problem. Maybe you're right. Maybe I am destined to be one of the bad guys."

Tristan sighed, shaking his head. "You're not a bad guy, Brando. You just want to be accepted, like the rest of us. Who knows? Maybe if the roles were reversed and I was the one with the powers, I'd be doing the same thing. At the end of the day, it's not about how many times you slip up. It's about whether or not you're willing to do anything about it. That's what makes a villain in my book. Someone who's willing to do the wrong things for the wrong reasons and isn't willing to change anything about it. And from the sounds of things, that's not either of us. So why are we the bad guys in each other's stories?" Tristan shrugged. "Maybe we don't have to be."

"All right, everyone! I hope you were all able to engage in some deep discussion regarding the topic of good and evil," Professor Tullage commented before walking toward the table in the middle of the room. "I wanted to begin class with this topic because I find it to be highly relevant to what we are about to do next."

"As you all know, while there are those who fight for justice, equality, and freedom, there is also the subset of individuals who fight for the opposite. These people are coined 'villains', and in our case, 'super-villains'. While it may appear cartoonish and silly, I assure you, there's nothing comical about a metamorph who turns for the worst. While we have the capability to do wonderful things, the capacity for destruction is that much more enhanced as well."

"One of my gifts has been to delve into the minds of others, navigating through their thoughts and discovering information which would otherwise be inaccessible. It took me years to master my abilities, and over time I learned to take others with me into these cerebral journeys. Which brings us to today, where we will be going on a field trip—through the mind!" With that, Professor Tullage grabbed the edges of the sheet and pulled them off dramatically, revealing a glass box beneath. The class let out a collective gasp as they stared into the transparent rectangle.

Contained inside of the box was the body of an aged man, his head shaved bald, and his skin slightly wrinkled. He had a grey tinge to his skin and a deep frown upon his smooth face. He was of average build and height and didn't appear to be anything unusual. Except for his hands. His hands and arms were completely covered in scars and burn marks as if he had stuck his hand inside of a deep fryer, the grotesque deformities a stark contrast to his otherwise normal appearance. His eyes were closed, and he seemed to be asleep, although his chest was barely moving. He had a thin, black ring made of metal around his neck with a beeping blue light contained within.

"The shell that lies upon this table belongs to the criminal mastermind known as The Shifter! For those of you who are unfamiliar with the name, The Shifter was a notorious criminal in the 70s. Known for his ability to physically alter his appearance, the man formerly known as Herbert Parrish abused this talent to the extreme, staging anything from high profile heists to strings of murders."

"It took a team of daring and brilliant metamorphs to eventually draw Parrish out from hiding and take him down, but it was not without its cost.

Several lost their lives in taking down this criminal, and it took years to eventually track down all of his past crimes."

"What's that brace around his neck?" Sofi interrupted.

"Excellent question, Ms. De Rossi. When applied to an individual, the brace emits a frequency of soundwaves which enters through the skin. When the waves hit the cerebellum, it literally begins to scramble the electrical signals throughout the body, causing a complete shutdown of bodily function aside from basic necessities, such as respiration and circulation. It puts the wearer into a perpetual coma, and this device is worn by all metamorph criminals who have been captured and detained by our law enforcement. The criminals are secured in this state within a secured location that only the Council members are privy to."

At this, Professor Tullage walked over to the side of the room and turned off the lights. "Place your heads upon the table and close your eyes." Tristan crossed his arms on the table and put his head down, shutting his eyes. "Take deep breaths and try to empty your thoughts. Relax...let your mind wander where it will...relax..."

Tristan breathed in deeply and tried his best to clear his mind. He felt his body grow heavy as the seconds ticked by. The room was silent except for the sounds of Professor Tullage's instructions, and Tristan began to lose himself in her words. Her voice seemed to grow louder, filling the room. Suddenly, an image flickered into his mind. It was blurry and fleeting, like an unfocused camera, but it had been there. A few seconds went by, when suddenly the image popped into his head again, this time more vivid. "Reeeelllaaaxxx your miiinnnddd...." Tristan felt his body drifting into a sense of nothingness, when the image reappeared, this time completely focused and clear.

Tristan was in a room of total blackness watching a small boy stand before a mirror. The boy was short and gangly, with unkempt hair and tattered, dingy clothing. Tristan couldn't say how he knew, but he understood that this boy was a younger Herbert. The boy seemed to be entirely focused on his reflection in the mirror, a look of curiosity upon his face as if he were confused at what stared back. The boy began to playfully mash his face together with his hands, slanting his eyes and pointing his nose up while pressing in his cheeks.

Tristan thought the boy was just being silly at first, until he realized the boy's features remained distorted even after he removed his little hands from his face. The boy now looked like he had smashed his face against a glass door, his features unrecognizable from earlier. After a few seconds, his face gradually began to restore itself to its natural state, the boy grinning and laughing before starting over and manipulating himself all over again. A sense of giddy playfulness and excitement rushed through Tristan, a world of wondrous possibilities opening before him. Gradually, the image began to lose focus, and Tristan blinked, back in the classroom again.

What just happened?! Tristan lifted his head, looking around to ensure he wasn't going crazy, however, based on the shared expressions of his class-mates, he was not alone in his thoughts. What he had experienced was real. Not only had he seen it within his mind, he had experienced it. He had felt what young Herbert was feeling at the time, as if the feeling were his own.

"What you all just experienced was a mind meld. It is an extremely del-icate and intricate technique to master and requires a very strong telepath-ic mind in order to control and sustain. In the hands of an untrained in-dividual, it can result in lost memories, merging of brain images, and most concerning of all, implantation of ideas." Tristan gulped at the thought. He could only imagine the ramifications of having the thoughts and ideas of a serial thief and murderer ingrained into his own mind.

"While you are within his memories, you will also begin to experience the emotions that he had during that moment in time. For many, this is a brief and temporary side effect of the mind meld, however the longer you remain within the patient's mind, the more permanent the results, especial-ly for individuals who tend to be more empathetic. Thus, it is important that the trained individual is also cognizant of time in the material world."

While Tullage explained, Juan was practically falling over his seat, hanging on to her every word. "Can this technique be learned or is this something innate?" he questioned.

"A bit of both, Mr. Parra. Now, for this next portion, we will be delving into darker memories, so be aware of the subsequent emotions you may ex-perience. Let's get back into a state of relaxation, and we will begin."

This time, knowing what to expect, the process went much faster. Hardly a minute had gone by when Tristan was back in the room of endless darkness. Tristan saw Herbert before him, however now he was a bit older, at least thirteen, although he still seemed quite small and gangly for his age. He still had a disheveled look to him, but something was different. It was his eyes. His eyes were no longer the gentle, playful eyes of an innocent youth. His eyes seemed harder now, colder and full of a hidden rage. These eyes had seen things. Terrible things. And this time he was not alone.

He was sitting at a wooden dinner table, his hands by his sides, while he stared blankly at the meager meal before him. The plate was half full of what appeared to be spoiled meat and cheese covered in mold. A sense of revulsion washed over Tristan, the boy's shared sensations beginning to take hold. A taller gentleman came into the picture, directly behind him, stumbling out of the shadows. The man was haggard and looked worn. The bags under his bloodshot eyes and unkempt facial hair revealed more than words could say. A strong scent of liquor permeated Tristan's nostrils.

"Watsa matter, boy? I put this here food on the table for ya to eat. Why ain't ya eatin'?" he growled. His low, menacing voice sent chills down Tristan's spine, and his heart began to race.

"I'm not hungry," the teenage boy mumbled.

"Sir."

"What?"

"I'm not hungry...sir."

The boy quickly corrected himself. "Sorry, sir. I'm not hungry, sir." For a moment, the man seemed to bristle with rage, but he kept quiet and nodded to himself, muttering something under his breath. He walked away, stepping back into the empty darkness behind the shaking boy. Once the father passed out of sight, the boy appeared to relax, breathing out a sigh of relief. Tristan felt the sense of dread leave him and began to relax once more.

Without warning, the father suddenly burst out of the darkness holding a belt, and with one smooth motion, brought it down upon the unsuspecting boy's head. Herbert was thrown out of the chair from the force of the blow, and Tristan watched in horror while the enraged father swung the belt down, time after time, upon the screaming boy, his mouth practically frothing in his frenzy.

"I'll teach you to disrespect me, boy! I work my butt off, day after day, to put food on this here table! If I put food in front of ya, yur gonna eat it! You hear me boy?!"

Tristan tried his hardest to pull away from the scene but regardless of where he turned, the image stayed before him. Finally, the father stopped his assault, spitting a wad of tobacco juice on the floor where a pool of Herbert's blood had formed, the battered teen sobbing hysterically in a protective ball. The man slowly turned away, walking back into the darkness before Tristan heard the sounds of a door closing and a car eventually driving away.

Tristan had a sickening feeling in his gut at the sight before him, as poor Herbert slowly picked himself back up. As much as he wanted to reach out and help him, Tristan could no sooner comfort the image as he could go back in time. The boy's face was a bruised mess, but what made it worse was the fact that due to his abilities, his facial features were more distorted than normal, his eyes, nose, and jaw aligned at awkward angles. Tristan watched Herbert painfully restructure his malformed face, the sobs slowly starting to settle down. Once he had finished, Tristan observed the boy's puffy eyes and saw the remaining humanity gradually slip away. The boy had seen enough. He had experienced enough. This was the straw that broke the camel's back.

"This was a pivotal moment in Herbert's life," Professor Tullage said, suddenly appearing beside him. "Abused by his father for years following the untimely death of his mother, Herbert grew up in a household of constant fear and unpredictable rage." As the image of Herbert began to lose focus, Tristan made out the shapes of his classmates joining him within the room of darkness. "His father suspected that there was something different about his son, but he tended to ignore the boy's abilities. Often times, he appeared to question whether or not Herbert was actually his son or a result of an affair, leading to many of his outbursts of violence. DNA testing would eventually confirm the father's suspicions, although he never discovered this fact."

Professor Tullage waved her arms at the blurred image of Herbert, bringing his face back into focus, as if wiping a smudge off of a window pane. "Behold, the face of innocence taken. A boy with a remarkable gift, which given the right environment and mentoring, could have become one of the great heroes of our time. Instead, he underwent a painful transformation from a joyful, little boy to a scared and angry adolescent. This is why this university is so important. It not only allows us a place where we can find a safe, understanding environment, it also allows us to save the lives of those who would ordinarily stray off this path."

Professor Tullage was turning away from Herbert's image when Juan stepped forward. His eyes appeared glazed over, and he seemed to be moving as if in some sort of trance. *Come to think of it, how was he moving?* Tristan tried to move his body but found that he could not budge from where he was positioned. Turning his head, he found that the other students were also in a state of suspended motion. Juan seemed to be the exception, which Tullage seemed just as surprised about. "Psyborg, how did you learn—?"

"There's something else there," Juan whispered, continuing to move past the teacher, his focus entirely on Herbert's face. "Something...deeper...I see it..." The boy paused for a moment before suddenly a faint glow began to emit from the fingertips of his right hand. Professor Tullage's face quickly went from a look of inquisition to complete horror.

"Psyborg! No!" she cried out, but it was too late. The boy's hand shot up, and his fingers gently touched the visage of Herbert Parrish, sending ripples across the room. Tullage rapidly spun around, sending out waves of psychic energy and forcing the other students back. Tristan was mere feet away from Juan, however, and couldn't escape the ripples' effects.

Tristan's stomach lurched, the room suddenly collapsing upon itself, and he felt himself fall forward into a pit of pure nothingness. Tristan could barely hear the screams of terror around him while his fellow classmates disappeared above. He felt himself twist and turn into the sea of darkness, flashes of random memories flickering within his mind's eye.

Plummeting down the hole, an orange glimmer appeared below, the color seeping in along the edges and swirling into his surroundings. As he continued to fall, the screams coming out of his mouth were gradually drowned out by the sound of another familiar voice screaming. Suddenly, Tristan felt a tear in the space below him, and he was immediately thrust into a room of smoke and flame, the heat of the surrounding air blasting into his face. Smoke enveloped his nostrils and his eyes burned with tears staring at the scene before him.

He immediately recognized the wooden dining room table, as well as the bound figure whose screams were now muffled by the masking tape that secured his hands, feet, and mouth. What he didn't recognize was the grotesque smile of the teenage boy standing beside the table, laughing. Herbert had his father's belt in one hand and a canister of gasoline in the other. The boy had morphed his face to give it an elongated jaw, sharp eyes, and devilish features. Herbert looked down upon the bloodied and smoke-covered body of his father before slowly dousing the terrified man in gasoline. The boy laughed louder the more his father protested, the surrounding flames licking hungrily over the body.

"PSYBORG!YOUNEEDTOPULLBACK,NOW!FOCUS!HONEINONYOURMEMORIESANDRELEASEHIM!

Tristan winced as the image before him exploded in a flash of light, sending his body flying back in slow motion into a sea of white. He closed his eyes at the brilliance of the light, but could not stop the images from entering his thoughts. A dark-haired, young boy gleefully holding his mother while she spun him around. Light. The boy crying beneath his bed, holding his head in pain as he tried to stop the millions of voices from invading his mind, his mother pleading for him to come out. Light. The boy, alone and frightened, hiding in the closet while the furniture in the living room outside levitated off the ground. Grey.

Tristan was flying now, racing through time and space. At this point, he couldn't tell whose memories were speeding past him in a blur of smoke and fog. Everything around him was covered in a thick grey smog, and he was moving horizontally now, rather than vertically. In a last gasp of effort, Tristan tried to focus his mind and hold on to something, any memory that he could find. Concentrating with all his might, Tristan felt a hard jerk on the back of his neck, and he was suddenly thrown backward onto the ground.

Tristan paused for a moment, chest heaving from the journey's intensity. He couldn't even tell if it was solid ground underneath his body, the surface completely obstructed in a thick grey mist. Composing himself, Tristan sat up, observing these new, alien surroundings. Everything was grey and shadows as far as the eye could see, and Tristan felt completely disoriented. *Where the hell am I?!*

To his right, Tristan's ears picked up on what he thought were whispers. He couldn't make out their exact location or to whom the voices belonged to, but he did sense that they were coming from nearby.

"Hello? Is anybody there?!"

There was no response, but Tristan could hear the volume of the voices increase. Tristan stood up shakily and forced himself to try and move toward the voices. There was definitely someone out there, and from the sounds of it, it seemed like two people were having a conversation.

Tristan had perhaps taken five steps forward when he noticed two shapes forming directly before him, not more than fifteen feet away.

"Hey! Can you hear me?! It's Tristan! I need help! Who are—?!"

"We have access to one another again. I was able to provide a distraction earlier today and hacked into the mainframe. It won't be long now." Tristan couldn't recognize the voice, the acoustics of his surroundings altering the quality, but something about it felt familiar. He stopped dead in his tracks, a feeling of sudden coldness and dread creeping into the pit of his stomach. He didn't know why, but something was telling him to stop calling out. Something was wrong. He shouldn't be here.

"Very good. You've done well, my boy," the other voice said. "They trust you and will never suspect a thing. Soon, this school will fall, and our opening will come." The second voice seemed older, darker somehow. More menacing. Tristan had never heard it before, but the hairs standing up on his forearm let him know his feelings were justified. He had stumbled onto something big. "Once we get our hands on the key, we'll be able to revive him. It's only a matter of time until he awakens, and when he does, this world and everything in it will be ours for the taking. The way it was meant to be. You just need to make sure you hold up to your end."

"Of course, Shadow. You know my loyalty is only to the Legion."

"Good. We were beginning to worry that you were forgetting why you came to the Academy. Do not let yourself forget who your real family is. These...children are a means to an end. If you wish to truly fulfill your potential, your path lies with us."

"Don't worry, Shadow. You know I've never been one to let my guard down. I'll make sure to continue my work infiltrating their system, and then—!"

Suddenly, the second figure jerked his head to the side and raised his hand. "Silence! What was that?!" The first figure seemed surprised and glanced around.

"What was what? I didn't hear anything. I wasn't followed, I swear!" The second figure slowly turned his head, searching for something.

"No...not here...not out there..." He slowly pointed a long, slender finger at his temple. The figure's head quickly snapped in Tristan's direction. "Here!"

BOOM! Tristan felt a force rock him backward, sweeping him off his feet. Tristan was lifted up in the air, feet facing the shadowy figure, and he was suddenly whisked toward the shape. Tristan strained with every ounce of willpower he could muster to stop his trajectory, and he felt himself slow down while the world around him shot forward. Tristan screamed in terror, shadowy fingers inching closer to his feet, and he felt as if his mind was tearing in half. The figure was close now, maybe three feet away.

WAITITHINKIHEARHIM!

Tristan heard a familiar voice boom in his head, and for a moment, everything froze. The dark, menacing figure looked around, frightened, before stepping back and disappearing into a grey mist.

IFOUNDHIM!TRISTANHANGON!IVEGOTYOU!

Tristan looked up as a beam of light began to crack in the air above. He felt something pull on his body as he floated upward, slowly at first before picking up speed. Soon, he was zooming into a world of light, eventually crashing down onto the hard marble surface of the classroom.

Chapter 18: The Mole

It took Tristan several minutes to gather his bearings and comprehend Professor Tullage's explanation for what had occurred. All the while, Juan knelt beside the supine Tristan, babbling uncontrollably about how sorry he was. "It was my fault, Juan. I should've anticipated there could have been adverse reactions having another telepath within the group. I had severely underestimated your abilities and how attuned you've become over the past few months." Tristan could make out the mutterings from the confused classmates around them, and from the looks on their faces, they were just as concerned about him.

He hadn't said a word since coming back, his mind slowly recovering from the journey it had just experienced, which the professor explained was normal. "When we mind meld, we tend to enter into a state of psychic reality, one where we maintain an ephemeral state of being. We can only move or manipulate the environment based on how strong we are mentally. The average person will remain in a suspended state, while the more powerful telepaths are able to move around and alter their surroundings. While I have entered minds with other telepaths, I've yet to do so with a student capable of movement, much less manipulation of the patient's mind. It can be very tempting for a beginner to become entranced in the memories of the patient and attempt to pull deeper into the psyche."

"I was able to withdraw the other students before they were pulled into the scene, however, you were too close and were drawn in. We tried to extract you from the memory, but it seemed you became lost within the mind stream and began to filter through the collective consciousness within the island. It took us a while to find you, but I was able to pinpoint your location and retrieve your mind before you had gone too far."

"I'm so sorry, Tristan! I didn't know! I didn't mean—!"

"It's okay, Juan. I'm good. Really," Tristan finally said, a collective sigh of relief exhaled by his classmates at the sound of his voice. "I was a little shaken up, but I'm fine. As weird as it sounds, I think I just need to sleep this one off."

Professor Tullage smiled at this and nodded. "I think that's enough excitement for one day, class. I hope you were able to learn something aside from the fact that even metamorphs can make mistakes." The class murmured in agreement before packing up their belongings.

As Tristan sat up, a hand shot out in front of him, offering help to his feet. Tristan glanced upward to see Brandon's relieved face above.

"Next time you want to get us out of class early, try not to pull the old 'losing my mind in the abyss' trick. It's played out."

After gathering his belongings, Tristan tried his best to maintain a relaxed, normal demeanor, but within his head, his thoughts were still racing over what he had just witnessed. That evening at dinner, Tristan sat down with his friends and told them what had happened, intentionally leaving out the part about the two mysterious figures. After what he had witnessed, he didn't trust speaking out in the open like this. Tristan nonchalantly cleared his throat and subtly leaned forward.

"Listen, I don't want to make this weird or anything, but I need to talk to you guys alone. There's more to the story, and I think it might be best if I explain it somewhere where we can have...more privacy." His three friends exchanged glances before nodding in unison. Without drawing attention to themselves, the four finished up their meals and made their way out of the mess hall.

Tristan led the way as he guided them to the hammock area of the campus. There was no one around, and it gave them a place where Tristan could speak openly without fear of anyone overhearing their conversation. Once he felt that there was no one within earshot, Tristan confided in his friends the events that had taken place that afternoon within his psychic state. His three companions listened intently, hanging on to his every word, and did their best to hold off interrupting unless they needed clarification on something.

A part of him expected his friends to look at him like he was crazy and tell him that it was all a result of a delusion. To his surprise, however, they all stared back gravely at him. Belle was the first to break the silence.

"Tristan, I get that what you saw was sensitive information, but you need to tell Professor Tullage. Like now."

"Seriously? I mean, who knows if this was real or not? It could have been a part of Shifter's mind that I fell into or something."

Belle frowned at this response. "It doesn't sound like it, Tristan. From what you've described, you weren't in Shifter's mind after the fire, and it seems like you may have stumbled onto something. What it is, I don't know, but your best bet for an answer would be the woman whose expertise happens to be in telepathy."

"Belle's right. I think you should talk to Professor Tullage," Dan agreed. "Who knows if what you saw was real or not, but it didn't sound good regardless. I'll be honest, it's kind of freaking me out. There's someone here on this island that's trying to take out the defenses? For what? And for who? This might be even worth talking to Winter about, from the sounds of it."

"Easy there, big fella. I'm not going to Winter about anything. He'd probably think I was making it up or put me on some kind of suspension until we sorted things out to make sure I wasn't losing it. And like I said, I don't even have enough information to go off of. What am I supposed to say? 'Hey guys, just a heads up, while I was taking a psychedelic trip through the mind of a serial killer, I accidentally fell into a secret meeting between two shadows who want to infiltrate the island in order to get some key which will help them take over the world'? Yeah, that sounds great!"

Tristan turned to Christian, in a last ditch effort to find someone who would convince him that what he saw was some freak misunderstanding. Instead, he saw a look of concern across the face of his best friend. "Sorry, bro. I'm with them. I don't think this needs to go to Winter, but it wouldn't hurt to at least get a little more information from Tullage. Maybe see if you recognized any of the figures. You said you felt like you knew one of them, right?" Tristan slowly nodded. He couldn't quite put his fingers on where or how, but he felt like if he had a little more time and training, he could have pinpointed the initial voice.

"Look, I don't want to jump to any conclusions, but let's say this is real and there is someone here on the island that may be a mole. You said that the person is someone here people trust but has done a good job of keeping people at a distance? To keep from getting too friendly with them? Maybe I'm crazy, but that sounds like someone we know a little too well..."

Belle said the words before Tristan could get them out of his mouth. "You can't be serious, Chris?! Are you really thinking that Gabe could be the mole?"

"Look, all I'm saying is that it would make sense. The kid is always talking about how metamorphs should be out in the open running this planet and bullying other metamorphs who aren't as strong as he is. He's a leader, so people trust him, but he comes off as a showboating bigot so he barely has any friends other than his crew. In my opinion, it fits."

Despite his initial reaction, Tristan had to admit, Christian had a point. However, Tristan didn't want to start thinking down that path. He knew Gabriel could be a jerk sometimes, but this seemed a little too nefarious, even for him. "Fine. I'll talk to Tullage. Tonight. I'm not sold that Gabe would be the culprit, but if what I saw was real, maybe Tullage could help me decipher who is behind all of this."

It didn't take long for Tristan to find the professor's office among the several doors that lined the fourth floor. Although it was a quarter to eight, a few of the professors still seemed to be in their offices, preparing their lesson plans for the next day. Tristan took a deep breath before knocking on her door.

"Come in, door's open!" a familiar voice responded, and Tristan turned the knob, stepping into the rather cozy office. The marble floors were a smoky color, and several bookcases lined the walls, packed to the brim with psychology textbooks and journals. There was a large, circular tan rug in the middle of the room, upon which a long dark couch and two comfortable looking armchairs stood. The professor had a small desk in the far corner of the room behind which she sat, going over her notes.

"Tristan! What brings you up here this evening? Tutoring hours have long passed!" Tristan nodded apologetically.

"Sorry to bother you so late, professor. I was hoping to get a moment of your time. I just needed to speak with you in regards to what happened to me today." A look of concern crossed Tullage's face as she removed her glasses.

"Is everything all right? Are you suffering any side effects from this afternoon's events? Have you been having issues with your memories?"

"It's okay, Professor Tullage. I'm not having any side effects or memory issues. At least that I know of." A look of relief passed over the professor.

"If that's the case, what brings you in here, Mr. Davids?"

"I might need to sit down, if you don't mind. This may take a while."

Professor Tullage gestured for Tristan to sit on the couch while she crossed the room to sit across on one of the armchairs. Tristan proceeded to explain his encounter to the professor while she patiently listened. Tristan tried his best to not omit or forget anything he had witnessed and managed to get through the entirety of his tale without so much as a pause. Once he had finished, she continued to sit there quietly, her brow furrowed in concentration.

After what seemed like an eternity, Tullage took a long blink and, just like that, seemed to relax. "I apologize for the delay, Tristan. I was trying to process what you were telling me while piecing both our memories of the event together to try and get a clearer picture. I'm sorry, I usually ask permission when analyzing a mind, but in this case, I needed you to be as unguarded as possible in order to make out some of the images."

Tristan was shocked at the fact that he had never felt the professor in his mind, even for a moment. *How strong is this woman?!*

"Wait, so you're saying you believe me?"

"Of course I believe you, Tristan. I was there! I pulled you out. In fact, I had already reported the incident to Principal Winter earlier this evening." A part of Tristan's heart jumped at this, wondering how the unpredictable headmaster would respond. "Currently, we are looking into who the culprit could possibly be, but it's been difficult. You have a very strong mind, young man, and that was one of the main reasons you're able to stand before me this evening. Thankfully, you were able to call out for help and resist long enough for me to arrive in time. I only was able to make out the barest of features on your assailants before they escaped."

"After pulling you out, you seemed fine and hadn't brought up what you witnessed. I was initially concerned that you had lost part of your memories of the event. I'm relieved to see that's not the case. In fact, your detailed explanation of what you saw has helped me immensely, and I should be able to get more information out to Principal Winter. While there's still much we don't know about these individuals, your memories will be vital in tracking them down. Thank you for your honesty."

Tristan felt a wave of relief over her words. "Thanks for listening, professor. It means a lot that you took the time, and I hope I've been able to help."

Before Tristan could leave, he felt that he still had one nagging question in his mind that needed to be asked. "Hey, professor. I had one other question to ask before I left."

"Of course, Tristan. Ask away."

"For some reason, you've fought for me from the very beginning. You were among the first to allow me step foot onto this campus. So my question to you is...why? Why did you say yes?"

Professor Tullage leaned back against the chair and seemed to think to herself for a bit, contemplating her response. "Tristan, do you know about my family history? Or the history of the Magnificent Seven?"

"I know a little bit from what you told us during your introduction. Everything I know about the Seven, I've read from the comics Mr. Peters gave me."

Tullage laughed softly and shook her head. "Let me give you a little bit of information that may answer your question."

"Your grandfather, Captain Thunder, had already formed the beginnings of what would eventually become the Academy as we know it. While the professors at the time taught the students during the school year, they spent their off months moonlighting as vigilantes, doing their best to be as discreet as possible. They had decided that rather than handle petty crimes within their respective cities, they would join forces and use their powers to combat the rising tide of evil metamorphs throughout the world. The seven individuals were your grandparents, Captain Thunder and Lady Starlet, and their five friends: Thoughtknot, Magnetron, Grizzly, Dr. Illusion, and Giant Girl."

"Together, they were a force to be reckoned with, and while they managed to keep their identities a secret, they did draw the attention of the U.S. government. After much debate, the government and the Seven agreed upon a pact. The U.S. would not interfere with the missions of the Seven to keep the hostile metamorphs at bay, in exchange for the government's protection and secrecy. This worked out for both parties. The government was able to get rid of some of the most powerful villains in existence, while the Seven were able to have the government cover-up their exploits and keep metamorphs under wraps.

"Sadly, the Seven would ultimately fall apart, allowing other metamorphs to fill in the roles of teaching at the Academy. I don't know for sure the final chapters of the other five, but I do know what happened to Dr. Illusion and Thoughtknot. The two had fallen in love during their time as a team, and upon retiring to the mountains of Colorado, they had me. I, too, was a child prodigy from a proud lineage of metamorphs.

"Unlike you, I had developed my powers from an early age, and I learned to master them at a level that surprised even my parents. I was immediately enrolled within the Academy and excelled from the moment I stepped foot on campus. Unfortunately, between the mounting pressures of my professors and the isolation of my classmates, I began to gradually lose my grip on my emotions, causing my abilities to become...dangerous. Both to myself and those around me."

"It took me a long time to get back to a point where I wasn't constantly drifting in and out of the psychic realm and unintentionally manipulating the minds of others. I had help...from a friend. With time and his guidance, I was able to regain control over my emotions and my mind. By the time I was allowed back into the Academy, several years had gone by. My old classmates had graduated, and I had to start fresh, a child prodigy no longer."

Professor Tullage gave a gentle smile and continued, "It took a long time for me to be at peace with where I am now. Our peers can be cruel, and our elders can place too much on our shoulders. It's never easy having to live up to your family name, Tristan. Embracing it is half the battle."

"What's the other half?"

"Learning to discover who you are without it."

Suddenly, the professor's head snapped to the side, her eyes focused intently on the nearby door. "Tristan...do you know if you were followed up here?"

Tristan immediately looked to the door and thought he heard the sounds of footsteps running away. Tristan quickly glanced at Tullage, who gave a nod of confirmation, and he immediately shot out of his chair and burst out into the hallway. He did a quick sweep of his surroundings but saw no one within distance. Nothing seemed out of place until his eyes caught the sight of the stairway door slowly closing shut. Tristan sprinted around the circular floor, closing the gap within a matter of seconds. He slammed open the door and could just make out the sounds of rushing footsteps below, as the unknown spy made their way down the stairwell.

Tristan flew down the stairs, jumping and skipping over as many as he safely could without breaking an ankle. He heard the door slam below him, and he cursed under his breath. By the time he reached the first-floor doorway, he was breathing heavily, but his adrenaline pushed him onward. He threw open the door and began to run to the sound of his target, audible footsteps coming from the area of the library. As soon as he turned the corner, Tristan ran smack into a seemingly surprised Gabriel, who was thrown back by the collision.

"Watch where you're going!" the flustered boy said, face red with anger.

"My bad, Gabe! I didn't mean to run into you! I was just—I had to—look, did you see anybody come around this way just a few seconds ago?"

"Seriously? It's like 8:30 right now. Nobody's trying to be here unless they have to. Stop running down the halls playing hide-and-seek with your friends."

"Dammit, Gabe! Did you see anyone or not?! I don't have time for your crap right now!" Gabriel stiffened up immediately, his facial expression hardening.

"You better check your tone, Tristan. There's no professors here to save you from getting swung on," he snarled.

Suddenly, Tristan grew wary, pausing to look around. It appeared that they were the only two people on the floor. "Where were you just now, Gabe?"

"Mind your own business, *yarpie*. The hell do you care?"

"I don't. It's just funny that you said no one just hangs out around here unless they need to. So why were you here?"

"Man, I was in the library studying! What's it look like, genius?"

Tristan glanced down at Gabriel's empty hands. "Where are your books?"

For a moment Gabriel paused, and Tristan could see his brain starting to spin. "I left them in the room by accident. What's it to you?"

"For some reason, I don't believe you, Gabe. You can either tell me what you were doing here tonight, or I'm going to have to take you up on that offer."

For a moment, neither of them moved, their bodies tensed and ready for the first person to throw a punch. Tristan watched Gabriel start to shift his weight to the left, and as Tristan began to prepare his counter, he heard the sounds of the cafeteria door open and a familiar voice call out.

"Hey, lovebirds! You two getting ready to slow dance?" Tristan turned to find Christian polishing off a handful of wings and smiling at the two boys. "Man, I come here for a snack, and I get a show too! This is turning out to be a great night! Go ahead and start it off, Trist! What you don't want, I'll finish!" he said with a menacing smile. Tristan could feel the temperature in the air slowly begin to drop.

Out of the corner of his eye, Tristan could see Gabriel shiver slightly. "Man, I don't got time for this nonsense. Y'all ain't worth the trouble." He marched past Tristan, making sure to bump his shoulder when he walked by. Watching the boy storm out of the front entrance, Tristan made a mental note: Gabriel wasn't simply on his list of suspects. Gabriel had now become enemy number one.

Chapter 19: Climbing the Ladder

As much as Tristan wanted to continue his pursuit of Gabriel and his mysterious mentor, it was not to be, the next few weeks a brutal exercise in multitasking when it came to his academic and athletic demands. Once they reached October, teachers began to plan ahead for their upcoming midterm exams which only helped increase stress levels. Competitively, Tristan and his team were facing a tough gauntlet, between two second-year teams and a third. The first week had them facing off against Team Eboue, a second-year team who were undefeated. Led by Manu Eboue, aka Granite, they were a physically imposing team.

Granite was from the Ivory Coast, and the tall, muscular boy could physically transform his skin into a granite-encased outer shell that was nearly impenetrable. Warthog, a short, swarthy boy from Arkansas was his second-in-command. Sporting a red Mohawk and tusks on either side of his mouth, what he lacked in size, he more than made up for with enhanced strength. The other two were less physically intimidating, however, they were technically superior when compared to their teammates. Dodger, an athletic boy with reddish-blond hair, had the ability of enhanced reflexes, while Acrobat looked like a brown haired gymnast, smaller but built like a tank. He had the gift of super agility, which allowed him to leap, bound, and tumble around his unprepared opponents.

Going toe-to-toe with them was what they wanted, but Tristan had other ideas. That Friday evening, their chosen environment turned out to be an intimidating, yet beautiful landscape within the northern mountains of Russia. While he despised the cold with a passion, a part of him was actually relieved, as he immediately analyzed the situation and devised a game plan that would potentially best their opponents. Deciding to perch above a rocky overhang overlooking a small lake within the mountainous region, Tristan and Belle eventually managed to draw out the aggressive Team Eboue to them. Unbeknownst to their opponents, Dan lay in hiding, and once Team Eboue had all gathered onto the mountain crag, the strongman let out a roar of fury before slamming his mighty fists into the ground beneath them.

Earth, ice, and stone rained through the air as Tristan flew backward from the force. He lost all sense of direction while his body spun like a rag doll, floating through the air before plummeting downward. The plan worked to perfection, Belle controlling the waters below them and manipulating the liquid tentacles that wrapped around the two before carrying them safely toward the shore beside the lake. Their opponents were not so fortunate, however, crashing into the frigid waters where Christian had been eagerly awaiting their arrival from the shore. Dipping his hands into the lake, he managed to turn Team Eboue into popsicles in under a minute, earning him an official total party knockout.

Following their match-up with Team Eboue, Tristan was worried that his friends were growing in confidence and knew he needed to stay on his guard to keep them from complacency. It didn't take long for his fears to be allayed, however. If Team Davids' matchup with Team Eboue was an exercise in tactical supremacy, their battle against third-year squad Team O'Brian that next week was their personal showcase.

Team O'Brian was led by Timothy, aka Shamrock, a diminutive Irishman whose unique ability was to shrink himself, which seemed cooler in idea than actual application. He was joined by Spike, a lanky Jamaican boy with blond dreadlocks, who was probably their best player. Spike could literally generate wooden spikes which protruded out of his skin and fired out like projectiles. Unfortunately, they were rounded out by two other classmates with subpar powers, Casper and X-ray. Aside from having less than intimidating aliases, Casper had the ability to run through solid objects, and X-ray had eyesight that caused him to see through everything.

Placed in a jungle scenario, Team Davids had to find their way across the hot, muggy landscape before spotting their opponents hiding in the foliage. Team O'Brian had taken a page out of Tristan's book and tried to bait them into falling into an ambush, but Tristan had already suspected as much. Before long, with Belle entrapping Spike in a globe of water, Dan hurling Shamrock through a tree, Christian solidifying Casper within a bramble of bushes, and Tristan overwhelming X-ray with a flurry of blows, the incompetent Team O'Brian were easily dispatched. As critical of a leader as he was, even Tristan struggled to nitpick about their win after that match.

They currently stood at 4-0, a great start, especially for a first-year team that no one had given any attention to. Tristan was determined to prove that their current run of form was no fluke. In fact, their next matchup would be the perfect opportunity to prove this fact.

They would be paired up against Team Carell in this third week of October, and Tristan knew that this would be their strongest test to date. Aside from being one of the prettiest girls among the second-year class, the auburn-haired Tiffany Carell, had a team of absolute quality with barely a weakness among them. Born with beautiful, greyish wings, Tiffany, or Windrider, was able to pull off speeds that rivaled even the fastest avian species.

Tiffany was joined by the Illusionist, Pause, and Pitch, all of which were more than capable of disrupting a team on their own. The Illusionist was a tall, gangly boy who wore lots of makeup and dressed in a purple suit usually reserved for a circus ringleader. He had the power of sensory manipulation, his pores emitting an undetectable toxin which could cause those around him to experience sensory disturbances, or illusions.

Pause was a short, pretty African-American girl who Tristan learned was a once highly recruited track sprinter. Her real power lay in her hands, however, not her feet. Similar to Christian, Pause had the ability to freeze her opponents, one touch able to hold an opponent for several minutes.

Last, but not least, was Pitch, a brunette bombshell with an amazing voice to match. Pitch had the power to hit vocal ranges which could literally incapacitate those around her. Her high-powered shrieks were known to break glass and, rumor had it, even stone when she really put her effort into it.

During the week, Tristan tried his best to not appear nervous in regard to their matchup, but by now his friends could tell when he was on edge. Of all the matches they'd faced, this one would be determined more based on individual skills. And as a leader, Tristan would need to learn to trust in his friends' abilities. Even though he wasn't sure how their next matchup would go, Tristan was sure of one thing: regardless of the outcome, his friends would give Team Carell a run for their money.

When Friday rolled around, Tristan was in a much better mood and more relaxed. They were scheduled to be the final matchup that evening, and Tristan couldn't have been more relieved once the bell rang, announcing their turn to enter the battlefield. He had heard that Professor Meulman was one of the guest judges tonight and was interested in seeing what the eccentric teacher could come up with. Whatever Tristan had imagined, he was not prepared for what came next.

As the battlefield began to shimmer and take shape, Tristan felt a subtle change in the climate. The room became quite windy and cold, the air slightly thinner and more difficult to breathe in. Then came the not-so-subtle change in altitude. The two teams could only watch as they were suddenly rocketed upward into the air atop two large platforms. As the platforms rose into the sky, each one split directly in the middle and pulled apart, separating each team in half. Tristan and Dan barely shifted over in time to avoid falling off their side of the platform while Belle and Christian drifted further away. Each platform that they stood upon began to expand, widening out to the point where they mimicked giant rectangles.

Once the room fully integrated into the designed scenario, Tristan came to realize what he was witnessing. Each group was now atop their own separate building, four in total with two team members per building. There appeared to be no way down into the structure itself, and they looked to be trapped on the rooftops of these skyscrapers. While there was plenty of space to move around, there appeared to be no way to actually get across to the next building.

Tristan walked over to the edge of the building and looked down. Rather than seeing roads or the tiny pinpricks of the people below, all he could make out were thick clouds beneath them. He felt uneasy at the sight, uncomfortable with the reality of not being able to view the ground below. Belle and Christian were about two hundred feet away from them, while the two parts of Team Carell were to his right. When the commencement bell rang overhead, Tristan's mind was a complete blank.

For a few minutes nothing happened, both teams utterly confused at the scenario before them. It seemed more like a brain teaser than an actual battleground. Tristan rubbed the back of his head, trying to force his brain to think. There was no way they would be placed in a scenario with no opportunity to actually battle. Thinking upon that, if there was any professor who would try to pull that off, it would, in fact, be Meulman.

While Tristan ran scenarios in his mind, Windrider unfurled her majestic grey wings and lifted up Pitch, both girls navigating toward Tristan's platform. A realization crept into Tristan's mind: Windrider had the ability to traverse across the battlefield, carrying her teammates over one at a time. The problem was, if she attempted to carry them over to Belle and Christian, she exposed herself to a long-range attack from one of Belle's water spheres. If she took the Illusionist or Pause to Tristan and Dan, they also were in danger of being quickly overpowered upon landing. However, by taking Pitch to Tristan and Dan, she had given herself the advantage with the one thing they couldn't compete with: a long distance attack.

All of this information flooded Tristan's mind, and he quickly turned around to his friend, who seemed unaware of the impending danger. It seemed like a thousand scenarios were racing through his mind all at once, but Tristan forced his brain to quickly analyze and process the one with the best probable outcome.

"Samson! I need you to listen to me and do exactly what I say, when I say it! Got it?!"

"Sure. What do you need?" Tristan took a deep breath and tried to steady his heartbeat. He had no idea if this was even possible, much less if it was going to work.

"You know how we have you train in the water? To see how strong you are and how far you can push back the waves?" Dan shrugged and nodded, his eyebrows raised quizzically. "I need you to do something similar. Except I don't need you to split the water. I need you to split the air." Dan frowned, understandably confused at the request.

"How the heck am I supposed to do that?"

"What's the loudest you've ever tried to clap?"

"Dude, you've gotta be kidding me..."

"Look, this is the best I've got. You can part a damn ocean. Now I'm gonna need you to disrupt the sound barrier before Pitch shatters our eardrums." Dan shook his head in disbelief.

"Is that all? Just push back a sonic wave with a round of applause? Anything else you want me to test out while we're here?"

Tristan grinned. "Well, funny you should ask..."

It took a total of fifteen seconds to pitch his idea to Dan, who had reluctantly agreed to go along. Tristan ran back to the end of the building and faced Dan, who was patiently waiting at the front to commence their defense. Windrider and Pitch were about fifty yards away at this point. Like he had anticipated, Pitch opened her mouth, and a loud scream emanated from her vocal cords. It was like getting slammed in the face with a garbage bag full of sand, Tristan nearly knocked off of his feet from its sheer power. A loud siren felt like it was going off all around him, the very air reverberating from the strength of her sonic blast.

Dan turned his watering eyes toward Tristan, his face showing concern regarding their plan. Tristan held out both hands to his friend and mouthed out the words "ten seconds". Dan nodded and awaited the countdown. Tristan followed the oncoming girls, trying his best to ignore the increasingly painful headache that was building up between his temples, and once they crossed the thirty-yard mark, he took a deep breath.

"Now!" Tristan screamed, although he knew Dan could not hear him, and began to sprint forward, praying he could time this correctly. Dan was facing the girls, looking slightly foolish as he attempted to clap his hands in their direction. *Seven, six...* Tristan was halfway across now, and it was getting more difficult for him to run, each sonic wave resisting his forward movement. Dan was growing red with effort, but Tristan could now make out the sounds of his hands. *Five, four, three...* Dan wound back, his arms slowly spreading out past his sides as his chest expanded outward. Tristan could see the faces of their opponents at this point, Pitch focused on maintaining her yell while Windrider looked simply confused. *Two, one...*

"NOW!" Tristan cried out, and whether he heard Tristan or not, Dan simultaneously brought his hands forward with all his might. There was a loud clap, like the sound of thunder, and the vibrating air before them simply stopped, splitting in half straight down the center. It was the strangest sight Tristan had ever witnessed, this cone of pulsating acoustics literally diverting itself around the two boys. The disturbance continued to push forward until it reached Pitch herself, causing her head to rock backward, momentarily stunned from the force of the opposing blast.

For about three seconds, Dan's response had stopped Pitch's voice dead in its tracks. That was all the time Tristan needed. At this point, he was already a step behind the now turning boy. Tristan lowered his torso, spreading out both arms before him, and the powerful grip of his friend's hands clutched the back of his suit. He felt Dan start to twist and a sudden forward surge, his feet leaving the ground. Tristan quickly threw his arms to his side, and Dan launched the boy at the unsuspecting girls with all remaining strength. Tristan squinted his eyes as the wind whipped across his face, his skin forced backward from the pressure of the air before him.

By the time Tristan managed to blink, he was mere feet in front of his oncoming targets. Instinctively, he adjusted his body, flipping his legs before him and simultaneously bending his knees. The next thing he knew, his knees were waist-deep in the gut of Pitch, who could only manage to let out a guttural whimper while the sounds of snapping ribs filled the air. The collision shocked the unsuspecting Windrider, and she reflexively let go of her current passenger. The force of the impact caused Tristan to flip back upright, and he immediately threw his arms forward, desperate to grab on to anything to stop him from joining Pitch. Luckily, he managed to get his hands around one of the steel boots of Windrider, and he held on to her as if his life depended on it.

Pitch barely let out a scream, fading away into the abyss below. Windrider roared in fury and immediately attempted to go after her friend, preparing to speed dive toward the clouds. Forcing his brain to stop thinking about where he actually was and what he was doing, Tristan thought back on to the past week's lessons in Defense Mastery and their focus on submission moves, the heel hook in particular. It was Tristan's best bet at the moment, but he needed to set himself up before he lost his opportunity when she dove.

As she started her downward arc, Tristan tugged down on Windrider's leg and threw his legs upward, flipping himself upside down. He immediately wrapped both his legs around hers, placing either foot into the bend of her knee. Keeping a tight lock on her leg, Tristan adjusted his hold on her boot, placing her foot underneath his armpit. His head was now facing the clouds below, and Tristan did his best not to throw up all over the place.

"Damn it, Davids!" Windrider screamed out while she soared upward, violently spinning and jerking around in an attempt to throw Tristan off of her. "What the hell are you thinking?! You're gonna get us both killed!"

Tristan looked up and grinned, despite himself. "I'm actually okay with that!"

With that, Tristan placed his forearm under Windrider's heel, cranking his arm up and toward his body. Arching his hip, Tristan applied all the pressure he could muster to the girl's ankle. Windrider responded the same way all the students had when having the move performed on them in class: she screamed in pain and tried to tap out. Except there was no tapping out here. There was only one way out of this arena, and that was the purpose behind Tristan's plan.

Within a matter of seconds, Tristan had correctly evaluated that he was essentially useless in this environment. He had no way of traversing to the other buildings and could not compete with the powers of his opponents should they find their way over. What he could do, however, was be a sacrifice. Both teams had a team member who could effectively travel themselves and others across the divide, and for Team Carell that person was Windrider. By losing Windrider, Belle would become the only person capable of moving people from building to building using her water control. Tristan had no doubt that Belle would figure out this fact, and if Tristan could take Windrider out of the match, he was handicapping them to the point where they could not recover. Even if that meant taking himself out while doing so.

Tristan heard the scream of pain coming from Windrider as she tried her best to break his hold, but the further she attempted to fight against it, the deeper he was able to get into the lock. Writhing in agony, Windrider began to plummet downward, unable to control her flight. Tristan didn't want to cause any structural damage, but at the same time, her thrashing was forcing him to hold on tighter to avoid being thrown off. The two dropped like rocks, the clouds below quickly closing their distance.

Continuing their speedy descent, Tristan smiled to himself, imagining what his friends and the audience were thinking right now. With Windrider's screams of pain still ringing through the air, the clouds finally dissipated and the cold steel ground appeared below, coming towards him like a train. *Yeah...this is definitely going to hurt.*

The first thing Tristan saw when he came to was not what he had expected. He was floating in some kind of warm, orange goo within a large tube made of glass, wearing only a hospital nightgown and breathing mask. He was attached to several lines of tubes and wires that connected to a variety of machines, and the liquid was pulsing, sending out a faint ripple that created a strange sensation throughout his body whenever it passed through. He appeared to be in a large steel room that was devoid of anything except for these monstrous devices. He felt like he was in some sci-fi monster laboratory, except that he was the alien creature the scientists were experimenting on. Unable to move and still trying to process everything that had happened, Tristan immediately closed his eyes and fell back into a world of darkness.

The next time he opened his eyes, Tristan was back in the familiar triage room that he usually frequented following a Battledome match. There was no one else around him besides a few nurses who were walking around checking equipment. He no longer had any crazy tubing or wires hooked up to him, and he was, surprisingly enough, feeling much better. Tristan looked up and down his body, shocked to see that he had no marks or scars from the event except for a few mild bruises here and there.

"Excuse me, ma'am?" he called out to the nearest nurse.

"Ah, Mr. Davids! Glad to see you're awake. That was a heck of an injury you sustained last match!"

"Is everything all right? I mean, am I all right?" he asked hesitantly.

"Of course you are, sweetie. Due to high altitude scenarios, the Battledome flooring is insulated with a special shock absorbing material, designed to instantly absorb all of the force of an impact and distribute it within itself. When it does, it simultaneously releases a gelatinous material which encapsulates the individual upon impact. You never actually strike the ground, but rather get placed in a suspended animation gel. Unfortunately, depending on the height, there's still a strong chance of suffering several broken bones and concussions. You suffered a few facial fractures, as well as a few ribs and your clavicle, but that's what the ICU is for. With our technology, we were able to non-surgically repair your tendons and bones within a few hours."

Tristan frowned. "So it's really only been a few hours?"

"Heavens no, dear! It's Sunday evening! We fixed and stabilized you within a few hours, but you've been sleeping it off for nearly two days! That's not unusual for that to happen, though. Usually the more traumatic the injury, the longer the patient needs to rest. Now, are we ready to get you outta here and back home with your friends?"

Tristan nodded enthusiastically at this, eager to get back to the comforts of his dorm and see his friends again. After being discharged, Tristan left the medical facility and was walking to the arena exit when he spotted his teammates up ahead. The moment they saw him, the three friends rushed over to greet Tristan, excited to see that he had fully recovered.

The four friends proceeded to head over to the Academy, where dinner was still being served. Once the team sat down to eat, they filled Tristan in on how the match had wound up finishing. After Tristan had taken out two of Team Carell's members, Belle and Christian had combined their abilities to create a frozen disk and, using Belle's water control abilities, transported the team across to where Pause and Illusionist awaited. It didn't take long for them to finish off the match, boosting up their place amongst the season standings.

Over the space of a weekend, Team Davids had become the talk of the school, viewed as serious contenders within the already talented first-year class. While he wanted to relax and enjoy the moment of triumph, Tristan knew this was fleeting, and that next week could be a much different story. Their last match before the bye week was against Team Parra, and Juan's team had a strong chance of pulling out the victory.

Juan's team was known to use advanced tactics, utilizing headsets to communicate with one another, which was not deemed an unfair advantage by the judges. Early on in the match, Juan would read the minds of their opposition, communicating the opposing gameplan to his teammates and guiding them through their counter tactics. While a highly effective technique, Tristan did note that this plan did have a major drawback: Team Parra was reliant entirely on Juan and had no real game plan of their own going into battle. Juan was their sole means of devising an improvised plan, and if anything happened to their communication lines, they were effectively neutered.

This was not to say that the team was powerless. Juan's powers had grown by leaps and bounds, and rumor had it that Professor Tullage herself was mentoring him in the art of telepathy and telekinesis. As for the rest of Juan's team, Hawk was a Native American boy with long, flowing hair and the ability to transform into a bird of any sort. Apollo was an athletic, muscle-bound student from Greece, whose perfect aim was an underrated ability that he used to great effect. Nearly every kind of potential projectile was a serious threat in his capable hands. Lastly, there was Hopper, who towered over her compatriots at 6'3. An avid basketball player, her ability to leap over long distances did not go unnoticed, although it was not nearly as effective in the Battledome as on the basketball court. Combined, the four made for a tricky matchup, but Tristan knew that whatever game plan he devised, it would need to require handling Juan above all.

One week later, Tristan found himself in a clichéd Asian dojo, complete with Chinese tapestry and bamboo flooring. They were a mere twenty feet from their opponents, which meant that once the bell rang to start the match, they would be attacking almost immediately. If they executed the plan well enough, they could have this match won within eight minutes, but if they failed to keep Juan distracted, they would be in a bit of a tricky situation. Tristan worked hard to clear his mind space before the beep went off. *Game time.*

Like a rocket out of a cannon, Dan and Belle immediately shot forward on the offensive. Belle, water vials uncorked, had already begun to form several large tentacles of water before her, which she was whipping forward at Juan. Running beside her, Dan, launched himself into the air before bringing down his meaty fists onto the ground in front of them. The force of the impact exploded the flooring ahead, sending debris flying in all directions and seismic waves flowing in the direction of the opposing team leader. Taken aback by the speed and ferocity of their focused attack, Juan immediately had to go on the defensive, running and dodging the oncoming whips and waves. Concerned for their team leader, Apollo, Hawk, and Hopper rushed to his aid, hoping to alleviate the pressure.

Tristan sprinted to the side of the dojo, curving around to flank their opponents, making sure to use the confusion to his advantage. While Belle and Dan continued their assault, Christian had fully transformed, and Tristan could feel the sudden drop in temperature as his friend closed his eyes and concentrated. This particular technique required a lot of focus, especially since Christian needed to target a particular area for their plan to work.

Belle and Dan were now about five feet from Juan. Hawk had morphed himself into a large falcon and was launching himself at Dan, his giant claws slicing gashes across the large boy's forehead. Apollo was throwing blunted projectiles as well, attempting to slow the tank down. Jumper was in midair, prepared to come down upon Belle, while Juan was frantically trying to avoid the attacks before him, under too much pressure to use his powers and read their minds.

Christian's chest continued to expand with air, and Tristan silently prayed that his friend could pull this off. As the two teams came together, Belle released her hold upon the water whips, commanding the vines of water to explode in the directions of their four opponents. The water sprayed across the faces of Team Parra simultaneously, who were unable to dodge the spray in time. While the spray of water was more surprising than painful, it served its purpose for Tristan's plan.

Opening his eyes, Christian threw his head forward and released a hiss of air. Without warning, Tristan felt the cold snap burst through the room, the temperature shift nearly bringing him to his knees. It was as if a wave of winter suddenly passed through the room, and Tristan had to force himself to keep running in order to avoid violently shaking from the oppressive cold. The students gave a collective shudder and stumbled from the snap, each one of them trying their best to reorient themselves.

As quickly as it had come, the wave passed, and the temperature returned to normal. However, Team Parra came to an unfortunate realization. Aside from their faces and clothes feeling like they were on fire from the frostbite, Belle's water blast had gotten all over their earpieces, which had completely frozen over after the sub-zero temperature drop. The team could no longer use their headsets for Juan's directives. Tristan could see the frustration on their faces as Christian now joined the fray, all three team-mates focusing their attacks on Juan.

Juan understood that without reading their tactics and communicating the game plan to his teammates, they were not going to stand a chance against Team Davids. So he did the only other option he had available to effectively accomplish their strategy. Juan focused his mental energy, extending out to all three of his companions and integrated their minds together into a mind meld. Unfortunately, Juan had no idea what was about to happen next.

Tristan had circled around Juan and was now behind the unsuspecting boy. In one swift move, Tristan slid across the floor, throwing out his front leg into a sweep behind his opponent. Juan's legs were lifted off the ground from the speed and force of the impact, sending him flat on his back. Tristan grabbed Juan's forearm with both of his hands, forcing the boy's wrist upward toward the ceiling. Tristan threw his legs across the body of his opponent, one leg over the neck while the other went across his waist. Tristan bent both of his knees, securing the boy's arm and elbow between his legs.

Juan's eyes widened, realizing what was about to happen. They had been practicing this technique all week in Defense class, and this next part would not be pleasant. Using Juan's chest as a fulcrum, Tristan pulled the boy's wrist toward his chest and applied upward pressure from his hips. The result was a full-on armbar, and from the immediate screams of Juan, Tristan had him deep in the hold already.

Remembering his own experience in the mind of The Shifter, Tristan had correctly reasoned that if the members of Team Parra were all psychically linked together, they would feel the emotions and sensations of the one whose mind they were directly linked to. That meant that if their host mind felt intense pain, that experience would be relayed to the others, effectively incapacitating the team in one fell swoop. What Tristan hadn't anticipated was the aftermath of his takedown and how powerful Juan's mind was.

Tristan heard the screams first, all three of Juan's teammates immediately holding the sides of their heads and joining their fallen leader in singing a synchronized ballad of pain. They each fell to their knees, eyes closed, and bodies writhing on the floor in pain. Tristan's teammates all looked at each other, stunned, while Tristan continued to apply pressure. Tristan was excited that his plan had worked and wanted to make sure he could close out the game for them, however, he soon began to pick up that something wasn't quite right. The banners hanging above were all waving around violently as if caught in a storm, despite there not being a breeze flowing through the dojo. Tristan wasn't quite sure, but he felt confident that the walls themselves were vibrating, and he noticed small cracks appearing along the bamboo flooring besides them.

What the—?! Before Tristan could finish his thought, a wave of psychic energy exploded out of Juan's small frame, nearly flinging Tristan across the room had he not been holding on so tightly to the boy's arm. Juan let out a bestial scream, sending psychic shockwaves shooting through the air, vibrating the world around them like the ripples of a pebble dropping into a pond. Except this was no pebble. This was a boulder.

Tristan felt himself holding on for dear life while the force of the waves tore apart their surroundings with their fury. He saw the other students forcefully thrown back several feet, some going straight through the bamboo walls. Tristan's heart began to race, a pounding headache suddenly interrupting his thoughts with a burst of pain. Images began to flash through his mind, although they were pictures he did not recognize. Tristan heard himself scream in pain and the images threatened to tear apart his brain. The psychic waves began to pick up, sending out rapid pulses before Juan finally blacked out, releasing a massive shock which forced Tristan to finally let go.

Tristan felt like he was gently floating into a state of oblivion, white light filling up his vision. Looking to the side, he could make out Juan's falling body beside him. The boy seemed back to normal now, his eyes staring back at Tristan, his mouth no longer frothing. In fact, the boy seemed to be smiling. Tristan then realized that Juan was in his normal clothes. In fact, Tristan was also in his regular clothing of jeans and a t-shirt. *This isn't real. We're in Juan's mind space.*

"YESYOUARE"

"Dang it, Juan! Cut it out! Just talk normally. You know that stuff freaks me out!"

Juan laughed next to him, his body straightening out so that his feet were once again beneath him. Tristan also felt his body righting itself before his feet eventually hit the powder-white surface beneath them.

The moment their feet hit the floor, the two boys were in a familiar bedroom, the small wooden walls around them filled with pictures of a young boy and his mother. For some reason, Tristan felt as if he had been here before. There was something intimate about this particular place, almost home-like. Scanning the room, Tristan recognized certain objects: his favorite stuffed rabbit halfway across the floor, the copy of "Goodnight Moon" that lay flat on the tiny nightstand, and his prized blue blanket bunched up on the rocking chair. It took Tristan a moment to realize that none of these thoughts were his own but were coming from his friend beside him. Tristan also realized at this moment that they were not alone.

Lying there on the bed was the beautiful Hispanic woman that Tristan had seen before in Juan's memories, only this time she was no longer exuding her gentle, vibrant smile. This time she seemed a shell of herself, her hair completely gone, thin as a rail, and pale, sickly skin that was covered beneath the covers of her bed. She had a look on her face that was trying to exhibit strength but could not hide the fact that she was extremely weak and in a great deal of pain. Beside her was the small, tan boy who was holding on to her, his tiny frame shaking with sobs of despair. *I shouldn't be here. This is personal. I shouldn't be watching this.*

"It's okay," Juan said, his eyes glazed over. "I don't mind. It's been a while since I've been here, and I think I'd rather have someone with me this time." Tristan swallowed hard and nodded solemnly.

The younger Juan was probably around five years old at the time as he held on to his dying mother. "Please don't leave me, mama! Please don't go away! I'll be good, I promise! I promise I won't move any more stuff! I can control it!"

"Shhh! Hush, my baby. It's okay. Mama will be with you always. This is not your fault. You've always been the best boy your momma could have asked for. But God is calling me baby, and I have to go now. You've been so good watching over your mama, and I'm so very proud of you." The woman gave Juan a smile before a wave of pain caused her to break into a grimace. Little Juan sniffled and looked into his mother's eyes.

"What will I do when you're gone? How am I supposed to control it? I can't do it without you!" The woman reached out and held his wet face in her hands, gazing into his eyes.

"My Juaninto, mi oso lindo, you will be strong like you always are. You are so strong, even without me. You have mommy's powers, but you are more powerful than I ever was. You are going to do incredible things one day, baby. Don't be afraid of the gifts God gave you. I want you to promise me you'll keep practicing."

"But mama—!"

"No buts! Promise me." The younger Juan reluctantly nodded, tears continuing to stream down his cheeks. "Good boy! Your grandmother is on her way now to come pick you up, okay? I want you to be just as sweet to her as you always were with me. Now, I need you to be strong, okay? Momma has to leave now..."

The younger Juan again nodded his head, wiping away the tears in his eyes. He took a deep breath and did his best to put on a brave face for his mother. The young boy stared back at the still gaze of his mother, stone-faced, hoping his feigned strength would help instill some in her as well. For what seemed like an eternity, the two locked eyes in a moment that would forever be ingrained in Juan's memories. Tristan wondered how long it took the little boy to realize that his mother was no longer blinking and that the gentle rising of her chest had come to a stop.

Tristan looked away from the scene, trying not to let his friend see the tears that were slowly falling from his eyes. "Cancer is a hell of an opponent," Juan said, his voice cracking with restrained emotion. "You can't punch it in the face. You can't verbally command it to stop. It just...keeps going. Like a wildfire spreading through a dry forest, consuming everything until there's nothing but death."

"Juan...I'm sorry..."

"She was a very powerful telepath, you know. I never met my father. He left us before I was even born. She was the one who taught me how to use my powers, helped me get them under control whenever I would get overwhelmed by my gifts. For a long time, I was afraid to use my powers after she died. I didn't think I would be able to control them without her. I felt lost. Then one day, my grandmother sat me down and told me that I couldn't hide from my abilities forever, that they were as much a part of me as breathing. She told me that learning how to use them was a way of honoring the woman who gave me the gift in the first place."

Juan wiped his eyes with the back of his hand, and when he looked back up, his face showed an inner strength that spoke more than words ever could. "So I did, Trist. I'm still working on it. But one day, I'm gonna be the strongest telepath out there. I'm not gonna let her down. I promised her I was gonna be strong, and I intend to keep my word."

"I have no doubt you will, Juan," Tristan said, placing his hand on his friend's shoulder. "You'll make her proud."

The room around them violently shook, pieces of the memory falling into a sea of nothingness. The tremors grew more violent, and Tristan could feel the ground beneath his feet start to collapse, his body going into freefall.

"Now, I think it's time I bring us back to reality. Man, my arm is gonna be sore..."

Tristan came to find himself still dazed, his opponent a few feet nearby, unconscious. Tristan managed to get himself sitting back up, only to realize that the bell had rung for the end of the match. With Team Parra all incapacitated from the mind meld, Tristan had managed to pull off the victory. While they were exhausted following their win, Tristan and his team assisted the medics in getting Team Parra onto the gurneys and into the Medical Bay, where they remained until their opponents recovered. Tristan and Juan exchanged subtle nods of acknowledgment, neither one bringing up what had happened during the mind meld. It was a pivotal moment, a sign of respect not just between two team leaders, but two friends.

The next week was a bye, and he gladly gave his teammates a much needed week off. They had come through a tough gauntlet of matches, barely hanging on, but victorious nonetheless. They would face Team Perrotta the following week, and Cynthia was making every effort to remind Tristan of this fact every chance she got. Listening to her egg on Dan during class, he couldn't help but smile while the two bickered back and forth over whose team was better. In the end, he didn't mind the playful banter. He understood what drove it. Some were here to discover themselves. Others had come to fulfill a promise they had made to someone long ago. At the end of the day, they were all here to become better than they were prior to setting foot on this campus. And for Tristan, the sky was the limit.

Part Three: To Be a Hero

Chapter 20: The Legion

It seemed as if it were all a dream. For once in Tristan Davids' life, everything seemed to be firing on all cylinders. The bye week had begun, and Team Davids was the talk of the school, finding themselves in fifteenth place among the Battledome contenders. All the kids were buzzing about this, and Tristan and his friends soon found that more and more students were joining their mess hall table for friendly chats and even advice.

Christian usually found himself talking with the prettiest girls at the table, while Dan would get into his hourly yelling matches with Cynthia. Tristan always found the dynamic between the two fascinating: Cynthia, the only one who seemed to be able to get a rise out of the usually stoic Dan, while Dan seemed to consistently get the temperamental girl to end their bouts in a fit of laughter.

In Belle's case, all of this newfound attention naturally brought on a slew of upperclassmen who were eager to court and impress the first-year beauty. This threw Tristan off at first, the young man finding himself incredibly jealous before he realized how childish he was acting. They were really good friends, nothing more, and he was the team leader. Besides, it's not like they were dating or anything.

Ever since their matchup, Tristan and Juan had also become good friends. The two boys usually sat next to each other during Professor Tullage's class, alongside Sofi and Brandon, who had also continued to develop their friendship with Tristan. In fact, aside from his rivalry with Gabriel, Tristan had grown quite fond of Team Jackson.

Overall, things were looking up for Tristan. That is, until the following week, when Thursday rolled around, and they received some disturbing news.

"Did you hear about The Legion?!" Tristan and his friends turned to Will, who had just sat down excitedly at their table. It was halfway through lunch period, and the four friends had been sitting together with Team Perrotta, bantering amongst themselves over who was going to win tomorrow night's battle.

"What are you talking about, Will?" Cynthia asked, eyebrows raised.

"I was emailing my parents this morning, and they gave me a heads up to be extra careful out here. Apparently, The Legion has resurfaced and are planning some massive attack! No one knows what they're going to hit or where, but knowing their M.O. it's gonna be big!"

Tristan was thoroughly confused at this statement and looked around to see whether or not anyone else shared in his puzzlement. To his surprise, expressions of fear and uncertainty were upon many of their faces, even Christian. The only ones who seemed at a loss were himself and Dan.

"Not to seem like a total outsider here, but am I the only one who has no clue what that means? Who the heck is The Legion, and why should we be scared of him? Or her, not trying to be sexist."

"Seriously, Davids, we need to dig you out from underneath that rock you've been living under for the past sixteen years," Cynthia groaned. "The Legion isn't a he or she. It's a 'they'. And *they* are the largest, scariest group of super villains ever assembled."

Belle nodded beside him, chiming in, "They are basically super-powered terrorists that were big in the nineties before the authorities started catching up to them. If what Will says is true, we're in for some dark days ahead."

"Why is that? Why should we be worried?" Tristan asked.

"Because The Academy has always been a major adversary toward The Legion. However, they've never managed to set foot upon Island X thanks to its defenses. But that doesn't mean it couldn't happen. They've gotten close before, and they've had plenty of time to prepare if we are truly the next target," Emily answered.

An air of tension seemed to hang over the table following this, while Tristan's mind did a double take. *Wait a second, the shadows I had seen a few weeks ago spoke about The Legion! Had I stumbled upon their plans to take down the Island?* Tristan exchanged glances between his teammates, the shared looks on their faces letting Tristan know they were wondering the same thing.

After walking outside to their usual spot along the campus lake, Tristan and the team recapped what they had just heard from Will.

"Dude, if what he said was true, your vision makes more sense. There definitely has to be a mole on campus if The Legion is trying to make a comeback and take over this place," Christian said, glancing around to make sure they were not being overheard.

"We definitely need to get back to investigating what actually happened that day. We haven't made any headway at all since that week," Dan muttered. He was right. They hadn't even thought about the events of that week recently, their focus entirely on the slew of Battledome matches and maintaining their grades.

"What's there to investigate? It doesn't take a rocket scientist to know Gabe is in on this! He was there that night spying on Tristan and Tullage and couldn't even provide a decent alibi when he was confronted. I say we keep tabs on him ourselves and wait for him to slip up," Christian replied.

"Slow down, Sherlock," Tristan said. "We need to make sure he's our guy before we devote what little free time we have to stalking the kid. I can't stand being on the same campus as the guy, let alone wasting my life following him around if we don't need to."

"I agree," Belle responded. "Besides, didn't Professor Tullage say that she and Principal Winter would be investigating the incident?"

"Yeah, but who knows if they've found anything. Personally, I've never heard of The Legion since my family isn't involved in the metamorph community. I don't know about y'all, but I'd like to learn more about what it is we're facing," Dan said.

"Couldn't agree more, Dan. I think the next step is to take a look and see what we can dig up on The Legion. We have time to run over to the study hall before class. You guys interested?" The group nodded unanimously and began to walk back to the Academy.

The study hall was nothing short of a marvel of modern bookkeeping. Upon walking through the double doors, there was nothing but rows of books as far as the eye could see within the massive square-shaped room. The books were stored on mobile shelving units that were compressed against one another and ran along a magnetically powered track.

The dimly-lit room had a ceiling mimicking the night sky regardless of the time of day, creating an ambiance of tranquility and focus. The back of the room had a glass partition, beyond which was the school computer lab. The lab also contained tables and individual cubicles for studying, all of which were usually occupied by the large number of students who constantly rotated in and out of the hall.

Tristan found that fortune was on their side when they spotted the lone empty computer on the other side of the room. Walking through the automatic glass doors, the four made a beeline through the tables around them before crowding around the computer together. Tristan inputted his login information and awaited for network confirmation to utilize the school's online resources. Once Tristan's access was confirmed, he proceeded to go into the school's information database.

The database search engine was like Google, only a million times faster and more comprehensive. Tristan typed in "The Legion" and awaited the computer's response. For a few moments, nothing happened, which was strange given how quickly the database usually ran. To their surprise, two words in red font popped up on the screen instead: "Access Denied". The four looked at each other with confused expressions. *Access denied? Since when?* It wasn't like they were trying to look up anything illegal. Tristan tried again, thinking that it was just a mistake on the computer's part, but once again the two words shone across the screen.

"Here, let me try. Maybe your login isn't working right for some reason," Belle suggested. Tristan gave up his chair while she attempted to access the information through her login. Once again, they encountered the same result, only this time it said: "Access denied. Please see administrator if you wish to continue, otherwise, database privileges will be revoked."

"What the hell is this?!" Christian exclaimed. "They're seriously gonna revoke our access if we keep trying? This can't be real!"

"Hmm, this ain't right. Maybe we should try other keywords. Like 'metamorph terrorists' or 'supervillain groups," Dan suggested.

The team tried to go around the security detail, utilizing other phrases to find any information on The Legion, however, they had no luck. Any link that appeared to have some shred of information even related to The Legion came up "Access Denied", much to the chagrin of the four friends.

"This is crazy! I've never seen this happen before!" Belle exclaimed, throwing up her hands in frustration.

"Looks like we stumbled upon something we aren't supposed to know," Dan replied ominously.

"Yeah, but the question is...why? Why are they so worried about us finding out about these guys? What are they hiding?" Tristan questioned.

Suddenly, the school bell rang, snapping the group out of their thoughts. "All right, we'll try and figure this out later. Let's plan on meeting after class in the common room to see if there's anything else we can think of," Tristan decided.

The team agreed on this, and they quickly left the study hall. Class couldn't be over soon enough for Tristan, and after changing his clothes, he joined his friends in the common area. Upon entering, Tristan spotted his friends circled around Belle's laptop. They glanced at Tristan, pointing to the screen before them.

"Did you read the email?" Belle asked.

"What email?"

"Battledome has been canceled tomorrow, and the games have been rescheduled! Emergency meeting, bro," Christian replied.

"What?! They rescheduled our match?! Cynthia's gonna blow a fuse!"

"Probably literally," Dan said with a smile. Tristan walked over to where his friends were sitting and read the email that was open before them:

"Attention, urgent message to all Academy student and staff: There will be an emergency meeting scheduled for tomorrow, November 2nd, in the amphitheater. The meeting will begin promptly at 8:00 PM. Please make sure you are all there on time as this meeting is MANDATORY. Those who fail to attend will be disciplined accordingly, unless permission has been cleared by Principal Winter himself. As a result of the meeting, Battledome matches that had been scheduled for this week have been rescheduled. All those affected will receive a follow-up email in regard to your new match date. Thank you and have a safe and enjoyable time on campus!

Ms. Dorothy Dorregard"

After re-reading the message a second time, Tristan found himself stunned at the news. "Since when do we have school-wide emergency meetings? When was the last time something like that happened?"

"Probably decades, at least. They only assemble everyone on the island if it's something major. Like 'impending danger' major," Belle responded.

"Like 'potential Legion' danger?" Tristan asked, raising his eyebrows. Belle slowly nodded, the group exchanging glances and thinking back to what they had experienced in the library.

The following evening, Tristan and his friends hurried over to the assembly in the hopes of finding a good seat. Even thirty minutes early, Tristan could see that they would have to sit near the back of the amphitheater. The area was filled to the brim with staff and students, all eager to hear what the commotion was all about. Tristan spotted his brother and sister on the stage seated alongside the other professors, and he gave them a wave before walking over to where Juan was sitting, their group having saved Tristan's seats.

Once all of the seats were filled, Principal Winter stood up and strode to the front of the stage. His cold, blue eyes swept across the audience, confirming that everyone was accounted for. The imposing man cleared his throat and took a breath before beginning.

"Ladies and gentlemen of the staff, my wonderful students, thank you all for being here. I wish it were under better circumstances, however, that is not the case. As many of you have heard, there have been whispers of a re-emergence of a group of notorious metamorphs known as The Legion. The group was known and responsible for a plethora of terror strikes throughout the world and were hunted down for years by every major security force aware of their existence. Ultimately, a group of metamorphs, led by myself, was able to track them down and eventually confront them. While we were unable to capture them, the group was forced underground and eventually disbanded at the start of the new century. Unfortunately, it seems that our victory was premature."

Tristan heard several audible gasps from the audience around him as the principal continued. "There have been reports and visual confirmation of The Legion openly attacking a top-secret military outpost in North America. While we are still unsure of what purpose this recent activity served, we know what their mission has always been: to bring about the downfall of mankind and force us into an age of metamorph supremacy as their rulers."

"Because we have opposed them in the past and stand for the equality of all peoples, the Academy has often been a focus of their ire and hatred. In fact, we have it from a trusted source within the school that there have been sightings of a potential mole who is currently working with the terrorist organization. It is, therefore, my duty to ensure that you are all aware of the dangers that lie ahead and to make certain that you are all protected from these individuals. This Academy has never been breached by any opposing force since its inception. I don't intend to allow it to happen now."

Principal Winter turned and nodded at Ms. Dorregard, who pressed a button on the side of the stage, allowing for the projector screen to roll down and the video to begin. At once, the massive screen was filled with a grainy photo of five cloaked individuals, who appeared to be standing within a laboratory facility. All around them lay shattered equipment, scattered bullet shells, and dead bodies strewn across the floor.

"The Legion was officially formed sometime around the late 80s during a time in which metamorphs had decided to fully distance ourselves from human relations in order to preserve our peace and anonymity. Comprised of several loosely affiliated cells to avoid detection and capture, the main group of the Legion consisted of the five cell leaders: Jaws, Firestarter, Crystal, Bullet, and their 'Overlord' Shadow. The members came from all walks of life throughout the world, some even former students of the Academy that had been led astray by dreams of grandeur and promises of power. The Legion used fear and violence in order to spread their agenda and influence other metamorphs into joining their cause."

Winter pressed a button on the clicker he held in his hand, and the screen shifted to a terrifying image of a creature...no, a man, whose pale, wrinkly face covered the screen. The cloaked man had a hood over his bald head and had no hair at all throughout his face. His sunken eyes were red and beady, resembling those of a shark. He had no nose, instead two large slits where one should be, and another slit that cut through his lips, revealing the lines of tiny razor sharp teeth within. He looked like a monstrosity from some poor kid's nightmare.

"The image before you is of Jaws, whose main focus has always been on eco-terrorism. He was born in Russia, although we do not know much more about his background other than this. His birth name is Petr Stolvich, and he was born into a family of powerful arms dealers for the Russian mob. His metamorph abilities are breathing underwater, enhanced speed and strength while underwater, and enhanced teeth and nails, although there are reasons to believe the latter was surgically done to further his mystique."

The image on the screen shifted again, revealing yet again another disturbing sight. The photo was of a massive man, whose tall, muscular build dwarfed that of even Dan. His head and eyebrows were shaved, and he appeared to have tribal tattoos all over his exposed upper body. He looked like an Olympic bodybuilder with his physique except for the bizarre contraption he had attached to his body and the sheer volume of burn marks and scars that covered his face and body. The device started at his face and resembled a gas mask that began from the bridge of his nose and wrapped around his head, leaving only his dark, crazed eyes exposed. Several thick, long tubes ran from his face mask, along his arms, and down to a wrist strap that wrapped around both his hands. He made for quite an intimidating presence.

"Charles 'Chucky' Smith, aka Firestarter, is the next member of The Legion to be focused on, his main area of expertise being arson. Born in New York, Charles had no problems using his brute strength and savagery to intimidate those around him, finding odd jobs here and there as an enforcer for street gangs. Charles' ability to generate fire from his mouth would have made him scary enough, however, it went one step further on the day he literally blew off his entire lower face in a deadly firefight. He managed to wipe out an entire city block with his exploits, but the end result was the permanent ravaging of his face and body. He managed to find an underground plastic surgeon who operated on his face and created this contraption you now see before you. The device is designed to allow Firestarter greater control over his abilities, channeling the flames he breathes into the tubes that run from the mask and out from the straps on his wrists. The wrist straps act as literal flamethrowers and can handle any high-intensity blasts he sends out. He is a pyromaniac in the truest sense and is usually their man when it comes to acts of mass destruction."

The slide transformed into the next member of the terror outfit, this time displaying a beautiful woman in her thirties, whose pale white skin nearly matched her white hair. She had icy, blue eyes, thick, black eyeliner and dark, red lipstick that was in stark contrast to her complexion. The seductive smile she gave toward the camera gave Tristan chills more than it excited him, a dark, evil presence felt behind the look.

"This is Kiana Richardson, better known as Crystal. One of the newer members to the group, her ambitious and cold-blooded nature has allowed her to quickly climb up the ranks to become one of Shadow's favored soldiers. She was born in Texas to a family of wealthy cattle ranchers. Despite her affluent upbringing, Crystal was often caught on the wrong end of the law growing up, which her family made sure to have covered up. They attempted to have her enrolled in the Academy, however, she barely made it a month before dropping out, deciding that the school was not 'fit' to suit her needs. We believe that during her time here, she managed to get into contact with Shadow himself, who recruited her due to her potential. Her ability is seemingly simple but incredibly powerful. She has the ability to generate crystals and can summon forth the mineral out of nothing, helping fund the Legion financially through many of their operations. While she excels in the field, she is mainly used as a planner and organizer of The Legions attacks, taking on a more administrative role under Shadow."

Winter clicked for the following image, which showed a shorter, stocky man in a bizarre chrome-colored outfit that ran from the top of his head to his feet. The one-piece leotard came over his head and ended below his nose to partially cover his face, leaving his eyes and mouth exposed. On his hands were devices that appeared to be brass knuckles, except they were larger and came together to form one large point at the ends, like a triangle. The muscles beneath his suit could easily be seen, indicating this was a man who was in peak condition and could hold his own in a fight.

"Originally from Australia, Clarence Thomas, the metamorph known as Bullet, is a key member of The Legion and their main assassin. All information regarding his family and upbringing has been wiped from any known database, making him extremely difficult to track. This man has the gift of super speed that can only be accessed in short bursts, firing himself similar to a projectile. Using the custom made bracers around his knuckles, he can literally fire himself toward his victims, using his speed to impale them upon the ends. The end result is a wound similar to a shotgun round and just as deadly. Bullet has led the Legion's special ops group, specializing in the takedown of high ranking government officials and any deemed a high-risk threat. Which brings us to our final slide."

The last photo was difficult to make out. It was taken amidst what appeared to be an attack upon the government compound. It looked like the photo was taken at night without the use of a flash. Soldiers were running around with either terrified or pained looks on their faces. It was total chaos, the men attempting to escape from the confines of the room. Upon further inspection, Tristan discovered that there were in fact lights stationed above the room, however, their luminescence was completely neutralized by the darkness. It was then that Tristan realized that the darkness was coming from within the room itself, the center to be precise. If he looked closely, Tristan could barely make out the figure of a man in the middle of the spreading darkness. The figure had a tall, thin outline with long hair flowing from his head. All other distinguishing factors could not be revealed, but even from here Tristan could recognize the familiar outline as the one he had seen earlier this semester.

"This is Chandler Robbins, the group leader of The Legion. He goes by the name Shadow, which is fitting as his powers allow him to manipulate and solidify shadows. He is nigh impossible to track, able to cloak himself in darkness, and can use the shadows around him to shield and conceal him while attacking his victims. He is a master manipulator, as twisted as the shadows he controls. He is highly paranoid and compulsive, requiring perfection with any planned attack. He, too, was a highly recruited student for our school, however, his beliefs were deemed too radical and anti-human even then, and he was eventually removed. He is a big proponent for human subjugation and metamorph domination within our world, his life dream to establish a new world order in which metamorphs rule based upon their power levels, where the strongest determine the fates of those around them. 'Societal evolution' he calls it, and he truly believes it will spawn a golden age of metamorph development."

Winter turned to the students, stepping forward to the edge of the stage. "Needless to say, these are dangerous times. While my goal is to educate the students, the safety and protection of all those under my care is first and foremost. Starting tonight, we will be under an advisory condition, which means there will be a daily enforced curfew of 9 PM. All students caught out of the dorms past 9 will face disciplinary action for their disobedience. Battledome matches and after-school classes and programs will modify their schedules accordingly to meet these conditions."

"Also, starting tonight, all Level 1 students will be assigned nightly patrol duties alongside the professors. While we do not expect anything to come of this, it is our duty to ensure the safety and well-being of all those on this island. We ask that you be careful when out late at night and show prudence when utilizing our information network so as not to expose yourselves to any potential danger. We are all a family here on this island and must look out for one another. If you see or hear any suspicious activity, please make sure this is reported immediately to our staff or myself directly. I thank you all for your time and attention this evening. Have fun, study hard, and above all else, be safe."

With that final statement, Winter walked off the stage, leaving Professor Cam to take the microphone. "You are all dismissed, however, the following students are to remain behind in order to receive their patrol assignments. In alphabetical order: Aftershock, Axle, Bastion,..."

Tristan and his friends stood up, joining the rest of the crowd in exiting the amphitheater while the Level 1 students were listed off. Walking back to their dorms, Tristan and his friends reviewed the meeting.

"I guess it makes sense why they blocked us from learning about The Legion. If their main way of recruiting is through manipulation and propaganda, then it would be understandable that the Academy would try and neutralize it," Dan said.

"Still, knowledge is power. And the more we know about these guys, the more equipped we'll be should they ever try to attack," Belle replied.

"Man, it's crazy," Christian said shaking his head, "I've never seen metamorphs with power levels like them. They're way more dangerous than your average baddies, for sure."

Belle nodded in agreement. "Power 6 levels from what it looked like, maybe even 7."

Tristan turned to look at Belle. "Hey, Belle, what's that even mean anyway? 'Power 6' or 'Power 9'? I've heard people mention that phrase before."

"It's an ability ranking system that was actually designed by your sister, Tristan. I would've thought you'd known that!"

"There's a lot I'm still learning about my family," Tristan shrugged.

"Oh, well, it's no big deal!" she began, slightly embarrassed. "It just looks at a metamorph's abilities and grades them based on several factors: functionality, skill level needed to master it, intensity, and a few other miscellaneous categories. Power 1 is the lowest and represents those whose abilities closely mimic those of our human brethren. Will would be a great example of this. Power 2 through 4 are where pretty much all the kids at school stand. Power 5 and above are those who have exceptional abilities beyond the average metamorph. As much as it pains me to say this, Gabe may have that potential, for sure. As for Power 9, those don't exist anymore."

Tristan raised his eyebrows. "What do you mean?"

"There hasn't been a Power 9 metamorph since...well, your grandfather. He was the last of them. Power 9s were basically the gods of old. Those whose powers could literally transform the face of the earth and dominate its inhabitants. Power 9s have either all died or their gene pool has become so watered down that they no longer are created. Why, where did you hear about that?"

"Uh, not sure. Anyway, like you had said, the more we know about The Legion, the more prepared we can be if they try to attack," Tristan said quickly, aiming to change the subject before Belle pried any further.

Tristan stopped walking, the group following suit, and he scanned the area to make sure there wasn't anyone around to listen in. Once he was sure that they were out of earshot of anyone else, Tristan looked at his friends and said, "Listen, we all know that there's a mole on this island. If we discover who the mole is, we stop The Legion before they even step foot on our home. I say we continue our investigation and try and see if we can smoke out the traitor. Are you guys in?"

"Bro, you don't even have to ask. You know we have your back," Christian replied, the rest nodding in unison.

"Good. Because I don't know about you, but this Academy is the best thing that's happened to me in a long time. For once in my life, I feel like I've finally found a place where I belong, and I'll be damned if I let those assholes run through here and tear it down. I don't care what power ranking they are, they step foot onto our home...we're taking them down."

Chapter 21: Midterms

Tristan could tell that the next week was going to be a strange one from the very beginning. The entire school was on edge following the meeting. Tristan's parents had emailed him to be careful but had otherwise not given away any further information. Being on the Council, they were among those investigating the whereabouts of The Legion's locations and couldn't disclose anything to Tristan.

The cold feeling of the school was further enforced by the weather around them. It was the beginning of November, and the temperature was generally around the 30s at this point. Additionally, midterms were only a few weeks away, increasing the feeling of stress that was pressing down upon the students.

Between the upcoming midterms and his investigation into the mole, Tristan barely had time to look over their opponents for the week. They would be facing Team Kewell, a fourth-year team with a poor record of 2-4 and a reputation for poor sportsmanship. Led by Barry Kewell, a muscular, brown-haired Australian boy, the team was often discombobulated, each member doing their own thing under Barry's loose leadership. Barry, or Frostbite, had the ability to generate ice waves from his body, using them to either create a protective layer around his body or as an offensive weapon to freeze his opponents. He was joined by Projection, a tall, heavy-set girl with long black hair who could project visible images from her mind, Hedgehog, a short, small-framed Indian boy with the ability to generate long needles from his skin, and Cleric, a blond, surfer-looking boy from California who could heal others through his touch. Tristan wasn't too concerned about game-planning against them. Besides, there wasn't much to see on film as they rarely used tactics.

By the time Friday arrived, Tristan was ready to just get the match over with in order to get back to studying. Battledome season was nearly over, and Tristan's team had Team Perrotta as their final opponent before the playoff selection next week. If they won today, Team Davids could potentially lock their position in the playoffs, a feat no one had predicted at the beginning of the year. After going through their usual pre-game routine and entering the arena, Tristan was fairly certain he would be back in the dorms looking over his notes within the hour. What came next, nobody could have seen coming.

It began like any other match, the environment settling on a rainy, grassy plateau surrounded by stormy waters in what appeared to be Scotland. The opposing team wasn't visible from where they stood which gave Tristan some time to develop a plan. The party split into two groups, Dan and Tristan going after Team Kewell in an attempt to lure them back to Belle and Christian, who would be lying in wait to spring their trap.

About ten minutes into their reconnaissance mission, Tristan and Dan heard the cries for help coming from one of the edges of the massive rock. Near the end of the plateau's border was a downward sloping ledge that could be used as cover, and from where they stood, Tristan could see that the ground had completely given way due to the torrential downpour, causing a mudslide into the rocks below. That was where they spotted Team Kewell desperately trying to rescue one another from falling into the waters.

Ordinarily, this would be a good thing for Team Davids, however, glancing down at the rocks, Tristan spotted what they were so afraid of. There appeared to be a strange shimmer and static around them, allowing for a brief glimpse of the metallic rods and structures beneath. *There's a malfunction allowing for a break in the simulator!* That meant that if they wound up falling, they would no longer be landing in an area that contained shock absorbing material. They would be landing on actual, hard metal! *This is not good!*

Tristan found himself sprinting towards the chaos, Dan calling out behind him. He managed to reach the screaming students in time, who were clinging to one another amidst the mud and rain in a desperate attempt to form a makeshift human rope to pull themselves out of the mudslide. Tristan clasped the hand of Frostbite just as the boy was losing his grip on the wet ground. Tristan suddenly felt an onrush of cold flood his body, and the fear on Frostbite's face turned into an expression of pure satisfaction.

"Sorry about the mix-up, mate, but ya gotta do what ya gotta do, right? Thanks for the help!" With that, Frostbite pulled on Tristan's now frozen body, throwing him down the slope below. While he fell, Tristan could now see that Team Kewell had been pretending all along. Hedgehog was using the spines on his stomach to lodge himself into the ground and stabilize the team as they held on to him. Projection was at the end of the human chain, facing the water, where Tristan suspected she was creating the illusion of a malfunction within the simulator.

Falling helplessly, Tristan couldn't help but feel unbridled rage within the pit of his stomach. He couldn't believe that they had pulled a cheap move like that on them and that he had fallen for it. At least he didn't have much longer to dwell on it as the water rushed to meet his face.

It was an unfortunate way to record their first loss and wound up being a poor battle overall. After incapacitating both Tristan and Dan, Team Kewell spent the rest of the time hiding from Belle and Christian until time ran out. From what Tristan heard from the others, it was the first time in decades that a team was actually booed both during and after the game. Even the commentators seemed appalled by the poor showing.

The teams did not shake hands following the match, Tristan and his friends still fuming over what had occurred. It was an unwritten rule amongst the students that if ever there was a chance of actual life-threatening emergency within the dome, the safety of the students came first over the chance of winning. Baiting a trap was one thing, simulating a potentially deadly event was quite another.

Tristan didn't have much time to dwell on the loss, using the rest of the weekend to scour the island in an attempt to locate the mole's meeting spot. Tristan tried his best to see if there was any place he could identify from his vision, but there were still parts of the island that the first-years didn't have access to, the rest barricaded by metallic gates and barriers.

Monday soon arrived, and Tristan received the study guides for their upcoming midterms, which he was not looking forward to. Professor Fisher's midterms would be covering everything in World History from the Byzantine empire up through the Roman. For Meulmann's class, they would be writing reports on the subject of mythology with their choice on the topic itself. Professor Tullage would also be doing a midterm paper on the topic of good and evil and the motivational theory behind both. Tristan wasn't overly concerned when it came to these three classes. He was currently hovering between an A and a B+ average within those courses, and he felt fairly confident that he would do well in the next few weeks if he studied hard enough.

Tuesday's classes, on the other hand, were of more concern. Professor Stellios would be doing a live practical for her midterm, the students needing to sign up for individual time slots for private evaluations. Their midterms would be focused on teamwork-based testing, each student pairing up with a partner to demonstrate their ability to combine powers effectively. Tristan had already determined that Belle and Christian would be best paired together, seeing as how their powers were more likely to complement one another, while Tristan would be partnered with Dan.

Professor Coffman would also be doing a practical exam, during which they would be tested with a "surprise" attack, the form of which would vary from student to student. Although the idea of an unpredictable test was intimidating, Tristan was surprisingly eager to see what his professor would devise.

That week, Tristan and his friend spent much of their time juggling responsibilities. With midterms starting to take precedence, they needed to be smart with how they spent their time, between their investigation and preparing for the last match of the Battledome season. Cynthia made sure to remind Tristan and Dan that in no way would she be holding back on Friday and that she was looking forward to "sending Dan crying home to his corn fields". Dan would politely remind her that they raised dairy cows on his farm, sparking yet another back and forth between the two.

Before he knew it, Friday had arrived, and Tristan was ready for the evening's fireworks. Win or lose, this was going to be a great battle. Both teams seemed eager to prove themselves against the other, and after all of their time training alongside one another in class, they knew what to expect. Despite their friendship, both squads had plenty on the line to fight for. Despite not being guaranteed a spot, Team Perrotta's record of 5-2 could put them in contention for a wild-card spot if they won.

Smoke and Fog had become quite a nuisance for opponents, the twins having learned to consciously shift in and out of their gaseous forms. The

Designers had even developed a fabric that would phase with the boys, allowing them to pass through solid objects without losing their suits on the other side. Camo had also grown into her own, becoming quite adept at this stage at blending into her surrounding, alternating shades of color at will. Often used for reconnaissance work and setting traps, she was exceptional at sneaking around and ambushing their opponents.

As for Detonella, there were few students at the school with the sheer power level she contained. From where she was at the beginning of the year, Detonella had grown by leaps and bounds. She was now able to control her blast radius much better, varying the intensity and width of her explosions. Combined with her steadfast leadership and airtight tactics, she was a force to be reckoned with, a statement that could easily be applied to the group as a whole.

The evening's matchups drew a large crowd, nearly every student in attendance to see who would be making it to the coveted playoff spots. When the two teams walked out to the field, the crowd was at a fever pitch. Tristan and his team faced their opponents, locking eyes with Detonella while they waited for the scenario to generate. The girl was all business tonight, their friendship on hold for the next few minutes until that final bell chimed signaling the end of their battle.

During the last few seconds of the countdown, Tristan lost sight of Team Perrotta. The environment around the students appeared to form the top floor of a five-story building surrounded by a small parking lot within a major metropolitan development. The scene outside reminded Tristan of downtown Miami, the oppressive heat from the midday sun reflecting dangerously off the grey concrete and black asphalt below.

Tristan looked around the room, scanning for any sign of their opponents as well as any positional advantages they could utilize. From what he could tell, they were completely surrounded by your standard office cubicles, their opponents nowhere to be found. A hundred scenarios and calculations raced through Tristan's mind, each one analyzed and broken down meticulously in terms of their potential success rate.

Tristan had watched enough film of Team Perrotta and witnessed firsthand their strengths and weaknesses to understand which members of their group were a priority and how they would approach this scenario. He also knew that Detonella could also say the same of them. Therefore it came down to two things: They would need to anticipate what Team Perrotta would do, and they would need to be completely unpredictable at the same time. Tristan turned to his teammates just as the bell rang overhead, signaling the start of the match. "All right team, here's the plan..."

Tristan gave his team a few minutes to get themselves into position before he walked to the back of the office. He immediately spotted what he was looking for and made his way to the recognizable red square on the wall. After he had retrieved what he came for, he ignored the warning prompts next to the nearby device, grabbing the handle and pulling down. The screech of the fire alarm rang out as the sprinkler system immediately ignited, sending water shooting across the room from the ceiling.

Tristan walked away from the fire alarm and back to the center of the room, where the downpour of water was the most prevalent. He pulled up a chair from one of the nearby cubicles and sat down, awaiting the next part of the plan. It came as a relief when he spotted the familiar ghostly appearance of the Anderson twins slowly phasing through the door.

"Pleasure to have you guys join us! Come on in, the water's great!" Tristan said, smiling and extending his arms out in a gesture of invitation while leaning back on the swivel chair.

"Pretty bold move just giving away your location like that, Tristan," Tom said as they glided forward.

"Why is that?" Tristan replied with a look of feigned confusion.

"Look, Tristan, we're not idiots," Matt said, rolling his eyes. "We know what you're trying to do, and it's not gonna work."

"Really? Is that a fact?"

Tom scoffed. "You think you're the first person to try this trick on us?"

"What trick?"

"The old 'temperature change' trick. The one where you make the environment super cold so that our molecules slow down and make it harder for us to be able to enter our gaseous forms. That's been done, chief," Tom replied. "Let me guess, Vamp is somewhere hiding, ready to turn this room into a meat locker before you guys spring your trap to take us two down."

Tristan nodded thoughtfully at their idea. That actually was exactly what he had originally thought of doing. It made the most sense and offered the best chance of success. By lowering the room temperature using Christian's powers, they could decrease the speed at which the molecules within the twins' bodies vibrated, stopping them from phasing properly and allowing Tristan and the team to take them down. However, there was a big flaw in that rationale.

Despite causing their powers to falter, it wouldn't completely disrupt the boys' ability to phase out, and most importantly, it would require the team to expose themselves within a confined amount of space, something that would be disastrous should they encounter Detonella. She could easily take out the entire team in one fell swoop if she came to the twins' rescue. Even if she was the last person standing on Team Perrotta, the potential for a total team incapacitation was still high. She had done it before in the past, which was why Tristan was still sitting and smiling, shaking his head at Smoke and Fog.

"You guys thought that out quite well. That plan would make a lot of sense. However, if you two were smart, you probably were able to take a peek in here earlier without me noticing and reported back to Detonella, otherwise, you wouldn't have just sauntered in here like you did. Which means you probably have some backup. Maybe Camo is sneaking up behind me while you distract me from the front. She takes me out, while the two of you draw out the rest of my team. When everyone's exposed, Detonella comes in and—BOOM! Game over everyone, thanks for playing! Do I have the basic gist of things?" Tristan didn't need to see the subtle shift in the boys' eyes to know he had hit the nail on the head. After all, it was what he would have done.

"I love to play chess. Used to play it all the time with my dad. He would beat me mercilessly when I was younger, but eventually, I began to understand the game and the key concept behind it," Tristan continued, leaning forward slightly. "The key isn't to outsmart your opponent. It's to get them to outsmart themselves. You just need to understand them to the point where you can get into their heads, how they think and act. Once you do, you just make moves that force them to do what you wanted all along. You see I've been sitting here, talking with you both for the last few minutes or so, and I have yet to see or hear Camo splashing around while you two 'distract me'. Where is your backup?" The two boys glanced at each other, and Tristan could see their eyes quickly scan the room, realizing the hitch in their plan.

"That means the roles have been reversed somehow, and *I* am in fact the distraction. You see, this water up above, turning this room into an indoor swimming pool? It's not for you. It's for Camo. Ariel has the ability to control and manipulate it, which means she knows and senses anything the water touches. Including a pint-sized ninja sneaking around. Which is why I placed her in the closet toward the back of the room. I'm guessing at this point Camo is entrapped in a large bubble of water unable to get out."

On cue, a loud bell went off, signaling an incapacitation. Tristan said a silent prayer, hoping he was correct in his prediction and continued.

"But then what about Vamp? Why hasn't he shown up to freeze this place? The answer is quite simple. If you two are here scouting and distracting, and Camo is supposed to be taking point, then who is protecting your fearless leader?"

"Detonella would never let herself get caught by Vamp! She would see him coming and take him out before he got anywhere near her!" Matt lashed out angrily.

"That's true, she definitely would. Although the key concept there is 'see him coming'. Hard to really prepare for him if you don't realize he's been hiding in the air vent space above the ceiling. If your leader is in fact out there waiting on your signal, she's probably enjoying a nice, cool breeze right now. And by cool breeze, I mean subzero."

At that moment, a second bell rang out above, and the twins turned to watch the door that they had phased through completely frost over, encased with ice particles.

"Hope she brought a parka. Which now leads us to you." With that, Tristan whipped out the fire extinguisher that he had been hiding behind his back the whole time just as the boys spun around to face him. Still stunned at the turn of events, they didn't have time to react as they both received a face full of carbon dioxide. While not as effective as a cold front would be, Tristan knew that the CO_2 based fire extinguisher was good for two things: smothering oxygen and sucking out massive amounts of heat from an environment. He was no Einstein, but Tristan was fairly certain these two effects would be effective in messing with their abilities. It also helped to keep the boys distracted from the 235 pounds of lean muscle that had been hiding in the adjacent cubicle and was now blasting through the walls to take them down.

The boys never stood a chance when Dan tore through the cubicle walls like tissue paper and grabbed both of their heads, smashing them together like cymbals. The two boys immediately collapsed to the floor and remained completely still.

"Hot damn, it worked," Tristan muttered as two subsequent chimes went off above. He felt his stomach drop and vision swoon while the simulation faded away. The room transformed back into the arena floor, and the glass dome reappeared, revealing the raucous crowd outside.

"They did it! They did it! They're going to the playoffs! Team Davids retains the famed family's spotless record of consecutive playoff appearances!" Jay screamed on the microphone above.

Tristan breathed out a sigh of relief while his teammates tackled him to the ground in a large dogpile. Tristan could hardly breathe, the four of them screaming in sheer joy and excitement, but he couldn't have been happier. In fact, he couldn't remember a time when he had been happier. The feeling of making the playoffs after a grueling season was overwhelming. The early morning runs, the brutal workouts in the blazing heat, the nights poring over game film, it was all worth it for that one moment together. It also helped that Belle was currently wrapped in his arms, her head against his neck as she giggled and screamed in joy.

Following the match, Tristan and the crew paid their respects to Team Perrotta and after everyone had been patched up in the infirmary, the two teams made their way to the cafeteria for a celebratory late night meal. It was the perfect way to end the evening, and Tristan couldn't have dreamed of a better way to end the Battledome season. His heart filled with pride when he looked upon his teammates, who had fought so hard and sacrificed so much to be on his team, despite the odds against them. They had gone through the fires of adversity, and now their reward was just around the corner. Playoffs awaited.

Before playoffs arrived, the students needed to survive the rest of the semester first, the next two weeks absolutely brutal with exams. The time they had used for training and scouting out their opponents was now entirely devoted to studying. The first things Tristan and his friends decided to tackle were their midterm papers. Tristan decided to do his on the Norse gods, the history of Odin in particular, while for Professor Tullage's paper things were slightly easier, with the topic having already been previously discussed.

It took about a week to complete his papers, but Tristan managed to pull it off. The next week came sooner than Tristan would have liked, but Monday was fairly easy. Professor Fisher was first, Tristan starting right in on his World History exam. By the time he was finished, his head hurt from all the information, but the next two classes were a breeze, needing only to hand in their assignments to Professor Muelman and Tullage. Overall, he felt fairly confident that he had done well in his three classes but couldn't shake the feeling of dread when thinking about how tomorrow would fare.

Upon arrival to Professor Stellios' class the following day, Tristan and Dan made sure to go over their game plan before signing up for a time slot. They tried to beat the crowd to class in order to get an early slot and were fortunate enough to get the third available opening. They didn't wait long before they heard their names called, and Professor Stellios walked the two of them back into the classroom.

"All right, gentlemen, you may begin whenever you are ready."

Tristan took a deep breath and began. "This is a technique that we had used previously in the Battledome. We've been working on perfecting it and, while it's still a work in progress, we think it can have a lot of applicable uses."

"We will be using a wooden target I brought with us as a test subject," Dan said, taking out the large slab of wood he had been toting around and placing it before them. The wood was about 4 x 4 feet and around two inches thick. It had a red bulls-eye painted in the center of the board and was propped up by a triangular cut of wood they had attached perpendicularly to the backside. The two boys stood about twenty feet away from the target, Dan directly in front of the object while Tristan was a few feet behind him. Dan's part in this technique was the critical factor. He needed to apply just the right amount of force so as not to shatter the board and the perfect combination of strength and speed so as not to shatter Tristan.

"Let's do this," Tristan whispered to himself, saying a silent prayer in his head that he didn't go flying over the edge of the cliff instead. "Now!" he cried, sprinting forward. Dan took a quick lunge forward, bringing his arms back toward his left hip before immediately shooting them forward, hands together like he was shooting imaginary beams from his palms. Tristan heard the familiar "pop" of air as Dan created a small wave of wind before him, blasting the wooden target, which slid back another ten feet.

Dan quickly reached back to grab the front part of the onrushing Tristan's suit before lifting the boy into the air and flinging him toward the target. Tristan felt the roller-coaster rush of speed and tried his best to adjust himself midway through the air. Thankfully, his speed was nowhere near what it had been in the Battledome, and he was able to adjust his flight so that he could bring his legs before him into a forward kick.

Tristan felt his heel strike the target, and the wood shattered in half straight down the middle, wooden particles spraying everywhere. Unfortunately, this caused Tristan to close his eyes resulting in a crash-landing several feet away. When he finally managed to slow down from his awkward rolls and scramble back into an upright position, he found himself directly in front of a slightly amused Professor Stellios.

"We're still trying to iron out the kinks of the landing," Tristan mumbled breathlessly.

"Clearly," Professor Stellios replied, her eyebrow raised slightly. Tristan felt his face flush immediately before he dusted himself off and made his way back to his friend, who was doing his best to not snicker. Professor Stellios wrote down notes on her grading sheet while the two awaited her response. "While your idea is slightly above average, I honestly cannot see this as being effective in any scenario. I will be giving you both your grades and feedback during our next and final class of the semester. You two may leave now and head over to Self-Defense. I trust his exam won't be as hard on the hips, Mr. Davids."

At this point, Dan couldn't hold back a snort, and Tristan immediately stopped rubbing his sore butt, still stinging from the landing. Embarrassing tumble aside, Tristan was happy to see that Dan had performed his part to perfection, and a part of him was relieved to know that at least his friend would not be hampered by him.

The two boys left the room, wishing Belle and Christian luck on the way out, and walked over to Professor Coffman's class where they signed up for their practical. Thankfully for Tristan, this exam went much smoother than the last. He was placed in a scenario in which he was surrounded by armed assailants, simulated by volunteer third-year students. Tristan had to overcome at least three of the five masked students without the use of a weapon in order to pass. They may have been third-year students, but in Tristan's mind, the scenario was far from fair for his opponents.

Tristan had begun to separate himself from his peers in his Defense Mastery class over the last few weeks, and it showed during his exam as he dispatched all five opponents in under four minutes. Overall, he took a few good knocks but was able to handle himself well above what even the professor had anticipated.

Professor Coffman gave the boy a smile and shook his hand before releasing him from the class. "Needless to say, you've developed quite the reputation for your combat skills, Mr. Davids. Keep it up. Defense Mastery will pick back up following the break, but I expect you to continue to hone your skills. Don't let that talent go to waste, young man."

"Never. Thanks again for all your help, sir."

Leaving the room, Tristan gave his friends a thumbs up before heading back down the mountain for lunch.

The results from their exams went pretty much as expected. Belle aced all of them, scoring the highest amongst all of the students in the class, which was a huge boost for the team's cumulative score. Dan also had a solid showing, managing to pull off a high B average, Psychology being his only stumbling block. Christian happened to pull out a low B himself, his grade getting a large boost from his practical with Belle. Tristan also scraped by with a low B average, mainly due to his Defense practical and well-developed papers. Despite Professor Stellios failing him, it was enough to get him over the hump.

Now that exams were over and Battledome was on a break, Tristan had another task that he needed to handle, this one on a more personal level. It was late November, and they were now on break for the next month until January. Due to the Academy rules, the students weren't allowed to leave the island during their first year, but Tristan would have the opportunity to

FaceTime his friends and family for the first time since he stepped foot on the island.

When he was finally able to find some alone time in the dorm room, Tristan called his parents to wish them a happy Thanksgiving. They were spending the holiday in North Carolina with the rest of the relatives, and they were all thrilled to hear from him. They had been getting small updates here and there from Allen and Elaina, and couldn't be prouder to hear that Tristan had made the playoffs in his first year, as well as passed his midterms. Tristan couldn't help but notice the slight concern on their faces when they learned that he still had not developed any powers as of yet, but they did well to casually play it off and congratulate him nonetheless. Tristan felt happy to see his parent's faces again and felt a sharp throb in his chest when he realized how much he had missed seeing them on a daily basis.

Staring at the black screen following the call, Tristan reflected on his past semester and all that had happened to him. All of his struggles, all of his triumphs, all of his experiences had changed him. He believed in himself. He was a leader. His friends could rely on him, and every day he stepped on this campus was another day he was proving all of his doubters wrong. And that felt good.

Sitting there with a smile on his face, Tristan noticed the faint drizzle of white specks passing past his window. A few seconds later, the door flung open and Christian stood by the door, chest heaving. "Bro, it's snowing! Grab your gloves and your sweater! We're about to go ham out there!"

Tristan grinned, standing up to grab his gear. He was looking forward to a fun break with his friends, and he couldn't wait to see what the next semester had in store.

Chapter 22: The Fight of the Year

Over the next month, Tristan and his friends used every opportunity they had to take advantage of the downtime. Aside from Christian's late evening dates (Tristan swore Chris was determined to go out with every girl at the Academy at least once), the four friends spent nearly all of their time together. There were also the school-wide religious observances, the multitude of international students celebrating everything from Hanukkah and Christmas, to Kwanzaa. On Christmas Eve, the staff and students had their annual school-wide snowball fight. Starting in the early morning, the residents on the island participated in an epic snowball war against one another, no powers allowed. They were allowed to throw snowballs from sunrise to sundown, ending the day with a truce and celebratory meal in the cafeteria.

It was an amazing day, and the look of sheer glee on Belle's face whenever Tristan would get hit with a face full of snow was worth every ice-cold minute. Her laugh was intoxicating, and he couldn't help but join her, despite himself. Sitting together to celebrate the end of the battle and enjoying an amazing Christmas Eve meal, Tristan knew there was nowhere else he would rather be.

The next day, Tristan and his friends exchanged Secret Santa gifts when they awoke. The downstairs Academy shop had restocked for the holidays and had a surprising variety of gifts available to purchase for the students. Tristan had picked Belle and scoured the store searching for the perfect gift, finally deciding upon two items. The first was a necklace made out of shells with a dolphin carved out of aquamarine, which for some reason caught his attention. The second was "The Little Mermaid", the original fairy tale by Hans Christian Anderson. While he felt like Belle would like it, Tristan still felt a bit of nervous energy as they all unwrapped their gifts.

Dan opened his first, tearing open a large box filled with tissue paper and burst out in laughter, pulling out a pair of large overalls.

"I hate you, Chris. How did you even find these?"

"You'd be surprised at the variety they have at the Student Store. Now lift up the tissue paper for your real gift." Dan took out the white sheets and his jaw dropped. The large boy reached inside and took out a Green Bay Packers jersey with "Matthews" on the back.

"How did you...?"

"I know how much you miss being back home and watching all the games. We really don't get many channels out here, so I—!" Christian didn't get further before Dan enveloped him in a big hug. "All right, big guy! You're gonna break a rib!" he yelled indignantly, but Tristan could tell he was pleased with the reaction.

Next up was Christian, who opened his gift to reveal a framed photo of the four friends together. The picture had been taken following their last Battledome match when the four of them had jumped on each other in a dogpile. They were all laughing and shouting in joy, a moment in time which Tristan could only describe as perfect. The frame was outlined in silver and at the top were engraved two words: My Family. From the eager look on Belle's face, Tristan could tell that the gift was from her, but her expression quickly turned to one of disappointment as Christian simply stared down at the photo silently. The three awaited some sort of reaction from Christian before Belle let out a sigh. "I knew it. I should've just gotten you a poster of Jennifer Lawrence or something. This was a stupid idea."

To Tristan's surprise, Christian shook his head slowly before raising his gaze, doing his best to fight back the tears that were forming at the corner of his eyes. He quickly brushed back his long brown hair while clearing his throat and said, "No, Belle. Not at all. This gift is...perfect. It's...Sorry, I just never really had people I considered my..." His voice caught in his throat, unable to finish the words.

Tristan was next in the order and was thrilled to unveil a thick comic book underneath the Christmas wrapping. The words "The Long Halloween" ran across the cover page of a drawing of Batman overshadowing several images of his long-time villains. Tristan was blown away as he looked back at Dan.

Dan shrugged smiling shyly. "I know you liked comic books and stuff. I asked your brother, and he got me in touch with Mr. Peters. He suggested

I get you that one so he had it shipped over. From your reaction, I guess it's good."

"Good?! Good?! This—this is amazing!"

"I'd rather some Dwayne Johnson movies, but I'll take your word for it," Dan said with a chuckle.

Last, but not least, was Belle, and Tristan joined the others in a synchronized groan while she carefully peeled off each individual tape strip and unwrapped the gift. Taking out the book and necklace, Belle broke out into the most beautiful smile he had ever seen. Tristan felt his chest tighten as she threw her arms around his neck and gave him a hug.

"Oh, Tristan, I love it! Dolphins are my favorite and you even got my birthstone! This is perfect!" Tristan did his best to ignore his two friends, who were making kissy faces and pretending to make out with invisible partners across from them, and enjoy the moment before him. Her hair smelled like lavender and her breath was warm against his ear. Finally, Dan and Christian began to cough obnoxiously, and Tristan and Belle quickly broke apart, both of them slightly red with embarrassment. Despite the awkwardness of the moment, Tristan couldn't have been happier at the outcome, and he spent the rest of the day floating on air.

The school celebrated New Year with an extended curfew and a dance party held on the courtyard, which everyone attended. Despite being too nervous to dance himself, Tristan had a great time with his friends and was more than happy to watch Christian tear up the dance floor. Tristan was more intrigued at the sight of Dan and Cynthia pairing up for a slow dance but didn't have much time to gawk before Sofi ran up before him and dragged him out to the dance floor to join her. Tristan knew his face was flushed from nervousness and did his best not to step on her toes. If he did though, she didn't seem to mind and was more than content to lead the dance. It may have been his imagination, but Tristan could've sworn he saw Belle look slightly upset at the sight, but when he shot another glance her way, she was already dancing with Brandon. Gabriel, on the other hand, looked like he was positively fuming, which gave Tristan a slight feeling of satisfaction for the rest of the night.

The next week, school resumed, and things went back to their usual routine. All of the students received an email updating the team rankings for the semester, as well as their current progress at the school. Much to his excitement, Tristan found that, thanks to their Battledome heroics, his team had made the largest rise in rankings amongst their class, going from one of the bottom feeders to the second placed team, behind only Team Jackson. Along with their team rankings, the email also contained individual rankings, including feedback from their professors.

The only blip in an otherwise positive report came in regards to his ability scores, which understandably ranked dead last in the class. This was reflected in his feedback, where despite his professors praising his efforts in the classroom, even Professor Stellios, there was a strong concern over his lack of progress when it came to discovering his powers. While he was disappointed, Tristan understood where the professors were coming from. It was something that had been starting to gnaw at him as they neared the final leg of his first year, and he had thought by now he would have discovered his abilities. These concerns would be placed on hold, however, as the school received some surprise visitors at the beginning of February.

The students were in the middle of their lunch period, Tristan joined by Team Parra and Conrad. Dan and Cynthia were in the middle of drawing on Christian's face with a permanent marker, who was passed out following another long night out, when the sounds of the superjet could be heard outside. This piqued the interest of the students, who slowly filtered outside to see what the commotion was. Tristan was shocked to see a group of four familiar faces walking toward The Academy.

There was a short, old woman with wispy white hair and intense green eyes whose short steps were aided by a large, gnarled wooden cane nearly twice her size. Next to her was a tall individual, completely covered in a long white shroud except for eyes of radiant gold. Lastly, on the other end were two faces that brought a smile instantly to Tristan's face. Racing to his parents, Tristan could hear the murmur of the crowd around him.

"The Council? Here?"

"Is that really Madame Magi? Whoa, cool, it's The Radiant!"

"Holy smokes, Captain Comet and Gaia! They're really here!"

Tristan's parents flashed a huge smile, opening their arms as he joined them in a running embrace.

"Mom, Dad! What are you guys doing here?! How come you didn't tell me?! Do Allen and Elaina know?!"

"Easy, slugger!" his father laughed. "One question at a time. We're here on Council business, unfortunately. It was fairly last minute, otherwise, we would have given you and your siblings a heads up. We'll be staying on the island for the next two weeks, but sadly we'll be pretty much out of sight. We'll be locked in meetings for the most part, and due to the nature of our being here, visitation with you three would technically be—"

"Prohibited."

The commanding voice of Principal Winter rang out above the din of the crowd, and the students suddenly parted, revealing the grey-suited principal. Tristan felt a familiar feeling of vertigo coming on as the principal approached, and he did his best to shake off the queasy sensation. Principal Winter's stone face cracked into a smile when he arrived to shake the hands of Madame Magi and The Radiant, bowing respectfully at them. When he reached Tristan's mom, he was shocked when she brushed aside his hand and gave him a hug instead.

"Oh stop it, Morgan...it's been too long."

Winter seemed just as shocked as Tristan was and, for a moment, seemed overwhelmed with emotion. He quickly composed himself, murmuring, "It's good to see you too, Gwen." Tristan caught a look of rage sweep over his father's face, but the expression passed as quickly as it came. There was no handshake as Winter faced off against his father, the tension between the two clearly visible.

"Olly."

"Morgan."

"While I hate to break up this little family reunion, you're not to have contact with the boy during your time here. You are here on Council business: perform your independent investigation into the Legion's activities on the island and leave. While I understand that you and your kin feel the need to simply ignore the rules that we have in place, I must insist that while you are here on my island, you will follow my orders. Is that clear?"

Still maintaining his staredown with the principal, Tristan's father placed his hand gently on Tristan's shoulder and moved him to the side. The veins on the side of his temple were positively pulsing at this point as he glared lock-jawed at Winter. Winter returned the glare with an insincere smirk. "I'm glad to see you can still follow orders. Now, let's get to the conference room and begin. We have much to discuss."

With that, Principal Winter turned around, leading the Council members through the divided sea of students to the Academy doors. Tristan's parents both quickly glanced back apologetically, his father giving him a reassuring smile. After the Council walked through the Academy doors, Tristan was joined by his teammates.

"What the hell was that all about?" Dan asked.

"For real! Winter usually walks around with a stick up his butt anyway, but that was just awkward, even for him!" Christian agreed.

"Does he not like your parents or something?" Belle asked.

"I honestly don't know, but then again, it's not like me and the guy are on good terms anyway. Let's just get back to class. Hopefully, I can learn a little bit more about this 'investigation' that's going on from Professor Tullage since she's on the Council."

That plan, however, never came to fruition, the students finding a relatively heavy-set man in his mid-thirties sitting in Professor Tullage's chair that afternoon. He was one of the Ph.D. students studying under the professor and would be substituting for her while she was away on Council business. Tristan found that the same situation was true the following day for Professor Stellios.

Over the next two weeks, the whole island was shrouded in a state of mystery. Random students and teachers would be called into Principal Winter's office for questioning, often for hours at a time. It was strange having such an important and powerful group of individuals on their campus, yet be completely in the dark as far as their workings. It was especially frustrating for Tristan, knowing that his parents were involved.

As the second week came to an end, at last, there appeared to be something to take the students' minds off of the looming investigation. That Friday, Tristan and his friends waited with a crowd of other students, nervously staring at the blank screen before them in the lobby. Eventually, the screens flashed to life, displaying a large bracket detailing the matchups of all eight quarterfinalists. It didn't take long for Tristan to find his team's name still among the lower seeded teams. Tristan's eyes ran across the page, staring at the name of their opponents, and a surge of adrenaline beginning to course through his veins. He knew deep down it was going to come down to this.

"Wow, now that's some B.S.! Not only did they underseed us, they got us fighting against the biggest scrubs in the competition! How is this even fair? Might as well just hand us the trophy now!"

Tristan spotted Gabriel, who stood beside his teammates, drawing as much attention as possible.

"Ignore him, Trist. He's just trying to hype himself up before the match. The more he talks, the more nervous he is about his chances. He's not worth the trouble!" Belle whispered from behind him. Tristan took a deep breath. *She's right. Save your energy for the real battle.* Tristan turned away, indicating for his friends to follow him.

"Yeah, that's right! Turn around and run away! Stick that little tail between your legs and keep your mouth shut, just like your pops did!"

The room instantly grew still, and all eyes stared at Tristan, who had immediately stopped. "Dammit..." Christian breathed out, as his pupils began to blacken. The veins on Dan's neck bulged out, his face red with fury, and Tristan could have sworn the massive boy grew at least three inches. Even Belle appeared incensed, the water in the central fountain beginning to boil at a rapid rate. In fact, all of the students seemed taken aback at Gabriel's outburst. All of them, except for Tristan.

To everyone's surprise, Tristan let out a snicker before slowly turning to face Gabriel. Tristan approached Gabriel, clapping loudly as he grew closer, a smile spreading across his face. The confused look on Gabriel's face was priceless, and Tristan could see him noticeably tense up, preparing for a fight to break out. Tristan stopped inches away from Gabriel's face, his eyes locked in on the dark brown irises of his nemesis.

"I want you to know Gabe, I couldn't be happier that we're finally going to settle this once and for all. I'm so happy that you finally get your shot at me. I just want to thank you, man, seriously. If it wasn't for all of that, there's a good chance you guys would've wiped the floor with us next battle. I mean, you guys are the better team, right? Unfortunately, none of that is going to matter. Because you've inspired me.

"Every waking moment is now devoted to you. I'm going to break down every aspect of your game, every strategy you've ever run, every tactic you'll ever dream up. I'm going to get inside of that black hole you're trying to pass off as a brain, and I'm going to use it against you. I'm not just going to beat you next match, Gabe. I'm going to end you. And the sad thing is, you're not even going to realize it until it's too late, and my fist is already halfway through your jaw. It's going to happen so fast, the crowd will just be starting to clap as I'm stepping over your unconscious body on my way out of the arena. So thank you, again...for reminding me what I'm fighting for."

Despite the sneer on his face, Tristan could see the flicker of doubt quickly pass across Gabriel's eyes.

"Is that a threat, Davids?"

"Not a threat, Gabe. A promise." With that, Tristan spun around and began to make his way out of the building, his stunned teammates following closely behind. "Make sure you start your timer!"

Over the weekend, Tristan stayed true to his word, utilizing his free time to pore over every matchup Team Jackson had gone through over the year. All eight battles were broken down and evaluated down to every last detail. What he learned did not surprise him. There was very little game planning done ahead of time for Team Jackson. There really was no need. The team was built to be overpowered from the very beginning, and their sheer ability level far outmatched any opponent they would face in the arena. It was almost unfair.

Blaze was their ace in the hole, an assassin who started off every match with an individual solo effort, incapacitating any of the weaker or more troublesome opponents in the blink of an eye. Twister and Wolf were their heavy hitters. Combining the power of air with bestial strength, the two excelled when it came to distance and melee combat, respectively. Agayu rarely even needed to utilize his abilities, staying back to strategically lend a hand to any of the other three in order to ensure the balance was wildly tipped in their favor.

Watching them in action, Tristan could see why they were so confident in themselves and had to admit, he was impressed. Gabriel's improvisational skills were perhaps second only to Tristan. He was very good at observing his enemies and quickly exploiting their weaknesses. His only weakness seemed to be whenever he allowed his emotions to get the best of him. At that point, he simply reacted on instinct, all logic thrown out of the window. It was during this moment, Gabriel was at his most dangerous, but also his most vulnerable. And Tristan had a hunch of just how to use that to his advantage.

Sunday night, the students received an email stating that the Council had concluded their evaluation of the Academy. Unfortunately, they had not discovered any evidence of the mole or internal tampering of the school's defense system during their search. The good news, however, was that the imposed curfew had been lifted and security patrols were deemed no longer necessary. Despite the good news, Tristan still felt a little concerned that the council had discovered nothing. After all, if the most powerful metamorphs on the planet couldn't find anything, what hope did he and his friends have?

The results of the investigation were still running through Tristan's mind Monday morning, so it came as a surprise when he was approached by Ms. Dorregard during breakfast on behalf of Principal Winter. Gathering up his belongings, Tristan followed the old woman as she shuffled them back to the principal's office, where his door was propped open.

Tristan swung open the door, stepping into the familiar chambers, and was surprised to find they were not alone for this meeting.

"Mom?! Dad?! What are you guys doing here? I thought the Council had left?" Tristan asked after giving them both a hug.

"We delayed our departure until later this morning. We figured we would join you two for this little impromptu meeting, as we thought it'd be best for...all of us to contribute," his mother said, glancing between his father and Winter, both of whom seemed to actively avoid one another's gazes.

"Contribute to what? What's this meeting about?"

"Well, Tristan, we've sat down with Principal Winter here and gone over your academic results from the year," Tristan's father began. "While we're overjoyed at how much you've done as a leader and your results in the Battledome...we're a little concerned in regard to your abilities."

"We understand this isn't your fault, son," Gwen replied, placing her hand on Tristan's shoulder. "Still, we're getting to a point where we're beginning to wonder..." Mrs. Davids seemed to falter at this point, seeing the look of concern creeping across Tristan's face.

"...if you belong at this Academy," Principal Winter finished coldly. "A point I believe I had made nearly a year ago now."

For a moment, Tristan dreamed of launching himself across the table and putting the silver-haired principal into a headlock. He wondered how much trouble he would get in. *It might be worth it.*

"Look, Tristan, nothing personal—," Tristan scoffed loudly, and even Mr. Davids allowed himself an eye roll at that statement. "These are simply facts. You are currently the only student who has ever been accepted into the Academy without demonstrating a single metamorph ability. While there are those who are considered 'late bloomers', even they have all demonstrated some unintentional use of their latent ability earlier in their lives. We were all hoping—yes, Olly, even me,—that being immersed in this environment would help ignite whatever hidden ability you may have inside...but that doesn't seem to be the case. Unfortunately, we are beginning to run out of options here, Tristan."

Tristan glanced back and forth between his parents, a sense of betrayal rising in his heart. *So was this it? His parents had given up on him being a metamorph?* Principal Winter sighed, and for a moment, Tristan watched the facade fall apart, closing his eyes while he rubbed the years of accumulated responsibility on his forehead.

"We're coming to the point now where it's becoming more and more apparent that you are in fact...normal. And if that is the case perhaps this Academy is not the right place for you. We have decided to give you until the end of the semester to prove us otherwise, however if you cannot...I will have to ask you to leave."

When pressed about the meeting by his teammates, Tristan surprised himself by avoiding most of their questions and telling them that it was simply his parent's only way of saying goodbye while on Council duties before they left for good. Technically, it wasn't a lie, but as Tristan's guilty conscience told him, it certainly wasn't the full truth either. While Tristan could tell they hadn't entirely bought his whole story, they were at least content to let it slide for now. But it didn't take a rocket scientist for them to notice something had changed within Tristan after that meeting. He seemed more on edge, more brooding, and more obsessive when it came to perfecting every little detail between his schoolwork and Battledome preparation.

Over the next two weeks, Tristan pored over his schoolbooks, doing everything he could to try and stay ahead of the curve. Tristan was exhausted from all of his late night studying, struggling to stay focused in class, which just caused him to have to try harder to catch up with what he missed. He was often lost in thought, growing more agitated, getting more frustrated at silly mistakes the team would do during practice. He seemed to continuously change up his tactical approach, gearing their game plan to rely on him more and more. The more mistakes were made, the more responsibility Tristan took away from his teammates, until finally, Christian confronted the team leader after a particularly harsh training session.

"All right, if no one else wants to say it, I will. Tristan, what the hell is going on, man? What's with you? Ever since the Council left, it's like you've been a totally different person. Now I get that you put a lot on your shoulders as a leader, but at some point, you've got to be able to open up and let us in!"

"They're looking to kick me out."

The silence that followed Tristan's words was deafening, his teammates trying to process the softly spoken words.

"Wait, what?" Dan asked in disbelief.

"Winter. My parents. That's what the meeting was about two weeks ago. I have until the end of the semester to prove I'm a metamorph or else I'm out. End of story. That's why I've been on edge lately, why I'm pushing myself so hard. I guess, subconsciously, it's why I'm pushing you guys so far away from me. This place has been like a home to me...and you guys have been like a family. I just...I can't let all of this go without a fight."

"Oh, Tristan...why didn't you tell us?" Belle whispered as she placed her hand on his back. Tristan shook his head.

"I honestly don't know. Maybe I was embarrassed. I just don't want you guys worrying about me. You have enough on your plates without having to take on my problems, too. You guys have sacrificed enough by taking the chance of being with me on this team. I just don't want to let you guys down."

"Hey, don't you dare hang your head," Christian said fiercely. "If you go down, we all go down together, you got that? You're our captain, and we follow you till the end. We're in this together, and we're going to figure this out." Tristan was touched and even more surprised to find himself in the middle of a group hug, the four friends clinging to one another in a sign of solidarity. Tristan's chest swelled with emotion, trying his best not to let any tears fall.

"All right, that's enough. Trist, you need a Tic Tac, and Dan's bicep is starting to break my back. Belle, if you need to keep hugging me, that's okay. I understand if you need more comforting, take your time." The group groaned and immediately broke up, Belle giving Christian a slight slap on the cheek, as they turned around. "I'll take that as a no," Christian said, rubbing his face.

Tristan didn't remember much leading up to the match. It seemed like a surreal blur to him. The fireworks in the sky on the walk over to the Battledome, the fanfare as screaming fans welcomed them into the arena, the pyrotechnics as they stepped onto the field. All of the glamour and excitement surrounding the match was just background noise to Tristan. All he could focus on were the cold, confident eyes of Agayu from across the field.

Over the past few days, Tristan had taken his friends' advice, allowing them to break down the game film together. No longer did Tristan put the match solely on his shoulders, but rather allowed his teammates to open his eyes to things he had missed, ideas he had never thought about. While he still had the final call, allowing his teammates to lend their voice and thoughts made Tristan see things in ways he hadn't noticed before and allowed him to come up with a way to take Team Jackson down for good. As the field began to shift around them, Tristan simply returned Agayu's sneer from across the dome with a smile of his own.

Once the field finally came to a rest, the two teams found themselves perhaps twenty feet from one another, standing alone in a park setting. It looked like the typical neighborhood park where you might take your children to go play. A few sparse trees here and there, a jungle gym for smaller kids to run around on, and there was even a basketball court in the distance.

Tristan turned his face toward the beaming sun overhead, not a cloud in the sky. Perfect.

Tristan returned his focus to the task at hand, feeling more relaxed than he had felt in a long time. As the bell chimed overhead for the match to start, Tristan felt his teammates tense up in preparation for what would come next, and an emotion shot through Tristan's bloodstream like an arrow: confidence. *Ladies and gentlemen, start your timers.*

The second the chime went off, three things happened: Blaze became a blur, the air around Tristan became violently cold, and Dan's arm suddenly swung forward into open air. Things couldn't have gotten off to a better start. As anticipated, Blaze would be utilizing his speed in order to try and take out Team Davids' most troublesome player, Belle. What Team Jackson failed to realize was that Belle's water vials were surprisingly empty at the start of the match. In fact, they had collectively missed the pool of water that was now running across the feet of Christian and gathered a few feet before the team itself, hiding amongst the grass. When the chime went off, Christian immediately dropped the surrounding temperature to freezing, including the water beneath him, causing the liquid to instantly turn to ice.

Tristan wasn't positive, but he was fairly certain that running on ice in track shoes was never a good idea, but he was more than willing to test this theory out on Blaze. Tristan never actually saw the surprised look on the boy's face when his feet immediately lost traction and slipped across the icy surface. All he heard was the sickening crunch from the impact as Dan's expectant arm swung across Blaze's neck in a fierce closeline. Blaze's head snapped back, his dreadlocks flying through the air, and his feet completely left the ground. The boy's body landed somewhere several feet behind them, hitting the ground in a crumpled heap, motionless. A part of Tristan wanted to check and make sure the boy was still breathing, but Dan was already moving toward phase two of their plan.

Twister was already looking to counterattack, a swirl of air starting to spin beneath her outstretched arms. Given her particular ability and range, Tristan had figured she would be the next involved and a major headache for the team. Which was why Dan was already bringing his palms together, conjuring as much force as he could muster, and Tristan had already started his run behind his friend.

It was just like they had demonstrated during their midterms, only this time they had it down to a science. Rather than grab Tristan by the front and side-arm him forward, Dan underhanded him like he would a bowling ball, allowing for Tristan to start off in a position where his feet were already pointing at the target. By the time the air blast struck the stunned Twister, causing her to lose her focus on the whirlwind she was creating, Dan had just released Tristan, who made sure to keep his heels aimed at her chest. As Tristan felt the familiar sensation of insane speed, all he could think about was the look that would be on Professor Stellios face when she watched this on replay.

Tristan felt the soft belly of Twister instantly collapse from the impact of his boots and he made sure to not lock out his knees upon landing. He had been practicing his dismount over the week, allowing his knees to bend while he leaned forward, following his momentum into a forward flip. While Twister landed several feet away, a cough of blood escaping her chest from a likely collapsed lung, Tristan landed surprisingly gracefully on all fours. With no time to celebrate that epic dismount, Tristan quickly got to his feet, spinning around to face the two boys that remained. As two bells rang off simultaneously overhead, Tristan saw the surprised looks on his opponent's faces turn to pure, unbridled rage.

This was where things got tricky. Outside of the Battledome, Tristan knew Team Jackson were hotheads, especially Agayu and Wolf. And he knew of nothing more that would absolutely cause the two to lose their minds than to see Twister fall right before their eyes to the hands, or in this case feet, of Tristan. He had no means of physically stopping the two boys together, especially when they went into a full-on rage.

Based on the look on their faces and the fire in their eyes, it was apparent what Agayu and Wolf had in store for Tristan. Agayu yelled in anger as the glass vials around his chest literally shattered with emotion, the sand whipping around violently before coming together on his hands to form two mighty fists that Tristan was sure would feel like a Mack truck when they landed. Wolf let out a feral scream that morphed into a savage roar when the lanky boy transformed into the fearsome, powerful beast within. They surged forward, completely lost in their emotions, ready to even the score. Tristan knew this was what Agayu had been waiting all year for. Unfortunately, his rival would have to wait another day.

With their focus entirely on Tristan, the two enemies had completely forgotten about the other three members of Team Davids, who had been charging behind them in an all-out sprint. Tristan felt himself involuntarily flinch as Wolf reared back in preparation to launch himself, aiming to tear the team leader apart, when Christian, using all of his supernatural speed, came out of nowhere to throw himself on the monster's back. It was like a battle of the classic horror monsters as Wolf began to spin around and claw at his back in order to get Christian off of him. It was to no avail, as Christian dug his knife-like claws into the creature's meaty flesh.

Tristan watched in amazement as Wolf completely stopped moving, frozen in place, while the features of his best friend took on an even more demonic look. Tristan didn't have to watch the scene for much longer as Dan followed up a moment after. Christian was able to quickly detach himself from Wolf prior to Dan's massive fist making contact. "Sweet dreams!" he said with a smile. Wolf could only widen his eyes before being struck with a force of Herculean strength that sent him flying through the air and crashing straight through the nearby jungle gym in an explosion of rock, steel, and fury.

Agayu was unable to assist his friend as he brought down his fist of sand upon Tristan's face, ready to annihilate his enemy into an unrecognizable pulp. To Agayu's surprise, Tristan merely blocked the strike with his forearm, the sand crumbling off like a cookie, and side-stepped to the left while sweeping out his leg, causing Agayu to stumble. Confused at how he hadn't just shattered his nemesis' arm into pieces, Agayu quickly spun around, even more incensed, and threw down with his other arm. This time, Tristan merely caught the fist in mid-air with one hand, stopping it completely as the sand fell in a pile to the ground, a look of complete triumph upon his face.

It was at this point that Agayu realized how wet and moist his entire arm was. In fact, all of his remaining sand was completely soaked, unable to properly form into a solid mass. He had never even noticed Belle manipulating her water from afar, drenching and corrupting the very material that had made him so dangerous. While he heard the third bell go off in the distance, confirming the loss of his final teammate, Agayu was unable to truly grasp how dire his situation was until he realized he was now being held by the best hand-to-hand specialist in their entire class. It was over before he even had a chance to react.

Blow after blow landed in quick succession, as Tristan utilized his positioning, speed, and technique to deliver a martial showcase that surprised even him. By the time Tristan was done, Agayu was on his knees, face bloody and bruised, and he stared blankly up at the boy he had never before seen as an equal, his body outlined by the blazing sun above.

"How...how did this happen...? You're...not even...special..."

Tristan smirked and shook his head. "Nope, I guess not. And you wanna know the punchline? Now, neither are you."

With that, Tristan spun around, delivering a roundhouse kick to Agayu's jaw and sending his rival into a world of darkness to join the rest of his team. After Agayu's body hit the ground, Tristan turned to his teammates and calmly gestured for them to exit the arena. The four friends never let so much as a smirk cross their faces, leaving the field before the medical team even made it on. They didn't stay for the moment when the hushed crowd, who was still frozen in shock, finally roared into a frenzy at the sight of the timer which had stopped to confirm what was once thought impossible: 2:58.

Chapter 23: All Falls Down

Tristan knew that what they had done was special, but nothing could have prepared him for this. After their unprecedented result against Team Jackson, everything changed. They were no longer viewed as underdogs, but rather one of the greatest first-year teams to walk through these halls. They were actually considered favorites to win, even after receiving word that they would be facing the current title holders, Team Nguyen, in the semi-finals. No team had ever won a match in under five minutes, let alone three. To pull that off against none other than the highly-rated Team Jackson was unheard of.

After the match, things changed for Gabriel as well. The next week following the record-breaking loss, he displayed two black eyes and a rather swollen jaw. On the wrong side of history, Gabriel was now determined to make himself as inconspicuous as possible, no longer swaggering down the halls. His teammates, on the other hand, were able to recover from the loss, coming by Tristan's table during lunch to formally congratulate them in a display of class he had not expected. While it was nice to finally be respected amongst those at the Academy, Tristan should have known better than to think things would remain like this. There were stormy days ahead that would soon overwhelm whatever sense of goodwill he was experiencing.

Tristan had three weeks to prepare for their next match-up against Team Nguyen, however, he found himself struggling to remain motivated following their victory over Gabriel. He knew he shouldn't let the match affect his level of effort, but it was hard to get back on track after that massive high. It felt like they had already won the title, and he found himself procrastinating when it came to analyzing their next opponents. Besides, he had bigger things to worry about, especially when it came to his academics. In fact, his grades were becoming quite a concern this semester.

Tristan found it incredibly difficult to concentrate in class, his mind constantly obsessing on his inability to discover his powers, to the point that his grades were steadily dropping. Unable to focus, he often seemed disinterested or flustered when called upon, and the quality of his assignments was unusually subpar. It felt like the harder he tried to fight and hold on to his dreams, the more they were beginning to slip from his grasp, a vicious cycle that was leaving him emotionally drained and discouraged.

The one bright spot in those three weeks was Belle's birthday, which they were able to celebrate together over the weekend. With spring now here on the island, the flowers were in full bloom, revealing the tropical oasis they were used to seeing. It was ideal conditions to celebrate her day, and they spent it doing whatever she wanted. A day at the beach and a bonfire under the night sky was the perfect way for her to enjoy turning seventeen, and the three boys did everything they could to make sure she enjoyed herself. After opening her gifts, she thanked them, and the thought of losing that smile was enough to make Tristan want to work that much harder to prove himself as a metamorph.

Unfortunately, Tristan's rollercoaster month continued in much the same way, and by the time he managed to refocus on their matchup with Team Nguyen, it was already the last week of March. While he certainly wanted to win on Friday, Tristan found that this desire had taken a fall on his list of priorities. Finals were approaching, and he was currently sitting on a C+ average. Still, Tristan knew that his friends were depending upon him to come up with a game plan for the match-up, and he began to scramble to devise a tactic for their upcoming opponents.

Tristan decided to base their gameplan around Belle, utilizing her powers as aggressively as possible to give the other three an advantage over their opponents. With what remaining time they had, Tristan did his best to prepare his squad for the battle ahead, and when Friday arrived, Tristan had managed to even convince himself that his plan going to work. Minutes before the match, however, Tristan found himself in an endless loop, going through scenarios in his mind, all of them ending in possible disasters. For some reason, he felt like he was overlooking something.

What is my problem?! Snap out of it! Despite his best efforts, Tristan could not get himself out of these thoughts of self-doubt. *What if he had it all wrong? What if Team Nguyen didn't start off aggressively at all and bided their time instead? What if...?* Before he could dwell any further, the teams were called forth, and Tristan was soon standing in the arena, sweat dripping profusely down his forehead. The screams from the crowd were deafening. He could barely hear himself think. *Were the lights always this bright? He couldn't remember the last time he felt this lightheaded. Why were his teammates looking at him so strangely?*

The field began to transform before them, and soon Tristan was standing on a muddy cornfield in the middle of what appeared to be the Midwest. The sky above them was absolutely hideous, storm clouds overhead and rain pouring down like a monsoon. Tristan could barely see their opponents through all the rain, but from what he could make out, they struck an imposing figure. Panic began to rise up in Tristan's chest as the bell rang overhead starting the match.

The boys got into their defensive shell around Belle, Tristan and Christian swinging toward either side while Dan stepped to the front, keeping the girl squarely in the middle of them all. As lightning flashed across the sky, lighting up the field in bright light, Tristan could see from afar Port looking at them with a quizzical look upon her face. *That's right,* Tristan thought with a smile. *She's confused, wondering how they're going to get to Ariel now. No luck, sweetheart. You've gotta go through us first, and with this downpour, there's no way that's gonna happen.*

To his surprise, Tristan watched as Port simply shrugged and spoke a few words to her teammates before turning with a smile on her face. *What's she got to smile about?* Tristan thought, confused. That would be the last thought that ran through his mind that match. The next thing he remembered was watching Port flick her wrist, disappearing into nothingness, and the sudden jolt of a fist slamming into his face as blackness rose up to meet him.

It had been Tristan all along. It was what Tristan had failed to realize early on when anticipating the match-up. At this point in their development, Belle had the highest power level amongst the four and was considered their most powerful player. However, power didn't necessarily mean best. When it came down to it, Tristan had quietly become Team David's best player. He rarely made a misstep when directing his squad, had an innate ability to adapt to pressure situations on the fly, and his hand-to-hand skills were actually a major concern when it came to Team Nguyen.

Not expecting them to focus their attacks on him, Tristan was knocked out by Port within the first minute of the match. They were down a man and stuck in an exposed defensive shell like sitting ducks with no direction or guidance on what to do next. Tristan had left his team scrambling to adjust to the full-on offensive onslaught of Team Nguyen, who didn't hesitate to press their advantage. They spent the next ten minutes on the back foot, trying to hold their ground against the steady pressure of their opponents, who slowly wore them down and picked them off one by one. The team fought valiantly, but they soon fell to the more experienced Team Nguyen and were knocked out of the playoffs. And Tristan knew he was to blame.

His friends did all they could to lift his spirits and keep him optimistic about the upcoming exams, but his mind was in a funk as depression settled over him. With Tristan's decreasing grades, the team ranking was plummeting, a fact that was beginning to cause some tension within the group, especially Belle. Used to getting straight A's, each C and D+ Tristan brought back was pushing her limits of tolerance. While she didn't outwardly say it, she was losing her patience with carrying the team academically, him in particular.

When April came around, the fear of losing their team leader had created a strain on their team dynamics, and their once unbreakable bond was starting to show some cracks. Christian seemed the most impacted by the prospect of Tristan leaving. His typical laid back demeanor was starting to fade as exams drew closer. He seemed more fidgety and stressed, slightly more pale than normal. He would study on his own much of the time or go out for long walks to clear his mind. From the looks he often gave Tristan, it was like he was preparing for his best friend to leave them at any moment.

Tristan did as much as he could, pouring all of his efforts into his studies, and by the time finals week had arrived he was as prepared as ever for what could potentially be his last two days of class at the Academy. In Professor Fisher's class, their History test consisted of major historical points that occurred between the ages of the Roman Empire all the way to the British, while Meulmann's exam was a written essay of The Odyssey. The last test of the day fell to Professor Tullage, which focused on the final ten chapters of their textbook on the principles of psychology. All in all, while they were difficult, Tristan felt fairly good overall with his performance, leaving his classes in a much better mood than he had walked in with.

Tuesday's finals, on the other hand, were a much different story. In Professor Stellios' class, the students were required to sign up for individual sessions in order to demonstrate their best offensive move, utilizing their power. It was humiliating enough that he didn't have any powers to demonstrate, but the fact that he even had to sign up in order to stand before her in silence was enough to demoralize anyone. Tristan found it even more difficult to meet her green eyes than normal, filled with an emotion he couldn't stand to observe: pity. "Anything, Mr. Davids? Anything at all?" she said, practically pleading for him to produce a miracle, but all he could do was stare down at the ground before him and shake his head.

Needless to say, Self-Defense didn't go any better. The students were placed in individual scenarios in which they were at a disadvantage and needed to utilize their abilities in a defensive capacity to try to maintain for as long as they could. In Tristan's scenario, he was placed against two fourth-years who had cement skin and could throw concussive blasts, respectively. He lasted for a little over thirty seconds before Professor Coffman needed to intervene and stop the match, Tristan horribly outmatched from the moment he began. Frustrated and disappointed at how his day had gone, Tristan spent the day in isolation, resigned to his fate that was ominously looming ahead.

While semester grades were supposed to be released by the end of the week, Tristan already had an idea of what was to come when he received an email from Principal Winter asking him to report to his office the next morning. His stomach in knots, Tristan decided to skip breakfast entirely, not wanting to delay the inevitable. By the time he entered Principal Winter's office, he had already run through the scenario half a million times in his head. He had pictured Winter's smug, self-satisfied smile as he told Tristan how he had been right all along and to pack up his bags to leave immediately. What he found instead surprised him.

Rather than a gloating look upon his face, Principal Winter sat solemnly beside the window sill, lost in thought while staring at the beautiful scenery below. There was a disappointed look across his face, and it appeared he hadn't slept much. In fact, he looked downright weary. Tristan didn't wait to be told to sit, taking his place in his usual chair across the mahogany oak table.

Finally, Winter broke the silence by starting off with a sentence Tristan did not expect: "Did I ever tell you about my relationship with your parents? How we knew one another?" Caught off guard, and genuinely curious, Tristan shook his head with a frown.

"Your father and I knew one another long before your mother came into the picture. Olly was my best friend. I was actually the one who introduced the two of them." Winter reached across to his desk, turning around one of his framed pictures, revealing an old faded photo of four young teenagers celebrating winning the Battledome championship.

Two of the teens, Tristan didn't recognize, but he could pick out his mother's joyous smile from anywhere as she was being carried by a strappingly handsome young man who looked very familiar. It took Tristan a second to realize he was looking at a photo of Morgan Winter in a happier time, when his movie star looks had not been affected by the burdens and stresses of time. A time when he appeared to be genuinely happy carrying Tristan's mother in his arms while she held aloft the Battledome championship trophy.

"Gwen and I struck it off immediately, her personality infectious and a perfect complement to my strict, regimented mentality. She was the glue that held our team together and helped us dominate the arena. It was much the same when it came to the three of us, after I had introduced her to Olly. At first, those two butted heads constantly, believe it or not, but even your headstrong father couldn't help but give in eventually." Winter chuckled silently to himself, reminiscing. "We were the best of friends."

"What happened to you guys?"

"Life likes to throw obstacles in your way every once in a while. And sometimes, it throws mountains. During my senior year, Olly and I had a bit of a falling out over something, and unfortunately, there was no going back."

"Was the falling out...over a girl?" Tristan inquired, putting two and two together as he thought back on the way Winter interacted with his parents when they last saw one another.

Winter nodded thoughtfully. "Yes, you could say that. Either way, Gwen had to pick a side, and she obviously chose your father. And that was that, as they say. We didn't see one another or even talk for years afterward until Allen was born."

Tristan sat for a moment, silent, as he let this new information sink in. "Why are you telling me all of this?" Winter leaned back against the glass window as he met Tristan's eyes.

"Because I need you to understand that this isn't personal. For years I held a grudge against your parents, hurt by how our relationship had ended. I consumed myself within my job, rising up within the university as I assumed the role of its leader. I buried my past behind me, including all the fond memories I had with your parents. Fate, however, is not without a sense of humor."

"It wasn't long before your siblings arrived at this school, young, eager, and hopeful to learn. Initially, I had personal misgivings of allowing them at this school. I'm not proud to say it, but the thought of denying them entrance did cross my mind, but your mother managed to reach out and talk some sense into this old fool's head. Needless to say, those first few years were incredibly difficult for me. As you know, those two are spitting images of your parents, in both appearance and personality."

"So what, you hated them for reminding you of how much you hated my parents?"

"On the contrary. It was hard because it reminded me of how much I missed them. Your siblings were a breath of fresh air and a much-needed wake-up call for this old man. They performed above and beyond my wildest dreams, and I couldn't have been happier. I did my best to stay in touch with them even after they had graduated, and when two positions opened up at this Academy, they were the first two that came to my mind. They were phenomenal students to have during their time here and have been just as invaluable as part of the staff."

Tristan frowned, shaking his head as he ran his fingers through his hair. "So what's the deal with me then? Why did I get singled out? Why are you so hell-bent on getting rid of me?"

"Tristan, I promise you, nothing could be further from the truth. Whether you realize it or not, I have gone out of my way to try and work with the professors in finding a way to keep you at this school. Who do you think suggested to Arman that you be included in his Defense Mastery class? Jane and I have sat down nearly every week this year to revise her traditional lesson plan to somehow include you! But Tristan, my hands are tied here! Despite how much history your family and I have, these rules have been in place long before me! And I cannot allow my fondness for the past to affect my judgment in this case."

Winter sighed as he stared at Tristan with those steel blue eyes, a look of remorse behind them. "We've just got back your final grades. While you managed to do decently in your other classes, you failed your ability courses. This has caused a drop in your GPA below the required 2.3 you need to remain eligible at this Academy. I wish there was another way, Tristan, but I've run out of options. There will be a plane to take you back home this afternoon after you gather your belongings and escort you back home to your parents."

After saying his farewells to his professors, Tristan gathered his friends together in the common room of the dormitory, wanting to get it all over with at once. Like ripping off a Band-Aid, he told himself. Will had a hard time coming up with words, for once, and the usually emotionally distant Juan seemed distraught. Cynthia let out a stream of Spanish that Tristan was pretty sure was 90% obscenities, heat beginning to subtly radiate off of her body. Even the members of Team Jackson were stunned at the news, Sofi the first to give Tristan a hug, while Brandon and Malcolm shook his hand, offering words of encouragement.

After saying their farewells, his other friends respectfully left Tristan and his teammates to themselves, the three having said nothing so far. Belle was a wreck. She hadn't stopped crying, her eyes puffy from the tears. Tristan's heart broke at the sight, and he felt a stab in his chest at the thought of never seeing her again. Dan was silent, his arms crossed before him as he stared at the ground. Tears ran down his face, although he maintained his typically stoic expression. At this point, Christian was nearly in full vampire mode, his emotions clearly getting the best of him.

"This is bullshit! They can't do this! They're just gonna kick you out and fly you home today?! This can't happen!" he yelled out in frustration.

"Chris, I know you're upset, but there's nothing we can do. Let it go."

"No! It can't end like this! You're not getting on that plane! Stay here! You hear me! Just stay here!"

"Chris, I—!"

"Please!" There was a look of pain on his best friend's face that Tristan had never seen before, like a wounded animal. "Promise me you will not get on that plane...I just...I just need a moment..."

"Chris!" Tristan called out to his friend, but the boy had already started to sprint out of the room, no longer able to hold back his emotions.

"Let him go, Trist. Let him go. He's gonna need some time alone. I'll make sure to watch over him for you. I'll watch over all of them," Dan said solemnly. Tristan gave his friend a nod of thanks. Dan had always seemed unbreakable, but as he wrapped his giant arms around Tristan in farewell, he could feel his friend shake with emotions as tears fell on top of Tristan's head.

Dan slowly left the room, giving Tristan a subtle nod towards Belle, as he let them have their moment. Fittingly, Belle would be his final good-bye. Tristan wished he could hold her in his arms forever. To say the words he truly felt. To tell her how beautiful she was, how he couldn't take his eyes off of her. How he was blown away by her intelligence and her strength. But most of all, how he loved her heart, how she looked out for them and was always there when he needed her.

Tristan wished that he could say all the words that he felt inside, but before he could get them out, Belle rushed forward and wrapped her arms around him in a tight embrace. They held each other for what seemed like an eternity, the walls around Tristan's heart finally crumbling down. The two shook as tears now flowed freely, and Tristan allowed the wave of emotions he had been holding back to finally break through.

"Please don't forget me," Belle sobbed in his ears.

"Are you kidding me? You're all I think about," Tristan replied, suddenly embarrassed he had said too much. For a moment he felt the girl start to respond, but instead, Belle pulled away, giving Tristan a gentle kiss on the cheek. She placed her forehead on his, the two locking eyes, as she gave him one last smile before turning around and walking toward the girl's wing.

Tristan knew she wanted him to call out to her, to say the three words that were stuck in his throat and stop her from leaving. Before he could say anything, Gabriel stepped in through the door behind him. Tristan spun around and faced his rival, quickly wiping the tears that were still upon his face. He wouldn't give him the satisfaction of seeing him at his lowest. Not today, not ever.

"So it's true? They're kicking you out?"

"Looks that way."

For a moment neither spoke, the two boys standing in the air of uncomfortable silence. "I'm...sorry to hear that."

Tristan scoffed in disbelief. "I figured you'd be throwing a party to celebrate not having to see me anymore. Please don't patronize me right now by saying you're sorry to see me go."

To Tristan's surprise, Gabriel simply shook his head in response. Tristan frowned, confused. *Where was the sneer, the mocking comments? Where were the trademark cocky swagger and belittling remarks?*

"Look, I'm not gonna pretend to like you, Davids. We have a past that's never gonna change and can't take back at this point. You know how I feel about you being here and what you represent. But at the same time, I'm not gonna walk around and act like you never existed either. For God's sake, I'm in the history books now." Tristan smiled at this last comment while Gabriel took a deep breath and continued.

"Do I think you're a metamorph? No. But do I think you're a hell of a student and earned your spot?...Yeah. Yeah, I do. Good luck, *bro*." Giving a slight nod, Gabriel turned around and left Tristan for what would be the last time.

Once Tristan made his way over to the island shoreline where the plane awaited, the noon sun was already scorching hot overhead. The plane he would be taking home was different than the superjet used to previously bring him and his peers over to the island. This private plane was still quite large, about the size of a Gulfstream, with all of the technological upgrades Tristan was used to seeing from the school's property. Approaching the jet-black aircraft, Tristan saw three of the crew members debark the plane and hurriedly move in the direction of the Academy Training grounds. Due to their distance from him, Tristan couldn't make out all the crew members on the far side but identified a strikingly beautiful blonde with porcelain skin joined by a tall, handsome man with long, black hair.

Awaiting Tristan by the plane's staircase was a shorter man, whose compact size belied the muscular physique that was practically popping out of the pilot's uniform. "G'day, mate! Pleasure to have ya on board! You must be Mistah Davids!" the pilot stated in a thick Australian accent. Tristan nodded with a slight frown.

"You're not the usual pilot, are you? I think it was Condor that brought us over last time." The small Australian man laughed as he casually reached over to grab Tristan's luggage.

"I'm not nearly on Condor's level, but don't you take that to heart! He usually only flies the superjet. My name is Brett, and I'm responsible for the private flights in and out of the island. They're usually few and far between, so I'm rarely utilized during the year. Last flight I had was in February, escorting the Council. Come on in, mate. I'll help you with these bags," the man said with a laugh as he jokingly pretended to struggle lifting Tristan's belongings.

Tristan smiled at the friendly pilot and thanked him for the assistance before following him up the stairs and into the plane. The inside was as luxurious as he could have imagined, rows of plush leather seats with TVs all within the large, spacious cabin with ample space to move around. Once Brett shut the door behind them and placed Tristan's bags into a storage space near the front, Tristan turned to him and asked, "Aren't we going to wait for the rest of the crew?" The pilot shook his head after he locked the storage door and fixed his cap on top of his buzzed brown hair.

"They won't be joining us on this trip since we only got one passenger! They went to go deliver some equipment over to the trainin' grounds instead. We do have one other member of tha crew here today tho. He's over in the galley down by the tail end, doin' a little maintenance work to the plane."

Brett pointed to the back of the plane, where Tristan spotted a door leading into a small room where he assumed the food was made. From the circular window in the door, Tristan could make out the back of a large man working on something within. "Billy is hard at work back there, so best to leave him to his business, ya know? Otherwise, feel free to enjoy yaself! I'll be starting the plane now. Been a real pleasure, young man!" Brett said with a smile, extending his hands. Tristan returned the smile and shook the calloused, rough hands of the pilot before taking a seat.

Preparing to depart, he gazed out of the window, admiring the beauty of the island before him one last time. The plane engines roared to life and flipped downward, propelling the plane off the ground. Emotions swirled within Tristan watching what he once considered his home fade below him. After they had hovered slightly above the level of the mountaintops, the engines swiftly flipped back around in the forward position, a burst of light flashing out the end as they rocketed forward, leaving the small island behind.

Once the pressure of takeoff had released, Tristan felt the urge to go to the bathroom. He realized he hadn't gone all morning, in his rush to say goodbye to his friends, and his bladder was now none too happy. Unbuckling his seatbelt, Tristan walked to the back of the cabin. While there, he caught another shadowy glimpse of the man in the galley. *While I'm back here, I might as well introduce myself. I'm sure he won't mind a quick hello, seeing as we're gonna be stuck together for a while,* Tristan reasoned. As he approached the door, Tristan could have sworn he heard the slight beeps of someone adjusting a digital clock. Perhaps Billy was adjusting the kitchen timer for their meals.

After knocking on the door, Tristan peeked his head in. "Excuse me, Billy? My name is Tristan, I just wanted to—!" The words immediately caught in Tristan's throat at the sight behind the door.

He had expected to see a large, heavy-set man preparing the food and performing some minor repairs to the plane's cooking equipment. Instead, he was greeted by the sight of a man, whose tall, muscular build was overshadowed by the apparatus wrapped around his head, leaving only a pair of familiar eyes exposed. There were no kitchen tools or equipment back here, replaced instead by large amounts of beeping, flashing explosives.

"Oh, my God..." Tristan managed to get out before the man lunged forward. That was the last image Tristan remembered before things went black.

When Tristan awoke, he had a pounding headache and was lying flat on his back. Adjusting his eyes, he felt wetness behind his head. *What the heck happened? What was all that noise? Where was he?* Tristan tried to get up but immediately regretted it, a sharp pain exploding in the back of his head while a powerful throb burst forward along his right temple. Feeling the back of his head, Tristan's fingers came back with blood.

Firestarter! Tristan remembered what he had last seen and quickly leaped to his feet, trying to make sense of it all. The Legion was here! He was on the plane with two of them now! Mentally preparing himself for a fight, Tristan stood up and took in his situation. His tactical mind racing, he noticed several things of importance. First, the plane was vibrating wildly, the noise he was hearing coming from the open door of the aircraft. Secondly, the storage room had been flung open, revealing the empty hangers along the back wall where parachutes were supposed to be. The third thing Tristan realized was that he was now alone on the plane. How much time had elapsed, he couldn't tell, but the two men were no longer with him. Fourth, and perhaps most importantly, Tristan was stuck on a plane strapped with explosives. Looking through the front window in the open flight deck, Tristan added an addendum: He was currently flying straight toward the Academy, perhaps a mere mile away.

With no parachute available and no time to think, Tristan's mind shut down, pure survival instincts kicking in. Taking a deep breath, Tristan sprinted to the open door and did the craziest, most terrifying thing he had ever done in his life— he jumped out of the plane.

Chapter 24: Invasion

The insanity that followed was one Tristan would never forget. He was probably at 1000 feet above the water at this point, traveling near to 120 mph. The wind flailed around him, but Tristan managed to adjust himself so that he would be facing the water below feet-first, in a knife-like entry. His heart was pounding out of his chest, and Tristan felt like he was about to pass out from the rush of fear and adrenaline alone. It seemed like his insides were on fire, his body about to explode from the emotions coursing through him. The water came at him like a train, and Tristan felt his butt clench as he braced himself for impact.

The moment Tristan's legs struck the water, he felt pain shoot up through his body as the ocean enveloped him. His eyes firmly closed, Tristan wondered if he had died upon impact, but the intense, achy pain throughout his body served as a reminder that he was, in fact, very much alive. Even with the adrenaline coursing through his veins, Tristan could not mask the feeling that he had been hit by a cement truck. Through sheer willpower and survival instinct, Tristan forced his body to work and propelled himself to the ocean's surface above. It felt like an eternity, fighting through the pull of the current as his lungs began to burn for the fresh taste of oxygen. Right when it seemed he had hit his limit, his chest about to explode, Tristan's head tore into the afternoon air.

Tristan sucked in deep mouthfuls of precious oxygen, slowly taking in his surroundings and reorienting himself. As his eyes adjusted, Tristan found himself greeted by a sight that immediately stopped his heart. The island was ablaze.

"Oh, my God!" Tristan whispered, trying to identify any signs of movement upon the sands before him. He was a little less than a mile away from the shore, which ordinarily would have been an easy warm-up swim but for his body having just survived a near-death experience. *Seriously, how the hell did I survive that?!*

Tristan made out the tiny outlines of bodies moving around the school grounds, trying to escape the chaos as screams of fear and panic filled the afternoon air. Tristan began to painfully swim toward the island, a feeling of desperation and duty driving him to ignore his body's desire to shut down. He needed to get back to the shore as quickly as possible. Tristan had no idea how he could possibly be of any use to his classmates, but there was no way he was going to let his friends take on The Legion without him!

As he swam, Tristan spotted three bodies making their way in the direction of campus from the training ground properties. Two other bodies appeared from the surrounding tree line to join them, and based off their familiar outlines, Tristan recognized The Legion members. Students and staff ran around trying to pull others from the wreckage and control the surrounding fire, but no one seemed to be paying any attention to the approaching danger. Tristan tried to scream and get their attention, but he was too far off to catch anyone's ear, especially in the midst of all the chaos. By the time the Legion was close enough for people to notice, it was too late.

From where Tristan could see, there were perhaps thirty students and staff members standing beside the rubble of the campus entrance trying to put out the fires and offer assistance to the wounded, none of whom reacted in time. The Legion was about twenty feet away when they were identified, and barely a scream was uttered before they had incapacitated the entire group right before Tristan's eyes. Tristan screamed in fury as Bullet fired himself into the crowd, ricocheting off the surrounding bodies, one falling after another. Firestarter added to the mayhem, his hands alight with balls of flame, and the giant monster unleashed them upon the remaining survivors, the fireballs exploding upon impact. Thirty metamorphs were taken down in less than thirty seconds. And it had only taken two of them.

Tristan gazed in horror at the carnage, his eyes locked on the scene as a dark, inky cloud emanated from the feet of the tall, long-haired man Tristan had spotted earlier. The cloud spread and grew larger, creeping forward and enveloping the bodies strewn before them. Tristan couldn't believe his eyes as the still, unmoving bodies slowly sunk into the darkness and disappeared. *What the hell was that?! Where did the bodies go?!*

It was at this moment Tristan realized the reality of his situation. This wasn't just another match in the Battledome, and these were not your average metamorphs. These were elite-level killers who would stop at nothing to complete their mission and who had no qualms with eliminating anyone foolish enough to oppose them. Tristan had no idea what their end game was on the island, but it wasn't going to be good. He needed to be smart about what he did next. This wasn't a game, and his actions could be the difference between life and death, not only for him but others around him as well.

Tristan eventually got himself a few yards away from shore and made sure not to draw any attention to himself while he observed the five villains disappear into the smoke and confusion of the Academy grounds. Out of the corner of his eyes, Tristan noticed a girl's body slowly crawl out from underneath a pile of nearby wreckage. The girl stood up cautiously, glancing around before reaching beneath the rubble to help two other figures escape. To Tristan's immense relief, he recognized the shell-shocked faces of Sofi, Brandon, and Emily, who were scanning the area to make sure they were in the clear.

Once on land, Tristan began to wave his hands toward his friends, his weary legs struggling to maintain balance upon the sand. The three students finally noticed Tristan, their faces shifting from confusion to excitement, before sprinting to meet him halfway. Reunited, the three friends swarmed Tristan, embracing him while they bombarded him with questions.

"Dude, you're alive! I thought for sure you were on the plane when it crashed! How are you still standing?!"

"What is going on?! How did this happen?!"

"What are we going to do?! Where is everyone?!"

Tristan raised his hands, trying to get his friends to calm down. He needed a moment to gather his thoughts and piece together the situation before any action could be made. The fact that he now had a few others on his side definitely helped improve the odds of their survival, however, they needed to make sure they didn't blindly rush into further danger. Tristan took a deep breath to clear his head before answering their questions.

"Long story short, the plane was being crewed by The Legion. I have no idea how they managed to get onboard or what happened to Condor and his staff, but they've had to been at it for a while given the number of explosives they managed to secure on the aircraft. I managed to jump out of the plane before it crashed into the surrounding walls of the campus." Tristan stopped his friends before they could interrupt his last statement with a firm shake of his head. "Don't ask, just know that it hurt. This place is now under siege by those five psychos, and judging from what I just saw, the school doesn't stand a chance if they don't organize the high-level students and staff quickly. With all this chaos, I doubt anyone knows what's going on. It's the ideal time for The Legion to attack, while people are confused and vulnerable. We need to stick together, find as many students as we can that can give us a decent chance against these monsters while encouraging others to hide out in a safe location, maybe the weight room over in the Training Grounds. Once we have a large enough crew assembled, we can plan a counterattack, or at the very least, find a way to get all the survivors off this island before The Legion takes us all out. Make sense?"

The group nodded in unison, their expressions letting Tristan know they understood the gravity of the situation.

"Before we go, do you guys have any idea where the rest of my team might be?" The three shook their heads, and Tristan tried not to let his disappointment show. "All right, let's head over to the campus grounds, staying as concealed as possible."

The team ran to the school grounds, making careful consideration to stay close together and low to the ground. Once they passed through the initial smoke and haze, they were greeted by yet another horrific sight. The once immaculate grounds were nearly unrecognizable, the tree groves shattered and aflame while the grass was riddled with pieces of burning rubble and massive holes from their impact. Tristan could make out several forms running around in the distance, screaming and trying to find help.

What concerned him most was how empty the school appeared. Given how many students and staff were usually walking around on any given day, Tristan had expected to see the area completely full of frightened classmates, yet the courtyard was unusually empty. Identifying the shards of crystal glass and scorched earth around them, Tristan could see that there had been a struggle here. In fact, he could see that a clear path had been established headed in the direction of the Academy itself, where the sounds of explosions and screams could be heard. The fact that he could find no residual bodies told Tristan that Shadow must have consumed them as well, but what he was doing to them remained a mystery.

The sound of a nearby student crying for help broke Tristan out of his thoughts, and he gestured for the others to follow him. Tracking the voice over by the hammock area, Tristan discovered a group of about fifteen students huddled together, trying to pry a classmate out from underneath a tree that had collapsed upon their leg. The pinned student's leg was at an unnatural angle, and while he had never been the squeamish type around blood, Tristan had to keep his eyes away from the sight in order to keep his stomach from interrupting him.

"Everyone back away! We'll handle this! Twister, can you use your powers to lift the tree off of him?" Sofi shook her head, her face slightly green as she stared at the unfortunate boy.

"No can do, Trist. The amount of wind I would need to lift this up would probably wind up tearing the rest of the kid's leg if I tried. Besides, that level of precision isn't exactly my strong suit."

"Damn it! Even if we all tried, I doubt we could lift this thing cleanly. Wolf, you in the mood to go beast mode?"

"I'm trying, Trist. But honestly, I'm more shaken up than pissed right now. He doesn't want to come out."

"Perhaps, you should leave the heavy lifting to me," a familiar voice called out from behind the fallen tree, and before Tristan knew what was happening, the massive load was suddenly lifted off of the student, rising well above the body and giving the others a chance to slide him out. His muscles rippling, Dan casually tossed the giant tree aside before dusting off his hands. He seemed larger than life, somehow bigger than Tristan remembered as he gave his leader a wide grin. "So, you couldn't stay away, huh?"

"Hell, someone needs to make you look good." While he wanted to run up and hug the big guy, Tristan instead turned to the students who were trying to help their fallen comrade. "All of you, head over to the weight room! Try and carry your friend over there and wait for help! Any others that you run into, direct them to join you! Understand?" The group nodded in acknowledgment, assisting their classmate as they headed in the direction of the training grounds.

"As for you, Samson", Tristan began, "You're joining the rescue party. Any chance you know where some of the others are?"

Dan nodded, pointing to the dormitories. "Last I checked, Ariel was over there, trying to put out the fires and help get some of the students out from the debris. No clue where Vamp is."

"Then let's not waste any time!" Tristan said, and soon the five of them were sprinting toward the smoke of the dorms.

Approaching the building, Tristan could see what appeared to be a few dozen students working hard to control the bedlam around them, a few of which he recognized. Powerfist was lifting up large pieces of debris and pulling up trapped bodies, while Warthog and Granite joined him. Cleric was to the side, trying his best to heal as many people as were being placed before him, his skin unusually pale and clammy from the effort. Frostbite and Belle were on the frontlines, battling the flames with a combination of water and ice, slowly managing to overcome the blaze. Tristan did his best to not stare in wonder at the sheer power of Belle, the girl managing to manipulate nearly a dozen different tentacles of water from the nearby pond and sweep them across the flames.

Upon arriving, Tristan shouted out orders. "Twister, help Ariel and Frostbite get the remaining flames under control! Wolf and Samson, let's have you two work on digging through the rubble and breaking down some of the barriers! Camo, you and I will help transport people over to Cleric! Let's go!"

The team split into their assignments, Tristan and Camo entering the still smoking building, trying to stay low and cover their mouths to avoid inhaling the residual smoke within. Together, they were able to pull out several unconscious students, while directing others to safety. After what felt like an eternity, Tristan and his friends had managed to quell the dormitory fire and rescue the remaining students.

Once things seemed to be in order, Tristan looked to Frostbite and Granite to manage the rest. "We're gonna need you two to take over this group. Right now, you guys are the only other team leaders we've run into, and you'll be better equipped to manage the survivors if things go south. I have no idea how things are looking over by the Academy, but I'm not optimistic. We've got a group of survivors hunkering down over by the weight room and could use your help over there. Cleric, I know you're drained right now, and you've done a hell of a job so far. I know it's asking a lot, but I need you to keep it up and use those powers on the remaining students by the training grounds. Powerfist, Warthog, you're our last line of defense if things turn sour. Protect the others as best you can."

"What about you guys?" Granite asked, gathering up the students.

"We're gonna head to the Academy and see what we can find. We'll try and rescue as many as we can, but if we run into The Legion...well, I'm not going down without a fight, that's for sure."

Frostbite patted Tristan's shoulder and smiled. "We'll see you later. If I'm putting my chips on anyone, kid, it's you. Give 'em hell for me." Tristan nodded at his fellow leader before turning to his friends, ready to motivate them for what lay ahead. Before he could get out a word, he was greeted by the sudden rush of Belle's arms around his neck as she held on to him in a fierce hug.

"Oh, my God, Tristan, I thought you were..." Belle began, pulling away from him, her eyes starting to water.

"I know," Tristan replied. "I'm fine. I'm alive. We're gonna get through this."

Belle nodded and began to say something before Tristan stopped her. As much as he wanted to treasure this moment and tell her how he felt, he knew this was not how he wanted to do so. There was little time and so much at stake. "Don't worry, Belle. We'll have time, I promise. But for now, we've got to get over to the Academy and assess what we're dealing with." The girl nodded in understanding, and Tristan turned to the others. "All right, team, get your minds right. Let's do this."

Tristan and the crew hustled over to the Academy as quickly as they could while trying to remain undetected, managing to direct a few stragglers to the weight room along the way. A gnawing concern began to grow in Tristan's mind the closer they got to the Academy entrance, but it didn't hit him until they had reached the marble steps that were now broken, caked with remnants of ash and blood. It was the eerie silence that bothered him, the stillness of the once anarchic environment just a few moments ago. There was nothing good behind those closed doors up ahead, and they needed to prepare for the worst.

Turning to his team, Tristan asked, "What's another way into the Academy? We're definitely not announcing ourselves through the front doors, and I don't think there's access through the roof."

"We can try one of the cafeteria windows," Brandon suggested with a shrug. "Anyone know how to pop open a window?"

"I think we can manage," Dan said cracking his meaty knuckles.

"Stealth, not strength, Hercules," Sofi said with a smirk. "Let's make sure we crack it, not smash it." Tristan nodded in agreement, and the six of them snuck over to the side of the Academy, where they slowly peered into the open windows.

Immediately, they ducked beneath the sill. The cafeteria was currently occupied. In fact, the entire front lobby and entrance were occupied by the captured students and staff. It was clearly a hostage situation as the remaining students and staff were forced to sit, The Legion walking around them on patrol. Jaws and Bullet were going around zip-tying the student's hands and feet while Shadow had all of the staff members, including Tristan's siblings, bound in his inky substance to the walls, their bodies covered like an insect in a spider's web. All of the bodies Tristan had seen engulfed by the darkness earlier were also currently gathered along the wall, bound together like some sort of grotesque mash-up.

This was not good. With the staff members incapacitated, the students were no match against The Legion, especially with their hands and feet bound together. From what he had briefly seen, Tristan was unable to make out Principal Winter, Professor Tullage, or Professor Stellios among those captured. Perhaps they were somewhere nearby preparing a counterattack of their own. Regardless, Tristan knew there was no time to waste, and that they needed to do something to give their classmates a shot at escape.

"The classrooms," Belle whispered pointing above. "Second floor. I can use my powers to open up a window there, and Sofi can lift us up to reach it. We can sneak in that way." Tristan watched as Sofi bit her lip nervously.

"I can try, but I'm really not the greatest with that level of precision. I don't want to launch you guys across the building by accident."

Tristan placed his hand on the girl's shoulder, staring intently into her uncertain eyes. "You won't. I've seen you at work, Twister, and believe me, there's few students who have your level of skill. I trust you." Sofi gave Tristan a soft smile, nodding in gratitude.

The students wrapped around the side of the building, standing beneath one of the second story windows while Belle uncorked one of her vials. Her eyes glazed over as the water slowly streamed upward toward the window sill. Sweat began to come down Belle's forehead as she concentrated, directing the water to slide beneath the tiny crack of the window's lining. Closing her eyes in effort, Belle began to slowly lift the window pane upward, eventually forcing the glass window completely open. Releasing a sigh of relief, Belle broke her concentration, allowing the water to return back to her vial.

"All right, guys, hold onto your hats. I hope this works," Sofi muttered.

Her olive eyes turned completely white as she raised her arms gently upward. Tristan felt a strong breeze slowly stir beneath his feet and soon he was rising further and further into the air. Sofi's brow was furrowed in concentration as she conjured five more air currents to lift up the team members. Tristan found the ledge first, using the air current beneath him to climb into the empty classroom. Once in, he was able to grab hold of his classmates one by one and get them safely inside. Sofi was the last to enter the room, the girl collapsing into Tristan's arms from exhaustion.

"What now, boss?" Dan asked once everyone had settled into the room, five pairs of eyes staring intently at Tristan for their next directive.

"Now, we gather some intel on what's going on down there. Then...we make sure The Legion regrets ever stepping foot onto our home."

Chapter 25: An Enemy Revealed

"Where the hell is he?!" Tristan heard the yell followed by the sounds of a thump and subsequent groan. The six students had quietly opened the classroom door and slipped into the hallway, moving to the central ledge in an attempt to get a view of the events down below. Cautiously peering over the balcony, Tristan and his friends arrived just in time to watch Shadow deliver another blow to the already bruised face of Professor Coffman.

"Tell me where Nova is hiding! Speak, Crusher, or I swear I'll break every bone in your body before I dispose of you!"

Nova? Who was that? Tristan had never heard of anyone at the school going by that name before. Coffman coughed, a bit of blood coming out of his mouth before he stared back at the enraged eyes of Shadow.

"I've suffered worse at the hands of better men, Shadow. Your threats do not scare me. They bore me. Now, go to hell," Arman retorted, spitting a wad of blood into the face of his tormentor.

The room was deathly quiet, the four villains staring in shock at the disrespect shown to their leader. Shadow slowly wiped his face, his hands quivering in rage while the shadows around him shook violently. For a moment, Tristan thought this was the end, that he was about to witness the execution of one of his favorite professors. Instead, the long-haired man laughed, surprising everyone, Arman included. Shadow began to clap mockingly, encouraging his henchmen to join as well. Soon, all five were laughing awkwardly as Shadow slowly walked toward the students.

In a flash, Shadow extended his arms, releasing a long black tendril at one of the captive students, Tristan identifying her as Tiffany Carell. The black tentacle wrapped around the screaming teenager like a vice, lifting her into the air.

"Nooo!" Arman screamed, his typically stoic face transformed into one of agony. The girl screamed louder as the coils around her slowly tightened, feathers falling off in masses from her once lovely wings. Tristan's knuckles were white from how hard he was gripping the railing in sheer anger. *What kind of sick, twisted bastard attacks an innocent girl?!* Tristan heard several pops come from the girl's chest, and he tried not to throw up listening to the increasing screams beneath him.

"Enough, Shadow! I yield!"

"Then tell me where he is!"

"I don't know, you imbecile! I told you, I don't know! He never entrusted anyone but the Council members as to where his safe house was!"

"Well, as you can see," Shadow said, gesturing around him, "none of your so-called leaders seem keen on being here to talk to me. It appears as if the Council has abandoned you all, and unfortunately, I'm rapidly running out of patience. If Nova doesn't surrender himself within the next ten minutes, every minute on the dot I'm going to execute one of these little brats until he decides that his little game of hide-and-seek is getting too costly. And to prove my point..."

Tristan's friends all turned away as the sound of crunched bone filled the air, Windrider's screams cut off abruptly. Tristan continued to stare in horror, transfixed at the image that would forever be burned in his mind. The screams coming from his teachers and classmates were deafening, a surreal mixture of terror and rage at the murder of one of their own. As Windrider's lifeless body was released unceremoniously onto the cold marble floor, Tristan found himself shaking with an uncontrollable rage. He tried to clear his head and regroup but all he could see in his mind's eye was the image of that figure, broken and unmoving upon the floor.

"Shadow, this is Crystal! Do you copy, over?" Tristan heard a thick country accent come over a static-filled device, Shadow producing a walkie from his pocket.

"What is it, my love? Have you found Nova?"

"No, sir, but I think I've found someone who knows where his location is. I found the old, crotchety secretary that works for him. She's been hiding on the third floor in his office, trying to sneak a few of the students to safety. We managed to spot her before she got away with them. Would you like me to get the information now or would you like to do the honors?"

"Hmm, tempting but no. You go on ahead and start without me. Have yourself a bit of fun, and I'll be on my way up, dear."

"You're the best!"

Shadow turned to Jaws and Bullet, gesturing to the students. "Keep an eye on the insects. If any of them so much as whimpers, you have my permission to crush them."

"But you said—!" Arman began.

"As for the teachers, if I'm not back in the next few minutes, kill them first before setting this place ablaze," Shadow said with a dark smile. "I never liked this school anyway. Trust me, old man, the world won't miss it." As he walked away, Jaws called out to their leader.

"Shadow, what about the boy?"

"What about the boy?"

"Where is he? Shouldn't he be helping us watch these little punks?! After all, they are his classmates!" Shadow laughed at this, shaking his head.

"Please, you know he doesn't have the stomach for all this carnage, despite all his boasting. Not yet, at least. Besides, last I heard, he ran off to go find one of the students he had some unfinished business with. With that temper of his, I'm sure he's taking his sweet time exacting his revenge!" With that, the villain walked into the elevator, making his ascent to the third floor.

The room below was silent, the students and staff now monitored by Jaws and Bullet, and Tristan's mind was racing to decipher the words that had been spoken between The Legion. *Nova...his old secretary...had they been speaking of Principal Winter? If so, that meant that Ms. Dorregard was being held at the mercy of their captors upstairs in his office! As for the boy they spoke of, clearly they meant Gabe with all the talk of his "boasting" and "temper". And if that was the case, that meant he was going after...*

Tristan quickly swept the room with his eyes, hoping that he could spot his friend, but alas, Christian was nowhere to be found. If Gabriel had gotten to him during this time...Tristan was afraid of what torments the bully had in store for his best friend. They needed to stop The Legion, and they needed to do it soon. Lives were literally depending on it.

Surveying the scene below, Tristan could make out a few familiar faces from amongst the crowd. Cynthia and Will were huddled together in a corner, shaking with fear as they tried not to draw attention to themselves. The Anderson twins, Juan, and Malcolm were among those on the wall, unconscious and trapped in the giant cocoon of living bodies. Tristan cursed his luck. It looked like any student with even the potential of being a problem for The Legion had been dealt with by Shadow. Gabriel had clearly done a good job scouting out the problematic metamorphs during his time as the mole. The thought of him being behind all of this made Tristan sick to his stomach.

Lowering himself, Tristan motioned the team together. In a hushed voice, Tristan began to devise a plan. "Okay, let's brainstorm. I'm not sure how much you guys were able to pick up on what The Legion was talking about, but they're trying to find Principal Morgan. I know based on what Shadow said earlier to Gabe, they're looking for some kind of 'key'. Maybe Winter has it, and that's why he's hiding out, so that they can't get their hands on it."

"Wait, what?" Sofi asked, confused. "What does Gabe have to do with this?"

"Don't you see? He's the mole! He's the one who's been feeding The Legion all the information this whole time!"

"No way!" Brandon said adamantly. "I know Gabe! He might be a jerk, but he's not capable of this!"

"I know it's hard for you guys to hear," Tristan said, looking between Sofi and Brandon, "but it's true! All signs point to him being the mole, and right now, he's on his way to kill my best friend. I'm not about to sit back and let that happen, no matter how much history you guys share!"

"Look, before we even think about stopping Gabe and The Legion," Belle said, stopping Sofi and Brando before they began their retort, "we need to find a way to free the students and staff. They're operating on borrowed time right now. It's only a matter of time before more people wind up like..." Belle paused, swallowing hard. Tristan tried not to let the image of Windrider cloud his judgment as he continued.

"We need to distract them. Draw them away from the students. If we can get some of their zip-ties free, we start to filter people out of here, maybe even freeing some of the teachers in the process. Ariel, Wolf, can you guys—"

"I can do it."

Tristan stopped, surprised at the steel resolve in Emily's voice. She had been so quiet this whole time, Tristan had nearly forgotten she was here. The most reserved girl in their class, maybe in the entire school, was the last person he had expected to volunteer for such a dangerous task.

"Camo..."

"I got this, Trist. Trust me. I can grab a pair of scissors from the classroom and go around freeing the students. They'll never see me coming. I'll just need somewhat of a distraction in order to get into place."

"I think I can provide what you're looking for," Sofi replied. Tristan nodded. This could work.

"All right, Camo, do your thing. But if it even looks like you're about to be spotted, you bail. Understand?" The girl nodded in acknowledgment before running back into the classroom. She returned moments later with scissors and proceeded to sprint around the circular hallway to the staircase.

Sofi gave their friend a minute to get herself down the stairwell before she stood up and faced the Academy front doors. "Time to make an entrance," she said, throwing forth her arms. A blast of pressurized air swirled around her hands before shooting out into the glass doors. In the blink of an eye, the doors blew apart from the impact, shards of glass spraying everywhere, while a fierce wind whipped through the room.

"What was that?! Where'd it come from?!" Bullet cried out, his head swiveling around.

"Cover the door! We're under attack!" Jaws replied.

"Keep an eye on the hostages!" Bullet yelled back, darting to the opening. Distracted, neither one noticed the door to the stairwell quickly open and close, a blur of movement making its way into the room. Even with his knowledge of her presence, Tristan could not make out any part of Camo, the girl flawlessly blending into her surroundings. He did notice, however, the surprised looks of some of the students sitting beside the stairwell who found themselves suddenly free from their bondage. Thankfully, no one had done anything rash, the students looking at one another in understanding that something pivotal was about to happen. Unfortunately, while the distraction had temporarily caused their captors to lose their focus, it had also caused them to be more volatile.

Picking up on the shifting movement behind him, Jaws spun around, his jaws elongating as massive, razor-sharp teeth expanded in his mouth. The nails on his hands grew to the size of kitchen knives, their edges gleaming in the light. "We said no movement! The next person who budges gets sliced and diced right here! I'm not bluffing!"

At that moment, Bullet returned, a frustrated look upon his face. "There's no one around here! It's a diversion!"

"A diversion for what?"

Camo froze in place, realizing she needed to make an exit and quickly before she was found. Jaws stood still as a statue, his beady eyes closing as his nose slits expanded, sniffing the air. Beads of sweat streamed down Tristan's brow. *This was not good. Get out of there, Camo! Get out!*

Suddenly, in a blur of motion that could rival that of Blaze, the monster leaped into the air behind him – into the space where Camo lie hiding. The students parted away, revealing their freed extremities as Jaws dug his claws into the back wall. Tristan heard a scream and saw a splash of blood as Camo reappeared into thin air, crying out in pain from the dagger-like claws buried into her left shoulder. *Nooo! Camo!* So focused on their friend's plight, the rest of the team failed to notice Brandon step back from the balcony, grabbing his stomach in pain.

"It looks like we have ourselves a hero, Bullet!" Jaws cackled with glee, the students screaming in terror around him.

"That's a shame. You know what we do to heroes. Why don't you give these little bastards a sneak preview, while I tie them back up?" The grotesque creature gave a horrific smile to Camo, displaying all of his massive teeth.

"With pleasure!"

"Hey, Tristan," Tristan was so focused on trying to devise a plan to save his friend, he barely heard the shaking voice behind him. "I'm...sorry...but he's coming...oooWWWOOOHHH!"

The howl of a raging beast tore through the air around them, and before Tristan knew what was happening, two tons of pure fury had just flown through the air, pieces of the balcony blasted out before it. Jaws had perhaps a brief moment to witness the monster he had just unleashed before Wolf landed upon him. The villain managed to narrowly avoid being completely impaled to the floor but couldn't escape the massive gashes the passing jaws of Wolf made upon his chest. Camo slid to the floor, clutching her injured arm as the battle between the two creatures raged on beside her, Jaws doing everything he could to avoid the whirling claws of Wolf.

"Bullet! A little help here!" Jaws screamed out to his partner, who appeared transfixed at the sight of the werewolf. Snapping himself out of his stupor, Bullet placed on his knuckle bracers. He had just started to set his stance when a blast of pressurized air lifted him clear off the ground and out through the front entrance, his screams drowned out by the savage roars of Wolf. Tristan turned to Sofi, who had a smile next to her raised hands, and she simply shrugged. "I like watching the little fishy get chased by the dog."

"Tristan, upstairs!" Belle called to him, pointing in the direction of Principal Winter's office. "Mrs. Dorregard! We don't have much time!" Tristan nodded in agreement before looking at Sofi.

"Twister! Think you can give Wolf and Camo a hand down there? Try and get the other students to start freeing one another. I'll take Ariel and Samson with me to try and stop the others!"

"I always knew you were crazy, Trist," Twister said shaking her head in disbelief. "Go. Let's see if you can keep beating the odds, Captain Psycho!"

With that, Twister threw her legs over the balcony, summoning the winds to safely carry her downward, where she began to help the others.

Captain Psycho. That has a ring to it. They made it up the flight of stairs in a matter of seconds, the three friends praying that they could arrive in time to stop The Legion from taking any further lives.

Upon arriving at Principal Winter's office, however, they realized that they were too late. Ms. Dorregard's body was still, lying upon the desk on which she once worked. Belle and Dan let out a gasp of horror while Tristan screamed in fury and frustration, punching the wall in anger. He felt his emotions boil within him, ready to tear Shadow apart with his bare hands. They had been too slow. It was too late, and now The Legion knew where Winter was hiding. *How could he have let this happen?*

"Tristan, look!" Belle said pointing past the deceased assistant to the open door of the principal's office. Tristan looked in the direction that Belle was motioning toward until his eyes landed upon the sight of the principal's bookshelf. It appeared to be shifted slightly, revealing an opening just behind it.

"A hidden door? Where's it lead to?" Dan murmured behind him.

"Payback," Tristan growled. "Let's go."

The two followed closely behind as Tristan walked into the room and over to the bookcase, moving the wooden frame further to find a hidden staircase leading upward. Tristan could feel the cool breeze of the night air and just make out a faint light from the stars above. Tristan motioned for his friends to follow, and he began the quiet ascent onto the roof. Getting closer, Tristan slowly peered his head above to see what dangers awaited. He was greeted by an unexpected sight.

Rather than an empty marble exterior, the roof was instead covered entirely under a layer of soil. In fact, it wasn't empty at all, completely full of exotic flora of all varieties. The plants and flowers were all colors and sizes, some potted, while others were planted firmly in the rich, moist soil. The tiny garden utopia was enclosed by a retractable glass ceiling which was currently open, allowing the full moon to shine its light upon the scene. For all of the chaos and mayhem around them, this place was surprisingly...beautiful.

Tristan was broken from his wonder by the sounds of muffled voices up ahead. Maintaining a low profile, Tristan and his friends made their way onto the garden rooftop and snuck around to where the voices seemed to be coming from. Tristan could make out the sounds of a struggle, a familiar voice yelling out in pain before unleashing a string of curses. Hiding behind a thick, grove of fruit trees, the three students were able to observe the commotion ahead.

Tristan's eyes fell first to the two bodies of Professor Tullage and Stellios that lay perhaps ten feet before them. To his immense relief, he could still see their chests slowly rising, although they were both clearly unconscious. Next, he saw Shadow stepping back, a grin upon his face as he held a rather large vial filled with a dark red liquid. Principal Winter was on his knees before him, battered, while his arms were held by the massive form of Firestarter and Crystal.

"Finally...the key is ours. Soon, we will be able to revive him and restore the natural order that nature had intended for this world all along," Shadow said, his eyes reveling in the sight of the item in his hand.

"You're a fool, Chandler! You have no idea what you're trying to unleash!"

"My name...is...Shadow!" Dark tendrils whipped out across Winter's face, leaving two deep gashes across his cheek. "Don't ever speak my human name again! Or I'll leave more than just a mark upon that insolent face of yours! You should be happy! You should be joining me! All of this...is because of you! Because you sought to stop him! To stop evolution from taking its place! He was right! This world should be ours! We should be the ones in charge, not these...monkeys! Instead, you hide on this island, like cowards, behind your technology and aliases, unwilling to show the world the true glory of our species! Well, no more! Once we get this back to the lab, everything will change. He will rise from his frozen tomb, appointing me to command his army. And he will have his revenge."

Tristan looked at the vial within Shadow's hands. The key. If he could get his hands on it, Tristan could pull their attention away from Winter and his classmates. He just needed two things: a way to snatch it before Shadow could stop him and a way off this rooftop. Glancing back at his friends, Tristan began to formulate a plan crazy enough to work. *Captain Psycho, indeed...*

"You think you know him. You think you understand his ideals," Winter spat out. "You have no idea who you're getting into bed with. Ha! You think you're special, that you'll be his right-hand man? You're no general. You're Chandler Robbins, a delusional, unstable reject that I had to kick out of this school because you were too stubborn to listen when people tried to help you! You want to watch this world go to hell in a handbasket, that's your business, but the moment you attack my kids is when you make yourself an enemy far worse than you could ever imagine. You'll be sorry you ever left me alive, because I swear I will make sure I dedicate my life to finding and repaying you for every step you took upon these grounds!"

"My dear, old, fool of a teacher...who ever said I was leaving you alive?" Shadow replied incredulously, a large, bladed shadow shooting from his hand. Principal Winter's eyes widened before Shadow brought down his arm, aiming the blade at the man's exposed neck.

Just before the blade struck, a loud clap was heard, the force knocking over the surprised Shadow and knocking the vial into the air. Two spheres of water shot through the room, colliding upon the faces of Firestarter and Crystal, both of whom released Winter. Taken aback, Shadow felt the searing pain of boots smashing into his sternum, Tristan flying through the room like an oncoming car. The villain let out a cry of pain, thrown back several feet into a pile of thorn covered bushes behind him. Tristan landed flat on his back, the boy managing to snatch the vial from the ground where it had landed in the soft dirt beside him.

"Get him!" Shadow screamed behind Tristan, who was now scrambling to his feet and racing back to his friends. Enraged and desperate to recover their belonging, Shadow unleashed lines of dark spikes at Tristan while Firestarter and Crystal threw out streams of flames and glistening daggers, respectively.

Tristan's heart leaped to his throat, realizing how he had misjudged his attack. He had hoped his little improvisation would have thrown them off a little bit longer, but these were not the inexperienced students he was used to facing on a weekly basis. While he needed to get over to Dan as quickly as his feet could carry him, his friend was still a good fifteen feet away.

Suddenly, time seemed to slow down around him. For a moment, Tristan watched all of these fatal objects moving steadily toward him, and he wondered if this was what it was like before someone died. He felt a familiar feeling of vertigo, a rush of nausea creeping upon him. *I know this feeling.*

That's when Tristan noticed the faint glow out of the corner of his eye. Slowly adjusting his head, Tristan saw the chest of Morgan Winter glowing softly with a radiant light so bright it nearly blinded him. The closer he stared the more the world seemed to spin around Tristan. It felt as if Winter was drawing him in. Not just him, but everyone and everything. *Nova... This is your power!*

Tristan watched in amazement as the shadow blades seemed to falter, flickering in and out before crumbling into dust. The flames sputtered in the air, unable to spread any further. The shards of crystal veered away from the boy, their ends deflecting into the empty air beside him. Tristan couldn't wrap his head around what the principal was doing, but he did know this: he was saving Tristan's life.

As quickly as it started, it was over. Morgan let out a cry of pain, absorbing the flames while daggers of shadow and crystal sunk into his body, and the man fell backward, grimacing in agony. *No!* Tristan thought, ready to turn around, but he was already too far at this point, Dan's hands grabbing the front of his shirt. Before he could call it off, Tristan felt himself lifted off of the ground and into the night sky. He was soaring, hanging on to the vial for dear life while he flew over Academy. He could hear cries of fury behind him as he cleared several trees below, the nearby lake coming up quickly.

Tristan prayed that this would work, as they had never before tested how far Belle's reach could go. If this didn't succeed, they'd be scraping Tristan's body off of the bottom of the lake in the morning. He closed his eyes and prepared for the worst when he felt the soft tendrils of water wrap around his torso, slowly decreasing his speed. He breathed a sigh of relief, the water lowering him gently to the ground below. Suddenly, a burst of flame lit the sky around the Academy's rooftop, and the water whips immediately dissipated, crashing Tristan down on the ground only a few feet below.

Panic gripped Tristan as he glanced back at the rooftop. *Belle! Was she okay?!* He prayed that his escape hadn't been at the cost of his friends but knew he couldn't dwell on it for long. He needed to hide. He needed to draw The Legion away from the school and give everyone else a chance to regroup and escape. It was the only way.

Tristan turned around and broke into a dead sprint, moving his legs as fast as they'd ever taken him, through the courtyard and past the rubble of the campus wall. Tristan raced to the mountain path, hoping to hide amongst the cliffs where his classes had been. His lungs burning, Tristan tried his best to ignore his aching body, which felt like it had gone through hell and back today. Despite all his training, he knew he was running on fumes.

Getting closer to the trail, Tristan heard signs of a struggle just up ahead. Two figures appeared to be dueling in the night a few yards away, the sounds of fists colliding ringing in the air. This didn't make sense. The Legion was behind him. There was no way they had gotten ahead! Confused, Tristan continued his run, and when he grew closer, realized the identities of the combatants.

Christian was stumbling backward, scrambling to regain his footing as Gabriel roared in anger before him. Gabriel shot forward swinging fists of sand, which Christian seemed to dodge using every bit of his enhanced speed and reflexes. As fast as he was, there was no way, he could escape Gabriel's aggression, and soon he was hit square in the jaw. His head snapping back, Christian tried to shield himself, but it was no use, Gabriel enclosing the boy's body in a block of sand.

"I'm gonna make you pay! You messed with me for the last time! You—!"

Gabriel's speech was cut short by the bone-crunching blow of Tristan's elbow to the side of his temple. The boy's eyes rolled back into his head, and he crumpled into a heap upon the ground, unconscious. Christian, immediately freed from the sand, stood up, shaking the particles off of his clothes. He glanced at Tristan, a look of sheer joy and relief on his face upon seeing his best friend. He ran up and gave Tristan a fierce hug.

"Tristan, thank God! You're alive! Dude, I thought you were on that plane! What are you doing here?! Where is everyone?!"

While thrilled to see his friend, Tristan shook his head furiously, pulling for Christian to join him. "No time to talk, Chris! We gotta get outta here now! The Legion won't be far behind us, and we've gotta hide!"

"What about this, jerk-off?!"

"Leave him! We gotta go!" Tristan cried and started to run to the trail.

"No! Don't go there!" Christian called back, moving in the direction of the jungle instead.

"Why not?!"

"If you go there, they'll pin you up in the mountains! There's nowhere else to go but down once you're up there! I've got a better idea! Come on!"

Christian sprinted into the lush greenery, and after analyzing the rationale, Tristan had to admit his friend had a point. He rushed into the thick, green jungle after him, trying to match Christian's enhanced pace.

After a few hundred meters, Tristan was exhausted. He could not keep up with Christian's speed and was slowly losing him in the thickness of the branches and leaves around him. He could no longer tell where they were, and he felt hopelessly lost. Calling out to his friend and ready to turn around, Tristan finally broke through the leaves into an open area, an old abandoned steel silo looming before him.

"In here!" Christian beckoned, opening up the door and racing within.

"Chris? Where did—How did you find this place?" Tristan asked, trying to catch his breath while moving to join his friend inside. There was something oddly familiar about this place, although Tristan knew he had never ventured out this far before.

Upon entering the silo, Tristan was greeted by near darkness, the only lights coming from the holes in the dilapidated roof above.

"Chris?!" Tristan called out, his eyes struggling to adjust.

"I'm here, man! Don't worry! We can hide out in here until daybreak! Hopefully by then, The Legion will have given up trying to find us and retreated." Tristan's mind was racing, trying to process his surroundings.

"Chris, I don't know, man. Something about this place doesn't feel right. Where are we?"

"It's an old abandoned hanger they used back in the day. It's been out of commission for decades. I stumbled upon it one day when I was out hiking with a date."

Tristan rolled his eyes, knowing full well his friend couldn't see him. *A date? Typical Chris.* Still, Tristan couldn't shake this feeling that he was missing something yet again. "Like I said, we should be good here, bro. As long as we stay put, the key should be safe with us."

Tristan felt the hairs on his neck rise, his heart skipping a beat. His throat went dry as he slowly turned to the sound of his friend. Tristan swallowed hard, a sense of overwhelming despair filling his heart.

"Hey, Chris?"

"Yeah?"

"I never said I had the key."

Suddenly, the air around him grew unnaturally cold, Tristan's breath immediately visible. The steady footsteps of his best friend led him under the light of the night sky from a rooftop opening. There was no mistaking the sadness in those black, empty eyes.

"Oh, Tristan. Why couldn't you leave well enough alone?"

Chapter 26: Electro

Tristan felt the world around him crumble in hopelessness, a pain echoing deep within him. He had never felt a betrayal cut as deeply as the one unfurling before him. *How could he have missed it? How could he have not seen through the lies? This couldn't be happening! He knew Christian, they were best friends!*

"How long? How long have you been working for them?"

"Tristan, it's not that—"

"How long?!"

There was a pause as Christian held his head, his dark hair falling across his face. "Years now...since I was ten. After my last stint at a foster home, the night I discovered my powers. I ran away while they were calling my social worker to come pick me up. All I could think about was getting out of there. I knew I never wanted to go back into the foster system. I was sick of the betrayals, of being tossed aside after a few weeks or months by some family who felt I wasn't worth the effort! All because of things I couldn't control! So I ran. I ran as far as my legs could take me. And that's when I found them. Or rather they found me."

"They knew I was a metamorph. They'd been keeping watch on children within the system who displayed characteristics of the Deus gene, and sure enough, I was among them. They thought I was special, my abilities uniquely suited for their needs. They valued me, Tristan. Do you have any idea what that feels like?"

Tristan swallowed hard and nodded, all the while checking his pocket to make sure the vial was still securely there. If he could keep Christian talking, he might be able to locate another way out, hopefully make a run for it, and lose the boy in the midst of the dense jungle.

"So then what? They just gave you a big hug and welcomed you into their warm, happy family?"

"God, no! Are you kidding?" Christian chuckled. "It was miserable! They tortured me relentlessly. Beat me into submission until I was nothing but their dog! They trained me how to use my powers, how to unleash the monster within. For years I worked under them, doing the occasional odd job in between training until finally, it was my turn to step up to the plate. And when it came to infiltrating the island, there was no one better suited for the mission than a prospective student."

Tristan shook his head in disgust, staring at a face he no longer recognized. "So it was all just a ruse?! All the laughs, all the tears we shed, all that talk of us being a 'family'? It was all just a lie!"

"No!" Christian replied with an intensity that surprised Tristan. "No! Those memories, those moments were as genuine as I've ever been! Coming into this mission, I had one goal, one objective: to find a way into this academy, scout out the defenses, and aid The Legion in sneaking in. I never expected to meet you guys. To actually find myself enjoying the life I had fabricated. Believe it or not, Trist, you are my best friend. You were the first person I'd met that looked at me as more than just a mistake, more than just a weapon. You saw me in all my flaws...and still took me on as your teammate. As your friend."

"Then why?! Why didn't you stop?! Why didn't you just turn them in?!"

"Because I can't! Don't you get it?! This isn't just some group of disgruntled metamorphs throwing a tantrum! This is an organization who truly believe in their ideals to the point of risking everything in order to accomplish their goals! This is bigger than me, Trist. Hell, this is bigger than them. If you had any idea what they were really doing, you would know that I don't have a choice. I'm already in too deep.

"The world is about to change, Tristan. For the better. And The Legion will be at the forefront of it all! Soon, metamorphs will no longer need to remain in hiding. We can be free to walk out into the world the way we were meant to...as its rulers. We won't be seen as freaks or monsters, but rather as gods among men. We were meant to rule over these humans, Tristan. To lead them into a future where we're in charge. Look at what they've done to this world! They're slowly destroying it with their wars, their pollution, and their destruction of its resources. They can't even get along with one another based on skin tone or political lines! They need us! They need us to save them from themselves! Don't you see, Tristan? The world will be so much better when we're in charge. We're not the villains here. We're the heroes. We may not be the ones they want, but we are what they need."

"So how does killing innocent metamorphs fit into your master plan for world peace, huh?! How do you justify murdering your own people, Chris?! Because there's a host of kids who lost their lives tonight, who will never see this utopia of yours, all because The Legion thought they were expendable, and as far as I'm concerned, your hands are just as dirty as theirs!"

Christian turned his head to the side, jaws clenched. "Paradise wasn't built in a day, Tristan, and it damn sure doesn't come free. There will always be a price to pay in war and believe me, friend, the war is coming. Are you sure you're on the right side?"

"What's that supposed to mean?" Tristan asked.

"I mean, how much do you really know about the history of this school and its founders? Winter and the staff, they're the ones who write the textbooks, the history of our people. They're the ones who dictate the rules of our society and feed you the propaganda, the ideals they force you to inherit. But what about the truth, the real stories behind these so-called 'heroes' you all idolize and aspire to be like?"

"What are you talking about?"

"Tristan, if you only knew the truth behind it all, what really happened all those years ago, you would never look at this place the same. You would see the Council for the cowards that they are and know that The Legion are the true saviors of our people. Stop trying to fight us, Tristan. Join us, and you can witness the truth for yourself! Who knows, maybe Shadow can even unlock your abilities! You can be a part of something special, Tristan! You can be special! Isn't that what you've always wanted?"

Silence hung in the night air as Tristan stared into the pleading eyes of his friend. A part of him wanted to believe Christian, to believe that he wasn't just a monster, a pawn caught up in the devilish schemes of a madman and his demented crew. Perhaps Christian was right, and the school was flawed, the school leaders subtly brainwashing and manipulating the students into blindly following their views of the world. Maybe the world would be a better place if metamorphs stopped hiding and took the responsibility of leadership for themselves.

Tristan wanted to believe his friend so badly, but all he could see was the cost, the price that was paid in the pursuit of this so-called ideal world. A world where people like Windrider would no longer have any part because men like Shadow existed. "Sorry, Chris," Tristan finally said, shaking his head, "but I thought I was part of something special. And I'll be damned if I let you take that away from me."

Tristan spun to face the door, ready to sprint out into the night in the hopes of losing Christian, but as he did a loud pop echoed out into the air.

"No!" Christian screamed, his voice echoing across the room, as Tristan suddenly felt something strike his shoulder and a searing pain ripped through his upper arm and chest. The force blew him onto his back, and he felt a warmth spread across the area. Tristan lay on the ground, unable to catch his breath, while a wave of nausea flowed through him. His vision swam before him, and he stared at his shoulder, blood flowing freely from where it appeared he had been shot. No, not shot. Not exactly anyway.

A pair of silver boots stood beside him, Bullet's masked face sneering above. "'Ello, mate! Hope you wasn't planning on goin' anywhere! The party's just begun!"

Tristan groaned in pain, unable to respond. Tristan knew he needed to find a way out of here, but his brain could barely function at the moment. He flipped over on to his stomach and attempted to crawl away, the sounds of laughter filling the air. They were here, all of them. There was no escape. He felt the hands of Bullet reach over to pat him down, eventually finding the vial of blood in his pocket. All Tristan could think about was how their efforts had been in vain. All those lives, all his friend's suffering, and there was nothing he could do to stop this from happening.

Tristan flipped back around, trying to prop himself up with one arm, as he looked into the downcast eyes of the boy he once considered his best friend. The tears flowed freely down Tristan's face now, a mixture of rage and sadness, the anguish of betrayal only intensifying the pain in his arm.

"Aww, poor baby's gonna cry! He don't like it when we laugh at him!" Bullet mocked, delivering a swift kick of his heel into the gaping hole in

Tristan's arm. Tristan immediately went back down in a scream of pain, nearly vomiting from the agony.

"That's enough, Bullet! Get away from him! You've made your point!" Christian yelled out from across the room, his eyes narrowing in fury.

Bullet glanced at Christian, a dangerous gleam in his eyes. "Easy there, schoolboy. You best remember which side you're on. You don't give the orders around here. Last I checked, you were still the whipping boy. If I were you, I would remember my place real quick, before you join your friend here in an unmarked grave."

The man's threat hung in the air while Christian's fangs gleamed in the darkness of the room. The tension was palpable, and Tristan wondered whether the two were really about to attack one another.

"Enough, you two," a voice cut through the silence. "Play nice. As much as I would enjoy watching you fight over who gets to sit in the front seat, Daddy has other plans for this evening."

Shadow stepped between the two, the darkness in the room appearing to respond to his very presence, intensifying in tone. Bullet and Christian immediately seemed to relax, deciding to hold off their spat for now, while the true alpha of the pack took over.

Tristan again tried to force himself up while Bullet delivered the vial to the awaiting hand of Shadow. *This can't be how it ends,* Tristan thought. Maybe if he could distract them, hold them off long enough, he could buy himself enough time for someone to discover them. It was the only option at this point.

"What the hell do you want with that thing anyway? It's not even a key. It's just a vial of liquid," he muttered, willing his body to work as he got on to his knees. Shadow laughed again, his eyes never leaving the vial.

"Oh, my dear boy, how little you know. This contains the blood of a certain Morgan Winter, a man whose DNA holds the 'key' to unlocking the most powerful being to walk this world since the time of Zeus. This isn't just some liquid," Shadow stated, looking Tristan dead in the eyes. "This is the very future of the world."

Tristan grunted, slowly picking himself up and standing on two very wobbly legs. He coughed, blood spraying out, but managed to maintain his uneasy footing. "I don't want your twisted future, asshole. None of us do. If you really think that this is how your 'perfect order' begins, on the graves of innocents, then you really are as delusional as they say."

Shadow laughed again, his pearly white teeth a stark contrast to the blackness gathering around him. "Oh Mr. Davids, who said you would be invited to this world of mine to begin with?" he asked incredulously. "Look at you! Why are you even here? You're nothing but an over-privileged reject, allowed at a school where you don't belong simply because you have a fortuitous last name!" The Legion all started chuckling at this while Shadow continued to mock the quivering boy before him.

"Look at you! You're not special. You're just some kid trying to stand up for his friends. Why the hell would I ever want such a waste of space in my world? You don't deserve it!" he spat in disgust.

"Shadow...please." Tristan heard the worried tone in Christian's voice, "Have mercy upon him. You know who he is...perhaps he could be of use to us!"

Shadow scoffed. "That's quite an ask, boy. Even if he is a Davids, he is a far cry from the once proud bloodline of his family. Still...I am not without reason. There is a chance that he could be of use. Our restored leader may even be quite pleased to see him." Shadow's eyes seemed to reconsider Tristan.

"What do you say, Mr. Davids? Would you like to die here on your feet along with all the other useless fodder on this island...or would you like to come with us, to serve our new lord in a world one could only dream of?"

Now it was Tristan's turn to chuckle. Despite the roaring pain in his arm and his dire circumstances, he couldn't help himself. The answer was so easy. Ignoring Shadow, Tristan stared right at the face of Christian, shaking his head confidently.

"Thanks, but I think you know where you can take that offer and shove it. I'd rather die here on my feet, a hero, than live on my knees in a world where I'm the villain."

Shadow rolled his eyes, shaking his head in disbelief. "Have it your way."

With that, Shadow shot forth his arms, releasing sharp tendrils of darkness speeding in Tristan's direction. Oddly enough, Tristan felt calm. He had failed, but at least he would leave this earth knowing that he never gave in. Closing his eyes, Tristan readied himself for the tar-like blades to tear through him like a hot knife through butter. Instead, he heard a muffled thud and a spray of grainy substance splashed across his face.

What the hell? Tristan wiped off his face and opened his eyes. Where there once was an open space before him, now stood a shifting wall, the imprints of the shadow blades within it. A wall of sand.

"What the—?!" Shadow began, but before he could finish, a massive wave of sand roared through the open door of the hanger, crashing into the unsuspecting bodies of The Legion. The villains flew back in a heap, tumbling over themselves at the fury of the swirling sands around them. The wave was followed by six giant spears of sand that shot through the air, aimed at The Legion. Shadow managed to recover in time to create a protective shield upon which the sand spear broke, but the other five received a load of rock-hard sand to their chest.

Without missing a beat, Gabriel sprinted into the room and firmly planted himself between the Legion and his classmate, manipulating the sand wall to merge onto his body and form a suit of armor.

"Sorry to break up the party, but if anyone is gonna kick Tristan's ass, it's gonna be me!"

Tristan felt a grin spread across his face, despite himself. Say what you want about him, Gabriel sure did know how to make an entrance.

Shadow roared in anger, a sword of darkness forming in his hands as he charged forward, while the others scrambled to their feet. Gabriel sprinted to meet him, creating a sand sword of his own, and the two metamorphs clashed in the middle of the room. They swung their weapons, the blades colliding, shattering upon impact and dissipating into the air. Gabriel did a forward roll, coming up and swinging a giant fist of sand into the stomach of Firestarter, the large man actually doubling over in pain. Gabriel spun to the right, swinging out his left leg to sweep the oncoming Crystal right off her feet. As the woman fell onto her back, Gabriel summoned forth a hammer of sand, bringing it down onto her stomach. Crystal let out a groan of pain as the air deflated from her chest, Gabriel already prepping his next counter.

When Bullet fired at his back, Gabriel was already raising up a defensive wall. Once Bullet struck the sand, Gabriel twisted his hands, shifting the wall and manipulating the trajectory of the henchman's flight. Rather than shoot through Gabriel's back, Bullet instead rocketed into the face of the unsuspecting Jaws, whose jaw cocked to the side abruptly, a jagged tooth coming loose from the impact. Focused on holding off the other five, Gabriel nearly missed Christian's follow through, the boy leaping into the air to sink his claws into Gabriel's side. Gabriel dipped low and spun around in one swift move, bringing his elbow up to connect with Christian's open jaw. Christian's neck snapped back from the blow, blood spraying into the air as the boy howled in pain, his fangs finding their way through his own lips.

It was unreal seeing Gabriel in action, taking on the entire Legion by himself as he sought to keep the two of them alive. He was far stronger than Tristan had ever realized, and he seemed to effortlessly control his abilities, launching one attack after another while keeping their enemies at bay. The battle continued to rage for several more seconds, Gabriel furiously manipulating the sand around him as fast as he could to deal with his attackers. While Gabriel probably could have held on for even longer, Shadow had other ideas.

Rather than continue his attack on Gabriel, the villain turned his attention to Tristan, who could only spectate. Reaching back to form a whip out of the darkness, Shadow swung his arm forward, the long, thick rope lashing right into the side of Tristan. Tristan heard a loud crack ring through the air and all of the oxygen he held immediately left his body. His vision swam as he struggled to breathe, intense pain and heat searing through his thorax. His rib clearly broken, Tristan slumped to the ground, clutching his side in agony.

Gabriel, looking back to see his fallen classmate, immediately disengaged from the battle. Trying his best to avoid the blows of the other five villains, he rushed back to defend Tristan. With Gabriel's back toward them, the villains simultaneously fired off their abilities in an attempt to finish him off. Once he reached the incapacitated Tristan, Gabriel spun around and called forth a defensive wall to protect them both, using all of his strength and will to halt the oncoming attacks. Tristan watched the flames of Firestarter, the glass shards of Crystal, the frost wave of Vamp, and the black blades of Shadow all collided at once into Gabriel's wall, his classmate crying out as he absorbed them all. The room seemed to light up as the metamorphs called forth all of their abilities in the ultimate battle of wills, both sides unwilling to yield. And still, Gabriel held on.

How his classmate managed the feat, Tristan had no idea, one first-year against a room full of master assassins. He screamed and roared, digging his heels into the crumbling ground beneath him, sweat streaming down his fatiguing muscles. But as awe-inspiring as Gabriel was in that moment, even he had his limits. Glancing back at Tristan, he looked tired, his muscles beginning to shake from the effort. For the first time since they had met, Tristan saw fear in Gabriel's eyes.

"Sorry, Trist...I wish I could've...done more..."

There was a flash of blinding light, and Gabriel's wall came crashing down around them, his classmate taking the full force of the combined powers. "Noooo!" Tristan screamed, but his voice was drowned out by the explosion around him. Tristan was lifted off his knees by the force and thrown to the back of the hanger, Gabriel's limp body following close behind. The sounds of crashing walls and crumbling pieces of roof filled the air while debris rained down around them.

"Tristan!" Christian cried out.

"Leave him! He's a goner!"

"But—!"

"I said leave him! We have a plane to catch!"

Lying on the ground, his own blood pooling beneath him, Tristan could barely make out the silhouettes of The Legion making their escape. All six of them. While the world he knew fell apart around him, Tristan found himself staring at the unconscious face of the boy he once saw as his enemy. *How could it have come to this?* Then, things went dark.

When his eyes finally did open, Tristan was surrounded in pitch black. His head throbbed something fierce, and he found himself unable to move. His entire lower body was pinned beneath a large sheet of tin roofing, and between this, his damaged shoulder, and broken rib, there was no way he could see himself getting out of this predicament. Coughing up dust and blood, Tristan tried to move his head while his eyes adjusted to the darkness. Gabriel was still a few feet away, his body also covered in debris from the collapsed building. The boy wasn't moving.

Unable to turn his eyes away from the sight, Tristan found himself barely able to cry, his body starting to shut down as he lay in the darkness. Death
was imminent. They had failed. He had failed. He had come to this school
in the hopes of becoming a superhero, just like the ones he had always read
about, to be like his family. He had come in the hopes that he would find
a place where he finally belonged. But Winter had been right from the beginning. He wasn't a superhero. He wasn't special. He didn't belong here.

He had no powers, his home had been destroyed, and there was a good
chance he would never see his classmates again. Hell, even his best friend
had betrayed him. To top it off, he had let The Legion walk off with an item
so powerful it would allow them to change the world as they saw fit. It was
all over, and Tristan was to blame.

Tears of anger and despair ran down Tristan's face, and he let out a sob.
His lower body was beginning to go numb. Struggling for breath, images
floated through his mind:

His family, eating lunch with his teammates, hanging out on the beach
with Belle.

His meetings with Principal Winter, jumping out of the airplane, the
winter snowball fight.

Mr. Peters, getting bullied at his old school, Gabriel laying down his life
for him.

All of these images of his life running through his mind. And more.

Bitterness at Christian for betraying them all.

Despair at his current state of helplessness.

Sadness for all of the classmates he had lost.

Regret for all the words he never said to Belle.

Fear of death, the uncertainty of what comes next.

But above all else...pure, unbridled anger at the unfairness of it all. This
wasn't how it was supposed to end. It couldn't be. He wouldn't let it.

Tristan began to feel a familiar burning sensation inside of his chest,
a sensation he had felt before when he first sparred against Gabriel, had
fought against Machina, and when he leaped from the airplane. A burst of
emotions that spread like wildfire, moving through every fiber of his being. A ray of determination that began to crack through the darkness of his
mind, breaking through the very pores of his body. A spark igniting in his

core that seemed to expand until his eyes grew hot and his very skin seemed to sizzle. It didn't just consume him, it became him. Tristan embraced the feeling, a primal roar escaping his body, and just like that—the darkness turned to light.

Several minutes had passed since the Legion had abandoned Tristan and Gabriel to their fates, the six villains quickly approaching their target which lay just before them: a small, private plane along the coast of the island. Shadow seemed in good spirits, the rest of the team talking amongst themselves, reveling in the anticipation of the glory that awaited them back home. The only one who seemed downcast was Christian, who appeared sullen and distracted, the boy not saying a word since they had escaped the collapsing hanger. Shadow waved his arm in the air, signaling for the pilot ahead to start the engine. The man was one of their human henchmen, one of many devoted acolytes whom they had brainwashed into serving them in the hopes that they could remain in their master's good graces once the new world order was established.

A rumbling of thunder was heard overhead, causing Shadow to look to the clear, starry night above. The man frowned, slightly confused.

"Aww, what's wrong, my liege?" Firestarter said, slapping the tall man on the back. "Not a fan of flying in a storm?"

"Shut up, Firestarter!" Crystal retorted, coming to Shadow's defense. "I hate flying in bad weather, too!"

This resulted in the four senior members arguing over how likely it was to crash a plane in inclement weather. The heated debate caused Shadow to roll his eyes in annoyance, appearing to ignore the comments of his subordinates.

They were nearly there when Shadow stopped abruptly, the others following suit. His eyes narrowed, a strange look within them. He turned back to the direction they had just come from, scanning the horizon. Slowly, he reached into his cloak and took out the vial of blood, handing the precious cargo to Christian.

"Take this, dog. Bring it to the plane and get in. Now." Christian frowned but did as instructed.

"What's the matter, boss?" Bullet asked. Shadow lifted his arm, staring intently at the raised hairs which stood on end like porcupine spines.

"Something's wrong."

Suddenly, a massive flash of light came thundering down from the skies, the bolt streaking through the air in the blink of an eye before making impact somewhere in the jungle. An explosion of blinding light followed, the force of the impact causing the island to tremble, and The Legion stumbled backward from the subsequent aftershocks. As the dust settled around them, the villains looked around in a panic unsure of what to make of what they had just witnessed.

"What the hell was that?!" Jaws screeched.

"Nothing good," Shadow murmured.

Shadow could have sworn he saw a flicker of movement, a blur that had shot out past the treetops, but scanning the sky, he couldn't spot anything besides the stars. That's when he noticed one of the stars moving toward them. The tiny dot seemed to grow in size and brightness as it neared, streaking across the night sky.

"Ready yourselves! Something is com—!" Shadow cut off abruptly as the star disappeared. A few seconds passed, The Legion holding still expectantly.

"Boss, what was that?" Bullet asked.

Suddenly, the ground exploded before them in a flash of light, the impact sending the group flying off their feet. Sand and earth rained down in a flurry, and the air buzzed around them. The villains felt their hairs stand on end, the static flowing through the air, as they stared at the glowing form before them.

The light coming from the figure was so intense it nearly blinded them, yet his outline was one that appeared oddly familiar. The air surrounding him crackled with electricity, sparks igniting all around him. He was like a god of old, his muscle-bound form literally exuding power while light shone from his very pores. He lit up the night by his mere presence, flickers of lightning flashing all around him. The ground trembled beneath his feet, the sand flowing away from his body in ripples like the water's surface. He had no pupils, his eyes ablaze with fiery light, and his hair slowly flowed in a constant wave. There were wounds on his body, but he seemed not to notice, able to move around without issue. He carried a body in his powerful arms, which was slowly beginning to stir.

Gabriel gradually opened his eyes, barely able to keep them open due to the light's intensity as he came to. Squinting, he started at the sight before him, nearly jumping out of the arms had his broken body allowed him to. The form smiled down upon him, and a voice reverberated into the night air.

"Relax, Gabe. I've got you. You don't have to fight anymore. You've done enough for one lifetime. It's my turn to return the favor." Gabriel's eyes widened in shock, and he slowly nodded his head. The Legion scrambled to their feet while the god lowered Gabriel's body to the ground, standing back up to face them.

"Oh...my...God," Christian whispered from the plane, a look of awe upon his face as he recognized the figure. This was no god. This was his friend. This was Tristan.

"Well, well, well! Look who decided to join the family. Haha! I knew there was something special about you, boy! You are a Davids after all!" Shadow said with a smile. Tristan continued to stand before him in silence, stone-faced. The Legion glanced around nervously, while Shadow cleared his throat. "I guess you should be thanking me! Looks like you just needed a little push to get you on the path to discovering your potential! Imagine what else you could learn under my guidance!"

Tristan tilted his head, a small smirk of amusement pulling at the corner of his mouth. "Gee, thanks."

"Yes, uh, well, my offer to join us still stands! Come with us and join in the splendors of the coming—!"

"Yeah, I'm just gonna stop you right there, douche-face. I really don't need to hear your come-to-the-dark-side spiel again, once was enough. Last I checked, you left me and my friend for dead and were responsible for the destruction of a place I called my home. Not sure how things go in that fantasyland in your head, but out here that makes us enemies." The very air around Tristan seemed to catch fire as electricity surged around him furiously. "Now, here's *my* sales pitch."

Tristan turned his palms upward, and a flash of lightning roared through the air, striking Jaws square in the chest. The creature's eyes went wide with shock before his body flew back, striking the side of the plane. He let out a moan, smoke escaping his mouth as his eyes rolled into the back of his head. He slowly slid to the ground and collapsed, a gaping, burning hole smoldering where his chest should have been. The eyes of his teammates flashed with panic, their jaws agape at the sight of their partner so easily dispatched.

Bullet was the first to react, roaring in anger at the loss of a friend, and he shot himself at Tristan, ready to finish the job he had started. In a burst of speed, Bullet was already inches from striking the fatal blow to his heart, when Tristan shot a glance in Bullet's direction.

With a cry of pain, the villain realized, too late, that as fast as a bullet may be, light travels faster. The remaining members of the Legion watched while Bullet suddenly ricocheted out away from Tristan, his flaming form flipping through the night sky before eventually crash landing several yards away, smoke streaming from his still form.

Tristan turned back to the rest of the Legion, a look of disappointment upon his face. It was almost too easy. He sprinted forward, his feet moving at a speed he had never before experienced, toward Firestarter. Streaks of lightning shot out behind him, and Tristan closed the distance between him and the brute in the blink of an eye. Firestarter just managed to react in time, throwing forth his palms, the flamethrower tubes releasing a torrent of fire. Simultaneously, Tristan launched himself straight up into the air, leaning forward into an acrobatic flip that allowed him to completely clear the stationary giant in one graceful bound.

Twisting his body in the air, Tristan landed effortlessly on both feet, now facing Firestarter's back. He placed his hand on the man's weaponized contraption and sent a surge of electricity throughout the pack. Like setting off a firework, Firestarter shot forward like a blazing rocket, his contraption exploding across his back as he flew over the sand. The man landed face first in a heap upon the ground, his screams ringing in the air while the flames consumed his skin. Firestarter leaped to his feet, his body a massive fireball, and he tried to get himself into the nearby water. He managed to get within a few feet of the shoreline before eventually collapsing with a thud, a final groan escaping his flaming lips.

Pushing the horrifying image to the back of his mind, Tristan continued to press his advantage, turning now to the nearby Crystal and launching multiple bolts in her direction. With each strike, Crystal brilliantly parried, calling forth crystal shields to deflect and absorb the blasts. Tristan continued his pursuit, making note of Shadow, who was attempting to sneak around him. Tristan fired off several more salvoes in quick succession, causing Crystal to nearly lose her footing before she stepped back into the waters.

Parrying the last blast, Crystal let out a cry of frustration. "Enough! Don't you get it, you little brat?! Your little light show has no effect on my crystals! You've lost! You and your friends are over with! Can't you see what we've done to this island?! You should have left this stupid school when you had the chance!"

Tristan raised an eyebrow in response. "Hmm, that's ironic. You should have never left. You could have learned a valuable lesson: always mind your surroundings." With that, Tristan let loose a surge of lightning in the water surrounding Crystal. The woman cried out as her body stiffened immediately, absorbing every current Tristan sent out.

Tristan heard the cry of anguish behind him after Crystal's steaming, twitching body sunk into the waters. A flood of darkness rose behind him, Shadow summoning every inch of blackness around him, and he channeled his full power into annihilating Tristan. Tristan slowly turned to his final enemy, facing down the oncoming darkness with surprising calm and poise. The darkness struck Tristan head-on, Shadow's eyes burning with rage and his mouth frothing with murderous desire. His expression quickly changed to one of disbelief, however, at the sight before him.

All of his rage, all of his power, all of it channeled into one force focused on destroying the insolent boy before him. And it had no effect whatsoever. In fact, none of it had even touched him. Instead, Tristan simply stood in the same position, the darkness swirling around his body and unable to pierce the light that shone throughout his body. Shadow glanced at Christian, who appeared to be frantically screaming for the pilot to take off. Watching his only means of escape rise slowly into the night sky above, it all seemed so surreal to Shadow. How had it come to this? How had he been bested by this insignificant teenager?

As he stared at the approaching form of Tristan, Shadow managed to spout out the only question his muddled mind could think of:

"What the hell are you?!"

"Who, me? I'm just a kid who's willing to stand up for his friends."

Tristan broke out into a sprint, his glowing body cutting through the darkness like a knife, the screams of Shadow drowned out by a single thought that ran through his mind. Remembering a familiar scene almost a year ago to the date, Tristan smiled to himself as he leaped into the air, bringing down the fury of the skies in a single punch. *It's hero time.*

When Tristan's eyes finally opened, he found himself in a warm, comfortable bed. The sunlight outside was poring through the slits of the window shades beside him, and there were the sounds of chirping birds indicating the arrival of morning. Slowly glancing around and gathering his surrounding, Tristan realized he was in the school infirmary, apparently the only one still here. He was no longer wearing his regular clothes, wrapped in a hospital gown instead. All he heard was silence from within the facility, and when he started to lift himself up, he felt a dull throb within his shoulder and side. It was nowhere near as bad as when he had initially hurt it, however, it was a nice reminder that the events from before had indeed taken place. Which meant...

Smiling to himself, Tristan lifted his hands to his face, calling forth small waves of electricity from his palms. It was amazing, this feeling. He had done it. He truly was a metamorph. Rising to his feet, Tristan noticed a small, handwritten note beside his bed:

"Please see me before you leave, Mr. Davids. I will be waiting at the place where we last met... Principal Winter"

Tristan threw on the extra pair of clothing that lay on the chair nearby and slipped on a pair of sandals that were beneath the bed, making his way out through the hallway. Upon opening the doors and breathing in the warm, summer air, Tristan walked to the Academy observing the new look of the school grounds. The place still looked like it had been through a war, rubble and upturned earth seen all across the campus, but there were already workers in place, cleaning and rebuilding the once proud courtyard. Even the dormitories were slowly being put back together, large cranes moving steel beams back into place. Thankfully, the Academy hadn't suffered too much damage, from what Tristan saw when he walked up the marble staircase.

Passing through the lobby, Tristan made sure to avoid the area where Windrider had fallen. He wasn't ready to relive that memory just yet. After taking the elevator up to the third floor, Tristan walked into the Principal's office, briskly moving past the now vacant desk of Ms. Dorregard. The bookshelf was already propped open for him, and Tristan made his way up onto the rooftop veranda. There he was greeted by the welcome sight of Principal Winter, in full suit, pruning his rose bushes.

"Ahh, Mr. Davids! I see you're up! It's been a while since we last saw one another. I was beginning to think you might never wake up."

"Where is everyone, sir?" Tristan asked, furrowing his brow.

"Summer break! We can't keep everyone here forever!"

"Summer break? Wait a second, what day is today?"

"The 1st."

"Of May?!" Winter nodded in reply. "You mean to tell me I've been unconscious for the last two weeks?! Jesus, I missed my birthday!"

"After you had run off, the Legion incapacitated us before going after you. Barely clinging on to life myself, I awoke to the sound of thunder and a flash of light upon the beach. By the time I had managed to get myself over there, you were unconscious, the entire Legion defeated by your hands."

"What about my friends? Are they—?"

"They're all fine, son. They're all fine. In fact, it was a battle all on its own trying to get them to leave your side and go on vacation. They care for you deeply, you know. Friendships like that are hard to come by these days. Make sure you treasure it." Tristan nodded, swallowing the lump in his throat.

While Tristan processed this information, Principal Winter continued his gardening. "You know, Tristan, that was a hell of a performance on your part. Without you, this school would be only a memory, and I wouldn't be standing before you today. We all owe you a great deal of gratitude. Your bravery in the face of danger and leadership in the midst of adversity allowed us all to survive the Legion's attack. Though it pains me to know that we were betrayed by one of our very own and my heart still mourns for those who lost their lives in the battle, my soul rejoices knowing that, in the end, good indeed won the day."

The man turned to face Tristan, his usual trademark frown replaced by a warm smile and continued. "Tristan, I have to say, despite my initial misgivings, I'm happy you proved this old fool wrong."

"What? That I had powers all along?"

"No," Winter said, shaking his head, "That you never needed them. Don't get me wrong, unlocking your abilities is no small victory, but the fact that you managed to take on the most dangerous metamorphs on the planet and throw them for a loop using only your wits says quite a lot about how much I've underestimated you."

"Thank you, sir. That means a lot coming from you. But honestly, I would have never gotten the chance to discover my powers if you hadn't saved me that night. What was that, Principal Winter?"

The grey-haired man chuckled softly. "That was me trying to remember my way around a fight. They called me Nova, back in my day. I have the ability to create literal black holes, physical rifts through space and time. Along with that, I can pretty much become one myself, dampening or absorbing the powers of others. It's an ability that can be difficult to control, especially if I am emotional, so I try not to use it much."

"Is that also why you come off as so distant?" Tristan asked uneasily. The principal shot him a sideways glance and raised his eyebrows. He did, however, give a curt nod in acknowledgment.

"So what happens now, sir?"

"Well, it's up to you, Mr. Davids. Personally, I feel that you've more than earned your way back into this Academy. That is, if you'll have us." Tristan grinned and nodded his head. "Good! I'll have one of our jets fuel up to transport you to where the rest of the students are currently, over on Nani Isle, another one of our locations just north of here."

"No need, sir. If you don't mind, I'd like to try getting there myself."

"Very well, Mr. Davids," Winter replied, giving Tristan a playful grin. "You remind me of him you know."

"Who, my father?"

"No. Your grandfather. You have the same abilities as he did. Hopefully, you prove to live up to them."

Tristan nodded but felt the need to ask one more question. "One last thing, sir, I've always wanted to ask."

"Yes?"

"That first day at the Academy, when you told the students my testing scores...did I really score the highest in the class?"

Winter chuckled aloud, shaking his head. "Heavens no, Tristan. You were middle of the pack, at best. You did score the highest in one particular area though. The best we had seen in years, a perfect 20: potential. By the way, did you ever decide upon your metamorph name?"

Tristan walked beneath the skylight and paused briefly, the name popping into his head naturally. Smiling into the sun's rays, Tristan replied, "Definitely. The name's Electro." With that said, Tristan leaped into the air, bolting through the opening and into the clear, blue skies above.

Thank you so much for taking the time to read Metamorphs: Return of the Legion, the first in my four-part series! I hope you enjoyed the book and are looking forward to the next installment!

Please make sure that you leave a book review as it will help bring more fans to the world of Metamorphs and be sure to sign up for the newsletter included in the link below to receive a FREE E-BOOK, be entered for FREE GIFTS, and be among the first to know about BOOK UPDATES!

Thank you all again, and until next time, keep imagining!

-Yuri Jean-Baptiste

Newsletter link: YJBLiterary[1]

---

1. https://mailchi.mp/c35f63fbf8d1/yjbliterary

Don't miss out!

Visit the website below and you can sign up to receive emails whenever Yuri Jean-Baptiste publishes a new book. There's no charge and no obligation.

https://books2read.com/r/B-A-CUMH-YTVW

BOOKS 2 READ

Connecting independent readers to independent writers.

Also by Yuri Jean-Baptiste

Metamorph Anthologies
Metamorphs Anthologies: Volume 1 (Episodes 1-10)

Metamorphs
Metamorphs: Return of the Legion
Metamorphs 2: Ripple Effect

Watch for more at https://yjbliterary.com/.

About the Author

While Yuri Jean-Baptiste may have spent his adolescence growing up in beautiful Fort Lauderdale, FL, he mainly lived in the magical fantasy and sci-fi landscapes his imagination created. A voracious reader and movie-lover, Yuri spent much of his childhood years world-building and concocting adventures before being forced to grow up. Lucky for him, he met his true love, Jennifer, who dared him to imagine again and pursue his dreams of becoming an author. Married in 2015, Yuri now lives in Durham, NC, with his wonderful wife and two dogs, although he devotes much of his time within his now fully-developed worlds. When he is not writing his novels, Yuri can be found channeling his inner nerd, playing Dungeon's and Dragons and Magic: the Gathering with his friends.

Read more at https://yjbliterary.com/.

59531261R00214

Made in the USA
Columbia, SC
05 June 2019